FOURTH
DAY

FOURTH DAY

A CHARLIE FOX THRILLER

ZOË SHARP

PEGASUS BOOKS
NEW YORK

FOURTH DAY

Pegasus Books LLC
80 Broad Street, 5th Floor
New York, NY 10004

First Pegasus Books cloth edition 2011

ISBN: 978-1-60598-275-5

10 9 8 7 8 6 5 4 3 2 1

Printed in the United States of America
Distributed by W. W. Norton & Company, Inc.

Zoë Sharp was born in Nottinghamshire, but spent most of her formative years living on a catamaran on the north-west coast of England. She opted out of mainstream education at the age of twelve and became a freelance photojournalist in 1988. She turned to crime writing after receiving death-threat letters in the course of her work, which led to the creation of her no-nonsense heroine Charlie Fox. Zoë lives on the edge of the Lake District, where she and her husband, a nonfiction writer, have recently self-built their own house. Zoë blogs regularly on her own website, *www.zoesharp.com* and also on the award-nominated *www.murderati.com*.

For Andy, with all my love

FOURTH
DAY

CHAPTER ONE

Nothing brings home a sense of your own mortality like being locked up alone in the dark.

Which was, of course, precisely why they'd done it.

My entire world had shrunk to these four rough-rendered walls. The room was barely the length of the narrow cot that filled one wall and took up almost half the floor space. The bed base was welded to the frame, which itself had been bolted to the floor. There was no window, just a stainless steel toilet in one corner, a small cold-water sink in the other, and a steel door in between with no handle on the inside.

Apart from that, there was just me alone with my thoughts.

Without sight, every sound became amplified. The quiet rustle of my torn shirt as I moved, the creak of the compressed foam that formed my mattress. I could smell my own sweat, the rising odour from the toilet pan, and the musky dampness of stale air conditioning.

The only lighting provision came from spots recessed into

the ceiling and covered by anti-tamper grilles. The switch that controlled them was somewhere on the outside. They'd taken away my watch, so my grasp of time had grown hazy, but there seemed to be no logic to the pattern of my artificial nights and days.

Right now, someone had decided it was night, but maybe they just liked keeping me in the dark. Or maybe they were getting their own back.

I sat on the bed, directly facing the doorway, back to the wall, with my knees hunched up and my bare feet tucked in, staring into the confronting darkness as if searching for answers in the visual static.

I flexed my hands out before me. Although I couldn't see them, the knuckles of my left felt stiff and inflamed. I probably should have iced them. If I'd had any ice.

I probably should have done a lot of things.

I rolled my shoulders, felt the sharp stab in the back of the joint where I hadn't got a decent break-fall in fast enough, the long burn of torn muscles in my forearm and thigh, the tenderness of fresh bruises that were rising just about everywhere. If the fluid puffiness along my cheekbone was anything to go by, I was well on the way to a belting black eye.

But, all in all I was still intact, still together – physically, at least. I told myself it was nothing I hadn't been through before, in one form or another.

But not quite like this.

The resistance-to-interrogation exercises I'd undergone in the army had been just that – exercises. Brutal, frightening, but ultimately little more than visceral make-believe. This was different. There was no instructor with an armband about to walk in through that door and tell me it was all over, pass or fail.

And the one person who might conceivably have come to my rescue, as he had before, was the last person, right now, I either wanted or expected to see.

You asked for this.

That I couldn't deny. After all, I had gone willingly into the cult calling itself Fourth Day, apparently well briefed and well prepared for what lay behind their walls, except for what I might find inside myself, if I was forced to look deep enough, for long enough.

And Randall Bane was the kind of man who could force you to take that look.

I've come face to face with some pretty scary people in my time. Stone-cold killers. People who would go straight through another human being because it troubled them less than going around. But for Bane, the man behind Fourth Day, I had a feeling that mere surrender was only the beginning of what he wanted from me.

The soundproofing was good enough that I didn't hear them coming. The first indication of company was the metallic slither of the bolt on the outside of the door dragging back, then a bright white spike as the leading edge cracked open and light flared in through the widening gap.

I shut my eyes, brought up a shielding hand to my face, to give myself space as much as anything else. By the time my sight had readjusted enough to see past the shelter of my fingers, Bane himself stood leaning in the doorway.

His arms were folded across his broad chest, smooth-shaven head slightly tilted. His back was to the light so I couldn't see his face, but I knew by his stance that he was watching me intently.

'Going to lend a hand personally with the softening-up process this time, are you?' I asked lightly, aware of the rawness in my throat. I let my wrists drape over my knees, striving to keep the tension out of my arms. 'Or are you just here to watch?'

Bane gazed at me without emotion. There was no hurry to him, no impatience. Everything in here adjusted its stride to fit with his.

'This was all so unnecessary, Charlie.' His voice was deep, neutral, almost without class or nation, and seemed to fill all the corners of the room.

'Yeah, well, you can't say I didn't warn you.'

'You did,' he allowed. 'And then you put three men in the infirmary.'

But there was no disgust in his voice, no recrimination. His curiosity was almost palpable. If I'd failed to get his attention before, I certainly had it now. I blanked out what I'd had to do in order to achieve that aim.

I shrugged, carefully. 'Maybe I just don't like being manhandled.'

'You don't like letting go of control – on any level,' he corrected. 'That scares you, doesn't it?'

'Don't you think it should?' I countered, striving to match his matter-of-fact tone but only reaching weariness. I let one hand lift briefly and flop again. 'Hey, you're the one who's three men down. You tell me.'

'Perhaps,' he agreed. 'But in your case, you know that if you lose control – of the situation, of yourself – people die. How many is it now? Do you even keep a count anymore?'

Sitting with my back hard up against the blockwork, I felt the moment my heart rate began to climb. *How could he possibly know that – any of that?* I stared at him and said nothing, and Bane nodded as if I'd spoken anyway.

'Ah yes, I know who you are, Charlie. More to the point, I know *what* you are.' His voice was utterly calm. There was nothing in it for me to latch onto, to rail against. It was as if I could feel myself begin to slide down a steep sheer surface into oblivion with nothing to arrest my descent. 'Did you think that story you concocted would hold for long?'

I gave a mirthless laugh. 'Longer than this, clearly.'

'Some things you just can't disguise,' Bane said gently. 'And ordinary young women do not carry the kind of old knife and bullet wounds that you bear without an extraordinary history of violence.'

Apart from the fading jagged scar around my throat, the other reminders etched onto my body of that violent past were all well hidden. Thinking about the circumstances under which Bane might have seen them brought a sudden tightness in my chest, an ache in my hands that fast became active pain. I realised I had them clenched into fists.

Scrabbling for grip, I said, 'I've saved more lives than I've taken, if that makes any difference.'

'Is that how you justify it to yourself?' he murmured. 'How interesting.'

He began to turn away, this audience over. Then he stopped, halfway into the light now, so I could see his brooding expression for the first time. It did little to reassure me.

'Tell me, Charlie, do they haunt you – the faces of the ones you killed?'

I tipped my head back against the wall. 'Does it matter?'

For a long moment we locked eyes, and there was profound disappointment in his level gaze, like I had let him down. Maybe it was shame that made my face heat. Or maybe not.

'To you, it should,' he said at last, finally allowing the steel to brush surface. 'What do you hope to gain from this attempt to infiltrate our community, Charlie? There is nobody here needs protection from anything – except possibly from you.' He smiled, a little sadly, and asked in that utterly calm and reasonable voice, 'Can you suggest one salient reason why I shouldn't follow my first instincts and rid myself of you at the earliest opportunity?'

I swallowed. Now came the risk, the gamble. 'You think I've come here simply to spy on you?' I said, keeping it flat, devoid of emotion. 'Alone and unarmed?'

'Oh, I think you've given a more than adequate demonstration of your...fitness for any such task,' Bane returned. 'What other interpretation can I put on your presence here at this time?'

At this time...

'I've told you already,' I said with a tiredness I didn't have to fake. 'I came because I thought you could help me.' If that was no direct lie, it was as much of the truth as I was prepared to tell him.

'You will not accept my help because, deep down, you do not want it. All I see in you is rage and sorrow, and without them you have nothing to sustain you.' The coolly delivered assessment sliced all the deeper for its icy objectivity.

I looked down at my hands, noticed for the first time I

had blood under my nails that didn't seem to be my own.

'It's better than feeling nothing,' I muttered. 'Or, I thought it was.'

'Ah, and now, suddenly, you've had some kind of epiphany,' Bane said with an edge to his voice that, in a lesser man, might have stooped to sarcasm. 'When, exactly, did you reach this desire for such a fundamental change in your life?'

I'd been warned, before I'd gone into Fourth Day, that I'd need a story within a story. I'd expected Bane to break through my primary cover, if not so easily, and I'd considered and rejected a number of options before finally deciding, at the last possible moment, what to tell him. The truth – or a version of it.

I raised my head very slowly.

'When I discovered I was pregnant.'

Smoothly, he stepped forwards, loomed over me and, before I could react, his fingers had brushed down the side of my face, lingering almost delicately at the swollen area under my eye. I flinched, and he caught my chin, his grip deceptively light. I wasn't fooled for a moment, but refused to give him the satisfaction of trying to twist free, of letting him see how badly he frightened me.

He stared straight down into my eyes and stripped my soul bare.

'There,' he murmured eventually, 'that wasn't so hard, was it – that first step?'

I glared back at him until my vision began to shimmer.

He sighed, a quiet outrush of air. 'We'll continue this later, I think. When you've had a little more...time to consider.'

He released me and stepped back into the corridor

outside my cell. I resisted the urge to rub the skin where he'd touched me, but could still feel the imprint of his fingers. He nodded to someone I couldn't see, and the door closed him out with the heavy clang of finality, leaving me in darkness once more.

With no pride left to hold them back, the tears streamed hotly down my face. Because, much as I hated to admit it, what Randall Bane had said was absolutely true. For years I had allowed my anger to drive me forwards, to dictate my thoughts and override my actions. It had brought me inevitably to this point, as if seeking the means of my own destruction. My timing, as always, was impeccable.

Alone again in the dark, I thought a good deal about life and death.

But mainly about death.

CHAPTER TWO

The first time I saw Fourth Day's California stronghold was through a pair of Zeiss ten-power binoculars from a little over six hundred metres out. I was propped on my elbows amid the dusty scrub, feeling the gathered warmth of the earth releasing up slowly into my body.

It was mid afternoon in mid January. Everyone had told me to watch for the chill factor, but I'd just been on assignment in London, where it had been mostly cold and sleeting and miserable. In the current windless fifty-five degrees, I was a basking lizard by comparison.

'How's our target?'

Sean's voice was low, clipped, at my shoulder. He spoke without moving, without even a vibration. There was a preternatural patience about him that made him a master at covert surveillance operations such as this. He could have laid up for days, watching, waiting, if he had to.

'Still in position,' I said. We were taking turns to keep obs and it was easiest to pare our blips of conversation down to emotionless terminology. At least, that's what I told myself.

I scanned across the area in front of us, keeping my movements slow. We were in the south with the sun behind us, where the twin lenses of the binocs would not readily catch and return the light, and where people were less likely to stare long enough to spot us in our careful concealment.

The compound itself was a huddle of squat prefab buildings, rather like construction site Portakabins, clustered around a dusty central courtyard. I assumed that was a defensive layout, although the building walls didn't look able to withstand a hard-kicked football, never mind stronger ordnance.

There was an accommodation block to one side, and a main building with a higher pitch to the roof that I took to be some place of worship. Apart from that, all it needed was a flagpole and it could have been a barracks.

Throughout our observation, there had been activity in the compound. The land was not suitable for large-scale agriculture, but citrus and avocado trees had been planted around the buildings, fanning out into the scrubland beyond. From what we could see, there was also some kind of hand-dyeing fabric thing going on. Rainbows of it hung out to dry, draping listlessly in the still air.

The men and women who formed Fourth Day's membership appeared to share the labour equally, with little regard for traditional male and female roles. And so, in the centre of the compound, on a bench set beneath an ancient juniper tree with a group of children clustered round his feet, sat a man who'd been identified to us as Thomas Witney.

Witney sat slightly hunched forwards, leaning in towards his class, some of whom looked as young as four or five.

His file had listed him as a teacher by profession, probably a good one. He spoke with animation, using his hands to give additional shape and colour to his words. I couldn't help but wonder at the doctrine he was spouting to hold their attention so absolutely.

He wasn't a big man, with a close-shaved head tanned to caramel. He looked so different to the photograph we'd been given that we had initially hesitated over confirming acquisition of our target.

The old picture had showed an altogether thinner, paler man, with a haircut designed to cover his inadequacies, and thick-framed glasses. He'd discarded both somewhere along the way. It was only his prominent Adam's apple that had finally settled his identity.

Now, in khakis and a baggy hand-knitted sweater the colour of old moss, he looked a far cry from the successful vice-principal of an exclusive private school. Before he'd dropped out, gone in, gone under.

Amid all the other activity, I didn't initially clock the girl who came out of one of the buildings with a still-chubby young child balanced on her hip. She was perhaps in her early twenties, small and dark. Her movements had a furtiveness about them, like a feral cat that's consented to domestication but isn't entirely happy to walk in human footsteps.

But Witney caught sight of her the moment she emerged, and I saw his hands falter as his thought process stuttered. A momentary hesitation, then his attention returned to his little al fresco class. But from the stiffness in his back, the sudden self-consciousness in his movements, it was obvious he was minutely aware of her.

The girl jiggled the child as she carried him around the edge of the dusty square, frequently glancing towards Witney. I read nothing but anxiety and distraction in her body language.

'Report,' Sean said, reaching for the camera with its telephoto lens.

With a wrench of effort, I closed out the image of the girl and the child. 'We still have eyes on our target, but he's surrounded by civilians. Minors,' I added, just in case that wasn't enough. I glanced across at Sean's face, all hard planes and angles. 'Lucky coincidence, or deliberate defensive position?'

'Does it matter?' Sean asked, the last vestiges of his Lancashire accent flattening his vowels. 'Either way, he's going to be bloody difficult to extract.'

'Of course it does. Whereas one is unfortunate, the other means they know we're coming for him, in which case—'

'Two Bravos,' he interrupted as movement flared in my peripheral vision. 'Inbound. North-east corner. Rifles.'

Still keeping it slow and smooth, I eased the glasses across. Two men had stepped into view between the buildings. One was tall, with skin so black it had a tinge of blue. He was built like an American football player, that impression emphasised by the way he carried himself. The other man was smaller, lighter skinned, with overtones of several races in his Eurasian features, combining to give him a certain regal air. From the way they interacted, the Eurasian was in charge, and it wasn't just the way they were dressed that set them apart from the other occupants of the compound.

Both men wore desert pattern camouflage, like you'd buy from any outdoorsman store or military surplus supplier for a weekend's hunting. But the long guns in their hands were not shouldered on their webbing straps, the way returning hunters would carry them, but cradled ready, like a patrol.

'M16s,' I said, and moved up to focus on their faces. 'When the hell did Bane bring in armed guards? Can you get a shot of them?'

Sean already had the viewfinder to his eye, adjusting to compensate for the falling light. The shutter release was set on continuous. It whipped quietly through a rapid series of shots as the men advanced. If they were on any databases, we would ID them.

I panned back and found we weren't the only ones following the progress of the pair. Witney had stopped all pretence at instruction, hands resting limply on his thighs as he watched them pass. In contrast, his spine was tense enough to crack. I felt rather than saw him start to sweat.

The group of children still concentrated on their teacher as the two men walked by. The Eurasian man raised a hand from the stock of his gun in what might have been no more than a friendly wave, a casual salute. Or might not. Witney nodded in jerky reply.

A couple of his pupils also cheerfully returned the wave. The sight of men with unshouldered weapons was obviously so common a sight to the children in this place that it didn't even warrant a second glance from the others.

That alone was enough to chill me to the bone.

I reacquired the girl with the baby. Like Witney, she too had faltered, her gait more uncertain now. Her unease communicated itself to the child who stiffened in her arms and began to struggle. There was a long pause, then a thin high wail reached us.

The two men with the guns halted, both turned almost blindly towards the sound. The big guy took a step in her direction. The girl whirled, hunching over the child as if to hide or protect it, and scurried towards the building from which she'd emerged, with the little figure clutched tightly in her arms. I watched her until she was all the way out of sight, feeling the wrench of isolation as the closing door cut off the child's screeching cries.

'What?'

I glanced across, found Sean watching me with darkened, piercing eyes. I could read nothing in his face.

'There was a possible threat to the woman and the child,' I said, aware of a sudden tension in my shoulders. Aware, too, that it was a thin excuse.

'Maybe those two just don't like the noise,' Sean said, choosing not to call me on it. 'Can't say I blame them for that – it goes right through you.'

I hid the flinch, said quickly, 'It's designed to get your attention, otherwise we'd have all died out by now. I just didn't like the way they looked at her.'

'We're not here to save them all, Charlie,' he said, flat. 'Don't let yourself get sidetracked. Our focus is on Witney. One at a time, OK?'

I didn't respond. We watched in silence as the impromptu class came to an end and Witney led the dozen or so children inside in what seemed unnaturally ordered pairs. Every other class group of kids I'd seen was more like a controlled explosion. I opened my mouth to comment, if only to try and ease the pressure shimmering between us, when the cellphone in my breast pocket began to vibrate. It was all I could do not to gasp at the sudden buzzing against my ribs. I reached up and tapped the receive button on my wireless earpiece.

'Fox.'

'Charlie – sit rep?' The voice didn't need to identify itself for me to recognise the cultured New York tones of Parker Armstrong. Sean's senior partner. My boss.

'It's quiet,' I murmured. 'We've had eyes on the target all day – and much good it's done us. He hasn't left the compound and he's never alone. Looks like Fourth Day have got themselves some additional security.'

'He's under guard?' Parker asked, terse.

'Not exactly,' I said dryly. 'If we're really unlucky it could be more in the nature of a human shield. Oh, and someone needs to update the guy's file. Just how old is the picture you showed us?'

There was a pause, an uncharacteristic hesitation, unusual enough for me to pick up on it. 'Five or six years,' he said at last, and there was a trace of reluctance in his voice, hardening as he added, 'It's what we had available, Charlie.'

Safely unseen, I let my eyebrows climb. Sean caught the gesture and fired me a warning glance of his own.

'O...K,' I said, knowing this was not the time to pursue the cons of outdated intel. 'How long do you want us to sit out here and wait for a slip-up in the security arrangements?'

'I don't,' Parker said dryly. 'Pull out for now. The rest of the team should be landing shortly. I'll bring everyone up to speed as soon as you get back.'

He cut the connection without wasting time on goodbyes, which was indicative of urgency, I judged. Parker was nothing if not unfailingly polite.

I glanced to Sean. 'Right, we're out of here,' I said. His only reply was a raised eyebrow of his own. 'Parker's promised a briefing.'

'About time,' Sean muttered, taking his weight on his elbows and beginning to inch himself backwards out of our makeshift hide.

Even without the binoculars trained directly on the compound, I caught the flash of colour below us and we both froze, ignoring the natural reflex to duck back into cover.

The girl we'd seen with the distressed infant came bursting out of the doorway from the main building, arms windmilling, as though she'd just jerked herself to freedom. Of the child, there was no sign.

She hit the ground running, clenched fists pumping up to full speed, heading straight for our position. Unless she jinked, in less than four hundred metres she'd literally trip right over us.

The reason for her flight was only a couple of seconds behind her. The pair we'd seen with the M16s barged out of the doorway and started in pursuit. No longer armed, the two men were no less menacing empty-handed. And they didn't waste their breath shouting. They knew she wasn't going to stop unless they forced her to.

My hand snaked behind me to the SIG P228 that lay concealed in the small of my back, made sure it would glide out of the Kramer inside-the-waistband clip. 'Sean—'

'Hold your position,' he cut in through clenched teeth. And just in case that didn't dissuade me, he reached over and grasped my arm at the wrist. I tensed under his grip, felt the iron resistance.

This time of year, sunset was around five and the light was dropping fast now, grainy in its descent, smearing the contours of the terrain into deception. Two hundred and fifty metres from us, the girl misjudged her step and went sprawling. A proper face-plant in the dirt. She lay winded for maybe a second, then she was scrabbling onto hands and knees. Small whimpered sounds of fright escaped her as her pursuers gained and pounced. The Eurasian guy, lighter and faster, grabbed her shoulder. The big black guy latched onto her outstretched arm, yanked her upwards.

Automatically, all the right defensive manoeuvres unveiled behind my eyes, a rapidly expanding blur of sound and motion, as if someone had fired up an instant wireless link between us, so that I was right there, inside her head, inside her body.

Physically, we couldn't have been more different. Where she was dark, I was fair. Where she was skin and bone, I'd worked hard to acquire muscle without bulk. There was maybe five or six years between us, but it seemed like a generation in terms of mindset and experience. She had already given in, but I had sworn a long time ago that I would never again submit.

So in my mind's eye I watched my own ghosted image swarm over her and take command.

An elbow into the long thigh muscle of the one who's grabbed my shoulder, dead-legging him. A clenched backfist up into his groin and he falls away. His partner's thinking capture, not containment. The big guy's trying to pull me to my feet. So I let him drag me up, swing me round, ignoring the hold he's got on my arm. He's not got a decent lock on yet. Big mistake.

The instant I'm up far enough to use my feet, I do so, exploiting his own grip for added momentum. A swift, hard, downward stamp to the outside of the knee, hearing the graunch and splinter as the joint collapses.

I shake him loose, and then I'm off and running again. Free, and filled with a fierce, raging pride...

My vision cleared, heart rate slowing. Two hundred and fifty metres away, the girl was still on her knees in the dirt. The men still had her by the arm and shoulder and she'd drooped under the burden of capture. She was weeping, great wracking sobs of wrath and heartbreak. Briefly, I considered another challenge to Sean's restraining hand again but, with a last squeeze, he let go, withdrew.

I turned my head, found him watching me intently. And suddenly that cool gaze angered me. Not just his confidence that I wouldn't do anything to jeopardise our purpose here, but because he was right. If I wasn't professional enough to ignore such distractions, then what was I?

But there were questions here. What was Thomas Witney's connection to the girl, I wondered? Were the guards there to keep people out, or keep people in? And what were they afraid of?

Sean's eyes flicked back to the girl, and her captors. They had her on her feet now, were leading her towards the building she'd so nearly escaped, one on either side. Her keening had reached a pitch where she was almost incoherent with it, losing coordination along with whatever burst of energy had fuelled her failed attempt. They were forced to support her, keep her upright as she stumbled along, pliant, between them.

Just as the three of them reached the doorway, it opened

and a new figure stepped out. Sean had the camera to his eye and I heard him suck in a sharp breath as he recognised the newcomer. It was hard not to.

Parker had shown us pictures of Randall Bane, but they were poor-quality images, snatched perhaps from a moving car, through glass, on the fly. They'd showed a man with a high-domed head, close shaven in the style that his follower, Thomas Witney, seemed to have taken to heart.

But by contrast, the man behind Fourth Day was tall, well over six feet, and fast approaching fifty. The covert photograph had been taken as he walked along a city street with a long stride that flapped the skirts of a well-cut overcoat around his legs. He had been surrounded by people but somehow elevated above them. Command radiated from him like a Roman general.

If I'd been staring at him through the scope of a sniper's rifle, I wouldn't have needed to see his badge of rank to know he was a high-priority kill.

Now, Bane folded his arms almost delicately and waited for the girl to be brought before him. The men let go of her when they were only a couple of metres away. Without their support she dropped straight to her knees, shoulders bowed so the vertebrae of her spine formed a peak at the back of her neck, utterly subjugated.

A cold fear pooled in my belly. I'd seen this pose before, in South America, and the Balkans, and the parts of Africa they don't mention on the wildlife documentaries. When he reached towards her, it took a blinded moment for my mind to recognise that his hands were empty.

Instead of the execution I'd been half-expecting, Bane touched the top of her head, so lightly it was almost a caress.

She lifted her face very slowly, fearful, and then through the magnification of the glasses I saw wonder there, as if she, too, had been expecting a bullet. He said something, only a few words, and let his fingers skim the side of her cheek with a softness that made me shiver.

He spoke again, receiving a downcast nod in reply, then held out his hand to her and there was something vaguely sensual about the gesture.

After the briefest irresolution, the girl put her hand in his, allowed him to help her to her feet, slide his arm around her shoulders. The four of them went back inside the building. The door closed behind them with a faint rattle that was barely audible at our current distance, amid the clicking of the insects all around us, and the rustle of a sudden winding breeze.

Beside me, I heard Sean hiss out a long breath. When I looked back across, it was to see a muscle jumping in the side of his jaw. His head turned slowly to meet my eyes and I put words to what was going through both our minds.

'Jesus Christ,' I muttered. 'Just who the hell *are* these people?'

CHAPTER THREE

It was a question I repeated later, after Sean and I had hiked out of Fourth Day's land on the edge of the San Gabriel Mountains, retrieved our rented 4x4 from a rest area, and gone hand to hand with traffic on Interstate 210 that crawls across the northern edge of the city of Los Angeles. Two hours later, we were back in Calabasas, where Parker Armstrong had set up his temporary base of operations.

Calabasas nestled into the hills of Santa Monica just above Malibu, and Parker had arranged use of an eight-bedroom mansion, part of an upmarket gated community on the outskirts, not being one to slum it if he didn't have to.

Although it boasted magnificent views and undoubted seclusion, the house had been built into what seemed like the side of a cliff, which struck me as a precarious location considering California's uncertain geology. Nobody else seemed overly concerned that we might be woken suddenly in the middle of the night to find ourselves at the bottom of the nearby canyon.

'Fourth Day was formed back in the Fifties,' Parker said now. 'Nobody's quite sure of their original doctrine except it's a fairly black-and-white interpretation of good and evil. Hence the name.' His voice took on that of a preacher from his pulpit. '"And God made two great lights; the greater light to rule the day and the lesser light to rule the night... And to rule over the day and over the night and to divide the light from the darkness... And the evening and the morning were the fourth day." Book of Genesis.' He shrugged. 'I'm paraphrasing, but that's the gist. Read into it what you will.'

'When do you get to the bit about scaring young girls half to death?' I murmured.

Parker frowned. 'Well, they managed to convince some wealthy donors to bankroll them, claimed some success with delinquency and drug addiction. For a time they kept pretty much to themselves, stayed below the radar, but by the mid Eighties things had moved in a more extreme direction.'

'How extreme?'

Parker glanced at me for a second, as if gauging how much I needed to know. Unusual, because as a rule there was little hesitation about him. Tall enough to appear deceptively slim, Parker hid a wiry frame beneath well-tailored dark suits, and a calculating brain behind an often bland expression. A native New Yorker, he was good-looking without being outright handsome, seeming able to subtly alter his looks, his voice, even his age, almost at will. He'd greyed prematurely, which I'd learnt was a family trait, but his gaze had aged faster still, cool and watchful. He and Sean were very much alike in that respect.

'There were rumours of rape and incest among the

followers, use of hallucinogenic drugs, widespread abuse.'
He smiled but it didn't reach his eyes. 'You name it, these
people made an art of it.'

I thought again of the girl's fright, and her despair. 'How
come these damn cults never advocate abstinence, chastity,
and *not* marrying your own prepubescent granddaughter?'
I said, wry more than bitter. 'And why didn't someone shut
them down?'

'Various people tried – relatives, mainly,' Parker said, and
I heard a flinty echo in his voice. 'But nobody could prove
any of it, and Fourth Day's lawyers made 'em wish they'd
left well alone.'

'So that was it?' I demanded roughly. 'They were just
allowed to do whatever they liked, so long as it was behind
closed doors?'

'Eventually, they couldn't keep a lid on it. A group of
former members got together and threatened legal action
about eight years ago. Fourth Day settled, but it finished
them.'

'That's not what we've been seeing,' Sean said, pouring
coffee from the filter machine on the credenza. Good coffee
was Parker's vice and his virtue. This particular grind was
full and rich and dark, the smell of it alone reminding me
of New York pavement cafés in the summer with the beat
of traffic echoing against the high stone and steel and glass.
Sean handed me a cup and sat on the arm of my chair with
his own, close but not quite touching.

Compared to Parker, Sean was wider, heavier, more
overtly aggressive in his make-up. Time in the corporate
world had given considerable polish to his working-class
origins in a small northern English town, but there was still

no mistaking what lay beneath the surface gloss.

We were using the Great Room as the nerve centre. It had an eighteen-foot ceiling and one wall made entirely of glass, which looked out over the lap pool and the far distant hillside of similar, exclusive and excluding homes. Parker had hit the switch for the massive full-length curtains as soon as we'd arrived, and they hadn't been opened since. We were not here to enjoy the view.

One end of the room was dominated by a huge fireplace that had apparently been lifted wholesale from a French chateau. A motorised home movie screen was dropped down in front of the chimney breast. There was a laptop hooked into the projector, into which we'd downloaded the pictures taken during the course of our surveillance.

Now, Sean leant over and selected one of the digital images. A distance shot of Fourth Day's compound flashed up onto the screen in cinema-quality high definition, half a metre high.

'Everything we've seen of them, from armament to vehicles, shows they're well equipped, and their gear is either nearly new or at least of good quality and looks well maintained,' he said, raising an eyebrow in Parker's direction. 'What happened to revitalise them?'

'Randall Bane happened,' Parker said flatly. 'After the settlement, Fourth Day was broke. Bane bought up the land and buildings for a song. It was assumed he'd turn it into a private ranch, but he kept things up and running, and nobody's heard jack about the cult since.' He reached for the laptop himself and put up the original picture he'd shown us of Bane.

Maybe it was because I'd seen him for real, but that

covert photo didn't begin to do justice to the presence of the man. Where Sean – and Parker, come to that – could radiate menace as naturally as breathing, Randall Bane was something else again. Something I couldn't quite put my finger on, except that it made me thoroughly uneasy.

I glanced at Parker, found his eyes fixed on the figure on the screen. It could just have been the projected colours that made his gaze seem suddenly very hard and bright. 'Bane's kind of an enigma. It's rumoured he made his money in the more volatile areas of the Middle East and the former Soviet Union, but nobody knows for certain and, needless to say, those countries are not exactly free and easy with the United States when it comes to information traffic. You would have thought somebody, somewhere, would have a file on this guy a couple of inches thick,' he said, 'but nobody seems to know who he really is, or what he's doing running a two-bit cult in California.'

'What about the other two guys we saw today?' I asked, taking a sip of my coffee. 'Any luck identifying them?'

Parker pulled his eyes away from Bane's likeness and clicked up a picture of the two men we'd seen with the M16s. 'The black guy's name is Tyrone Yancy. Ex-Marine. Dishonourable discharge in 'ninety-eight. Was having an affair with his CO's wife. When the CO found out, he slapped her around some. Yancy broke the guy's jaw. Since then he's worked construction, militia training, security, whatever comes along that needs muscle.'

'What about the other guy?' Sean asked. 'Of the two of them, I would have said he was in charge.'

'John Nu.' Parker's eyes flicked to ours. 'A Brit. Another ex-military man. Corporal in the Parachute Regiment. Saw action in the Balkans and failed Selection for the SAS twice. Left five years ago and has been working the private military contractors' circuit ever since.'

'A mercenary, then,' I murmured. 'Sounds like Bane surrounds himself with interesting people.' I glanced up. 'You said he left five years ago, so how long has he been with Fourth Day?'

'Just the last six months. Bane suddenly started recruiting additional security. Took on eight guys, including these two.'

Sean frowned. 'How does Thomas Witney fit in to all this?'

'He's just a guy who suffered a family tragedy and decided to take a little time out from the world,' Parker said, and there was the blur of evasion beneath the quiet words. 'Apparently, it was never supposed to be a life-changing event but there were...complications. Now our client wants a retrieval and they're prepared to go to considerable trouble to achieve it.'

'Yeah, but how much trouble are they expecting *us* to go to?' Sean asked. 'From what we've seen of Fourth Day, they're prepared for something – almost as if they're expecting an incursion of some kind, and taking on people like Yancy and Nu confirms that. So, just what are we dealing with?' His tone was deceptively mild. 'You haven't exactly been forthcoming on this one, Parker.'

'I'm sorry to go all cloak-and-dagger on you guys,' Parker said stiffly. 'But the client's kinda paranoid when it comes to confidentiality.'

'He must be,' Sean said, and there was definitely a touch of bite to him now, like a prowling shark. 'Seeing as you haven't even told *me* who the client is.'

I glanced up from my coffee in surprise. Sean might be a junior partner in Armstrong-Meyer, but he was a partner nevertheless. And Parker wasn't usually so secretive.

Parker's right eye twitched fractionally, narrowed down. 'That's not important,' he said. 'What *is* important is that we extract Witney as soon as possible. You've told me yourselves what the situation is in there. He's nervous of something, surrounded by armed guards. He may have gone in voluntarily but, from what you've seen, it kinda looks like he's having second thoughts.' He stopped, took a breath. 'I have given my personal assurance to the client that we will get him out again – no matter if he's willing or not.'

It was as close as I'd seen him come to temper. The bark of it was enough for silence to form uneasily around the edges, like frost.

Keeping my voice bland, I asked, 'Why the hurry?'

Parker's head snapped round, and for a moment I thought his tongue would follow, then he seemed to shake himself, said without inflection, 'If there's something on your mind, Charlie, spit it out.'

'The picture you showed us at the original briefing was of a very different man to the Thomas Witney we've been watching,' I said. 'And he didn't get that way overnight. How long, exactly, has he been behind the wire, and why the hurry to get him out now?'

Sean glanced at me and I caught the barest flicker of surprise on his face. Then he fixed Parker with a dark gaze, echoing my own enquiry.

Parker sighed.

'Witney went in to Fourth Day a little over five years ago,' he admitted.

'And you were going to tell us this piece of information when, exactly?' Sean's voice was never more deadly than when it was soft as now.

Before Parker could answer, there was noise in the hallway and one of the three-metre-high front doors swung inwards, signalling the arrival of the rest of the team. Parker quickly crossed to greet them, not hiding his relief at the interruption. I glanced up at Sean.

What's going on?

I don't know.

The two men came in, said their hellos. Joe McGregor I'd worked with before on numerous occasions. A young black Canadian who'd been through two tours in Iraq on exchange with the US Third Infantry, before deciding he'd had enough excitement. As he dumped his kit down on the tiles he nodded to me and Sean with the wary friendliness I'd grown to expect, ever the total professional.

But the second man was someone I'd never thought I'd see back out in the field. Not just on this job, but ever.

Bill Rendelson had been one of Parker's first close-protection officers, had worked alongside him right up until a radical extremist group sent a parcel bomb to the businessman he was protecting on a trip to South Africa, four years ago.

I'd seen the photos in the file. The bomb missed its intended target but, in doing his job, Bill left his arm behind in the ruins of a Cape Town hotel suite, and his active service career along with it. The right-hand sleeve of his jacket now hung straight and flat from the shoulder, clipped together halfway down just to make the point.

Since the amputation, he had adapted his stance to cope with the uneven distribution of his weight, giving his blocky torso a slightly twisted look that mirrored accurately, I'd always felt, his state of mind.

Neither Parker nor Sean seemed surprised to see Bill, but maybe they just hid it better than I did.

'OK,' Parker said, once rooms had been allocated and bags carried up the overly grand Scarlett O'Hara sweeping staircase. We were back in the Great Room, the only background music provided by the coffee machine gurgling through a fresh cycle. 'Now you're all here, I can bring you up to speed. First of all, it's been pointed out to me that I should start with an apology.'

An almost imperceptible ripple went through the assembled group. He settled us with a cool stare, said, 'I've made it a rule never to send people in on surveillance operations – on *any* kind of operations – without adequate intel, but I've done that here.'

'Why?' It was Sean who asked the question, calm and without judgement. Their earlier clash might never have occurred.

Parker glanced at him for a moment and I had a brief mental image of two glaciers impacting with slow but inevitable force.

'Because time is not a luxury at our disposal in this case.'

'Why the rush, boss?' Joe McGregor asked, unconsciously repeating my earlier question.

'As you know, we've carried out these kind of snatches on cults before, on behalf of parents of misguided children, but our target now is a whole different ball game.'

He brought up two new images on the screen, side by side. The first was the same picture of Thomas Witney that he'd shown to Sean and me before we'd begun our watching brief. The second was a covert surveillance picture, taken earlier that day. I was struck again by how much Witney had changed during his time in the cult.

The original snap had been taken at some formal occasion. One of Witney's hands was wrapped tightly round the stem of a champagne flute, with the awkward grip of a man more at home grasping the neck of a beer bottle. He looked uncomfortable to have been caught on camera, and despite the half-hearted smile, an air of misery hung over him like misted rain.

'This is Thomas Witney,' Parker said, for the benefit of McGregor more than Bill Rendelson. It was probably Bill who'd collated the initial data. I glanced across at him, but the big man sat without any sign of impatience on the leather sofa, coffee in his hand, attention on his boss. Only when Parker put up the newer picture did Bill give the screen a long scrutiny.

'Witney went in to Fourth Day because he believed that the cult in general – and Randall Bane in particular – was responsible for the death of his only son, Liam.'

Another picture came up, of a young man in a scruffy olive drab jacket. Standard student wear from Vietnam to the present day. The shot had been taken on a university campus. He was standing in a group, listening intently.

He was centred in the frame, the faces of the others slightly softened by the narrow field of focus. The boy looked no older than nineteen or twenty, a thin serious face and naturally pale skin that held a flush of red along his prominent cheekbones.

'Liam Witney became involved with the cult while he was a student at UCLA, dropped out of college and then became a self-styled eco-warrior,' Parker went on. 'He joined a radical group who call themselves Debacle, died a few months later during a protest against oil exploration in Alaska. Witney believed Bane *encouraged* Liam in this direction and, against advice, decided to infiltrate Fourth Day in order to prove it.'

'Was he a cop?' McGregor asked.

Parker shook his head. 'A schoolteacher,' he said. 'But he'd been to the cops and gotten nowhere. He felt, rightly or wrongly, that because the boy had been engaged in illegal activity at the time of his death, there had been only a cursory investigation by the law enforcement agencies. He decided to go it alone.' Parker's expression hardened. 'Witney left instructions that if he didn't come out voluntarily inside six months, he was to be extracted – by force if necessary.'

'So what happened?' I said.

Parker cast me a fast, dark look. 'He cancelled,' he said shortly.

There was a long pause, and then Sean asked with quiet sarcasm, 'And nobody thought to question his state of mind?'

Parker's face tightened. 'Well, it's sure being questioned now,' he said. 'And that's why we have to get him out of there, fast as possible.'

There was something about the inflection, the emphasis, that tugged at all of us, but it was Bill Rendelson who said it. 'Boss, when you say "we" I hope you don't mean—'

'I'll be going in with Joe and Sean and Charlie,' Parker said calmly. 'I want you here running comms, Bill. I can't think of anyone I'd rather have handle that end of an operation.'

Bill shrugged the compliment aside as a poor attempt at flattery, scowling. 'To hell with that,' he snapped, jerking to his feet. 'You can't have both the agency's partners in the field at the same time. It's crazy!' His gaze was scornful as it swept over Parker, more so as it then flipped between me and Sean. 'It's bad enough that you're putting Charlie in when—'

'That's enough,' Parker said, cutting Bill dead without troubling to raise his voice. He had that kind of knack. 'Charlie is one of the most capable operatives we have. I'm putting her and Sean in together because they're damn good at what they do, and I trust them not to let any personal feelings they might have for each other interfere with their ability to do their job. If you can't do the same, Bill, you'd best speak now.' He glanced pointedly at his watch. 'There's still time for you to catch a flight back to New York.'

It was cruel, and very unlike Parker's normal measured stance. Something flared and died in Bill's muddy eyes, then he shook his head and subsided, shooting me a quick, poisonous glare that bothered me more than it should have done.

He knows.

I busied my hands with putting down my cup, aware of a sudden coldness that had nothing to do with efficient air conditioning. When I looked up again, it was to find Parker watching me minutely.

'You OK?' he murmured. It was casually put, and could

simply have been in response to Bill's obvious hostility over the forthcoming operation. But it wasn't.

'Of course,' I said, forcing a smile. 'I'm fine.'

Sean, meanwhile, was interrogating all of us with a silent lethal gaze. I kept my face neutral and hoped that, for once, his ability to read me like an open book was going through a dyslexic phase.

CHAPTER FOUR

'What's going on with you and Parker?'

It was later – late, in fact. I lay alongside Sean in the half-light of the bedroom we were sharing.

'Going on?' I echoed carefully. 'Nothing, and I bloody well hope you're not implying—'

'Of course not,' he said. 'But he's clearly concerned about you for some reason.' He lifted up onto one elbow, stared down at me in the gloom, as if feeling his way, and added softly, 'Tell me.'

I drew in a quiet breath. 'After we got back from Texas, I suffered a few side effects from...what happened there,' I said, which was fine but hardly went the distance. 'You were away – Mexico. I didn't want to distract you while you were on the job.'

'But that was before Christmas,' he said, and maybe it was because of the darkness but I heard a mix of emotions in his voice – bafflement, with a touch of accusation. 'And you told Parker but not me.'

'I ended up in hospital for a check-up,' I admitted,

which skated so thinly over being an outright lie it was in imminent danger of falling through. I shifted uncomfortably, glad he couldn't fully see my face. 'So, of course Parker knows – the company insurance scheme had to pay for it.'

'And that's it?' he said.

My hesitation was fractional. 'Of course.'

He sighed. 'If there's anything that will affect this operation, Charlie, I need to know.'

'There's nothing,' I said, more firmly, rolling onto my side away from him, even as a little voice in the back of my mind whispered, *'Coward.'*

His hand stroked smoothly across my shoulder, thumb sliding into the slight indentation of the old bullet wound in the back of my scapula, tracing its outline like a rosary. I knew then, beyond any doubt, that he loved me, despite or possibly because of my flaws and imperfections.

So, why did that realisation bring a wash of silent tears oozing past my eyelids?

I lay quite still while I fought this inconvenient burst of unwarranted emotion, and gradually his caress slowed. Eventually, he leant down and pressed a kiss into my hair, murmuring, 'Goodnight, Charlie.'

I didn't answer, even though we both knew I wasn't sleeping, and I felt the mattress stir as he turned on his side away from me. I knew all I had to do was roll over and reach for him, but I just couldn't do it and I had no idea why.

If he'd kept the job out of the equation, I thought in desperation, perhaps I'd have finally found a way to tell him the truth. That when we'd returned to New York from the events in Houston three months before, I'd found myself pregnant with his child.

'Well, there's no doubt about it – you're pregnant,' the young doctor said. 'I would say seven or eight weeks.'

Still reeling, I muttered, 'It's seven and a half.' And when she raised her eyebrows, I added, 'I may not have a medical degree, but I can still count.'

'Well, er, congratulations?'

This last was hesitant, definitely a question. She must have realised from my face that her diagnosis was not exactly the outcome I'd been hoping for.

'Thanks.' Suddenly glad I was sitting down, I stared dully at the corner of her desk where the cheap veneer had split to reveal the chipboard underneath. Well, you can't expect solid hardwood furniture in a free downtown clinic.

My father, who had long since escaped the UK's underfunded state medical system for the rarefied atmosphere of private practice, would have been horrified to see me in such a place. I had no intention of ever telling him I had cause to be there.

The doctor sitting opposite looked about eighteen, a Chinese American with a long, thin neck rising giraffe-like from the shapeless collar of her white coat, and dark circles under her eyes. Now, she sighed, twisting in her seat to face me, and I saw her check out my ringless hands, clasped together in my lap.

'Do you know who the father is?'

I gave a lopsided smile, assailed by a brief but vivid flashback to a half-wrecked hotel room in Boston, of the exultation in Sean's eyes as we'd lost control of everything, including our senses, in the heat of fury and passion. 'Oh yes,' I said, 'I know.'

'And are you still in regular contact with him?'

I nodded.

'But you don't want him to know that you're expecting his baby.' Another statement, disappointment in her tone now, maybe even a little anger on behalf of all those expectant mothers who'd sat in this very same chair and didn't have a choice in the matter. Because they didn't know. Because they were scared. Because they'd been betrayed or abandoned or rejected out of hand.

That shook me out of my stupor a little. 'You can tell that from my test results?' I said sedately. 'Wow, you people are good.'

She capped her pen, tossed it onto the desk and sat back, the action causing her plastic chair to bounce slightly, like an old-fashioned rocker. 'Look, you're wearing a good watch and expensive shoes. I'm guessing you don't need to come here unless you wanted to keep this quiet.'

I was wearing the Tag Heuer Sean had given me when we'd first moved into the Upper East Side apartment, and soft brown leather ankle-length boots under my jeans, bought in a sale at Saks. Everyone told me I'd got a bargain, but they'd still cost what seemed to be an indecent amount of money, even when I'd mentally converted it back into sterling. So, I could see her point.

I let out a slow breath. 'You're right,' I said. 'I don't want him to know.'

'Why not? I mean, is he married?'

Sean and I had discussed the subject of marriage only

once, on a two-day drive to Texas, under threat and on the run. *'I don't think I'm good husband material,'* he'd said. *'And, if genetics are anything to go by, I'd make a lousy father.'* The ironic thing was, at the precise moment of that conversation, it was too late. I'd already conceived.

'Only to his job,' I said, closing that mental door. 'We both are, come to that.'

'Ah,' she said with the faintest trace of a sneer. 'And you feel having a baby will disrupt your career?'

'I work in close protection,' I said flatly. 'I'm a bodyguard. My job is to put myself between the client and the threat, regardless of personal danger.'

How can I do that, without hesitation, if I've a child to consider? This won't just disrupt my career – it will finish it.

'Ah,' she said again, more soberly now. 'I see.' There was another long pause and we sat listening to the bustle of phones and pagers and babies crying outside her office, and the buzz of traffic coming up from the street. 'You're from England, aren't you?' she said then. 'Is your status here in the United States dependent on your work?'

I nodded. 'I would most likely have to go home.'

'And the father, I take it, might not want to follow?'

I thought of the newly installed ARMSTRONG-MEYER lettering in brushed stainless steel on the maple panelling behind Bill Rendelson's desk. Ever since Sean had been manoeuvred out of the army and set up on his own, he'd been working towards this point. A partnership in a highly regarded New York agency with a prestigious international reputation. I'd already nearly ruined things by getting him, and Parker, embroiled in a huge scandal involving my parents the previous autumn. This might just be the final straw.

'No,' I said. 'I couldn't guarantee that he would.'

'Then you have a big decision to make about your future, and that of your baby,' she said, suddenly looking very tired. She pulled open the top drawer of her desk and picked out a couple of leaflets, put them into my hands. I glanced at the top one. It offered advice on terminating unwanted pregnancy. The second was a list of clinics who would perform such a procedure.

Mouth suddenly tasting of ashes, I lurched to my feet, spilling the leaflets on the desktop. The open drawer, I noticed, was full of them.

The young doctor eyed me with concern. 'Take them – think it through,' she urged. 'You need to consider all your options, however unpalatable you may find them at the moment.' She hesitated. 'Surely, as a bodyguard, you have to do that, don't you?'

'Yeah,' I said, finding my voice and not recognising it when I did, 'but murdering the principal is never an option.'

CHAPTER FIVE

We went in to Fourth Day two nights after our initial recce. Sean at the rear, Joe McGregor and Parker Armstrong to the centre, and me on point.

Parker was old-fashioned in some ways, but there was no gallantry at play. Sean and I had done the bulk of the recon work and knew the ground. Parker simply picked me to lead because I was physically smallest, minimising our chances of detection.

We'd carefully chosen dark disruptive-pattern-material camouflage to suit the terrain going in, and aid our exfil. Particularly if we were in a hurry, or under fire. The last thing we seriously expected was that Fourth Day would use deadly force to protect the compound, but we planned for it anyway.

Each of us wore body armour under our fatigues and McGregor had an M16 to give us comparable range and rate of fire to the weapons we'd seen the guards carrying. Its use was strictly a last resort, Parker had warned, and not something he wanted to explain to the local cops.

As well as our usual semi-automatics, we all carried TASER stun guns as a non-lethal alternative. Parker had several ampoules filled with various pharmaceutical concoctions, including enough horse tranquilliser to knock out half the runners in the Grand National if he had to.

We hiked in just as the sun dipped below the far horizon, using the last of the light and a hand-held GPS. Sean and I had already programmed in waypoints during our daylight recces. We knew the planned route was clear of undue hazards or easy opportunities for ambush.

The moon came and went behind fast-moving high cloud. Our shadows followed suit, rippling like liquid over the uneven ground. The local weather service had predicted an almost clear night, so we carried our night vision equipment rather than using it.

We moved as quickly as silence would allow. Less than twenty minutes after leaving our drop-off point, the four of us were overlooking the darkened compound. We confirmed our insertion to Bill Rendelson, monitoring comms traffic from a van pulled in behind a small roadside bar a mile away. Parker glanced across at Sean. 'You're sure about Witney's location?'

'Ground floor, third window along, to the left of the main doorway,' Sean said immediately, taking no offence. No harm ever came from double-checking.

Parker nodded to McGregor. 'Eyes and ears, Joe,' he said, and the three of us ducked out of cover and ran, bent low, across the open ground towards the building, leaving McGregor to watch our backs.

We reached the door through which I'd seen Randall Bane emerge only a few days before. I tried the handle to check it was locked, jerked my head to Sean. He moved up, a lock pick set already in his hands. Within moments, the tumblers had yielded and the door swung open to reveal a spartan lobby.

Sean and I had already checked that Fourth Day did not use a CCTV monitoring system, which would have been my first request, had I been in charge of their security. I reminded myself that Nu had failed Selection twice.

We were still careful as we slipped quickly over the threshold into the main accommodation building. We stayed wide once we were through, to make targeting more difficult.

There was enough light from the windows to see the contours of the room. The sparse furniture was functional but not shabby, and modern air conditioning was unobtrusively keeping the internal temperature down to a comfortable cool level.

Despite the lack of a personal touch, the interior of the building bore out our earlier observations of a revitalised organisation. Even the lino gleamed to a high-buff shine like a barracks floor.

Parker would have stepped past me towards the left-hand corridor if I hadn't put out a restraining arm. For a moment I thought he might insist, but he surrendered point at once, indicating with a slight bow that I should go on ahead. I moved past him into the corridor, putting my feet down with utmost care, counting the doorways which corresponded to windows on the outside of the building. Fourth Day might have enjoyed an injection of funds over the last few years, but that didn't mean the inmates got bigger cells.

We flattened against the wall outside the door to the

room we knew to be Witney's, and I sent up a quiet prayer that he wasn't fooling around with anyone that we didn't know about and hadn't suspected. Or at least that he didn't regularly spend the night away from his own bed. With Parker's potted history of the cult in mind, nothing would have surprised me.

The door was solid, secured with a simple lock that was child's play for someone with Sean's nimble fingers. Then we were pushing the door open. Parker and I went through the gap first, leaving Sean to pull the door almost closed behind us and keep a watch over the corridor through the crack.

The window had no curtains, which was how we'd been able to pin it down to being the correct room in the first place. Now, illuminated by the ghostly moonlight, I caught an instant snapshot of the layout of the narrow space Thomas Witney had called home for the last five years. A small desk, a straight-backed chair with a pile of clothing folded neatly on the seat, a single bed, and a side table containing only a book and a glass of water.

Witney lay sprawled beneath a thin sheet, apparently relaxed and unaware. Carefully, quietly, Parker reached for one of the ampoules he carried and broke the seal.

But some people are alert to even the smallest sound while their body rests. As we closed on him, some animal instinct jolted him into wakefulness. Witney reared up from the covers, body in spasm as though responding to a nightmare, and saw us. Instantly, I heard him suck in a breath to shout.

I took one fast onward stride and launched, landing with one knee in the vee of his ribcage to punch the wind out of him, hands going for his mouth, his throat. Parker grabbed his arm, jabbed the needle of the ampoule into bare flesh and squirted the contents into the former schoolteacher's heightened system, where his accelerated heart rate began to distribute it like an express courier service. I wrestled Witney's head into a chokehold, subdued him long enough for the drug to take effect.

Ten milligrams of a premed relaxant like midazolam, even whacked into muscle rather than direct into a vein, was more than enough to induce the sedated compliance of an average adult male in a little over a minute, but not enough to knock him out. We had a half-hour hike back out to our collection point. Far better not to do that with a deadweight unconscious body to carry if we could avoid it.

I waited for Witney's struggles to slow and weaken before I let go and rolled sideways off the bed. Parker helped the now unresisting man to sit up, while I grabbed his things from the chair. The lightweight shirt and trousers had the soft feel of constant laundering. I checked the pockets and dumped it all in his lap. Parker squatted in front of him.

'Thomas,' he said gently. 'We need for you to get dressed now and come with us. Can you do that?'

Thomas Witney raised his head only with great effort, seeming suddenly very tired, like an old man, but he managed a laborious nod. Parker nodded back with grim satisfaction.

We helped him dress, recognising his clumsiness as lack of coordination rather than deliberate delay. When his boots were laced, we moved him towards the doorway. Sean opened it a crack and peered through, then gave us an abrupt *wait* signal.

We froze. My eyes were locked onto Sean for the first

sign that we'd been compromised. The seconds stretched as they ticked by, with Witney swaying slightly between us.

Finally, Sean closed the door, latching it in absolute silence, and turned back to us.

'Remember the girl with the kid?' he said to me.

How could I forget?

He nodded as if I'd answered out loud. 'She's just walked down the corridor to another room at the end. Last door on the left. Is that her room,' he demanded, eyes raking over Witney, 'or somebody else's?'

Witney's head turned vaguely in the direction of his voice. 'Bathroom,' he mumbled.

I exchanged a quick glance with Parker. Witney was slow on his feet. Too slow to risk dancing him down the hallway in the time it took the average person to go to the loo in the middle of the night.

'We wait until she comes back,' Parker said.

'We should get her out as well,' Sean said, his gaze on Parker now, intent.

Parker let out a long, fast breath. 'Don't go off the reservation on me now, Sean,' he warned in a fierce whisper. 'We do not have time for this.'

'You didn't see her. How Bane was with her.' Sean's eyes flicked to me, as if for backup. 'The opportunity's there. We should make time.'

'Look, Sean—'

'She won't go.' Both of them stopped dead at my quiet interruption, turned their focus onto me.

'Why not?'

I returned Sean's fierce gaze without flinching. 'Did she have the kid with her?'

He shook his head.

'Then she won't go – not without her child,' I said. 'Trust me on this, Sean.'

'You're talking about Maria.' Witney's voice was slightly dreamy, as it might be for a man who'd just been shocked from sleep, but otherwise he sounded calm and coherent. He nodded with slow gravity. 'She needs to stay here – with her family.'

Sean gave a short grimace of frustration. 'Parker—'

'No...and that's an order.'

I'd never heard Parker pull rank before. Maybe he'd never had to. Still, I thought Sean would stand his ground, but with a last hooded stare, he nodded shortly, turned away.

A few moments later we heard shuffling footsteps pass along the hallway, a door open and close. We gave the girl, Maria, enough time to regain her bed, then slipped out, shepherding Witney along between us.

Sean relocked both the door to Witney's room and the main entrance as well, once we were outside, to confuse pursuit.

Just when we could have done with some cloud, the moon now glowed strongly. The most dangerous time was crossing the open area of the compound, when we were caught full in the glare of the reflected light. It bounced back up off the pale sandy ground with the brightness of winter snow.

Parker and I forced Witney into a stumbling jog, one on either side of him. I had one hand on the pressure points at the back of his neck to keep his head down and give me advance warning if he tensed to resist. There was nothing.

Then, about halfway across the open courtyard, McGregor's voice came into my earpiece in an urgent whisper. 'Security patrol!'

We reacted instantly, dragging Witney down into the shade of the only cover available – the ancient juniper tree with its wooden bench. We flattened ourselves into the shadow thrown by the trunk in the strong moonlight, and froze, keeping Witney beneath us both for his protection and our own.

We heard the scuffing of two sets of booted feet, ambling across the dirt, listening intently for a change in cadence to indicate surprise or discovery. I shut my eyes briefly, willing my heart to slow so my body gave no betraying quiver. I'd learnt a long time ago that the most outrageous levels of exposure in the field can be countered by simple immobility.

The footsteps of the two guards arced nearer, then began to fade. We didn't move until McGregor's voice came again. 'Clear!'

By the time we'd scrambled up and reached McGregor's position, I was flush with sweat that had little to do with exertion. McGregor took the rear to cover our retreat, Sean now on point. We closed in to a diamond formation around Witney, moving with the kind of practised ease you can only achieve when working with people you'd trust with your life.

But there would be repercussions for Sean's little mutiny over Maria, I knew. Although Parker might appear easy-going on the surface, that didn't mean he took insubordination lightly.

And there was a part of me that was fiercely glad Sean

had made his stand for the girl. It heartened me in a way I couldn't quite define.

Maybe I will be able to tell him, after all.

Over our comms link, Sean put Bill Rendelson on alert. By the time we reached our retrieval point, there was a van with blacked-out windows waiting to collect us, along with two identical decoys. We piled Witney into the back of one and all three vehicles took off in different directions. We were pretty sure we'd escaped detection so far, but there were no guarantees it would stay that way.

Our driver was another of Parker's operatives, Erik Landers – ex-military, as most of them were. He drove to make progress without attracting undue attention, and we sat in silence in the rear, swaying to the lurches of the soft suspension over the undulating road surface.

The back of the van had bench seats fitted along both sides, facing inwards. I was to one side with McGregor. Witney sat opposite, with Parker and Sean close on either side of him.

I glanced at my watch, calculating. That dose of midazolam would give us around four hours of docile obedience before it wore off. And when it did, Witney would have no memory of his abduction, or of any of us, which was a useful by-product in this line of work.

The ex-schoolteacher had hunched in on himself, but was otherwise showing no physical ill effects from the drug. He seemed tired and distracted rather than doped up, but everyone reacts differently to chemicals in their system.

At least, that was what I told myself, when the

headlights of a passing car pierced the front screen and swathed across us, revealing that while he sat quiet and apparently accepting of the events that had overtaken him, Thomas Witney's face was wet with helpless silent tears.

CHAPTER SIX

'Good morning,' I said, putting the breakfast tray down onto the low table in the centre of the guest suite. 'How are you feeling?'

'Annoyed and bewildered, I guess,' Thomas Witney said dryly from the far side of the spacious room.

I glanced across and found him sitting on the floor with his knees up in front of him and his back to the wall. He was facing the long window that led out onto the balcony. The balcony doors stood open, the breeze causing the muslin curtains to belly inwards like seaweed in a soft current. He was out of direct line of sight of the opening, but could still see out across the canyon. He spoke without immediately taking his eyes away from the view.

Witney had re-dressed in the same simple clothes of the night before. He wore no watch or jewellery, and his feet were bare.

There was something slightly faraway in his expression, as though he was trying to pick out the melody of a half-remembered song, played quiet at the periphery of audible grasp. I stood back from the table, waited until he finally turned his gaze onto me.

'Wouldn't you be?' he asked.

'No,' I said frankly, noting the lack of bitterness in his voice. 'To be honest, I'd be bloody livid.'

He didn't rise to that, instead said with near indifference, 'May I ask how long you intend to keep me a prisoner here?'

It was a familiar question. I'd done a few cult extractions since we'd joined Parker's outfit, and the people concerned were rarely pleased by their change of circumstances, initially at least.

'You're not a prisoner, exactly, Mr Witney,' I said. 'But it's perhaps not in your best interests to leave us just yet.'

He reacted to that, but only to get to his feet with an easy grace that brought to mind a gymnast or a dancer. He crossed the room lightly until only the low table separated us, stood with his hands folded together in front of him. He wasn't a big man and we were of a similar height. In the old pictures I'd seen of him, his hair had been dark, slightly floppy. The remaining shadow of it on his shaven skull indicated that it would have been retreating fast at the corners, leaving a pronounced widow's peak.

'Not a prisoner?' he repeated then, and he smiled, a sad little upward quirk of his lips. 'So the large gentleman with the gun under his arm lurking at the top of the stairs would not try to prevent me from walking out the front door, hmm?' He jerked his head towards the open window. 'Nor the one by the pool?' His eyes flicked over me, casual, almost dismissive. 'And you...?'

'Charlie,' I supplied.

He inclined his head a fraction, acknowledging a lie untold. 'And you, Charlie,' he said with an expressive flick of his fingers towards my right hip under my open jacket. 'Will you use that gun you carry, if I go against your wishes?'

I hid my surprise, looked him straight in the eye. 'I won't have to.'

He let his eyebrow lift. 'Maybe,' he said, and let his gaze drop very deliberately to the tray, as if that was the end of it.

I'd half-expected that he would ignore breakfast as some kind of protest, but he inspected my offering with apparent interest. The food selection was nothing fancy, but included toast, coffee in a disposable cup, croissants, and fresh orange juice. Anything that could be eaten without giving him the potential weapon of a knife and fork. He paused, then picked up the plastic glass of juice and held it out to me enquiringly.

I took the juice from him without comment, took enough of a swallow to satisfy his concerns, handed it back. He gave me another of those little bows and drank in careful sips, casting a somewhat jaundiced eye over the lofty proportions of the room as he did so. Compared to his little cell at Fourth Day, this place must have seemed a palace.

'So, Charlie, would it be too much of a cliché to ask where am I? And how did I get here?'

'You don't remember,' I said, more a statement than anything else.

He frowned, the first outward sign of disturbance in those unnervingly smooth thought patterns. 'No,' he said slowly. 'I went to bed at home last night at my usual time, in my usual way, and everything was normal. And when I awoke...it wasn't.'

'You were in the compound of a cult,' I said instead. 'Locked in your room and surrounded by armed guards. Surely that hardly counts as "at home", Mr Witney?'

'Your definition of "home" clearly differs greatly from mine,' he returned calmly. 'However you choose to label Fourth Day, at least Randall Bane never spied on us.' He flicked his fingers towards what I'd thought was a very well-hidden CCTV camera in one of the light fittings. 'Randall offered me sanctuary when I needed it most, when the rest of the world had betrayed my trust. How else would you have me think of it but as my home?' And before I could answer that, he added, 'The key, incidentally, was on my night table. All you had to do was knock.'

I paused, tried to remember seeing a key, failed.

A lie, then. Aimed at me, or himself?

'So if Fourth Day is all sweetness and light, why did you lock your door at night?'

'To keep out strangers.' The response was immediate, but again there was that slight shift in stance, uncomfortable. I considered calling him on it, should have done so.

'Don't you miss it?' I asked instead. 'The life you had before Fourth Day?'

'What life? A job I'd grown increasingly disillusioned with, and a marriage that was already crumbling before....' He stopped, smiled that sad little smile again, clasping the orange juice with both hands, as if afraid they'd give away his secrets if he turned them loose. 'There was no life before Fourth Day,' he said. 'There was only an existence of sorts.'

I put my head on one side, searched his features for sign of irony, found none, and said with care, 'What about Liam?'

He stiffened. 'What about him?'

'Five years ago you were *so* convinced that your son's involvement with Bane led directly to his death,' I said, needing to push now the first cracks had begun to show, 'that you hounded every government agency you thought might listen. And when none of them did, you went in to Fourth Day yourself – to find evidence against Bane.'

'And instead I found truth,' he shot back, colour in his cheeks now. 'Is *that* why you came for me?' He snapped the empty plastic glass onto the tray and waved an all-encompassing hand to the house, the guards, me. 'All this trouble, when all you had to do was *ask* and I could have told you that Randall Bane *was not* responsible.'

'So who was?'

'I don't know.' Witney's face shut down. He shrugged, letting his palms fall outwards in supplication. I read evasion in the shift of his shoulders, in the way his eyes slipped away from mine. 'The past is behind us,' he said, but it rang hollow, like a mantra with no faith behind it.

'Liam was your son,' I said, stubborn. 'Is he so easily forgotten?'

Witney's head jerked up in anger then, affording me a glimpse of the man who'd been willing to sacrifice everything to find a reason for a pointless death.

'You are not a parent, or you would have no need to ask such a question.' His voice was frigid and colourless, almost without emotion.

Not a parent... Oh God, if only you knew...

He looked right at me as he spoke, and because of that he caught the violent swirl of emotion that flashed into my unguarded face. His eyes widened as he made the kind of leap I didn't want – and couldn't afford – anyone to make.

'You have children?' he demanded. 'I'm—'

'That's none of your business,' I cut in, brusque.

'Maybe not. But you must realise that no parent should ever outlive their children.' He paused a moment, choosing his words with the utmost care, then said softly, 'If I'd had the chance I'd have laid down my life for Liam's, without hesitation. As it is, nothing I can do on this earth will bring my son back. Throwing my own life away to go after who might have been responsible would have been an insult to his memory. Randall Bane helped me to come to terms with that. To finally let my son rest.'

There was a curious intensity to him, as if he was trying to convince himself as much as me. *But how do you rest?* I wondered. *Knowing that you failed him.*

'So Bane persuaded you to give up,' I murmured. 'How convenient.'

He shook his head. 'Bane helped me,' he said. Then offered, more tentatively, 'He could help you, too.'

'Oh, I've seen the kind of help he offers to young women, thanks,' I said, and felt my lip begin to curl. 'Tell me, do they all run screaming from him, or is Maria the exception? For that alone I'd gladly see him taken down.'

His head reared back. 'Leave Maria alone,' he said, sharpness to his pleading. 'She would be harmed more than you can know if you try to take her away from her family as you did me.' He watched me for a moment, as if trying to judge how much truth I took from that, then he said suddenly, 'What was it that you used to abduct me, by the way? Presumably some kind of psychoactive drug – Rohypnol perhaps, or some other form of benzodiazepine?'

This time I didn't trouble to hide my surprise and his mouth twisted. 'If you did your homework on me then surely you must know I was a schoolteacher. I may have started my career with general science, Charlie, but over the past five years I have been called upon to teach my little group of students a broader spectrum of subjects – chemistry among them.'

I remembered the rapt attention of his outdoor class under the old juniper tree and wondered what the hell he was doing bringing up that particular area of chemistry amid them. Before I could voice the question, even if I'd a mind to, Witney turned and said casually, 'I assume, from the lack of interrogation now, that you used the opportunity presented by such a drug to learn everything you wished to know?'

I shook my head. 'You talk as if this is some kind of extraordinary rendition, Mr Witney,' I said. 'To the people I work for, this was a simple rescue.'

'Is that what they told you?' His voice held a hint of pity. 'But if that's the case, why leave it so long? When Liam first entered Fourth Day, I did some research into cults. You will no doubt have done the same and found out, as I did, that the longer you leave someone on the inside, the greater the psychological trauma when you get them out.'

I tipped my head on one side. 'I thought you didn't like the cult label?'

'Not when it doesn't fit. I didn't know, then, what Randall Bane was trying to do,' he said, earnest now. 'But perhaps you should be asking yourself why wait until now to "rescue" me?'

'I'm the wrong person to ask,' I said. 'We were hired to get you out, no more than that.'

'So, you're mercenaries?'

'No – specialists.'

Witney's gaze was suddenly intent. 'Whatever they're paying you, Randall Bane will double it to deliver me back.'

I raised my eyebrow. 'You're worth so much to him?'

'He looks after his own.'

'I'm sorry,' I said slowly. 'You know I can't do that.'

Nodding, Witney asked quietly, 'And when they've gotten what they want out of me, what then?'

I didn't have an answer for him. He saw as much in my face and nodded. But as he did so, something flared in his eyes. They flew to a point over my right shoulder, to the open doorway and the balcony, his expression lunging into fearfulness.

It was so neatly done, so well-focused a piece of classic misdirection, that he almost had me. Automatically, I started to twist, reaching for the SIG, and in that fraction of a second Witney had closed in and was suddenly all over me.

He deflected my arm down and away with an almost negligent, open-handed blow and stepped in hard against my body with his own, hooking his heel behind my ankle to force me off balance while his other hand slipped beneath my jacket for the gun.

And as he did so, his hand brushed against the underside of my breast. It didn't matter that it was probably a wholly unintentional caress. I still jerked, an involuntary spasm, saw in his eyes that he'd felt it.

Muscle memory and training took over. Already overbalanced, I used the momentum he'd created, throwing my weight back to accelerate my rearward arc. As we went down, I twisted my hands into his thin shirt to control our joint descent. His fingers just managed to touch the SIG's pistol grip and closed on empty air.

As we hit the tile and began to roll, I transferred my hold to his arm and pivoted on my shoulders like a break-dancer. By the time the pair of us stopped spinning, I had a straight-arm lock on his left wrist across my thigh, with one foot wedged firmly into his armpit to keep it on stronger than was strictly necessary. I told myself it was purely for containment.

'Jesus, Witney,' I growled, shaken by the speed and polish of his technique. 'Are you trying to get yourself damn well killed?'

Since my other heel was pressed down hard onto his windpipe, it was a question to which I did not expect an immediate answer. I kept him pinned for a few seconds longer, mainly just to prove I could, then released him. It took him a moment to get his breath back. By the time he sat up, rubbing at his throat, I was on my feet again and well out of reach.

'I don't need to try,' he said at last, still gasping. He levered himself onto his feet, not so graceful now, and for the first time, when he looked at me, I saw bitterness and despair. 'You've done that for me, by taking me out of there.'

'You're safe here,' I said, losing patience as a sudden memory of Randall Bane reaching out towards the kneeling girl bloomed and withered inside my head, leaving behind it a sense of restlessness like a bad dream. 'I don't know who you think is after you, exactly, but we can protect you.'

He studied me for a moment, frowning, eyes running slowly over me as though he couldn't quite marry my image with what just happened, then he shook his head, and I saw his face close up. 'I doubt it.'

I suppressed a sigh of exasperation and didn't press him. 'Whether you realise it or not, we *are* trying to help you,' I said tartly. 'What did you think that little performance was going to achieve? Even if you got past me, there are still half a dozen others out there to contend with, as you pointed out.'

'We are judged not by what we achieve, Charlie, but what we attempt.'

'What am I supposed to say to that?' I demanded. 'Nice try?'

Over at his original position by the wall, he put his back to it and slid down until he was sitting at the base, knees tucked up in front of him, arms wrapped around his shins. He'd drawn that air of eerie calm around himself again like a cloak. I'd turned away before he spoke.

'Bane can help you, Charlie, if you'd only let him.'

I jerked a hand up. 'Oh no,' I said quickly. 'I'll overlook the attempt to overpower me, Witney. In your position, I probably would have done the same. But, if you try to convert me, now that really *will* piss me off.'

I stalked over to the door, rapped on it and waited for McGregor to work the lock from the outside. When I looked back, it was to find Witney's gaze still fixed on me. I jerked my chin towards the tray I'd left behind.

'Enjoy your breakfast.'

CHAPTER SEVEN

We moved Thomas Witney out of the Calabasas house that afternoon, in a convoy of three near-identical armoured Chevy Suburbans with anti-ballistic glass and run-flat tyres, and barrelled north on I-405, heading towards Santa Clarita.

Getting Witney into the vehicle had been done carefully, but he didn't give us any trouble. We'd backed the vehicles into the huge garage that took up the whole of the lower ground floor. Sean and McGregor had brought him down and bundled him straight in, Sean sliding into the rear seat of the centre vehicle alongside him, as much to ensure he didn't get any ideas about leaving us prematurely, as for his own protection.

I was behind the wheel of the chase car, with Parker Armstrong riding shotgun. In a conservative dark-grey suit that contrasted with his short-clipped hair, Parker had a quietly prosperous air about him. He could have been a banker, or a lawyer, or a businessman, especially with those ever-watchful shrewd eyes hidden behind wrap-around sunglasses. But the casual observer would have been hard-pressed to point to close protection as his stock-in-trade. Unless they jammed their face right up against the limo-black tint on the windows, that is, and saw the MP5K slung casually across his lap.

The shortened version of the Heckler & Koch MP5 sub-machine gun was ideally suited as a close-quarters weapon within the confines of a vehicle, which was why Parker favoured it. As well as my SIG, I had an HK53 compact assault rifle down the side of my seat, in the gun rack the vehicle armourers had thoughtfully provided for the purpose. When they'd said the Chevys came fully loaded, they'd meant it.

I kept checking my mirrors for signs of a tail amid the jostling traffic, noting the drivers of half a dozen makes and models who seemed eager to match our speed and course. Maybe they just thought we might have some big-shot Hollywood type on board and they were craning to catch a glimpse.

Not that we were expecting trouble. No more than usual. I certainly wasn't expecting it to come from inside the vehicle.

'You let him get to you,' Parker said then, out of nowhere.

I'd been concentrating on keeping the Chevy close enough to the car in front to practically exchange paint, and he caught me way off balance. 'Excuse me?'

'Witney,' he elaborated. 'You let him get under your skin.'

'If he did, I handled it,' I said shortly.

Parker gave a slow nod. 'That you did,' he agreed with

a flash of very white teeth against his tan. When I glanced over, he added, 'That takedown was as fast and nasty as any I've seen – I was impressed. But that wasn't what I meant.'

'Oh?' I fought not to let my alarm show, kept my hands steady on the wheel, eyes flicking between the driving mirrors and the massive rump of the Suburban that seemed to fill my forward view. It was a difficult balance between keeping far enough back to have reaction time if we came under attack, and not giving anyone chance to muscle between us.

Parker sighed. 'Just be thankful I was the one monitoring the feeds this morning, and not Sean,' he said. He waited until he saw the hint of colour, the sudden heat in the tips of my ears, before he let me off the hook of that accusing gaze. He slipped off his shades, tucked them into his top pocket as his voice turned gentle. 'You gotta tell him, Charlie.'

'What? That Witney tried to land one on me?'

'No, that he scored a direct hit with that crack about parental responsibilities.' He paused, added with a gentleness that almost undid me, 'If it was me, I'd want to know.'

Would you?

My breath hissed out. 'I've never planned to keep anything from Sean,' I said. 'I've just been searching for the right moment.' It sounded lame when I said it. But the right moment never came. And by the time I realised that, it was much too late.

'Search harder,' Parker said, grim. 'If the hospital hadn't called me, I wouldn't know either, would I?'

No, you probably wouldn't. 'Did you tell Bill Rendelson?' I asked, remembering that bitter glare.

'I didn't have to,' Parker pointed out in a steady voice.

'All agency paperwork comes across Bill's desk – including medical expenses.'

Damn. And how long can he be relied upon to keep that little titbit to himself?

'All right,' I said, defeated. 'As soon as we're done here, I'll find a way to tell Sean.'

'If you feel that's best,' Parker said. Was I being over-touchy to read such scepticism into such a short response?

I took my eyes off the road for just long enough to throw my boss a cynical glance. 'How long do you think he'd keep his mind on the job, Parker,' I said tightly, 'if I dropped something like that on him now?'

'Sean's a professional,' Parker said, confident, reaching for his sunglasses, sliding them back on. 'He wouldn't let it affect him.'

Yeah. But there was a hollow ache somewhere high under my ribcage that I recognised as anxiety. *Maybe that's just what I'm afraid of most.*

CHAPTER EIGHT

Our destination was a part-completed parking structure on the outskirts of Santa Clarita. On that much, at least, Parker had briefed us before we left Calabasas. There, we would hand Witney over into the care of our mysterious client, saddle up and head back to New York.

I wasn't sorry to be going home.

It still struck me as odd to think of Manhattan that way. The time I'd spent teaching self-defence classes to women in a run-down seaside town on the north-west coast of England seemed a lifetime ago. Several lifetimes, if you wanted to look at it that way. And not many of them happy ones.

But there was something about New York that sang to me. The colour and the noise, the friendly profanity, the chance to slip unnoticed as a sharp blade through the crowd.

On the surface, Los Angeles seemed too shiny by comparison, too evenly tanned, its teeth too straight and too white. It was a city altogether too prone to admiring its own reflection in designer store windows as it cruised the main drag, and wouldn't admit to anything rotten at its core.

'Boss?' came Erik Landers's voice over the radio from the lead vehicle. 'This is it?' There was enough doubt in his voice to make it a question.

'Affirmative,' Parker said, terse, into the mic. 'Top floor. Stay alert, people.'

'I don't like it,' I murmured, looking at the sagging security fencing, the weeds forcing up through the cracked concrete. 'I hope you took payment upfront on this one, Parker.'

'Trust me, the last thing this particular client is going to do is try to double-cross us, Charlie,' Parker said. 'He just likes to keep things kinda covert, that's all.' But when I glanced across I found him craning forwards to check out the high angles and knew, despite his reassuring words, he didn't like the set-up any more than I did.

So, why agree to it?

The three Chevys clambered slowly over the uneven ground, soft suspension wallowing through the iron-hard ruts. According to Parker's intel, the parking structure was part of an overambitious retail development project that had stalled into a morass of legal wrangling. Meanwhile, the concrete blanched and crumbled as nature did its concentrated best to reclaim what had been taken.

The mesh gate blocking the entrance to the structure now stood drunkenly open, the chain that had once secured it cut through with neat precision, dangling from the pulled-back hasp with the redundant padlock still attached.

We climbed steadily up the darkened series of ramps towards the roof, the Chevys thumping over badly fitted expansion strips, their tyres protesting each tight upward corner until at last we broke through into sunlight again.

The roof was a wide, flat area of rippled concrete, mapped by tar lines and scattered with the abandoned debris of slipshod management.

You could certainly see plenty from up here, from the distant rush of building traffic on I-5, to the distinctive beige and orange livery of a Southwest Airlines 737 lifting off out of the grandly overtitled Bob Hope International Airport in Burbank. I didn't have the time or the inclination to admire the view.

Three vehicles were already in position on the otherwise deserted rooftop. Two more blacked-out Chevy Suburbans that had probably come from the same custom workshop as our own, and a dusty old mid-Eighties' Ford Econoline panel van. The van, as much rust as paint, looked perfectly at home in its current surroundings, which was, no doubt, why it had been chosen.

We pulled up with a decent distance between us in which to dance. Immediately, the front passenger door of one of the opposing Suburbans opened and a lone figure got out. He was tall, made taller by a ramrod-straight back and parade-ground stride. His grey hair still Marine Corps-clipped, silver moustache the same. He, too, was wearing dark glasses against the bleached-out glare, and for once I was glad of the barrier. I knew from experience there was nothing to be gleaned from this man's stone-cold gaze.

'Epps?' I said, almost a whisper. I turned, staring. 'We've been working for *Epps*?'

Parker gave a single staccato nod, bit out, 'We still are.'

I'd never been sure exactly what position within the US

government security services was held by Conrad Epps. I doubt there were many who could offer a comprehensive job description, and fewer still who wanted to know.

But when my father had got himself into a mess on this side of the Atlantic the previous autumn, Epps was the one who made it all go away. I had no illusions that Epps had acted for any reasons remotely related to altruism or sentimentality, because I was pretty convinced he was a man devoid of either quality. If it hadn't coincided with his interests to help us, then nothing I could have said or done would have made him lift a finger.

And now, if the stiff distaste on Parker's face was anything to go by, he'd called in the marker for that happy quirk of fate.

Epps's team climbed out of their vehicles and assembled like a well-drilled display behind him. Four men with regulation shaded eyewear and regulation haircuts, wearing long, dark raincoats despite the cloudless sky. Two more got out of the old Econoline, more casually dressed, but clearly Epps had bought these men from the same factory store as the others. There were no firearms on show, but that didn't mean they weren't close.

I heard Parker let out a quiet breath, saw his knuckles flex, then he slid the MP5K into the footwell and opened his own door. As he stepped down empty-handed onto the baked concrete, he was nothing but calm. The rest of us followed suit. Sean got out of the centre Chevy and held the rear door ajar for Witney, so Epps got his first look at the object of this cloak-and-dagger exercise.

Epps stilled for a moment, removed his sunglasses as if making sure, then nodded.

'Mr Armstrong,' he greeted, raising that deep voice just loud enough to carry. 'Good job.'

'Thank you, Mr Epps,' Parker returned gravely. 'I trust this wipes the slate clean between us.'

'That would be a reasonable assumption on your part,' Epps said, which was neither confirmation nor denial. Perhaps he had learnt a long time ago never to speak in absolutes.

I'd moved up on Parker's left, close enough to see the way the corner of his eye narrowed slightly at the exchange. Even Epps, I considered briefly, would be a fool to push him too far.

Sean came forwards with Witney walking alongside him. The schoolteacher seemed older, greyer in the piercing reflected sunlight. That smooth coordination I'd noticed in him was gone, so he almost stumbled over the roughcast concrete beneath his booted feet, as though, whatever he'd been expecting, this wasn't it. When he reached Parker and Epps, he halted.

'A case of better late than never, huh?' Witney said with that sad little upward hitch of his mouth.

'Indeed it is, Mr Witney,' Epps said. 'I should have taken notice of you five years ago. For that, you have my apologies.'

Witney regarded him. 'If you had, we wouldn't be here now,' he said and the bitterness to his voice almost masked the desperation. 'There was nothing to find.'

Epps turned his head a fraction and fixed Witney with a very deliberate stare. A sudden apprehension riffled the hairs on my arms, the back of my neck.

'We'll know, soon enough,' Epps said and, without

shifting his gaze, louder over his shoulder, 'All right. Let's move this along.'

The two men from the Econoline stepped in and grabbed Witney's arms, one on either side. They were big men and he was not, and there was nothing gentle about the way they handled him.

'What do you want with him?' I demanded. 'What's he done?'

Epps shifted his icy focus onto me. I refused to flinch, despite the eerie sensation that you could look right through those bottomless eyes of his, all the way down into hell. Sean and Parker closed in on either side, as though that alone would stop Epps crushing me like an annoying fly if he felt the urge.

'As far as we are aware, Mr Witney is not personally responsible for any wrongdoing, but the information he is withholding is another matter,' Epps said, his voice chillingly neutral. 'At this time, we are taking a particular interest in the Fourth Day organisation, and we believe Mr Witney is... intimate with its command structure.'

'You're after Bane,' Sean said. 'Why?'

Epps shifted his gaze. 'I don't believe, Mr Meyer, that I am required to explain my actions to you.'

Witney, who'd faltered at the turn of events, now began actively to resist. The two men made what seemed to be only a fractional alteration in their stance, but their grip went from assistance to control in an instant. When the schoolteacher still twisted against them, they took him professionally to his knees and held him there long enough to zip PlastiCuffs onto his wrists behind him. It was interesting how much trouble he caused them for such a simple manoeuvre.

Almost as one, Sean and I stepped forwards. Two of Epps's people mirrored our actions, blocking our path. When we sidestepped, so did they. I thought of the gun on my hip, knew I'd probably be dead before I had it drawn.

'Please don't be foolish, Charlie,' Epps said, and his unexpected use of my first name was a threat all by itself. A whole collection of them. *I know you*, it said. *I know everything there is to know about you and the people closest to you, and I will use it – all of it – against you if I have to.*

To my onward shame, I stopped.

The two men manhandling Witney, meanwhile, reached the Econoline, opened the rear doors and threw him inside like a side of meat. Unable to break his fall, he landed face down, the air slamming out of him.

One of Epps's men rolled him onto his side so his feet cleared the door and I caught a glimpse of Witney's face. Not terrified, as I would have expected, but pale with boiling anger. The closing door cut short my view.

The men climbed into the front seats, cranked the engine, and headed for the exit ramp leading back down into the bowels of the building. The old Econoline sounded a lot sweeter than it looked.

I swung back to Parker, would have let rip had I not caught the hint of stress in his tight-lipped face.

'You will, of course, give us twenty minutes to clear the area before you move your team out,' Epps said to him, as though nothing of the struggle we'd just witnessed had ever happened. Officially, I don't suppose it had. 'We want to keep this low-key.'

For a long moment, I thought Parker would argue. I

wasn't sure whether to be relieved or disappointed when, at last, he gave a short nod and let his gaze drop away.

Epps dealt the barest glimmer of a smile, as if he knew precisely what such capitulation had cost. Knew, and didn't care. He cast a brief dismissive eye across the rest of us, then turned his back with an almost lazy disregard. His broad shoulder blades beneath the pale raincoat made a very tempting target.

We watched him walk away.

'Why didn't you tell us?' Sean asked the quiet question.

'About Epps?' Parker said, giving us both a tired smile. 'Why? What difference would it have made?'

I thought about my glib reassurances to Witney that very morning. *Not a prisoner, exactly...*I'd told him. *Not in your best interests to leave us just yet....* Would I have used those words if I'd known what was coming?

'What do you think is going to happen to him, Parker?' I asked. 'Do you honestly believe Epps is going to turn him loose when he's sucked him dry?'

Parker's face twitched, and there was just a tinge of the same sadness that had passed through Witney. 'No,' he said at last. 'I don't.'

Sean was still glowering. Parker let out a slow breath, looked about to say more, when there was a sudden flurry amid Epps's people.

His team were too proud to run, but one approached him at a swift jog, finger jammed against his earpiece. 'Sir! We have a situation.'

I saw Epps's purposeful stride hitch. 'What kind of a situation?' he demanded. 'They can have scarcely cleared the perimeter.'

'Er, that's just it, sir,' the man said, paling under that stony gaze. 'They haven't *reached* the perimeter. We can't raise them.'

And then everyone was running, and all those guns I'd sensed earlier were out and cocked and ready.

Two of the Suburbans belonging to Epps's team set off with a yelp of tyres, jolting down the ramp. I leapt for the driver's seat of our own vehicle, threw the HK53 to Parker and twisted the key in the ignition.

We followed Epps's men downwards with caution, not wanting to get mixed up in a friendly fire scenario. I kept the big Suburban to a walking pace, giving cover. Parker was to my left, the compact assault rifle pulled hard up into his shoulder, forefinger outside the trigger guard. In the driver's door mirror, I could see Sean with a similar weapon. Both men put their feet down carefully, softly, and their eyes were everywhere.

We found the Econoline on the ground floor with its nose hard up against the mesh security fencing near the entrance, surrounded by Epps's people. The engine was still running and the doors were open. The guy who'd been driving was slumped half out of his seat onto the concrete, feet tangled up with the pedals. In that position, the gaping wound to his throat had caused him to bleed out rapidly into the dusty concrete, like a sacrificial goat.

The other man had managed to get a couple of strides from the passenger door before going down. Epps was bending over him. As we reached the scene, he rose without expression, dusting his hands.

'Neck,' he said briefly. There was nothing in his voice and even less in his eyes.

I climbed down from the driver's seat, walked over and glanced into the rear of the Econoline. The only thing inside the van was a single pair of discarded PlastiCuffs on the scarred metal floor.

But Thomas Witney had vanished like he'd never existed.

CHAPTER NINE

At 6:45 that evening we stood by the door of a hangar at Van Nuys Airport, while the sun dropped fast behind the smoky hills towards the Pacific. I watched it bleed a trail of the palest blues and pinks, the colours absorbed by the stumpy control tower. Air traffic in and out of the airport seemed tireless and unending. In the rapid onset of dusk, the lights of the planes showed as fierce bright pinpricks against the darkening sky.

We'd stayed in Santa Clarita only long enough to carry out a fast but thorough search of the area surrounding the abandoned development. Plenty of time to realise that, if Witney was escaping on foot, he would have qualified as an Olympic-standard sprinter.

He'd also somehow managed to extricate himself from a set of PlastiCuffs, which had been applied by experts, and had concealed in his simple clothing a blade sharp enough to slash a man's throat, despite being thoroughly searched before we'd taken him out of the house in Calabasas.

Either we were all getting very sloppy, or he'd had help.

A shiver ran across my back, despite the day's residual warmth. If our security had been breached, who knew what form Epps's retribution would take.

With the cold efficiency I'd come to expect of him, Epps had called in a professional clean-up crew to deal with the bodies, and an enclosed trailer to remove the Econoline to a forensics lab. Then he'd brusquely ordered us to follow him. Parker had put McGregor in charge of his own team's continuing search, with two vehicles at their disposal. He was good, but we were not holding our breath on a result.

Parker had also left very specific instructions for Bill Rendelson, should the rest of us fail to return within a reasonable time frame. Nice to know the boss wasn't entirely trusting when it came to our client.

We climbed into our remaining Suburban, Sean at the wheel and Parker alongside him, and drove south to Van Nuys in a fast-moving convoy, using the high-occupancy vehicle lanes to cut through the evening rush. Epps's men kept us firmly boxed in all the way.

'So, did Witney jump, or was he pushed?' Sean asked eventually into the tense silence.

'When I spoke to Witney this morning, he certainly seemed to think that by taking him out of Fourth Day, we'd put him in some kind of danger,' I said. 'He told me Bane would pay us double what we were getting to return him.'

'Looks like he may have found a cheaper way.' Sean's reflected gaze in the rear-view mirror was filled with an angry reproach. 'And you didn't think to mention this before?'

'I was aware of it, so it was my call,' Parker said quietly, before I could answer. 'Besides, we were already taking maximum precautions. What more could we have done?'

But I heard the nagging worry underscoring his words.

'And he didn't give any indication of who – besides Bane – might have wanted him?' Sean persisted.

'No.' *But I promised him he'd be safe, that we'd protect him...*

Sean said, 'If it was a snatch, why uncuff him?'

'And if it was a rescue,' Parker responded grimly, 'why kill two men to effect it?'

At the airport, we bypassed normal security checks and were driven almost straight into this nondescript hangar, where Epps disappeared into an inner office without a word, and we were left kicking our heels. Enough of his men lurked nearby to disabuse us of any notion that we were free to leave. They were not what you'd call chatty.

Not a prisoner, exactly... The irony was not altogether lost on me.

Through the open doorway, I watched a small executive Gulfstream jet land and begin to taxi, and idly checked my watch. I thought again of the bloody scene in the parking garage. The kind of power Epps wielded, I knew that by now even the tarnished area of concrete would have been dug out and relaid, leaving no trace of something that never happened in the first place.

Had it been our fault?

Sean leant his head back against the driver's door of the Suburban and closed his eyes. 'Next time you take us for a picnic, Parker,' he said lazily, 'take us somewhere nice.'

'Yeah,' I said, 'and bring some food.'

That raised a smile which almost made it up to Parker's eyes.

'I'm sorry,' he said at last, tiredly. 'Epps was pretty damned clear on how he wanted this handled. I had to play it by the book.'

Sean gave an apparently casual shrug. 'Don't sweat it,' he said, eyes still shut. 'We all have our secrets.'

Parker's gaze briefly met mine, fell away.

'Any ideas why we're being kept hanging around here?' I asked quickly, flexing my fingers inside their gloves. As the sun disappeared, I reminded myself it was still technically winter. I would have jammed my cooling hands into my pockets, but didn't want the restriction just in case. The same went for buttoning my jacket.

'Looks like we might be just about to find out,' Parker murmured.

We turned to see Epps had left the office and was approaching with that precise military stride. From outside the hangar came the roar of another turboprop going through maximum revs for take-off. The rising growl of the plane's engines seemed to expand as Epps drew nearer. If I were more fanciful, I could almost have imagined he'd timed his entrance deliberately. He halted a few metres away and waited until the noise had largely abated before he spoke.

'Well, gentlemen,' he said, with barely a flicker in my direction. 'I think you'll agree that what should have been a clean and simple operation has turned into the mother of all cock-ups.'

'It doesn't necessarily follow,' Parker said with every appearance of bland politeness, 'that it was *our* security that was compromised.'

The cold stare Epps levelled in his direction was no less vicious for being short.

'Security *was* breached, somewhere along the line,' Epps said through his teeth. 'And the source is being ascertained as we speak. Heads will roll, gentlemen, you may be certain of that.' He left just long enough of a pause for the words to sink in, then hit us with, 'But right now your primary objective should be reacquiring your target.'

'Wait a minute,' I said. 'We completed our assignment and handed him over into your...*care*.' If Epps noticed the sarcastic emphasis, he gave no sign. 'Surely, if anyone needs to *reacquire* him, it's you.'

His head turned very slowly in my direction. 'I consider your task incomplete,' he said with an air of total finality.

One look at Parker's flattened expression was enough to dissuade me from argument – one I stood little chance of winning.

'Well, I do not, so if you want us to continue working on this,' Parker said, matching his tone, 'you're going to have to pay the going rate. The man who went into Fourth Day was a schoolteacher. The man who came out was something else again. This was not the job we were briefed to do.'

'I concur,' Epps said, surprising all of us. 'Which is precisely why we are here.'

He nodded towards the huge doorway, just as the Gulfstream G550 I'd seen land earlier swung its nose into view, rolled fully inside the hangar and powered down. The twin-engined corporate jet was sleekly arrogant, with its racehorse-slender body and high tail. As the distinctive whistle of the Rolls-Royce turbofans died away, the door cracked open. I fully expected another macho military type to come bounding down the steps.

Instead, the figure who appeared almost diffidently in the

doorway was a slim man with a long mousy ponytail and little round John Lennon glasses, like a throwback from the Sixties. He peered out at the assembled faces as if unsure of his welcome. With the prospect of facing Epps, I couldn't blame him for that.

He caught sight of the group of us over by the Suburban and raised a faltering hand in greeting.

'This is Mr Sagar,' Epps said as the figure came scurrying down the steps, a canvas satchel bumping against his hip. Epps's voice was dry and devoid of inflection. 'He is considered something of an expert on cults. That *is* my understanding?' he added ominously as Sagar reached us, a little flustered.

'Er, yeah, sure,' Sagar said, shaking hands all round. His hands were small for a man, barely bigger than my own, and his grip was brief but firm. He was older close up than I'd first thought, late thirties at least, but his boyish air was compounded by the quick, bright grin he flashed at me. 'Hi. Call me Chris.'

'And you reckon he can give us inside information on Fourth Day?' Sean asked.

Chris Sagar stopped fussing with his bag and straightened, the last of the dying light catching the lenses of his glasses and flashing fire.

'Of course,' he said. 'Seeing as how I used to be Randall Bane's second in command.'

CHAPTER TEN

'The first thing you gotta do is *never* underestimate the guy,' Sagar said, perching on the edge of his seat and leaning forwards, eyes flicking earnestly at the expressionless faces in front of him. 'That's just fatal. If there's an angle you can think of, Bane will have thought of it already, planned a way around it, made a backup plan in triplicate.' He paused, shook his head, hands linked together tightly in his lap. 'He's got a mind like a steel trap.'

'*Now* you tell us,' I muttered.

We were on board the Gulfstream, sitting dormant in the hangar. It was the nearest convenient place to hold a conference that had enough seating. Giant soft-leather armchairs that gave alarmingly when you sat on them.

Sean had not come aboard with the rest of us. He'd taken one look at the set-up and announced he'd stay with the Suburban to watch our backs.

Now, Sagar looked surprised, maybe even a little hurt. 'Hey, I briefed you people weeks, if not *months* ago.' As if to prove it, he flipped open the satchel, dragged out a

battered red folder and handed it across to me. I opened the
file, riffled quickly through a couple of neatly typewritten
pages, my eye lighting on key words like *weapons training,
indoctrination, unarmed combat, mind control, counter-
insurgency techniques*, before I grew aware of other eyes
boring into me, and dutifully passed it over.

Parker picked up the sense of it in a moment and glanced
at Epps, sitting impassively opposite. Of the four of us, he
was the only one who seemed at ease in his surroundings.
Maybe the two guys he had loitering by the jet's open
doorway helped him feel unthreatened. Suddenly, I was
grateful we had Sean to watch those watching us.

'Withholding vital intel jeopardised the safety and security
of my team,' Parker said with lethal calm.

Epps's gaze sliced across the narrow cabin. 'It wasn't
your team who were put in jeopardy, now, was it, Mr
Armstrong?'

For a moment the tension hummed between them,
was only broken by Sagar clearing his throat. 'Um...hey,
guys?' he murmured. 'Look, I don't know what's going on
here, and to be honest, I don't want to know. Is this some
interdepartmental jurisdiction crap, is that what this is?
No, don't tell me,' he went on, hastily, lifting his hands as
two heads winched in his direction. 'Forget I asked, OK?'
he added hastily. 'But – what with you sending this truly
outstanding ride to fly me down here from San Francisco,
when I would have been happy with a bus ticket – I just
kinda assumed you were finally taking my warnings about
Fourth Day seriously, and there was some urgency to this
deal, y'know?'

For the first time in our brief, arm's-length acquaintance,

Epps hesitated. Only fractional, but so out of character that it struck me clearly, even so. Those cold eyes flickered momentarily over Parker's shuttered face, then he said, 'There have been certain developments while you were in flight, Mr Sagar.'

Sagar's face went from anxiety to consternation and back again. 'Oh crap,' he said softly, eyes darting between us. 'You lost Witney, didn't you?' He sat back in his seat, chewing at the side of his thumb and staring out of the oval porthole alongside him as if expecting a view. 'Goddamn it,' he said with quiet compression. Then he sighed, made a visible effort to pull himself together, spoke under his breath. 'Well, that proves it, I guess.'

'Proves what, Mr Sagar?' Parker demanded, his patience worn to a thin veneer.

Sagar glanced at Epps as if for permission to speak. I didn't see the older man so much as twitch, but Sagar must know him better than I did. Sagar nodded, as if Epps had spoken aloud, and said, 'Look, I joined Fourth Day about a year or so before Bane took over, and I bought into it wholesale.' He broke off, shook his head again, took a moment to gather himself. 'I can't believe I was so gullible, but at the time...' He shrugged. 'That's why I've devoted myself to exposing these cults for what they really are, and why I've been working with Mr Epps's people.'

'So, what exactly *is* Fourth Day?' Parker said, voice neutral.

'It's all there,' Sagar said, waving to his dossier. 'When he first came on the scene, I thought Bane was a saviour – literally. He was promising to change the whole thing around, and I welcomed him, I admit,' he added, shamefaced.

'Wasn't long before I realised all he wanted was a base to recruit and train people. Very specific people. I know, because for a while I was in charge of the evaluation side of the operation, so—'

But I was already remembering Thomas Witney's uncanny reaction speed. He'd got close to me almost before I knew it – was it only yesterday? I was aware of Parker's eyes on me, even as I cut across Sagar's recall.

'Recruiting how?' I asked, ignoring Epps's poisonous glance. 'And training them for what?'

Sagar shrugged in apology. 'Look, I never found that out. Bane liked to keep things very...compartmentalised. I guess he felt he had more power that way. If the organisation couldn't run without him, he had ultimate control over it.'

'You said Bane was recruiting very specific people,' Parker said. 'But Thomas Witney was a schoolteacher before he went in to Fourth Day. What was so special about him?'

'He had focus,' Sagar said immediately. 'He had that kind of driven personality. You might think the strong ones are the most difficult to turn, but they're not. All Bane had to do was redirect that focus, that drive.'

'But to what purpose?'

Sagar shrugged helplessly. 'I don't know. By the time I was uneasy enough to be asking those kinda questions, Bane was already beginning to shut me out of the loop.'

'That,' Epps said, grim, 'is information we were hoping to persuade Thomas Witney to share with us.'

'But Bane got to him first,' Sagar said, looking twitchy. Even more so when Epps rose abruptly, reaching for his inside pocket, but all that came out of it was a silently lit cellphone. Epps checked the incoming number and strode away to the rear of the plane without excusing himself. My mother would have been appalled by his manners.

Sagar's eyes roved between Parker and me, bright with questions. 'So, are you guys like...FBI? CIA? Or some Homeland Security Black Ops outfit I don't wanna know about?'

'Private sector,' Parker said. 'Out of New York.'

Sagar's eyebrows climbed, then he began to nod. 'Yeah, that makes sense, I guess. Mr Epps calls you in so he has ultimate deniability, huh?'

'Let's just say we're good at what we do,' Parker said smoothly, 'and we owed him a favour.' To his credit, he managed to not even glance in my direction as he spoke.

'So, you went into Fourth Day and got Witney out?' Sagar's face fell and he added quickly, 'Um, if you don't want to talk about it, that's cool.'

'Yes,' I said. 'We got Witney out.'

'You, too?' Sagar said, eyes widening behind those little glasses. 'I mean, there's no reason why not, of course, but even so...wow.' He grinned again. 'I was never any good at all that kung fu stuff, y'know? I joined Fourth Day thinking that was one thing Bane could give me, but he never did. Man, there were a lot of broken promises.'

He sounded almost wistful for a moment, then the brightness was back in his eyes. 'How much trouble did you have getting to him? I mean, from what I hear, Bane's taken on a lotta security recently.'

'We had it covered,' Parker said, and while his tone was pleasant, something in it warned Sagar not to push.

'Yeah,' he said, sober now, respect in his voice. 'Yeah, I get that. So, what happened – you handed him over to Epps and *Epps* lost him, is that it? Is that why he's so pissed?'

We were saved having to answer that by the man in question snapping his phone shut to end the call and striding back down the plane.

'Well, Mr Armstrong, it looks as though your services will be required for a time longer,' he said, stony. 'My people have just found a short-range tracking device attached to one of the vehicles.'

Parker bristled. 'If you're suggesting—'

'One of *our* vehicles, Mr Armstrong,' Epps admitted. He paused, uncertainty an unfamiliar taste in his mouth that was not to his liking. 'The van being used to transport Mr Witney, in fact.'

I raised my chin and dared to look Epps in the face. 'And heads are about to roll, are they?'

Something venomous thrashed behind his eyes. 'They will if Mr Witney is not recovered and debriefed about the exact nature of Fourth Day's current activities,' he snapped. 'If he was taken – willingly or unwillingly – find out who has him, or where he's hiding, and get him locked down.' His gaze pinned Sagar to his chair. 'You will liaise with Mr Armstrong's people until this assignment is completed, Mr Sagar.'

'Hey, slow down,' Sagar protested. 'You don't understand! I agreed to compile a profile, that's all. If Bane knows I'm back, well...' he swallowed, let his eyes drop away. 'I don't wanna disappear, y'know? I was never trained for any rough stuff.'

'Don't worry, Mr Sagar,' Epps said, dismissive. 'Mr Armstrong's people are the best available.' Which might have been intended to reassure the man, but was a double-edged compliment if ever I heard one. 'You'll be paid a consultancy fee for your time and expertise.'

Parker rose. In the confines of the aircraft cabin, he and Epps suddenly seemed to be standing very close together. I was struck by their similarities – Epps a taller, heavier, soulless version of Parker. Out of the corner of my eye I saw the men by the plane doorway shift their positions slightly. Automatically, I got to my feet. Epps kept his eyes on Parker, completely without regard to me.

'Our marker was cancelled out the moment we delivered Witney,' Parker repeated quietly.

'Yes, Mr Armstrong, it was,' Epps said, showing his teeth. 'But we have a contingency fund for circumstances such as this, and I'm sure you'll be happy with the amount on offer. And let's just say I will view your extended cooperation in a very favourable light for the future.'

Parker allowed himself a cynical smile. 'Is that as close as you're going to get to saying, "I owe you one"?' he asked.

Epps eyed him briefly without response. 'I trust you'll provide accommodation for Mr Sagar during his stay,' he said instead, and glanced pointedly at his watch. 'Now, if you'll excuse me? I have to go tell two widows about the auto wreck on the two-one-oh this evening, in which their husbands have officially met their deaths.'

CHAPTER ELEVEN

Thomas Witney's body turned up the following morning, in a rent-by-the-hour motel room just off West Sunset Boulevard, barely twenty miles from where he disappeared.

Parker took the call and had us ready to move out inside ten minutes. It would have been faster, but Chris Sagar dug his heels in about wanting to tag along.

'I knew Witney,' he said simply. 'And, if I'm right, I know the man who had him killed.'

Parker treated him to a long, unforgiving scrutiny. The kind that normally had tough guys shuffling their feet awkwardly and avoiding eye contact. Sagar stood up to it no better than most.

'All right,' Parker said at last. 'Grab your gear. You're not in the vehicle when we're ready to move out, we leave you behind.'

Sagar nodded, grateful.

'Is that wise?' I asked quietly, watching him take the winding staircase towards the upper floor at a fast jog, ponytail jinking. 'Whoever's responsible for what happened to Witney may well have eyes on the scene, waiting to ID who turns up.'

'I agree,' Parker said. 'But somebody put a tracker on that vehicle, and if Bane is as good as Sagar says, he'll know who we are anyway. And he'll know Sagar was flown down from San Francisco in an agency jet. Taking him with us doesn't give Bane anything he doesn't have already.'

'It does give him one thing,' Sean said, and we both turned in his direction. 'An opportunity.'

Sagar only just made Parker's deadline, scrambling into the back of the armoured Suburban right as Sean was reaching for the ignition, which would have operated the central locking system, shutting him out. Sitting directly behind him in the rear seat, I caught Sean's assessing gaze in the rear-view mirror before he slipped on a pair of Wayfarers, masking his eyes, and cranked the engine.

We drove eastwards, through the Santa Monica hills towards the San Fernando Valley. Ahead of us, smog sat sullenly over LA like a nicotine ceiling. Sagar was silent for the first part of the journey, content to rubberneck at the southern California scenery. There was a slightly wide-eyed innocence about him. I hadn't quite made up my mind if I found it appealing or not. It was certainly contrasted sharply with the wary cynicism of the man I shared my life with, and those I habitually worked alongside.

'So...Charlie, isn't it?' Sagar said when we'd settled into traffic on Route 101. 'How the heck did someone like you end up in this line of work?'

'Someone like me?' I echoed, pleasant.

'Hey, I didn't mean...' he began hastily, stopped and took

a breath. 'Um, OK, my bad. All I meant was, you got the same look as these guys.' He gestured, a little helplessly, towards Parker and Sean in the front seats. 'Like you're waiting for it to go wrong all the time. It's not a look you see often in a woman.'

'It's called experience,' Parker said without turning around. 'Charlie's got it. And if it all *does* go wrong, you'll be grateful she does.' He did turn then, just enough to glance back across at me. 'He's all yours. Stay on him.'

Sagar shifted in his seat. 'Wow. Does this mean you're, like, my personal bodyguard? How does that work?'

I passed him a long look that he had no trouble interpreting, even through dark glasses. 'It works that if you do as you're told, you won't get hurt,' I promised crisply. 'Don't do as you're told, and I'll hurt you myself.'

Sagar went quiet. I couldn't quite work out if the prospect excited or frightened him.

As we drove inland from the Santa Monica Mountains and left the freeway, I was struck again by the duality of Los Angeles. Sunset Boulevard had a glamorous ring to it, but turned out to be a mashed-together mix of squat one- and two-storey commercial buildings and gleaming modern extravagances, with billboards and palm trees competing for silhouette room against a harsh blue sky.

The motel was on an intersection and boasted thirty rooms arranged around a central courtyard. The fat man in yesterday's clothes who was slouched behind the front desk told us he had ten rooms shut down for 'routine maintenance', but to my eye there was no sign of any kind of maintenance going on, routine or otherwise.

The construction was cheap and insubstantial. There

wasn't anywhere I would have chosen as good cover in a firefight, and the whole place had the faded-out shabbiness you find in the tropics, where constant good weather proves just as hard to repel as bad.

As we drove round from Reception, there were two police black-and-whites parked to the right of the courtyard, bristling with antennas and intent. A sunglassed cop was leaning against one of the cruisers, heavily muscled arms folded across his chest as he watched us pull up on the tar-webbed asphalt.

We climbed down from the Suburban carefully, taking in the terrain. I moved in alongside Sagar. Behind the barrier of my own darkened lenses, my eyes roved constantly across the surrounding buildings, looking for gaps in the reflections from the glass. Open windows were always easier to spot in a country where air conditioning was the norm. According to the temperature read-out on the office building across the street, it was already sixty-eight degrees, providing an almost creamy warmth. It was hard to remember we were only weeks past Christmas.

The cop's body language told me that whatever cooperation Epps's influence had secured was being offered grudgingly at best. In the back of one of the cruisers, a German Shepherd had gone into a slavering barking frenzy at our approach, which the cop totally ignored.

'You Armstrong?' The question was aimed at none of us in particular, the delivery just a little too studiously disinterested to be wholly convincing.

When Parker nodded, the cop jerked his head towards an open doorway a little further along the row. 'Detective Gardner is waiting on you,' he said. He gave Chris Sagar and me a fast dismissive once-over. 'You might wanna leave the civilians outside.'

'Thanks,' Parker said, moving past with just enough hint of a smile to have the cop's brow creasing at the joke he'd missed.

I felt Sagar's hesitation as we neared the doorway. 'You don't have to go in,' I murmured, but he shook his head vigorously.

'No,' he said, swallowing, 'I do.'

Inside, my overriding impression was of thinness. Thin fabric curtains; thin stained coverlet on the bed; thin stick furniture that had been cheap when it was new and was now being asked to hold together well beyond its time. The TV remote was bolted to the bedside table. By the splits in the unconvincing wood veneer surrounding the base, the fixing had withstood several attempts to forcibly remove it.

The cramped room was made more claustrophobic by the presence of another uniform, a crime scene tech with a camera and flashgun, and a compact dark-haired woman in cargo pants and a casual cotton jacket. I pegged her instantly as the cop in charge without needing to catch a glimpse of the shield hooked into her belt. Even in a crowd, there was a certain space around her. She looked up as we loomed in her field of view, bone-weary rather than actively hostile, jaw working gum.

Gardner gave the same jerk to her chin as the cop outside. 'You Armstrong?' she repeated, gaze lingering long enough that she'd know us again.

'Thanks for holding for us, Detective Gardner,' Parker said, stepping forwards with his hand extended. 'We appreciate the heads-up on this one. I hope it's been made clear to you that we have no intention of horning in on your investigation.'

Gardner flashed a brief smile. She had very dark eyes that were bright with unanswered questions, framed by impressive lashes, long and curving. 'Pity,' she said, laconic. 'We topped four hundred homicides in LA last year. I was kinda hoping you spooks were gonna take this one off of our hands.'

'No such luck,' Parker said, sidestepping the detective's misapprehension that we were part of Epps's crew. 'Can we take a look at the body?'

'Sure. He bought it in the shower – neater that way, huh?' Gardner said, leading the way into the en suite bathroom. If I'd thought the bedroom was small, the bathroom was minuscule by comparison, lined in small white stretcher bond tiles badly mildewed along the grout lines, the taps covered in a fur of limescale.

Thomas Witney was crumpled into the far corner of the low bath, stripped naked, his hands bound tight behind him with wire. The way it had sliced deep into his wrists told me he'd fought long and hard against the restraint. But if the marks on his body were any indication of what had been done to him, he'd had good reason to.

'Ain't pretty, is it?' Gardner said with that lazy quality cops everywhere adopt as a means of self-protection. 'They sure went to town on him.'

'They didn't have the time to be tidy,' Sean said, crouching to scan the body with eyes that were as cool and flat as his tone. 'He was only snatched yesterday. Whatever they wanted out of him, they wanted it fast.'

'And I'd say they got it,' Parker said, grim.

'Yesterday?' Gardner queried, her own gaze narrowing.
'We found some older injuries on him – there, on the throat
and around the left arm, see? The doc reckons those pre-
date the others. Thought that was maybe how they grabbed
him – some kind of chokehold. Know more once they get
him on the slab.'

Sean got slowly to his feet, and I had a feeling there was
trouble in the very deliberation of his movements. I glanced
at Parker, but his face was professionally blank.

'How did he die?' he asked.

The detective's bright gaze flicked between us, curiosity
bubbling. 'Gunshot,' she said after a moment. 'You can't see
it with his head resting against the tiles like that, but right
temple, close range. Small enough calibre not to splatter his
brains all round the tub. Like I said, keeping it neat. We
might get a match when they pull the round out of him, but
I wouldn't bet on it. These guys were pros.'

'Taking a risk, though, weren't they?' Parker said. 'Doing
that to him here.'

Gardner grunted in what could have been amusement,
waved an arm through the open doorway to the bedroom.
In the wall above the bed I noticed several old bullet holes,
cracks in the plaster radiating outwards from each of
them.

'You think?' Gardner said. 'Nobody woulda heard a
damn thing. I guarantee it.'

'I gotta go,' Sagar mumbled suddenly. I turned to find
him pale and sweating, hands fluttering to his face.

'Get him outta here,' Gardner said quickly, more resigned
than angry. 'Don't let him hurl on my crime scene.'

I scooped a hand under Sagar's elbow and fast-walked

him out into the bleached brightness of the courtyard. On the other side of the parking area was a set of vending machines and a bench. I headed him across to it and plonked him down in the shade, then slipped my sunglasses back on and stood a couple of feet away with my back slightly towards him, staring outwards.

The muscled cop and the K9 cruiser had gone. A dark-tinted van marked 'Coroner's Office' had taken its place. Two men in disposable suits were wheeling a trolley towards the crime scene. Other than that, there was no activity. If any of the other rooms were taken, the occupants were too blasé, or too wary, to gawk in front of the police.

The current live information hit my retinas and was processed by one part of my brain, but another part replayed the image of Witney's body, crumpled in the scuffed bathtub. The whole thing ran inside my head like a scene from a movie, disconnected from reality, from the life he'd once had. It seemed a shabby way to die, amid your own filth and fear and pain. I hoped, when it was my turn, I went out quick.

Of course, I'd already given death a trial run and been mildly disappointed not to recall anything about the experience. No long tunnels, no bright lights and harp music, no deep voices calling my name. Just a big black zero.

So the records show, I flatlined for almost two minutes after being shot twice on a job in New Hampshire, shortly before Sean and I started working for Parker. It had been almost exactly a year ago, I realised, and wondered if I ought to mark the occasion like some kind of macabre rebirthday.

Behind me, Sagar was sitting hunched over, gasping in

the dry air. Without comment, I dug in the front pocket of my linen suit trousers, brought out a roll of cash and fed a single into the vending machine.

It was another of Parker's rules that we always carried enough of a float to buy our way out of trouble if the need arose. Beyond anything else, it was amazing how much smoother egress from a busy restaurant could be achieved if you tipped the waiter thirty per cent upfront to make sure your food arrived at the same time as your principal's, if not slightly before. Most of the people we were assigned to protect were not prepared to sit around while their bodyguards finished eating.

My selection thunked into the chute at the bottom of the machine. I dug it out and handed it over without taking my eyes off the surrounding area.

'You blame yourself, don't you, Charlie?' he said quietly at last. I glanced back, found him taking a sip of his Mountain Dew. His colour was better and his eyes had turned shrewd behind those little round glasses. 'If you want to blame anyone, blame Bane. He's the one responsible for all this.'

'He shouldn't have had the chance. If I'd done my job better, Witney might still be alive.'

'Hey,' he said, chiding. 'You didn't... I thought Mr Epps was the one who...?'

'It still feels like it's on my watch,' I said. 'Like it's on my head.'

Sagar rose, stood alongside me, his eyes fixed on the open doorway to the room where Thomas Witney died. 'You liked him, didn't you?'

'Yes, I did,' I said. 'And you know what pisses me off the most?'

He shook his head. Across the courtyard, the two coroner's men reappeared, manoeuvring the wheeled stretcher between them. It now contained a black body bag, loaded and strapped into position.

'The waste,' I said bitterly. 'Witney never told us anything about what was happening inside Fourth Day, because it wasn't our job to ask. And Epps never got the opportunity.' I watched the body being loaded into the van with impersonal efficiency. The doors slammed. 'Witney never wanted to leave that cult. If Bane was so bloody desperate to prevent a possible security breach, he didn't have to torture and kill him. All he had to do was take him home.'

CHAPTER TWELVE

When we got back to Calabasas, it was to find Epps waiting for us. He was leaning casually over the table in the Great Room, picking his way through our intel with his back arrogantly towards the hallway.

Joe McGregor was standing awkwardly nearby, himself flanked by the two security men who habitually accompanied Epps. McGregor threw Parker a look of embarrassed apology as we came in, received a head shake by way of reply. There wasn't much short of tear gas could prevent Epps coming in and doing as he pleased.

'It would seem that locating Thomas Witney did not prove as difficult as I envisaged, Mr Armstrong,' Epps said when he heard our footsteps, waiting until we were almost upon him before he straightened, turning to add with a mirthless smile, 'although, naturally, I would have preferred him returning in a more…viable condition.'

Sean's stride never faltered, he just kept moving, crowding in on Epps until they were bumping toes. Two pig-headed people, equally refusing to give ground to the other. Sean paid no regard to the reaction of Epps's security detail, totally ignoring the Glocks that suddenly appeared in their hands and pointed unwaveringly in his direction, trigger fingers inside the guard.

Sometimes, Sean's utter lack of fear was what frightened me most about him. Would he still take those risks, if he was a father? Would that condition make him more than he was? Or less?

'If you had given us even *half* the story on this, from the beginning, Thomas Witney might still be alive. As it is, we've just come from the scene and you can take my word on it that he didn't die pleasantly,' Sean said through his teeth. 'Now, I don't expect someone like you to give a shit about that, but two of your own are also dead because of the mistakes that were made here and, if nothing else, the payout to their families ought to make a significant hole in your budget, so don't you think it's time you told us what the *fuck* is going on?' He ended on a bark, cast a contemptuous glance at the nearest gun barrel, three inches from his left eye, and added an almost jeering, '*Sir.*'

For a long suspended moment, Epps didn't speak. In many ways, he and Sean shared the same underlying phenotype. The same genetic predisposition to violence, present at birth, developed by military training and honed by experience. But where Sean's behaviour was tempered by a basic honour code, Epps's personality was so balanced on a knife-edge that I had no idea how he would react to such blatant insubordination. Anything from amusement to execution – it could have gone either way.

Instinctively, I eased a few inches sideways so I was fractionally in front of Chris Sagar, keeping my knees soft and my weight evenly spread. Sagar didn't react. He was watching the scene unfold with a frozen stillness, like a spotlit rabbit.

In my heart, I yelled silent warnings to Sean, but in my head I knew I'd do more harm than good by interfering. Sean had always walked his own path, finely judged his own risks.

As he'd done, it seemed, in this case.

Epps's eyes flickered, enough for his men to lower their weapons. He raked Sean with a final disparaging stare before dismissively turning towards Parker. 'You might like to consider putting your boy here on a very short leash,' he said. 'Before he gets you into more trouble than you can handle.'

'Oh, I don't think so,' Parker said easily. 'Sean does his best work when he's off his chain.' He gave what had every indication of an open smile, taking years off those severe features. 'And besides, he has a valid point, and we already asked you nicely once. Time you levelled with us, Epps.'

Epps sighed. 'There's nothing left to say that you need to know. Thomas Witney was our original lead into this investigation. He approached us after his son died. Without him, we hit a dead end.' He stepped around Sean and headed for the hallway, pausing briefly to add, 'Take your team and go home, Mr Armstrong. You're all done here.'

By my shoulder, Chris Sagar stiffened. 'So, that's it?' he demanded faintly, and I heard a tremble in his voice. 'After everything *I've* done on this, the bastard *walks*, is that it?' He shook his head almost savagely, like a wet dog, voice rising in pitch and volume. 'I've spent months collecting information for you. You know what Bane's doing. I've told you – about the way he selects people, trains people. As sleepers – as terrorists, for God's sake!'

He tried to dart past me, to get to Epps, but I grabbed his upper arms and parried when he tried to paddle away. He never even looked at me. His eyes were locked on Epps, pleading now. I heard the bud of tears in his voice, the desperation. 'He had Witney picked out for something special – something big. You've *got* to stop him. I...'

Whatever else, telling a man like Epps that he'd *got* to do anything was never going to be a winning strategy. Sagar saw Epps's face darken, realised his mistake, and stammered to a halt.

'The evidence, whatever that might be, died with Witney,' Epps said at last, voice glacial. 'Until we have something else – something fresh – the investigation will remain open.'

'Open doesn't mean active,' Sagar muttered, not entirely cowed. He risked another glance. 'What about the land in the desert Bane's so desperate to keep people out of, huh? He could have a whole camp of al-Qaeda out there for all you know—'

'Well, you see, that's just the problem we have here, Mr Sagar – we *don't* know,' Epps cut in, snap to his voice for the first time. 'I've already bent the rules as far as I'm going to on this one and we're no farther forward than we were at the start. Except that I'm down by two good men, as Mr Meyer so eloquently pointed out.' The sarcasm twisted from his lips. 'In fact, we've taken a backward step, because Bane is now fully cognisant of our interest.'

He stopped, let his eyes track round the rest of us. 'We cannot afford another Waco,' he said flatly. 'Our only course is to pull back, keep a watching brief, and hope he does something stupid.' He paused. 'I have already devoted too much time and effort to Bane, and this is not our only concern at the moment.'

Sagar shook his head, more helplessly this time. I still had hold of him, felt him wilt under my hands.

'What about me – the work I've put in?' he asked, plaintive. 'Was that all for nothing?'

'Your cooperation with the federal government is duly noted,' Epps said. He reached into his inside pocket, brought out a thin envelope and slapped it down onto the corner of the credenza next to the coffee machine. I was close enough to recognise the Greyhound bus company logo. 'And you get a free ride home. I'd strongly advise you to take it.'

CHAPTER THIRTEEN

For maybe twenty seconds after the front doors closed behind Epps and his men, we stood in silence. Then Chris Sagar lurched out of my grasp and groped his way to the nearest chair like a man feeling his way in the dark. He sat hunched forwards, staring down into the terrazzo tile in front of his scuffed basketball boots.

In the periphery, I was aware of Parker ordering McGregor to pack his gear, telling Bill Rendelson to book us tickets home, first available. I caught Sean's eye.

So, it's over.

Not yet, it isn't.

He came past me with a single, unfathomable glance, halted in front of Sagar. The proximity forced Sagar to tilt his head back to meet his gaze.

'Talk,' Sean said.

'W-what?' The fear jumped behind Sagar's glasses before his gaze darted towards me, as if hoping I'd safeguard him against this new threat and realising I'd be part of it. 'What about?'

'About Fourth Day,' Sean said. 'About exactly what Bane's up to, that he's prepared to have three men killed to protect it.'

'Sean,' Parker said quietly. 'The job's done. Let it go.'

'It's never as easy as that, is it?' Sean said without inflection, not taking his eyes away from Sagar's. 'Witney's dead. Don't you want at least to know why?'

'I suppose, officially, we are still on Epps's dollar,' Parker said, considering. He moved alongside, stared down at Sagar. 'OK...talk.'

Sagar swallowed convulsively. 'Where do I start?' he asked with a tired smile. His thin shoulders flexed with the effort of putting out a long breath. 'Look, after Bane took over Fourth Day, he used to hand-select certain people from among his followers, sent them off into this area of wilderness for some kind of "special training", and before you ask – no, I was never among his chosen ones. I never knew for sure what went on out there, but they all came back different – the ones who came back at all.'

'But you must have had a pretty good idea,' Parker said. 'How did Bane explain the disappearances?'

Sagar shrugged. 'All he'd ever say was that their time with Fourth Day was at an end and they'd decided to go back out into the world.'

'And that never struck you as...a bit fishy?' Sean demanded.

Sagar flushed at the note of disdain in his voice. 'Look, you have to understand what it's like being inside of a cult. Bane demanded total obedience, that you place yourself totally into his hands, or you don't get into the place to begin with.'

Agitated, he got to his feet, brushed between Parker and Sean and began to pace, hands nervously atwitch, speaking fast and low as if in shame. 'He chooses people who need him more than he needs them. He singles out the vulnerable ones, the ones at the end of the line.' He halted, suddenly defiant. 'The ones who believe he can help them because they've no place else to turn and are going to welcome whatever he suggests with open goddamn arms, all right?'

'Is that how it was for you?' I asked quietly.

He nodded. 'Yes, if you must know. I was one of the lucky ones. I had friends who eventually got me out, got me help, but I was so under the spell of that place it was like being ripped out of the womb.' His eyes flickered around us, muttered, 'The outside world was the last place I wanted to be.'

Silence followed this plaintive outburst. He found he could no longer meet our steady stares, mine included. Muttering about getting his stuff together, he let his gaze drop and hurried away, clenched in on himself.

As he bolted up the stairs, his footsteps died away faster than his words. The echo of them lingered inside my head. I could absolutely understand the seductive lure of someone who might be able to fix what lay broken inside me.

And I thought of Witney – his reactions, his speed and his technique. Whatever Bane had taught him, out there in the wilderness Sagar spoke of, did Thomas Witney rank as one of the successes, or his failures? And what had been preying on his mind, that day we'd watched him teach his little class under the juniper tree?

Parker watched Sagar's retreat with narrowed eyes.

'So,' I said, 'what happens now?'

'We pack,' Parker said, succinct, turning so the rest came back over his shoulder as he strode away. 'The sooner we clear this place, the sooner we stop paying rent on it.'

I shrugged, would have headed for the stairs myself had Sean not touched my shoulder.

'Charlie,' he said. 'Got a minute?'

He jerked his head towards the French windows leading out onto the terrace at the back of the house. I followed him out of the air-conditioned chill and into the hazy warmth of early afternoon. In the greenery surrounding the lap pool I could hear insects buzzing, the distant noise of traffic from the nearby freeway, carried in on a faint ripple of breeze that stirred the air just enough to be pleasant.

Sean walked almost to the edge of the terrace and stared out at the far side of the canyon, where a row of similar palatial homes clung precariously to the steeply sloping ground.

'What's going on, Charlie?' he asked then, his voice hushed against the quiet and almost pained. 'Why all the secrets?'

His back was towards me, which was a small mercy. I ambled over to the fancy outdoor dining table, sat under the open canopy of the sunshade and waited until I knew I could keep my own tone even before I spoke. 'Secrets?'

'Witney,' Sean said. He turned away from the view to pass me an old-fashioned look. 'I know how to spot the marks left by a chokehold. I was the one who taught it to you.'

He came back towards me with that long, fluid stride, belying the amount of muscle he carried by the lightness of his step, the predatory grace. The sun was bright and I almost reached for my dark glasses, but knew they would provide little defence.

'He put up a decent struggle against Epps's people,' I pointed out, but the excuse lacked conviction.

'Not that kind of struggle.'

'Well, I—'

'Don't,' he said softly. 'Don't lie to me, Charlie. Parker told me what happened.'

Just for a moment, I thought Parker had overridden me and told him the whole story. It took a second of sheer fright before I realised Sean was talking about Witney's abortive grab for me.

'He had no right,' I said, feeling my face begin to heat.

'Parker had every right,' Sean countered. Until then, his voice had been calm and reasonable but now it began to crackle. Abruptly, he swung one of the chairs away from the table and placed it opposite mine, sat astride it with his arms folded on the back. He rested his chin, watching me with eyes soft as velvet, hard as quartz. 'You know what pissed me off the most? That you didn't feel it was something you should have told me yourself.'

'That's just it, Sean,' I threw back, wearing thin. 'What I was *feeling* was foolishness, if you must know – that Witney nearly got the drop on me. But he didn't. I dealt with it and I didn't think it was enough of a big deal that I had to come running to you with the story.' I shrugged, discomfited. 'Maybe, if I'd stopped to give it that thought, well, I would have handled things differently.' *Maybe.*

There was a long pause, then something flickered at the corner of Sean's mouth, just a glimmer of a smile. 'With Witney, or with me?' he asked.

I allowed my own face to relax. 'Both, probably.'

'What's happening to us, Charlie?' he demanded, and I sensed he didn't expect an answer – not from me, anyway. After a moment, he sighed, shook his head and let his eyes drift back across the canyon.

I shrugged again, wrapped my arms around my body as if I were cold, and said, evasive, 'Maybe I just don't like losing – anything or anyone.'

'We're in the life-and-death business,' he said, serious. 'It's unrealistic to think we're always going to come out on top. There will always be very bad days.' He eyed me flatly. 'Another time, *we* could have been the ones in the van.'

I looked away sharply, swallowed.

'You can't survive constantly looking back at what might have been, Charlie,' he said then, and his voice was gentle, almost coaxing. I kept my face averted and wondered if he'd ever know how achingly close to the truth of it he'd come. 'You just have to concentrate on what goes right, learn from the mistakes, and let the rest of it go, hmm?'

'I know,' I muttered, wondering if there'd ever be a time when the words *what if* would go through my head without making me want to weep. 'I'm sorry. All this...,' I waved vaguely to indicate the whole place, the whole situation. 'It's got to me this time.'

'I don't know what the problem is between us,' he said, hesitant enough to have me looking up. 'All I know is, it began before we ever left New York.'

I opened my mouth, but he cut me off, reaching out to take my hands in his.

'We've travelled a *hell* of a long way together.' He gave my fingers a final squeeze then reached up, almost hesitant when he was always so sure of himself, and ran two gentle fingers down the side of my face. Eyes too dark to have a colour were locked onto mine, as if pouring his will into me. 'And there's nowhere I can't go with you, Charlie. Nowhere I'd want to go.'

Tell him! screamed a voice in my head. *There will never be a better time than now.*

'Sean, I—'

'Sorry to interrupt,' Parker's voice came from the doorway, giving no indication of exactly how long he'd been standing there, eavesdropping. 'I've just had a call from Detective Gardner. They're bringing Randall Bane in for questioning and Gardner's offered to let us observe. Bill's gotten me onto an afternoon flight out of LAX and I'm cutting it fine as it is, but d'you want to go?'

There was the faintest pause. 'Of course,' Sean said then, rising. 'When?'

Parker checked his watch. 'Bane's on his way in right now, apparently,' he said. 'Gardner has promised to keep him on ice 'til you get there.'

Sean glanced in my direction.

'Sure,' I agreed, swallowing the bitterness of disappointment and relief. 'Why not?'

CHAPTER FOURTEEN

From everything I'd heard of Randall Bane, and what I'd seen first hand of the man during our recon of Fourth Day, I fully expected to find him relaxing in Detective Gardner's interview room with a phalanx of clever lawyers ready to tie the police up in knots, but that was not the case.

Instead, Bane sat centred and alone in the single upright plastic chair. He neither slouched nor sat rigidly. He didn't seem overconfident, not at all nervous. He didn't fidget, didn't look bored.

He simply sat.

Gardner had deliberately chosen this room, I knew, hoping to unsettle him. It was designed solely for interrogation, with the bolted-down table, bare walls, harsh lighting, and the mirror that obviously wasn't.

'You wouldn't believe the kinda scum I've faced across that table,' Gardner said, not taking her eyes off the obscured glass that separated us from the spartan place where Bane sat. 'Gang-bangers, rapists, murderers. There was this one kid, hacked two of his classmates to death with a machete just 'cause they dissed his sneakers. But this guy? He's something else.' She shook her head. 'Kinda gives me the heebie-jeebies, y'know?'

'Oh yes, I know.' Chris Sagar pushed his glasses up his nose with a nervous forefinger. Even in the low light I saw the sheen of sweat on his upper lip. 'Why do I need to be here?' he muttered. 'You don't need me for this.'

As he started to turn away, Sean put a hand on his shoulder.

'Stay,' he said. He, too, had not taken his eyes off Bane. 'You know him well enough to spot the lies.'

Sagar thought about protesting further, slid one look at Sean's face and subsided again, glowering. It was interesting to note how badly Bane unnerved his former acolyte, even a room away in a building full of cops.

When the door opened suddenly behind us, Sagar jumped. Another detective, a thickset guy with Mexican features, appeared in the gap with a bulky file in his hands. He jerked his head to Gardner, who excused herself and went over. The two of them bent over it, talking fast-and-low Spanish.

'If Gardner is hoping to shake him by making him wait, I don't think it's going to work,' Sean said, still watching Bane. 'He has the look of a man who'd outwait an alligator.'

'Did you *have* to mention the alligators?'

We'd once had the misfortune to be in the water at dusk with a lot of blood and a bunch of alligators. Dusk is when they come out to feed. I'd never forgotten their prehistoric grace, nor the dreadful certainty that every moment was our last. I was still uneasy in the water, even in swimming pools with crystal visibility, when I was as sure as I could be that nothing lurked beneath the surface.

I had that same feeling of unreasonable apprehension now.

Gardner finished her conversation and looked over. 'I'm gonna get this show on the road,' she said. She nodded to Sagar without expression. 'You stay put 'til we're done and he'll never know you were here, OK?'

Sagar nodded back, too grateful to react to the slightly mocking note in the detective's voice.

Gardner went out, closing the door behind her. A few moments later, the door to the interview room opened and she stepped through.

'Mr Bane,' she said, offering a brief smile as she came forwards, leaving the door not quite latched behind her. 'I appreciate you coming in. Thanks for waiting.'

Somewhere between Observation and Interview, she had lost the jacket and was down to rolled-back shirtsleeves, businesslike. She carried a Glock 9 mm high on her left hip. Bane's eyes dropped to the gun just once, as though marking its position, then he ignored it. If Gardner was disturbed by the man, up close, she hid it well.

'Just a few things I'd like to clarify from your statement, if that's OK?' she said, brisk but casual. Bane inclined his head slightly. We watched him closely for any more telling reactions to all this, but there was very little to see.

Bane was dressed well without any flash. He wore a collarless shirt in what could have been silk, fastened by a single pearl button at the neck, and a suit that was discreetly made to measure without being an obvious designer label.

He was still shaven-headed but, unlike Thomas Witney, would have had a generous head of hair. So, a conscious choice rather than a sop to vanity or pride. He had strange eyes, I noticed, golden like a cat's, and he suppressed his blink rate, either naturally or by design, enough for them to be hypnotically compelling.

'She hasn't read him his rights,' Sagar whispered, suddenly fretful. 'Why not? Anything she gets from him will be inadmissible. You see how Bane manipulates people, even in here. He—'

'She hasn't closed the door,' I said, cutting him off. 'Gardner can argue in court that it wasn't necessary because he wasn't in custody, and it stops him clamming up. Relax, Chris. She knows what she's doing.'

Over the top of Sagar's head, Sean passed me a cynical glance. *You think Bane doesn't know what she's up to?*

Of course. I was just hoping natural arrogance would get the better of him.

Gardner sat down opposite, her back to the mirror, and took a sheaf of photographs from the file, fanning them out on the scarred tabletop. I couldn't see what was in the pictures, but I could make an educated guess.

'Do you recognise this man?' Gardner asked. Her voice was softer, I noticed, as if hoping to lull Bane into underestimation.

Bane took a long look at the pictures without expression, studying each in turn. As he put the last one down, something close to pity flickered in his face.

'If I did not,' Bane said then, 'this would be a pointless exercise, would it not, Detective?' His tone suggested it was pointless anyway, but it was hard to pin down. I struggled to place the origins of that deep voice, compressed with power like a tightly muscled frame. Something about it zipped straight to the roots of my hair. Alongside me, I heard Sagar's unsteady hiss of breath.

In the interview room, Gardner shifted a little in her chair. I sensed her discomfort, knew Bane was getting to her just by being, and that fact annoyed her. She tilted her head, cop style, although her voice remained light. 'Humour me, Mr Bane.'

'His name is Thomas Witney,' Bane said. 'Or, it was. But, of course, you already knew that.'

'And when did you last see Mr Witney...alive?'

'Two days ago. He came to see me on the evening he disappeared from my property.'

My property. So, Bane's quasi-religious beliefs did not put him above avarice, it seemed.

'Disappeared, huh?' Gardner repeated. She made a show of frowning over the file. 'There's nothing here about you filing a missing persons report.'

Bane eyed her for a moment. 'We have learned from experience that LA's finest are neither interested nor effective when it comes to matters that concern us.'

Gardner's tone was cynical. 'You got some proof of that?'

'Naturally,' Bane said. 'Over the last year or so our community has been plagued by a spate of attacks, harassment, vandalism, scare tactics, but no official investigation has been launched.'

'News to me,' Gardner said. 'They still going on, these alleged attacks?'

'Not since I hired my own security personnel. They have handled things very effectively.'

A sudden vivid image of the girl, Maria, exploded behind my eyes. Her desperate flight brought short by the men sent to chase her down, and the terrifying delicacy of Bane's touch when she'd been brought back to him. What else did they handle, I wondered?

'And was Witney personally affected by any of this?' Gardner asked.

'He was injured in one of the early attacks. Run off the road on his way back from the city and ended up in the bottom of a canyon. His legs were broken.' There was nothing in Bane's voice as he added, 'The police claimed he must have been driving too fast,' but I heard the censure.

Gardner chose to ignore it. 'He mention he was worried about something more recent?' Gardner asked. 'He seem scared?'

'Not at all.' The denial came fast and easy, a little too much of both.

I glanced at Sean. We both remembered the way Witney reacted the day we'd seen him teaching his little class under the juniper tree.

He's lying.

I know.

'So, why'd he come see you?'

'He wanted to borrow a book. JD Salinger's *The Catcher in the Rye*.'

There had been a book on the bedside table in Witney's room, I recalled, the night we'd gone in to bring him out of Fourth Day. A slim volume with a largely red cover. I hadn't taken note of the title.

Gardner jotted it down. 'Why that particular book?'

Bane shrugged, the first animation he'd shown. 'It was next on the shelf,' he said simply. 'I am something of a bibliophile. Thomas had expressed a desire to work his way through the classics.'

'Well, everybody needs a hobby, I guess. Me? I'm more interested in philately – stamp collecting, y'know?' Gardner said casually. 'So he borrows a book, then rabbits. That worry you?'

'Yes,' Bane said. 'I thought it highly unlikely that Thomas would have decided to leave so suddenly, without a word, in the middle of the night, in just the clothes he stood up in. I assumed, of course, that he had been taken against his will.'

'Any signs of forced entry?'

'I expected none. The people who took him were, no doubt, experts in their field.'

'This was, what? Two days ago?' Gardner rubbed a dubious hand across her chin. 'And still you didn't file a report?'

'Would you have taken it seriously if I had?'

'Well now, he's a cool one, isn't he?' Sean murmured, and there was a certain heightened interest in his tone.

'You don't know the half of it,' Sagar mumbled, shifting miserably, as though just to stand within earshot of Bane was a painful experience.

'What makes you so sure Witney didn't just up and leave?' Gardner asked now, on the other side of the glass. 'Seeing as how he was free to come and go.'

Bane ignored the sly dig. 'Thomas was happy within our community,' he said. 'He felt secure there.'

'Secure from what?'

Bane paused before answering, as if gauging how far to let Gardner push. The detective sat back in her chair, looking relaxed, patient, as though there was nothing at stake.

'When Thomas first came to us, he was in a state of some emotional and psychological distress,' Bane said. 'We gave him time out, in order to heal, to find peace with himself.'

'That so?' Gardner said, her voice still pleasant. 'Only, I dug out an old report, filed by Mr Witney five years back, in which he alleges that Fourth Day in general, and you, sir, in particular, were responsible for the death of Liam, his son.' She sat forwards, opened the file and scanned what looked like a sheaf of old photocopies, leaving the pages on view. Bane would have needed superhuman willpower not to sneak a peek, but he didn't even glance at the top sheet, so temptingly displayed. 'The same Liam Witney who, shortly before his death, also joined your cult.'

That got a response. Something bright and quick snaked through Bane's eyes, concentrating his gaze into icy daggers that triggered my automatic flight response. I felt my blood pressure step up slightly as the adrenaline constricted my arteries, boosting the flow to my heart. Beside me, Sagar shifted from one foot to the other. Sean leant fractionally closer to the glass, the natural predator in him sensing weakness.

'Your information is incorrect, Detective,' Bane said, covering smoothly. 'Liam's unfortunate death occurred some months after he'd left our congregation.'

Gardner's voice was part mocking, part surprise. 'Is that how you see your organisation – some kinda church?'

'I prefer to think of Fourth Day more along the lines of a self-help organisation. But if a man knows himself, it does not matter what others call him,' Bane said, but there was a tightness around his jaw as he said it. 'And "congregation",

I believe you'll find, means simply an assembly of people.'

Yeah, nice theory. Shame about the practice.

'So, Liam was what?' Gardner asked, and I could tell by her tone that she'd registered the hit. 'Some kinda disciple?'

'Liam chose to be with us for a while,' Bane said, his emotions well back inside his fist now, held tight in check. His voice had regained that calm, almost hypnotic penetration, as though he was trying to project the force of his will directly through it. 'He was a young man trying to find his place, looking for the right path to follow.'

'And you helped him find it, huh?' Contrasting to Bane's restraint, Gardner's scepticism was unbridled.

'Some of us are lucky enough to find a path. Who can tell if it's the right one?' Bane said. He straightened his shirt cuff beneath the sleeve of his jacket. 'Liam believed he'd found his, and therefore his time with us was over.'

Gardner paused, making a play of flipping through the pages of the file, as if hoping Bane would feel the urge to justify what he had or had not done to counsel Witney's son. Sadly, he did not.

'So, let me get this straight. Two months before his death, Liam Witney joined a radical eco-group called Debacle,' the detective said, slapping the facts down cold and hard on the table between them. 'And now you claim he'd already left Fourth Day at that time? That you had no influence over his decision?' She looked up sharply. 'Thomas Witney sure as hell blamed you for that at the time. We got a whole box full of the complaints he filed against you, Mr Bane.'

'And yet no charges were ever brought,' Bane said, his

manner regretful but unshaken. He sighed. 'For a time, I believe Thomas blamed everybody. In the end, he blamed only himself.'

'Damn, he's convincing,' Sean allowed.

'I told you,' Sagar muttered in a strangled voice.

'We looked into it at the time, of course,' Gardner went on as if Bane hadn't spoken, 'but no evidence was found to support those allegations – something that caused Mr Witney a good deal of anger. Now, I'm sure you can appreciate, sir, the difficulty I'm having, putting that alongside what you're telling me now, that Mr Witney only felt safe when he was with you, when it seems that his original intention was not so much to join you, as to infiltrate your organisation in order to expose it.'

She sat back again, rocking, but it was not the hoped-for bombshell. Bane gave a slight smile, his expression almost sad at her childish attempts.

'Thomas came to us seeking truth,' he said. 'And – having found it – he decided to stay.'

'You expect me to believe it's really as simple as that?'

'Why not?' Bane said. 'You must be aware that when Thomas joined Fourth Day, he left instructions that if he did not return to the outside world of his own accord inside six months, he be retrieved from our evil clutches – by force if necessary.'

For the first time, a note of self-deprecation, a trace of irony, had crept into Bane's voice. His knowledge of Witney's safety net shouldn't have surprised me. If Witney had gone over, he would have confessed all to Bane.

'Before that time was up, Thomas arranged for a representative from this agency to visit with us. I thought

Thomas had successfully convinced him that he wished to cancel his arrangements.'

I glanced at Sean again. *Epps?*

He shrugged, frowning.

On the other side of the glass, Bane rose, smooth and elegant, and buttoned his jacket. 'Now,' he said, 'as you've been so careful to leave me an open door, unless you have anything else you wish to ask, I think we're done here.'

Gardner said nothing, just flapped a dismissive, distracted hand. Bane almost reached the doorway, then turned back.

'If you were looking for someone with an interest in removing Thomas Witney from Fourth Day's protection, and using whatever means they saw fit to find out what he'd learned during his time with us,' he said in that compelling voice, allowing his gaze to sweep across the mirrored wall behind Gardner's chair, 'then you may find it instructive to speak to that representative. His name, as I recall, was Parker Armstrong. He was part of some kind of specialist close-protection agency out of New York.'

My eyes flew to Sean's. 'What the hell...?'

'Tricky bastard,' Sean murmured.

Gardner didn't immediately respond, but I saw from the way her neck tensed just a fraction that this was news to her. And I knew Bane must have seen it, too.

'Maybe I'll do just that,' she said at last, grimly.

He nodded. It was entirely my imagination, but just for a second Bane's eyes seemed to lock directly with mine through the opaque glass, before he added, 'I'm sure you'll have no trouble in finding them.'

CHAPTER FIFTEEN

It took us a while to disentangle ourselves. Detective Gardner was understandably unamused that, in her opinion, we'd let her go into interview half-cocked.

There was nothing on record to prove or disprove Bane's allegation about Parker. Sagar claimed he'd never been privy to the meeting, although he could confirm something had taken place, a few months after Witney joined the cult. And afterwards, he said, Witney's training had begun in earnest.

It didn't help that Parker's plane had already taken off and he was conveniently unavailable to answer questions. I shied away from believing he'd deliberately withheld something so important. At the same time I couldn't help but remember his evasiveness over the whole assignment.

And, particularly, the way Witney's gaze had swept over Parker as much as Epps at the handover in Santa Clarita, his obvious shock, took on new resonance. *'Better late than never, huh?'* he'd said.

Because up to that point, I realised, Parker had been

careful not to let Witney catch a direct glimpse of him. Except during the extraction itself, and the midazolam would have ensured he didn't remember any of us the next day. Was that, I wondered now, cynically, why Parker had chosen to use it?

The only thing we could do with Detective Gardner was plead ignorance and let her blow off steam, patently disbelieving. We were well aware that was all she could do at this stage, with the spectre of Epps hanging over the whole case. I knew Sean was loath to call on the government man to intercede if it could be avoided but, fortunately, Gardner didn't know that. As we departed, I had a feeling that was the end of any cooperation we might hope to receive from the LAPD.

Sean left curt messages for his partner to call us. Parker's cellphone would have been switched off in the air, but even well after his New York arrival time, he still hadn't been in touch. With our own flights confirmed back to the east coast for the following evening, and most of the team already gone, we were just killing time until we could get to the office and have it out with him.

If it hadn't been for the presence of Chris Sagar, Sean and I might even have enjoyed our last night in the Calabasas palace. As it was, we kept a standard watching brief over him, almost out of habit. For his part, Sagar seemed edgy after his dislocated encounter with Bane. He stuck close, clingy as a dog just back from kennels, ensuring that any personal conversation was kept to a minimum.

Just before he hit the sack, Sagar announced, somewhat defiantly, that he'd like to go out for a run first thing in the morning. Neither Sean nor I objected.

'If I gotta sit for eight hours on a goddamn bus, I'm gonna stretch my legs,' he said, and I couldn't blame him for that. It was probably prudent of Epps not to waste government funds delivering him back to northern California by the same plush means as the outward leg, but it smacked of pettiness all the same.

'Suit yourself,' Sean said with a shrug. 'But I've got the letting agent coming by early to do a walk-through – make sure we didn't steal any of the fittings.'

'I'll go,' I offered, noting the little gesture of wry relief from Sagar. 'I could do with the exercise myself.'

So, with the not-yet-risen sun turning the sky ashy pink above the dew-glittered hills, I found myself out on the terrace the next morning. I was in an old polo shirt and sweats that included a hooded zip-up top, doing warm-up exercises.

Almost exactly a year previously, I'd taken a 9 mm round straight through my left thigh. At the time, the second bullet – the one that had gone tumbling through my chest cavity – had seemed the greater evil. Time had proved the leg injury more costly, both in terms of physio and temper.

I'd worked bloody hard to rebuild the wasted muscle carved out by the passage of the round through my flesh, to regain full mobility and strength. Even so, I knew the fact I walked entirely without a limp now was as much down to luck as it was to determination on my part. The bullet's path had somehow threaded past the vital nerves, bones and sinews. I could just as easily have been crippled for life.

A noise to my right had me straightening fast. I turned to see Chris Sagar in the open doorway. He was dressed in sweat pants and a vest and looked still half-asleep.

'Good morning!' I said with unnecessary cheerfulness.

'It is?' he grunted, stumbling out onto the terrace and flopping into some half-hearted quad stretches.

I lifted my left foot onto the back of a chair and folded my body down over my knee slowly. There was still tension in the underlying tissue, but overall the leg felt pretty much OK.

'You were the one who wanted to be up and at 'em at this hour,' I pointed out as I swapped onto the easy side.

'Did you have to remind me?' he groaned. 'I like the benefits of exercise, but that doesn't mean I have to enjoy the process, y'know?'

I raised an eyebrow as I rolled into a lateral stretch, aware of the solid weight of the SIG lying in the small of my back under my shirt. 'Well, if you've changed your mind, speak now. I'm happy to go back to bed.'

He grinned at me then. 'Hey, is that an invitation?'

'Only if you like your food liquidised and fed to you through a straw.' It was Sean who spoke, coming out of the French windows, barefoot and dressed in a loose black karate *gi*. He spoke lightly, but his eyes didn't entirely share the joke.

'Hey, sorry, man,' Sagar said, flushing. 'I didn't mean—'

'You don't need to apologise to me,' Sean said mildly as he came past us. 'I'm not the one who's likely to break your jaw.' He skirted the lap pool and moved out onto the open area of terrace overlooking the canyon, dropping almost immediately into the first of his formal morning *katas*, so practised that each move flowed into the next, brimming with a lethal grace and utter focus. The similarities between Sean's level of contained concentration and that demonstrated by Randall Bane were not lost on Chris Sagar.

'Uh, you all set?' he mumbled, as though trying not to attract Sean's attention again.

But for a moment my eyes were locked there, and my imagination had ghosted in a little figure alongside him, a tousle-headed boy perhaps, in a miniature outfit, scowling with the concentrated effort of matching his movements to those of his proud father.

Sean pivoted towards me. His face was a blank mask, his gaze inward, showing nothing. I forced myself not to pass a defensive hand across my belly.

'You OK?'

I turned to find Sagar watching me.

'Yeah, sure,' I lied, dry-mouthed. 'Let's go.'

CHAPTER SIXTEEN

I let Sagar set the pace, half-prepared for him to take off like a rabbit at a greyhound convention, but he didn't seem inclined towards heroics. We started out at a fairly sedate jog, only picking up speed once we realised our comparative levels of fitness.

We fell into a matching rhythm, pounding up the dusty shoulder of one of the winding canyon side roads. The temperature was perfect at this time of day, just cool enough to be pleasant and just warm enough to dry the sweat on our bodies almost as it formed. I tried not to think about the tobacco-tinged air I was sucking into my lungs.

Sagar had an awkward running style, almost shambling, but he covered the ground with deceptive speed.

'Why do this if you don't enjoy it?' I asked.

He flashed a sheepish smile. 'You wanna know the truth? Bane, that's why,' he said with engaging candour. 'He had this idea you should do something you didn't wanna do, every day, y'know?'

'Really?' I said, trying not to let the doubt show in my

voice. I took another half-dozen strides. 'Why?'

'He's big on this whole mind-and-body thing,' Sagar said. 'I mean, I hated getting out of bed in the morning to go run, but I did it because he always made me feel like I'd be letting myself down if I didn't. And I always swore I wouldn't do it if I didn't have to.'

'And now you don't have to?'

'Yeah,' he grumbled. 'I do it just about every day. That's the trouble with Bane. He spouts all this crap about you finding your own path, but you kinda get the feeling he's always there pulling your strings, y'know?'

'Like the book he'd lent to Witney, you mean – *Catcher in the Rye*?'

Sagar's stride faltered. 'You got that, huh?' he said and the sheepish look was back in full swing. 'I didn't want to bring it up, in case you guys thought I was making something out of nothing, but—'

'I know Hinckley was obsessed with the book before he tried to knock off President Reagan, and Mark Chapman had a copy on him when he shot John Lennon,' I said with a sideways glance. 'They do teach us how to watch out for loony stalkers in this business, you know.'

'Sorry, yeah,' Sagar said, flashing a quick smile. 'And there was this other guy – somebody Bardo – killed an actress called Rebecca Schaeffer,' he went on. 'He was carrying the book when he shot her.'

'Interesting, but hardly conclusive,' I pointed out, altering my stride as the incline steepened towards a left-hand hairpin, feeling my muscles begin to tighten. 'The thing sells in its hundreds of thousands. Not everybody who reads it is a lone assassin. Next you'll be telling me Bane had you listening to heavy metal so you could absorb the hidden satanic messages.'

'You can mock,' Sagar protested quietly, starting to lose his breath now. 'But you saw what he was like yesterday, Charlie. You felt it, just like I did. And you could tell he was lying about Witney being afraid, couldn't you?'

Denying it would have meant lying to him myself, and I wasn't prepared to do that just for the hell of it. I saved my breath for the hill.

Just before we hit the blind corner, I glanced back casually over my shoulder, as if checking for traffic. Three hundred metres behind us was a dusty Chevy Astro van in a self-consciously nondescript shade of beige. It hadn't been there the last time I'd checked.

I couldn't remember if it was a requirement to have a front licence plate in California but, if so, the van was in violation of the code. I caught a glimpse of two men in the front seat. They were wearing those hunting hats with a peak and ear flaps you can tie off under your chin. Technically, it might be winter but that was overkill unless your aim was concealment.

Uh-oh.

'Come on, Chris, enough slacking,' I said, keeping any alarm out of my voice. 'Time to pick up the pace, hmm?' and lengthened my stride.

Sagar's pride had him putting on a spurt alongside me, so we pounded through the turn in step. As soon as the van lost sight of us, I grabbed his elbow and flung him sideways towards the edge of the roadside. A sand-pitted steel crash barrier was all that separated us from the steeply sloping canyon side.

'Hey!' he yelped, baulking. 'What the—?'

I didn't answer. One look over the precipice was enough to tell me there was no escape that way. The ground was made up of loose earth and landslide gravel. It was punctuated by tenacious spiky vegetation and rocks big enough to cause serious injury if you lost your footing, but no use as decent cover. It was a long way down.

Swearing under my breath, I checked the road ahead. It ran straight for probably another five hundred metres before the next winding corner. The gradient would slow and tire us before we reached it. If this really was an ambush, they'd picked their location well.

I felt the reassuring weight of the SIG in the small of my back, debated for maybe half a second then reached under my shirt and drew it. Below us, the van's engine revved as the driver accelerated towards the corner, abandoning the stealthy approach.

Sagar yanked his arm free and stumbled to a halt, eyes on the gun a little wildly.

'Charlie—'

'For God's sake, Chris, keep moving!' I jerked my head to the far side of the road. 'If they make a run at us, get over the barrier there and back down onto the lower stretch of road.' It might be just as treacherous but at least it wasn't far to fall on that side, and from there the gradient was all downhill. It would take them time to turn the van around, or force them to continue the pursuit on foot. Anything to even up the game.

I swallowed down the shiver of tension invading my system. Everyone is afraid in a situation like this. Being afraid is normal. It's what you do with your fear that defines you.

'I'll hold them as long as I can,' I told him, hoping he'd get past the landed-fish stage long enough to take action. The image of Thomas Witney's tortured body bloomed large and ugly at the front of my mind. 'Go!' I snapped. 'Run like hell and do not come back for me.'

He might have been about to argue but then the van lurched into view, leaning hard as it loaded up the suspension through the turn, and the time for talk was over. There was no doubt in my mind now, even before the nose dipped under heavy braking, the front doors already opening.

I brought the SIG up, double-handed, and took two quick sideways steps to put Sagar at my back. My finger curved around the trigger, beginning to take up the mechanism, but I held my fire. Contrary to popular belief, taking potshots at a moving vehicle is a very hit-and-miss affair, especially with something as small as a 9 mm pistol, but our current threat assessment had come up minimal at best. A fact I now cursed silently.

I had thirteen rounds and no spare magazine.

When I glanced back, Sagar remained frozen to the spot for a moment longer, staring at the rapidly approaching vehicle with disconnected fascination. I shoved my shoulder against his, knocking him sideways, and that finally broke him out of it. He gave a kind of strangled cry and bolted for the edge of the road, but the van driver swung across after him. Panicked by the pursuit, Sagar tripped over his own feet and went sprawling messily to his knees on the stony surface of the road.

I just had time to consider that, whatever his role had been inside Bane's organisation, field agent wasn't it.

The van jolted to a halt with its front corner about

three metres away from us. I hesitated only long enough to identify my first target. Then the rear sliding door flew open, and the decision was made for me.

A man crouched in the opening. His face was half-hidden beneath a woollen cap and his shoulders spoke of well-muscled bulk. As he opened the door with his left hand, he brought a weapon up to firing position in front of him with his right. Whatever fear that plagued me finally evaporated at that point. Now the waiting was over, I surrendered to experience and sheer survival instinct almost with relief.

I aimed without thinking about it, a reflex action, and put my first two rounds into the centre of the man's body mass before he had a chance to fire.

He folded with a surprised grunt and dropped the weapon, which clattered somewhere onto the metal floor of the van. That same instinct told me to keep firing until he went down, but I was only too aware of my limited supplies and he was already falling away backwards, beginning to cough. I let him go.

Maintaining a sense of open spatial awareness is one of the hardest things in a firefight. Adrenaline constricts your field of focus until all you can see is the object immediately in front of your sights. Avoiding that tunnelling-down takes countless hours of training. Being regularly shot at for real helps, though. If you survive, you learn.

As it was, while I was dealing with the guy in the back of the van, I was minutely conscious of the front-seat passenger jumping down onto the road, the thump of his boots hitting the surface, the way he brought his arms up around the trailing edge of the door, hands clasped together as he swung towards me. A big black guy. As well as the hunting hat, he had on a bulky tan canvas jacket and jeans. Could have been a construction worker on his way to site.

Without a pause, I snapped my aim across and fired through the door glass, putting the first round into his upper arm and the second into his chest as he spun. He let go of the weapon in his hands, which landed on the asphalt amid a shower of broken window fragments. Then his legs went from under him. He slid down the bodywork with the blood gleaming dark against the tan of his jacket and shock in his face.

The driver should have been on me by now, but the cab was empty, the door standing open. I crabbed sideways round the front end of the van, keeping below the level of the glass, eyes everywhere. He might have seen his comrades go down and decided to scarper, but I wasn't betting on it.

I glanced at Sagar again as I edged past him. He was still on the ground, floundering, defenceless.

'Charlie, what the—?' he began, his voice high and loud, buzzing. I waved him sharply into silence, but it was too late.

The wheelman reared out from behind the van and charged us. He was wearing a dusty green bomber jacket and was slighter than the other two, carrying less obvious muscle.

As he appeared, he flung his right arm up and back and, at the same time, I heard a shell being racked into the chamber of a pump-action shotgun.

It was deliberate misdirection, that noise. It was exactly how an extendable baton is designed to sound as its telescopic segments unfurl and lock instantly into place. To paralyse by noise association and give the wielder time to deploy the weapon to full and devastating effect.

I shot the wheelman before he'd time to get within striking distance, knowing I had to take him down fast. Two groups of two rounds, body shots, fired as fast as I could work the trigger. Even so, momentum kept him coming, almost lurching into my arms as he stumbled and went to his knees at my feet. I jumped back, tracking him with the SIG all the way down. His face, contorted, was close enough for me to smell cigarettes and spice on his breath.

It was only as he fell, gasping, that I realised he wasn't dead. That none of them were dead and all of them should have been. I was using hollow point Hydra-Shok rounds that flared on impact to deliver maximum internal damage as they shed velocity. They'd all been on target. So...

Ignoring his yelp of protest, I punted the wheelman over onto his back and dragged open the zip on the bomber jacket. Underneath it, strands of yellow Kevlar tufted through the four holes I'd put in his lower chest.

Body armour.

There was no heavy-duty ceramic trauma plate in the pocket at the front of the vest, and if the way the wheelman groaned when I dug the heel of my hand into the centre of the grouping was anything to go by, he'd cracked a couple of ribs as a result of the multiple close-quarter hits.

I straightened, keeping hold of him, and kicked the baton out of reach. It hadn't been fitted with a baton cap and skittered happily off the edge of the roadway under the barrier.

'Come on, up!' I commanded, wrapping my fist into the back of the man's collar and hauling him to his knees. He resisted until I jabbed the business end of the SIG close up against his right eye. The end of the barrel was still hot enough to brand him where it briefly touched his skin. He double-flinched – first from the burn and second in case I shot him because of it.

'The next one,' I murmured, 'goes somewhere it won't grow back.'

He made a flutter of capitulation with his hands, allowed me to half-drag him round the nose of the van. When I let go he rolled onto his side, clutching his chest, and stayed there.

Yeah, sunshine, they don't warn you how much it hurts, do they?

The guy from the passenger seat was still sitting with his back up against the bodywork. Blood was seeping down his left arm but he made a flimsy attempt to block me as I checked under the canvas jacket. Sure enough, he was also wearing armour. I looked for the gun he'd dropped among the mess of glass, found it nearly concealed beneath his thigh.

But when I lifted it out, I found he hadn't been carrying a gun at all. The weapon was a TASER, capable of delivering a fifty thousand-volt charge at anything up to ten metres. I'd had the misfortune to be hit with one only a few months previously and it wasn't pleasant – plenty nasty enough to put you on the ground and keep you there. It didn't compete with being shot, but in my personal experience there wasn't all that much to choose between them.

I hefted the TASER for a moment, considering, then flung the stun gun out sideways, saw the passenger's eyes follow its looping trajectory over the crash barrier. Saw the fear jerk in them.

Then I heard a slight scrape from the rear of the van and took two quick sidesteps, bringing the SIG up again.

The first guy I'd shot was sitting up, legs splayed, rubbing uneasily at his chest. As I moved into view, he reached automatically towards his own fallen weapon on the floor of the van. Now I had the chance to look at it properly, I could see it was another TASER. If the lack of blood was anything to go by, he too had a vest. He was enough of a pro to freeze when he saw the gun in my hands and the intent with which it was being pointed in his direction. I'd already shot him once without hesitation, but still he weighed up the odds.

'Don't even think about it,' I said. 'Confucius say, "Man who wears bulletproof vest should not complain if shot in bollocks,"' and deliberately lowered my aim. His questing hand froze again, allowing me to edge forwards and pluck the stun gun out of reach. It quickly followed the baton and the other TASER over the edge of the road.

And, gradually, I became aware of the warm breeze coming up the canyon, stirring the desultory grasses that had sprouted by the shoulder. Above the ringing in my ears I heard the van's engine ticking as it cooled. The guy I'd winged in the arm was breathing more heavily than the others. Somewhere higher up, the gunshots had set a dog barking. The sweat that pooled suddenly at the base of my spine had very little to do with exercise, but I noted almost remotely that my hands were steady.

I backed up far enough to keep the three of them covered and pulled my mobile phone out of the zip pocket of my sweatshirt with my left hand, flipping it open and stabbing the speed-dial number for Sean's phone with my thumb.

As it rang out, I glanced across at my reluctant principal, still on the ground in front of the van.

'Do you want to ask them, or should I?' I said with a measure of calm.

'Ask them what?' His own voice was rough.

I jerked my head towards our attackers. 'Which of them reads JD Salinger.'

CHAPTER SEVENTEEN

Detective Gardner arrived twenty minutes after the first of the black-and-whites. She climbed out of her car and stood, hands on hips, surveying the taped-off scene with barely contained annoyance. She was wearing jeans today, boots with Cuban heels and a loose lightweight jacket that did a reasonable job of hiding the 9 mm on her belt.

Considering the possible connection to Thomas Witney's murder, I shouldn't have been surprised that she got the call-out on this one, but that didn't mean any of us had to be pleased about it, least of all her.

She glanced over to where I stood, leaning against the front wing of our remaining Suburban, Sean alongside me. I half-expected her to come charging over, but she was too much of a pro for that.

Instead, pulling on a pair of latex gloves, she ducked under the tape and did a brisk walk-round of the Chevy van, still abandoned in the middle of the road with the doors flung wide. The crime scene techs had carefully marked the position of every piece of ejected brass from my SIG, and were now busy photographing the bloodstains from the passenger's flesh wound.

Gardner seemed in no hurry to get to us. She spoke to the uniforms who'd been first on scene, was shown an evidence bag containing my surrendered gun, and others containing the TASERs and the extendable baton, which they'd recovered after I'd helpfully pointed out their existence and location. The baton had rolled as far as the gutter of the lower stretch of road before it had snagged in the scrub.

I shifted my weight, risked a look to Sean, but his eyes were on the detective as she leaned into the rear of both cars where the uniforms had cuffed and separated the suspects, spoke to them briefly. The front-seat passenger, watched over by a burly cop, was still being patched up by the paramedic crew.

They'd cut away his jacket to treat the arm wound, and the hole in his covert body armour was plain to see. He'd been turning, and my second shot landed slightly high and right of centre because of that. Without the vest, the trajectory of the round would have carved through his chest cavity on a lethal diagonal course.

He'd be dead, I thought. *They'd all be dead...*

Gardner looked closely at the hole I'd left and made some offhand remark to the paramedic, who laughed. We were too far away to hear, but it brought a scowl to the injured man's face.

Only then did she discard the gloves and stroll over towards us, stuffing her hands into her front pockets so the jacket was pulled back to reveal both gun and badge. She halted a couple of metres away and subjected the pair of us to a hard stare, head tilted.

'You people just cannot stay out of trouble, can you?'

'They came after us,' I said mildly. 'Not the other way round.'

She grunted, then asked with reluctance, 'Your guy OK?'

Sean jerked his head towards the rear of the Suburban and I opened the door. Chris Sagar was sitting hunched down nervously in the back seat and he looked up with a hunted expression, cringing away until he recognised the face peering in.

'You promised me Bane wouldn't know I was there,' he said to her, mournfully reproachful. 'What the hell am I gonna do now, huh?'

She stared a moment longer without expression, nodded and shut the door again.

'Lucky he had you,' was all she said, peeling the silver paper from a stick of gum and folding it into her mouth. 'So, you wanna let me have your side of it?'

'I've already given your guys a statement.'

'Humour me,' she said. The same words she'd spoken to Randall Bane in that interview room – was it only yesterday afternoon? A chill passed across my shoulder blades and I twitched it away.

Voice as level as I could manage, I delivered a clear, concise run-through of events, from the moment I'd first spotted the Chevy, to Sean's arrival, less than six minutes after I'd called him. And while I was talking, I clamped down hard on my emotions, not giving them a crack to slither through.

Gardner listened without interruption until I'd finished, occasionally jotting down comments in a slim black notebook.

'Why d'you call him first?' she asked then, nodding towards Sean.

'Because I knew he'd get here faster, and I was concerned about keeping three of them contained on my own unless I shot them again,' I said candidly. 'Just to be sure.'

She ignored my poor attempt at humour. 'You know these guys claim they were driving along, minding their own business, when you jumped out and attempted to hijack their vehicle at gunpoint?'

'Of course,' I echoed. 'We went out for a run and simply got too tired to walk back, is that it?'

'And how fortunate,' Sean added blandly, 'that they'd all taken the precaution of wearing body armour this morning, just in case of such an eventuality.'

I tensed. *Jesus, Sean! Did you have to remind her?*

But Gardner, still making notes, didn't outwardly react. She smiled almost in spite of herself, shrugged a shoulder. 'Tell me about it,' she said, wry. 'I think it's safe to say they're not the brains of the operation. And if it's any consolation, Charlie, looking at the evidence, I reckon it probably all went down pretty much how you say.'

'Thank you,' I said, without irony.

'But, what I still don't know is why.' Her expression hardened. 'And unless you people stop jerking my chain with all this, I'm gonna run you all in and sweat you 'til you drown in it.'

I resisted the urge to glance at Sean, kept my eyes focused on Gardner's, emptied my mind of anything approaching guilt.

'I have no idea why,' I said, which was pretty much the truth of it anyway. I shrugged. 'The rest of our team has pulled out. We're just waiting to go home.'

Gardner favoured us with her best cop stare a little longer, then sighed and shook her head, as though she'd given us our chance and we'd blown it.

'It wasn't a hit,' Sean said as she began to turn away.

Gardner stopped. 'How d'you work that out?'

Sean leant back against the Suburban's bodywork and folded his arms casually, as if we were discussing some utterly mundane subject. 'If that had been the case – and if it had been a serious attempt – both Charlie and Sagar would be dead.' Those expressionless eyes skimmed over me, even if something twitched at the corner of his mouth. 'No offence intended, of course.'

'None taken,' I said, equally grave. 'To be honest, I'd already come to the same conclusion. They should never have stopped moving. Just open up the side door as they came past and let rip with a couple of Uzis. They wouldn't even have to be decent shots. Just point and spray. No fuss...plenty of mess.'

Gardner's eyes drifted over to the squad car where the two men were sitting in the rear seats, bodies rucked forwards awkwardly from the restraints. I followed her gaze and remembered suddenly the way Thomas Witney's hands had been wired tight behind him. I blinked slowly, trying to clear the image. It proved stubborn.

Gardner's attention came back to me, sober. 'Lucky for you they weren't going for a hit, then, huh?' she said and frowned. 'But in that case...'

'It was a snatch,' I said. 'Hence the TASERs and the baton. They came prepared to subdue, not kill.'

Sean's eyes flicked to mine. *Not yet, anyway. Not here.*

You think I don't know?

Gardner gave that cool consideration for a moment, then nodded, closed the notebook and slipped it back into her pocket. 'We'll find that out once I get these jokers into Interview,' she said grimly, and gave me a final assessing stare. 'Like I said, Sagar was lucky he—'

Whatever she'd been about to say next was lost as her eyes moved past us, to a point further up the canyon road. Sean and I both turned to see a group of Suburbans bearing down on us at speed. Discreet black, with limo tint on the windows, they had government issue written all over them.

'What the hell are the Feds doing here?' Gardner muttered under her breath. She glanced at us sharply. 'Did you call them?'

'Not guilty,' Sean said quickly.

Sure enough, when the lead vehicle in the little convoy came to a halt alongside our own Suburban, it was Conrad Epps who stepped down onto the cracked asphalt, looking around him with supercilious expectancy. A general surveying the field where he's just decided a battle will be fought.

'Detective Gardner,' he greeted, his men fanning out behind him. He flashed some kind of official ID, fast like sleight of hand, and folded it back into his inside pocket, not bothering to look at her directly. 'Thank you, Detective. We'll take it from here.'

'The hell you will.' Gardner's voice was flat with outrage. 'On whose authority?'

'Mr Armstrong's people have been working for the federal government on this matter.' Epps's head swung very slowly in her direction. To her credit, she didn't back down. 'If I have to, I will get your chief on the line, right now, to quote the relevant sections of the Patriot Act to you, in words of one syllable,' he grated, 'but forcing me to do that will not have a beneficial effect on your long-term career prospects, Detective. That enough authority for you?'

Gardner paled. 'Yes, *sir*!' she said, lip curling. She turned back to us. 'Don't leave town, either of you.'

'On the contrary,' Epps cut in. 'I believe Mr Meyer has reservations out of LAX this evening.' He paused. 'I would strongly advise you and Ms Fox not to miss your flight.'

Behind us, Chris Sagar opened the door and slipped down onto the road.

'And what about him?' I demanded. 'Still planning to put him on a Greyhound bus?'

A muscle twitched in the side of Epps's jaw. 'Arrangements have been made for Mr Sagar to enjoy more...secure transport,' he said.

From Epps, that could have meant anything from a private jet to a sealed casket, and Sagar paled accordingly.

'I-I...um...what about my stuff?'

'I'm sure you can detour to collect your gear on the way to Van Nuys, Mr Sagar,' Epps said. He turned slightly and the driver of one of the Suburbans jumped out and held the rear door open. Sagar didn't need telling twice, but he hesitated awkwardly in front of me, hardly able to meet my eyes.

'I...' he began again, swallowed. 'Thanks, Charlie. You...um...saved my life, y'know?' And with that he scurried over to it, keeping his face averted as if trying to avoid eye contact with any of the men from the beige Chevy van. The Suburban did a multipoint turn in the narrow road and sped away.

Epps, meanwhile, had been taking in the spent brass and the bloodstains. When he was done he glanced at me fully for the first time.

'Good job this wasn't a professional crew,' he said, and strode away before I could think of a suitably cutting retort.

'Well, I'm kinda glad to know he has a problem with *all* women,' Detective Gardner said wryly, watching him go, 'and it's not just me he's pissed at.'

'Not exactly a people person, is he?' I murmured.

Gardner gave a snort, then reached into her pocket and pulled out a business card. She clicked her pen and scrawled something on the back of it.

'Here's my cell. You think of anything else you wanna tell me about this...' Her voice trailed off as she handed the card over, but when I tucked it straight into the side pocket of my hooded top, her gaze lingered meaningfully.

'... We'll call you,' Sean said.

We climbed into the Suburban and Sean started the engine. Epps's people were already transferring the prisoners to their own vehicles. The men who'd attacked us didn't look too happy about that but, I reasoned, if they were the ones responsible for grabbing Witney – and killing two of Epps's men in the process – they had every right to be anxious for their immediate future and personal well-being.

As Sean backed up and turned the Suburban around, I pulled the card Gardner had given me out of my pocket again and looked at it. On the front it simply said 'B. Gardner' and listed two phone numbers designated 'office' and 'cell'.

Frowning, I turned the card over. On the back, in an

untidy hand, she'd written, 'Malibu Seafood. PCH. One hour.'

'Gardner wants a meet,' I told Sean, showing him the card. 'Any idea why?'

But part of me wondered if she'd finally get round to asking the question I'd been dreading. The one I'd been waiting for ever since I fired the first shots into the guy behind the sliding door. The question I'd asked myself, with various stages of recrimination.

Sean glanced across, his expression unreadable. 'One way to find out.'

CHAPTER EIGHTEEN

Back at the house in Calabasas, a quick Google search revealed that 'Malibu Seafood' was a local fish restaurant, and 'PCH' was shorthand for its location on the Pacific Coast Highway – Highway 1 – which followed the twisting coastline all the way up to San Francisco. 'One hour' needed no translation.

Chris Sagar had already been and gone by the time we arrived back. I suppose the chance of another ride aboard that Gulfstream was too good to miss. Sean and I quickly finished our own packing, not that there was much to pack. The letting agent arrived for her walk-through just as we were leaving. I tuned out Sean's smooth excuses as I stowed our gear in the Suburban.

As he climbed behind the wheel, though, he was smiling.

'What?'

He unhooked his sunglasses from the rear-view mirror. 'I thought I'd take advantage of the lady's local knowledge and ask her about Malibu Seafood,' he said.

'And?'

'Best place for seafood for miles.' He put the Suburban into gear. 'She recommends the red snapper or the ahi tuna burger.'

'Well, at least if this meeting with Gardner is a washout, we can still get a decent lunch,' I said lightly, although the thought of food made me slightly queasy. I paused. 'Why exactly *are* we meeting her, by the way?'

He shrugged. 'Does no harm to extend an olive branch when our paths are bound to cross again sometime,' he said. 'Better, in that case, to have the local cops thinking of us in friendly terms.'

Yeah, Sean, but she's not just a local cop. She's Homicide...

Malibu Seafood didn't look like much from the outside. In the UK it would have been in a pass-by lay-by on the A1 somewhere north of Doncaster, with the wheels removed in a thin attempt at permanency and sophistication.

But out here it had an allure all of its own. Being right across the highway from the beach did it no harm, either. A sign outside the unprepossessing single-storey building boasted a fresh-fish market as well as takeaway and the Patio Café, which turned out to be little more than a raised decking area to one side, with a fabulous view of the ocean. Ordering a meal involved queuing up at the counter inside and collecting a number, which was then squawked through an external speaker when your food was ready. The restrooms were a hike up the parking lot.

I let Sean handle the food while I climbed the short flight of weather-bleached steps to the patio deck, partly sun-shaded by climbing vegetation. I'd grabbed a fast shower back at the house and my hair was still damp. I couldn't think of a better way to dry it than with the warm breeze coming up off the Pacific.

Detective Gardner – presumably 'B' to her friends – was the sole occupant at one of the rough picnic-style tables, tucking into a voluminous green salad, liberally draped with some of the biggest king prawns I'd ever seen, although I knew they were called shrimp over here. To me, shrimp were tiny pink crescents, usually served suspended in solidified butter, like prehistoric insects captured in amber.

I slid sideways onto the fixed bench opposite Gardner with my back to the trellis, and nodded to her plate.

'Looks good.'

She paused long enough to swallow and wipe her fingers delicately on a paper napkin. 'Is good,' she said then, well brought up enough to cover her mouth with her hand as she spoke. 'You find the place OK?'

'Why, were you hoping we wouldn't make it?'

She put down her fork and took a slurp of her drink. 'Depends,' she said, then, 'if you're planning to keep bullshitting me or not.'

'In that case, why don't you ask what you want to,' I said sedately, 'and we'll see if it stinks?'

As I spoke, I kept my eyes moving. Along the opposite shoulder of the road, a lone female jogger ran, eyes on the ground in front of her feet. I watched the passing vehicles, particularly vans or minivans with opening side-doors, or anything with the glass dropped towards the restaurant. Just because our attackers bungled things this morning, didn't mean there wouldn't be a second – altogether more serious – attempt.

I felt footsteps on the planking and Sean came up the steps and slid onto the bench alongside Gardner. She frowned at that, but he smiled blandly, not putting out any overt threat. We were early for lunch and, for the moment, we had the place to ourselves.

'How're we doing?' Sean asked me.

'I was just about to find that out.'

Gardner sighed. 'That bastard Epps has shut me down,' she said, rolling her shoulders. 'Totally. Bunch of his guys showed up and took everything related to the Witney crime scene – files, forensics, photos, even my notes. You name it, they boxed it up and carted it out of there.'

'What about this morning's little incident?' I asked.

She grunted. 'Won't even get as far as an official report,' she said. 'I've already gotten hauled in by my captain and told to hand everything over to the Feds and forget I ever heard about it.'

'So, Detective,' Sean said, linking his hands together on the tabletop and regarding her levelly, 'I assume from that – and the fact we're all here and not in your office – that you're off the books on this one?'

She gave him a cool stare that was probably inherited from her mother, but was all cop.

'What about those four hundred other murders you mentioned?' I asked. 'I thought you said you'd be glad to have the Witney case taken off your hands.'

'There's a big difference between giving something away and having it stolen,' she said flatly. 'I don't like being told how to run an investigation, and I especially don't like being told to stop running it. So...what gives?'

Sean and I exchanged a long silent look across the table.

Does it gain us anything to tell her?

I don't know. Does it gain us anything not to?

'OK,' Sean said at last. 'We can understand your frustration.'

And so we told her, carefully and with judicious editing, almost the whole story, from going into Fourth Day to extract Witney, to my 911 call after the ambush that morning. We admitted that Parker had kept his previous involvement with Thomas Witney quiet, even from us. That we hadn't known he was Witney's safety net, could shed no light on why Parker had chosen to leave the schoolteacher in the cult's clutches. Maybe that explained his delayed determination to retrieve him now.

In the middle of all that, our number came over the speaker and I made two trips to the little serving hatch to collect our food. Sean had ordered enough for an army and, I noted, had gone with the letting agent's recommendation of the Pacific red snapper. Without appetite, I'd picked fish tacos, assuming from the modest price that they'd be less substantial. I'd been wrong on that one.

'So that's why your pal Epps was so desperate to get those three guys away from us,' Gardner was saying when I returned with the second tray. She looked away sharply, anger plain on her face. 'Son of a bitch,' she murmured. 'He screwed up and he's covering his ass. What's the betting he'll have those guys on the first transport to Gitmo, just so's it never gets out that he lost two of his own?'

'I should imagine they're already on their way,' Sean said.

'Thing I can't work out,' Gardner said, 'is why they tried to abduct this Chris Sagar guy? I mean, if he's been outta Fourth Day for as long as you say, any information he coulda given you would be real out of date. OK, so whack him, yeah, that I can see. But kidnap? Why the risk? And what could he tell them?' She absently picked up a remaining shrimp from her plate, bit it in half and shook her head. 'Makes no sense.'

Sean sliced open his fish. 'What makes you think,' he asked calmly, 'that they were after Sagar?'

Gardner glanced between us and then went very still as that processed. 'You think they were after Charlie?' she demanded, not quite incredulous, but not far from it. Her gaze lingered on me. 'What makes *you* so special?'

I unwrapped my knife and fork. 'Thanks for that,' I said dryly. 'I've been asking myself the same question.'

'We know they aren't afraid to kill – Witney or Epps's boys,' Sean said. 'And yet, this morning they failed to adhere to the first most basic rule of attack.'

'Which is?'

'First kill the bodyguard,' I said, picking up one of the tacos and trying to work out how to get it into my mouth without ending up wearing most of it.

'Maybe they were doing their best,' she said, laconic. When I simply grinned at her, she added, 'Or maybe they were after both of you and never made it past first base.'

Sean shook his head. 'They didn't have the manpower. Not for a double snatch on a target with a professional bodyguard. Three men – including a driver – just isn't enough.'

'If Sagar hadn't tripped over his own feet when I told him to make a run for it, then as soon as we separated they'd have been stuffed – even with the TASERs,' I agreed. 'If it had been my op, I'd have wanted two mobile teams. Six men at the very least.'

Gardner picked up her fork again, winding the tines into her lettuce. 'OK,' she said then, reflective, 'I'll buy that for a dollar. Question is, why you? You said you spoke with Witney the morning after you grabbed him. Did he say anything? Give you a hint what Bane's up to that's suddenly gotten Homeland Security's panties in a twist?'

I shrugged. 'Witney knew his life was in more danger on the outside than it had been when he was still with Fourth Day, but he wouldn't be drawn on why,' I said, frowning. 'Was it coincidence, I wonder, that Witney was the one injured in the attack last year that Bane mentioned?'

'Alleged attack,' Sean put in. His eyes flicked to Gardner. 'I assume you checked up on his claims?'

She nodded. 'Witney was pulled out of a wreck on one of the back roads leading from Fourth Day's place. Claimed he'd been run off the road, but we never proved it one way or the other.'

'Witney seemed to think it was significant that it'd been left until now to get him out. He said Bane would double what we were getting to deliver him back. And he assumed we'd drugged and interrogated him while we had the chance.'

I looked up and found Gardner's eyebrow raised inquiringly.

'Which we didn't,' Sean said blandly.

'Whatever he knew, he told me nothing that would have been worth trying a grab raid to find out,' I finished, almost lamely.

'They tortured him,' Gardner pointed out quietly. 'He would have told them anything he thought they wanted to hear, just to make it stop.'

'You don't have to remind me,' I muttered.

I had a stark flash of Witney's body, left broken in the bath of a cheap motel, remembered his earnestness, his grief over his son, and his dignity. Something bubbled up in my chest and I reached for my drink to help force it back down again. Sorrow was never far from the surface these days. I looked away sharply, out over the gently rolling breakers, coming in slow and steady along the shoreline, tried to regulate my breathing in step.

'There was nothing you could have done, Charlie,' Sean said, tension pushing roughness into his voice. A warning. 'Don't try shouldering the blame for this.'

'Maybe that's not what she's feeling guilty about, huh?' Gardner said into the silence that followed.

'Meaning?' I snapped. But I already knew.

Sean turned to look at the detective, slowly, coldly, and something about the way he did it reminded me of Epps. In spite of herself, Gardner shifted slightly on her seat.

'Meaning?' Sean repeated softly.

She pushed her plate away, wiped her mouth again and rested her elbows on the tabletop, linking her fingers together. 'Exactly when did you realise those three guys were only carrying TASERs, Charlie?' she asked. She paused meaningfully, the way I could imagine her pausing with the gang-bangers and the rapists and the murderers she'd spoken of. 'Was it before or *after* you realised they were all wearing vests?'

I'd been expecting this, but I still hadn't found an answer. Not a convincing one, anyway.

'Probably both at the same time,' I said, then shook my head. 'No, I knew the driver was wearing something – or was on something – when he came at me. Four to the chest will normally stop just about anyone.'

'Stop them?' Gardner asked. 'Or kill them?'

'In close-protection work, your only concern is to protect the life of your principal,' Sean said, stepping in smoothly. 'We're trained to react to a threat, Detective, just as you are. To keep firing until the target goes down.'

It was interesting, I thought, that he made no mention of our shared military background, where the priorities had been slightly different – identify your enemy and get the first shot in before they do.

What are you trying to hide, Sean?

What do you think I need to?

Gardner took all this in with those quick bright eyes, storing away our every tic and reaction for future reference. She was intuitive and tenacious, neither qualities I wanted in someone who had me under a microscope.

'You know that if they hadn't been wearing those vests, and all we'd found on them were non-lethal weapons, you'd be cooling your ass in a jail cell right now – spooks or no spooks.'

In my experience of Conrad Epps, I felt she was vastly underestimating the range and scope of the man's authority but, I reasoned, now was not a good time to point that out.

'I know,' I said calmly. *And don't you think I haven't gone over it, a hundred times, since it happened?*

'You ever had a TASER hit, Detective?' Sean asked.

'Oh yeah,' she said, wry. 'In training. Hurts like a son of a bitch.'

'So, if you were faced with an assailant – *three* assailants – armed with them,' he went on, 'wouldn't you do whatever it took to avoid taking that hit?'

'Yeah,' she allowed, but her eyes were back on me. 'So, you knew they were TASERs?'

'Honestly?' I let out a long breath. 'No. You see a gun – or what looks bloody like a gun – pointed at you with clear intent, and that's enough. You react. You don't fixate on the weapon itself. It's just an inanimate object. You look at the person behind it. Their eyes, their hands, the way they hold their shoulders. That's what tells you they're going to shoot.'

She reached into her pocket and pulled out a packet of gum, regarding me with those cool, flat eyes as she unwrapped a stick and folded it into her mouth.

'Shoot? Yeah, sure,' she said then. 'But kill? The only one playing for keeps here was you.'

'If I'd been shooting to kill, I'd have gone for head shots,' I said grimly. 'Besides, how long do you think I would have lasted, if I'd let them put me on the ground?'

'Well, just be kinda thankful to your pal Epps that you won't have to argue that one in front of a judge.' She rose, automatically hitching her jacket free of the Glock on her hip as she did so, and swung her legs over the bench to get up without bothering Sean. By the end of the table she paused and gave me a half smile that came and went like a light.

'I saw what they did to him, Charlie,' she said. 'If it's any consolation, if it had been me, I woulda shot the bastards, too.'

CHAPTER NINETEEN

In the Suburban, heading for the airport, Sean said, 'Talk to me, Charlie,' as if he wasn't going to like what I had to say.

I turned away from glumly watching traffic through the side glass with my chin resting on my fist.

'What is there to say?' I asked. 'I overreacted. You and I both know it. And Detective Gardner certainly knows it, too.'

It took him a moment to reply. 'And what would you have me tell your father, your mother, if you'd hesitated and they'd got you?' he said, harsh. 'If they'd tortured and executed you in some shitty little motel, just like they did with Witney?'

My parents' long-standing, intense dislike for my profession had undergone something of a revision after the events of the previous autumn, when they'd been reluctantly forced to rely on me and Sean to act as their temporary bodyguards. Oh, they didn't like it any better now, but at least they had some understanding of what we did.

I tried to remember how my parents had gone about imparting their moral standards into their only child, but that part of my infancy remained obstinately blank. It could have been by osmosis. I glanced at Sean. Were we as capable of setting an example to the next generation?

'How about, "Well, at least she wasn't a murderer"? Not in the eyes of the law, at any rate.' Was that really my voice with its irritating, petulant note?

'Christ Jesus,' he muttered between his teeth, then let out a long breath. 'You know my first thoughts, back on that road in the canyon this morning, when I heard you run through your statement for the cops?'

He pulled out to overtake a slow-moving truck in the right-hand lane, accelerating hard into a gap that didn't really exist. You can get away with driving a little more aggressively in an up-armoured SUV.

'No. What?'

'*Textbook.* That's what I thought. It was textbook, the way you handled things. Fast, clean, accurate. An armed attack on a principal, three on one, and you wiped the floor with them.' He smiled a little. 'I was bloody proud of you, if you must know.'

My skin rippled. 'For trying to kill three people?'

'No – for doing your job! How many times have I told you, you can't afford to let emotion cloud your judgement in this business, Charlie? It almost killed you once, for Christ's sake.'

'That was different. You know it was,' I reminded him, quietly reproachful. 'The life of a child was at stake.'

Ella. The four-year-old daughter of a principal I had failed to save.

'Yeah, and you held your fire, not because it would have endangered the kid, but because it would have traumatised her to witness the result,' he said, flaying me with the truth of his words. His eyes, hidden behind the lenses of his sunglasses, were on the mirrors, the traffic. Anywhere but on me, and I was glad of it.

'She was four years old and I was doing my best to protect her,' I said at last, stiffly. Only then did he flick a glance in my direction.

'Yeah, well, sometimes you've just got to concentrate on saving them first and worry about the after-effects later,' he said. 'Like you did today.'

It wouldn't matter, I realised, what decision I'd made about leaving the business, about becoming a full-time parent, because Sean would still be involved. And who was to say that wouldn't still make me – and any child we might share – a target? A target who would grow up with a mother who habitually checked underneath her vehicle for explosive devices before making the school run, performed countersurveillance routines on the way to the supermarket, who had a gun-safe in her bedroom.

What kind of moral code would that imprint?

We rode on in silence, turning inland at the Santa Monica Pier and heading through Venice Beach and Marina del Rey, the traffic starting to build now as we began picking up signs for LAX.

Then I said, stark, 'I didn't know.'

'Didn't know you hadn't killed them?' Sean asked immediately. 'Or that they weren't carrying firearms?'

'Either,' I said with a mirthless little laugh. 'Both.' I paused, eyes fixed on the brake lights of the car in front as we slowed. 'And you know the worst thing? At the time...I didn't care. I saw the threat and just reacted.'

Just because it was textbook, doesn't mean it was right.

'You care, Charlie,' he said, not sounding quite so exasperated with me anymore. 'It's always been your Achilles' heel for this job – you care too much. And feeling nothing when you're in the middle of a firefight is just a skill you pick up. Don't knock it. Being calm under pressure is a good attribute.' He looked across, eyes hidden, face without expression.

'Feeling nothing when you have to make the decision to kill isn't the problem – trust me on that,' he said. 'The real problem comes if you start to enjoy it.'

The flight back to New York was five and a half hours, squeezed in next to two fat businessmen, who talked loudly in impressive management jargon that was nothing but empty words and hot air.

Sean sat two rows back, across the aisle to my right. The flight was full and we hadn't been able to rearrange our seats, but there are times when I'd swear Bill Rendelson booked us tickets like these on purpose.

We lifted out of LAX in the dark, banking hard over the city to reveal a million dots of light stretching out in a giant matrix to the far horizon. Still full of tacos, I declined the dubious evening meal, reclined my seat, pulled my blanket up to my chin, and willed myself to sleep.

It was a long time coming.

Every time I closed my eyes, I had a jumbled-up vision of the ambush, sometimes in slow motion, sometimes so fast the figures were little more than a blur. But, every time, I saw the rounds hit, and I heard again the noises my targets made as they fell.

Sean had lost his adverse reaction to death a long time before we first met. Since then, I'd watched him kill without hesitation or regret and, yes, there were times when I might even have said there was a certain grim satisfaction about him, too.

And while at one time he'd had disturbed dreams, close to nightmares, that saw him sweat and tremble in his sleep, I'd never seen uncertainty in him during his waking hours.

I thought again of Parker's warnings, to tell Sean about my condition, and to do so as soon as this job was over. Well, we were on the plane home. It was over now.

But I was filled with an overwhelming sense of dread that we'd have a similar conversation. A conversation that owed everything to a cold-blooded, pragmatic assessment of the facts, and very little to emotional gut reaction, which Sean seemed to hold in such low regard.

And I wanted emotion from him, like nothing else.

I'd lost the child I carried halfway through the eighth week, just two-thirds through the first trimester. Old enough to have a heartbeat, but not yet a gender. An entity but not yet a person.

It had happened suddenly and without warning, just as the weather turned colder and the month into December. About five days after my visit to the downtown clinic where the Chinese doctor had offered me the leaflets about terminating my pregnancy. My own body, it seemed, had ideas of its own on that score.

All I knew was that I'd collapsed in the street, bleeding, while I'd been looking at the Christmas displays in a department store window. After that, things were a slur of pain and indignities. By the time I came round in hospital to find Parker at my bedside, it was all over.

I'd had what the doctors referred to as a spontaneous abortion, a phrase which preyed continuously on my mind, as though I'd somehow willed it. It happened in about twenty per cent of first-time pregnancies, so they told me. There was no apparent cause. Just my body's way of rejecting a foetus that was, for whatever reason, unviable. There was nothing I could have done to prevent the loss of my unborn child, the doctors assured me, trying to comfort, nor to halt my miscarriage once it had begun.

The logical half of my brain completely understood and accepted their gentle explanations. But the emotional half, that was another story.

Sean had been away working and I'd begged Parker not to recall him. Not to tell him.

After all, how *could* I tell Sean I'd just lost his baby, on the run-up to Christmas, when I hadn't quite got round to telling him I was expecting it in the first place?

CHAPTER TWENTY

We were greeted by a thin daylight at JFK and a thirty-five degree drop in temperature. We collected our checked bags and walked out into blustery rain that had the smell of sleet about it.

Erik Landers was waiting to pick us up, looking lean and efficient in an immaculate grey suit and stark white shirt. He and Sean fell into easy conversation about the upcoming baseball season, still a couple of months away. We rode back into the city with the heater on full and the windscreen wipers hustling water off the glass. It seemed a world away from Los Angeles.

Landers dropped us off at our apartment, a stone's throw from Central Park on the Upper East Side. The building was owned by some rich relative of Parker's, which didn't narrow it down much. When we'd first moved to New York, he'd done considerable arm-twisting on our behalf to get us a lease on the place at a price we could afford.

As we took the lift up to our floor, all I wanted was a

hard shower and a soft bed, but knew only the former was on offer.

I stood under the needle spray of hot water for a long time, sloughing off the grime of recirculated plane air, and some of my weariness went with it. Not all, but some.

When I stepped out of the cubicle, it was to find Sean leaning in the bathroom doorway, watching me as he unbuttoned his shirt. Almost lazily, he hooked a towel off the rail and passed it across. I wrapped it hastily around my body, suddenly self-conscious to be naked in front of him in case he spotted the minute physical changes. He always did see too much.

'You OK?' he asked.

'Yeah,' I said with a quick smile, indicating the billowing steam. 'Better for that, that's for sure.'

'Mm, I thought you were trying to boil yourself, you were in there so long.' He came forwards to lightly grasp my upper arms, eyes on my face. 'You look a lot happier than you did when we left LA,' he said quietly. 'Seriously, Charlie. I'm glad. Sometimes life throws shit at you, and you've just got to put it behind you and move on.'

He stepped back, a look of wonder on his face. 'I mean, look at what we have here, hmm? When I was back in school, the best my teachers predicted for me was that I'd end up in the army, in prison, or dead.' He shook his head. 'But every day I wake up in this apartment, this city – with you – and I have to bloody pinch myself to check it's all real.'

'Yeah,' I said softly, smiling on the outside and weeping within. 'Maybe it's just good to be home.'

* * *

By the time we reached the midtown offices of Armstrong-Meyer, wrapped up against the slushy cold in overcoats and gloves and scarves, the laid-back warmth of the west coast seemed a distant memory.

Bill Rendelson, manning the desk in the plush reception area on the twenty-third floor, greeted us with his customary scowl when the lift doors opened.

Almost as if we'd planned it, Sean and I strode unhesitatingly across the expanse of tile towards Parker's office. As we swept past the desk, Rendelson was already half out of his seat in protest. Sean sent him back into it with a single daggered look.

'He's in, I take it?' It was barely a question. When we reached the door, Sean rapped his knuckles once, briefly, on the wood. Then he was turning the handle and we both walked in.

The office straddled the north-west corner of the building, and had been furnished by an interior designer with a clean modern eye and very few budgetary restrictions. It smelt, as always, of furniture polish overlaid with good coffee.

Parker was on his feet next to one of the large windows, talking on the phone when we barged in. He glanced across sharply and I saw him go still, but he smoothly continued his conversation, using the time to inspect the pair of us as though for imperfections. I resisted the urge to come to attention and saw Parker register that fact in the way his right eye narrowed.

Eventually, he ended the call and moved across without hurry to slot the cordless handset back into its base station on the desk.

'Sean, Charlie,' he greeted us calmly. 'You got back OK?'

Sean's head gave a tiny jerk of impatience, but when he spoke there was nothing in his voice.

'After everything you said to Epps about keeping secrets,' he said, 'it was a bit of a shock to find out you've been hiding the biggest one of all.'

Parker's eyes flickered to me, a gesture Sean didn't miss, I was sure of it. Then he said, 'We'll get to that. Tell me about this ambush.'

I let Sean recount the story while I helped us to coffee from the pot of Jamaican Blue Mountain on the credenza. We sat in the comfortable client armchairs, facing each other across a low glass table. Parker leant back, slightly angled towards both of us, giving his utter attention to Sean's verbal report. He didn't fidget or interrupt, hardly blinked until it was done. I was suddenly reminded of Randall Bane.

'I think we've smoothed things over a little with the LAPD, but I wouldn't run any red lights in that town for a while, if I were you,' Sean finished. 'We still don't know who those guys were and I'd guess we're not going to find out, if Epps has anything to do with it.'

'Epps already called this morning,' Parker said dryly, surprising both of us. 'The guys who tried to jump you are local talent, he says. Pros, but not high on the food chain. They reckon they were only recruited for the job two days ago and told they had to move fast.'

Sean said, 'Have they confirmed it was a snatch, not a hit?'

Parker nodded. 'They were given a reasonably accurate description of Chris Sagar and told just to grab whoever was with him. Their instructions were quite specific.'

'But they weren't told who this "whoever" might be?' I asked.

'No. Apparently, the guy driving, name of Delmondo, did the deal – and before you ask, a voice on a cellphone and a dead-letter drop for half of the money upfront. He said when they saw it was a woman, they thought they'd have it easy.' Parker glanced across at me and smiled. 'You kinda disabused them of that notion pretty quick.'

'If they weren't expecting resistance,' Sean said, 'why the body armour?'

'Standard operating procedure these days, according to Delmondo. These guys wear Kevlar like the rich wear Prada and Armani.'

'Good to know,' Sean said, and the casual tone of his voice sent the hairs prickling along my arms, because I knew exactly what piece of information he was tucking away for future reference.

Next time, head shots.

'How did they know where to find us?' I queried, and noted Parker's frown.

'They got a call to say you were leaving the house,' he said carefully. 'Picked you up from there.'

My eyes flicked to Sean's in dismay. I would have sworn the house was not under surveillance. We'd been automatically attentive. And, besides, the very fact that the whole estate in Calabasas was gated off, and had its own security, was what made it so ideal for us in the first place.

'There was nobody watching the house,' Sean said, before I could make the same statement. 'Not unless they had half a dozen teams on it and they were bloody well trained.' He shook his head. 'And if they were using so many people that we didn't make them, why not send more on the snatch itself, just to be sure?'

'Hey, I didn't say I agreed with Epps's take on it,' Parker said mildly. 'I'm just telling you what he said.'

'What were their orders, once they'd grabbed me?'

'To call for instructions on where to deliver you,' Parker said. 'They were pretty insistent that they weren't out to kill you.'

'Yeah right,' I said, mildly sarcastic, 'which is why they took *such* trouble to hide their faces.'

Parker raised an eyebrow at Sean, who shook his head. 'They knew there wasn't going to be any danger of Charlie identifying any of them afterwards,' he said. 'Even if they *allegedly* weren't going to finish the job personally.'

'I think it's safe to assume Epps's people will have questioned them kinda...closely on that,' Parker said gravely.

'What about the cellphone number of this mystery employer?' I said.

'Dead end. Pay-as-you-go number, probably stripped and dumped in a storm drain, soon as the job went south.'

'Does Epps think they're the ones who grabbed Witney, too?' I asked.

'They claim that was nothing to do with them, but maybe they're holding out because they know killing two federal agents will put all of them on Death Row for sure.'

'And has Epps put his own house in order and found out who put the tracker on the van Witney was in?'

'No,' Parker said. His lips twisted briefly. 'Or, if he has, he wasn't willing to share *that* information with me,' he amended.

We sat for a moment in silence, then Sean put down his

coffee cup and said flatly, 'OK, Parker, what's the real story with you and Thomas Witney?'

Parker sighed and sat forwards with his forearms resting on his knees, shoulders hunched. I opened my mouth to hurry him along but Sean, catching my eye, shook his head slightly.

Give him time.

For what? To remember, or invent?

Sean's glance was reproachful. He waited without impatience, but his eyes never left Parker's face. The coffee machine gurgled unexpectedly, like sudden indigestion. The siren of a fire engine ran the length of the street below us, echoing between the buildings.

At last, Parker looked up, loosing a breath. 'The Witneys came to me about Liam five years ago.'

'After he was killed?' I asked.

'No, it was after he dropped out of college,' Parker said, rubbing an absent forefinger along his temple. 'They were worried he might have gotten involved in drugs, something like that, and they asked me to find out.'

'Why you?' Sean said. 'Armstrong's has never been a private investigation firm.' He paused, head tilted. 'You had a prior connection.'

A faint trace of a smile appeared on Parker's face. 'Lorna Witney runs an oil exploration business,' he said. 'Family firm, I think, but she's a smart lady. Lotta grit. Degree from Columbus. We provided security personnel for their ongoing overseas projects.'

Sean said, 'The name doesn't ring any bells.'

'It won't. After she and Witney parted, she shifted her base of operations to Europe and I assume she now uses someone local.' He shrugged aside that dent to his professional pride.

'So, what *did* you find out about Liam?'

'That he'd come into contact with Randall Bane and had joined Fourth Day,' Parker said simply.

'Just like that,' I murmured. 'Wow, Bane must be even more persuasive than I thought.'

'Liam had been off the grid for six months,' Parker said. 'By the time we located him, Bane had him pretty much where he wanted.'

I remembered Thomas Witney's edge of regret over his son, asked, 'Why did they wait so long before they went looking?'

'Not the first time he'd pulled a stunt like that,' Parker said. 'The impression I got from his parents was they were not entirely surprised when he dropped out of college. They thought maybe it was some girl, but figured he'd be back when he needed money. It was only after they got his cut-up bank and ATM cards in the mail, they realised he was serious this time.'

'So they tried to get him out,' Sean said. 'Did they ask you to do an extraction?'

'Only after they'd tried just about every other way to get to their son,' Parker said tiredly. 'Which gave Bane plenty of time to move the kid elsewhere. By the time we went in, he was long gone. Next thing we heard, he'd turned up dead during some sabotage attack against an oil exploration project in Alaska. Real blow for his mother, considering her line of work.'

'Debacle, wasn't it – the name of the group he joined?' I said, remembering Detective Gardner's interview with Bane.

'Yeah,' Parker said. 'They claimed responsibility. Claimed Liam had been executed in cold blood and was a "martyr to the cause", as I recall, but I saw the reports. The boy was caught planting explosives and apparently tried to shoot his way out. Even I would have judged it a good kill.' There was bitterness in his tone. 'Witney blamed Bane's influence. He haunted the authorities, trying to get some action, became obsessed with bringing Fourth Day down, by whatever means. Eventually, he decided to go in himself.' He looked up. 'The rest you know, pretty much.'

'Oh, I think there are still a few important blanks,' Sean said softly. 'Like, why did you leave him there, Parker? Weren't you supposed to be his safety net?'

Parker didn't reply right away, just got to his feet and strolled over to the window, leaning against the deep reveal and staring sightlessly at the distant lanes of traffic. Another fire engine passed, then a couple of police cars. Must be quite a blaze.

'Sounds kinda bad, doesn't it?' he said eventually, his tone wry. 'What you gotta understand is how Witney was when he went into that cult. He was a man on the edge of reason. Lorna – Mrs Witney – was scared for his sanity. The doctors were talking about placing him in an asylum.'

'Bane told Gardner you went to see Witney, before the first six months were up, and Witney convinced you not to retrieve him,' I said baldly. 'Why?'

Parker turned away from the view, met my eyes. 'Because he was almost back to normal. Rational, calm, reasoned. He told me he was at peace and, looking at him, I...believed it.'

I let out a long breath. 'How do you know it wasn't some drug-induced torpor?'

'Credit me with some intelligence, Charlie.' Parker gave me a slightly old-fashioned look. 'I can spot a junkie, and Witney even let us draw blood from him. We had a private forensics lab in LA run just about every test they could think of. It was clean.'

'There are plenty of other ways to exert control over someone,' Sean said. 'You should know that.'

Parker sighed. 'Yeah, and maybe we should have ignored his wishes, got him out by force and put him through some kinda twelve-step programme, but ultimately, it was out of my hands.'

'Oh?'

'Mrs Witney made the choice to respect his wishes and leave him be.'

'His *wife*?' I demanded. 'Hang on, Witney told me his marriage was crumbling before he ever set foot inside Fourth Day. How the hell do you know her decision wasn't based on the fact that he'd gone fruit loop and she was delighted to see the back of him?'

Parker's gaze grew cool. 'Well, Charlie, looks like you'll have the opportunity to ask her. Mrs Witney is unable to travel, but she wants the full story on what happened. I've given her my word that someone from this agency will accompany her husband's body over to her home in Scotland for burial and give it to her,' he said, pronouncing 'Scotland' like it was two separate words, distinct and foreign. 'She wants him treated with dignity and respect. Be sure to extend the lady herself that same courtesy, won't you?'

CHAPTER TWENTY-ONE

Two days later, I landed just outside Edinburgh on a Continental flight out of Newark. Having been through the formalities, I stood in the rain watching as Thomas Witney's coffin was transferred, with deferential efficiency, into a sombre black Mercedes van belonging to the firm of funeral directors Lorna Witney had appointed.

Then I climbed into the passenger seat of the accompanying E-class belonging to the funeral director himself, and soon we were heading north for the Forth Bridge. I was still not entirely sure why I was here.

The funeral director was an elderly Scot called Graydon Meecham, tall and gaunt, his face was tailor-made for a black top hat and a wing collar. He also turned out to have a dry wit and a fund of stories about the funny side of the burial business. They made the two and a half hours it took to reach Aberdeen pass much faster than they might otherwise have done.

I saw the coffin safely tucked away in Meecham's cold storage. He offered a business card and told me, with a twinkle, that if ever I had a body to dispose of, I shouldn't hesitate to call.

'Can I run you up to your hotel, lassie?' he asked. 'Where are you staying?'

'There you have me,' I said, tucking the card away in my jacket pocket. 'I believe Mrs Witney was sorting something out. Could I trouble you to give me a lift over to her offices?'

He hesitated. 'Ah, there might be a wee problem with that.'

'Why?' I asked, a little coolly. 'Is it far?'

'It's not that, lassie. It's just, well, she's been having a spot of bother lately.' He squirmed like a schoolboy, glanced through his office window to the yard outside, where one of his lads was already washing the salt-streaked rain off the E-class, nestled amid the highly polished hearses. 'Environmental protesters of some kind, you know the type. They've been picketing the place, trying to intimidate visitors.'

'Ah,' I echoed, thinking of his obvious pride in his vehicles, and waited a beat. 'How about if you dropped me off just round the corner, out of sight?'

We drove in silence through the city centre. I think he might have been giving me the scenic tour by way of recompense.

The architecture was largely cold granite grey, which lent the city an air of hard-bitten dignity, of being hunkered down with its teeth gritted against the bitter wind coming up off the North Sea, all the way from frozen Scandinavia.

Even so, I got an impression of tenacious prosperity, whatever was happening to the rest of the UK economy.

I'd been keeping tabs on the news from home. 'Hell in a handcart' seemed to be the best general description.

The oil exploration company run by Thomas Witney's ex-wife was located in one of the industrial areas towards the east of the city. Here, the buildings were no-nonsense functional units, streaked with grey and no glitz. I wouldn't have wanted to leave a vehicle parked unattended for longer than I could help it. Graydon Meecham wasn't even keen on stopping. He swung the big car round in the mouth of a junction about a hundred and fifty metres from where I could see a small group of demonstrators, around fifteen or twenty of them with placards, gathered around a pair of closed gates set into the galvanised fencing.

'Good luck, lassie,' Meecham said as I climbed out, lifting the rucksack that was my only luggage from the footwell.

He was already driving away as I slung the rucksack over my shoulder and walked towards the gates, watching for patterns as the protesters moved and interacted as a group, pinpointing the natural ringleaders.

Not everybody at a demo wants to fight, and some will run if anything more serious than a scuffle breaks out. Others will join in once things have kicked off, but won't instigate. And then there's the aggressive subspecies for whom the prospect of violence is their only reason to turn out in the first place. Identifying such people in a crowd quickly, and then isolating and neutralising them, was part of the job.

In my estimation, there were two likely candidates here. One was a short squat guy, maybe in his mid thirties, with ginger hair and a close-trimmed beard. The other was taller, thinner, younger and blonder, and had the kind of tan you don't get by sitting out in your garden in the north of Scotland in January.

I reached the gate. At one side was a security intercom with a call button and a speaker, in a vandal-resistant metal box. I 'excuse-me'd' my way through to it and pressed the call button, waited for a response.

Although I couldn't see water, I got the impression we were near the harbour from the intermingling smells of fish and diesel and salt in the air. The sky overhead was filled with the raucous squabble of a thousand seagulls. It had stopped raining just north of Perth, and an uncertain sun had broken through the clouds. On the whole, it didn't make the place look any more welcoming.

'You don't wanna be going in there, kiddo,' said a voice close by my shoulder.

I wasn't surprised to find one of the potential troublemakers crowding in on me. The tall blond one. He had an American accent and a nice smile and bad breath, and was casually holding his placard face down over his left shoulder.

The placard consisted of foamboard nailed to a lump of two-by-two, which seemed excessive as a support unless he also planned to use it as a weapon. For that reason alone, I stayed close to him instead of stepping away, as he expected me to. If he decided to take a swing at me, better not to let him build momentum.

'Oh?' I said cheerfully. 'And why's that?'

'Why?' It was one of the girls who spoke. She had much more of a local accent, her voice intense and bitter. 'Because they're raping the planet, that's why. Not that people like *you* care – arriving in that gas-guzzling monstrosity!'

'And you all got here on bicycles or in nice hybrid electric cars, did you?' I asked pleasantly, nodding to the assortment of battered old vehicles parked along the opposite side of the road. Her only answer was a scowl. 'Thanks. I'll bear it in mind.'

The intercom buzzed and I pressed the button to speak, not taking my eyes off the blond guy with the placard. He had a real surfer dude look about him. If only he flossed. 'I'm here to see Mrs Witney,' I said into the microphone. I hesitated a moment, then added carefully. 'Tell her Parker Armstrong sent me.'

The speaker emitted a brief garbled message, something about someone being on their way, and went silent.

I didn't miss the way the surfer dude's eyes flared.

'Ah, an audience with the boss lady herself,' he said. 'In that case, kiddo, you can give her a message from us.'

'What kind of a message?'

They moved in then, started to jostle, bumping me, not outright rough but aiming to scare. I dropped my rucksack off my shoulder and waited to see which one of them would cross the line first.

In the end, it was the short squat guy, which came as no great surprise. Maybe he was trying to make up for being slower on the initial attack by being right up there in the second wave. We were almost on eye level with each other, a fact that did not please him.

He shoved the heel of his hand into my shoulder, trying to rock me back into the fencing. I rolled out from behind it, brought my hands up and reached for him, twisting his wrist round and up into a decent lock. Just enough to hold him immobilised with one hand, and make the others wary about coming to his aid. He went rigid with shock, rising on his toes, teetering as he tried to work around the pain.

'I don't like that message,' I said, speaking directly to the surfer dude, not missing the way one of the secondaries started to edge round behind me. 'You might like to tell your people to stand down, though, because the first one who tries anything, I'll dislocate every bone in your friend's right arm.' I paused, watched the doubt form in their faces. 'Up to and including his shoulder joint. He'll be having surgery for months.'

We stood like that for what seemed like half a day, while the gulls wheeled mocking overhead, until, at last, I heard hurrying footsteps on the other side of the gate, and the jangle of keys.

A couple of big guys in nightclub bouncer black wrenched the gate open. I waited a moment longer, then released the squat guy and pushed him away. He stumbled back, cradling his hand.

I grabbed my rucksack and stepped through the gate. The guards slammed it shut again after me.

'Hey, kiddo,' the surfer dude called as I started to walk away. 'That was only part of the message. Don't you want to hear the rest?'

I stopped, turned back, half-expecting insults and curious to see if they were ones I hadn't heard before.

He was smiling broadly at me through the bars of the gate, placard still balanced over his shoulder.

'Tell Mrs Witney she should have left well alone,' he said, his words more chilling for being delivered so evenly. 'Ask her what she gains by involving people like you. And what else does she have to lose?'

With that he turned and walked away, almost a swagger.

And as he did so, for the first time I was able to read the top part of the placard he'd been carrying throughout our exchange. I didn't get much of it – just the first word. A name rather than a statement.

Debacle.

CHAPTER TWENTY-TWO

When I was shown into Lorna Witney's office a few minutes later, my first impression was a woman of aloof restraint.

She sat very still behind an imposing mahogany desk, a plinth-like construction with the appearance of a solid block, like some kind of Mayan sacrificial altar. She didn't rise as I crossed the expanse of oxblood-red carpet towards her, just peered over the top of her reading glasses and waited for my arrival as if granting audience.

Thomas Witney's widow had a striking face, dominated by a slightly haughty nose, and dark-red hair cut short and feathered in an attempt to soften the austerity. She wore a severe grey fitted jacket over a cream blouse with an open neck, smart and businesslike. When I halted in front of her she took off the glasses and pushed back a little.

It was only then I realised she was in a wheelchair.

The surfer dude's parting shot outside took on new meaning.

'And what else does she have to lose?'

It was information that should have been in Parker's

briefing, I considered, but he'd said very little about this woman before sending me over here as a glorified courier. Surprisingly little...

I kept my face neutral as we traded names and regarded each other, a mutual weighing-up exercise, then she said, 'So, you're with Parker.' Her voice was low and husky, with the dust of rural Texas still running through it despite living over here for the last five years.

'I am.'

She digested my answer as if there was more to it, nodded shortly, then wheeled back and rolled out from behind the desk. The immaculate cut of her suit did not quite disguise that the upper half of her frame was all angles and muscle, her shoulders bulked out like an athlete by the effort required to work the chair, leaving her lower body narrow and wasted.

She could have had an electrically operated chair and saved herself the heavy lifting. The fact that she hadn't chosen the easy option was an interesting one, I felt.

'Thank you, for bringing Thomas back to me,' she said, a little mechanically. 'I'm...grateful.' The hand she offered was strong, the palm callused.

A strobe-lit image hit me, of that damn motel bathroom again, the smell of fear thick in the air like blood.

'I'm sorry for your loss, Mrs Witney,' I said, stiffly formal. *All of it.*

'What do you know about loss?' It was a snap response, but then she glanced across at me, her gaze assessing. 'No, I take that back. If you work for Parker, you probably know more than most.' She gave a tragic sigh. 'Thomas was effectively lost to me years ago. I guess I thought I'd accepted it.'

Maybe I was just tired, but something in that martyred tone rankled, made me less diplomatic than I probably should have been.

'But you *could* have had him back, couldn't you?' I said bluntly. 'If you'd wanted him.'

'Excuse me?' she bit out, icy calm. 'What, precisely, is *that* supposed to mean?'

My turn to sigh. 'Look, Mrs Witney, I've just flown three thousand miles with a corpse because Parker said you wanted answers. Well, so do I. I thought we'd skip the foreplay.'

Lorna Witney turned bone white, jaw jutting, so for a moment I thought she'd simply have me thrown out.

'What answers?' she asked eventually, through stiff lips.

'When your husband went into Fourth Day, you must have known how close to the edge he was,' I said. 'Why didn't you overrule his decision to stay – allow Parker to get him out, as arranged – unless you'd decided by that time you were better off without him?'

'That's not true! You don't know how Parker and I agonised—' She broke off, swallowed, then said in a low voice, 'Yes, the balance of Thomas's mind *was* disturbed, but it was like that before he ever set foot inside that place. *Way* before.'

But my mind had veered sharply at the way she flushed as she spoke. I saw the trace of guilt underlying her words, thought for a fraction of a second that she had indeed engineered her husband's convenient retreat. Then the truth of it hit me like a slap in the face.

'*You don't know how Parker and I agonised...*' Something about the way she formed my boss's name. Connection and memories...

'Wait a minute. Surely it was your decision, not Parker's?'

I'd half-expected a vehement denial, but the flush deepened. She had the very pale skin unique to natural redheads, a dusting of freckles across her cheekbones. The blush clashed horribly with her hair.

'My God,' I whispered. 'You and *Parker*...?'

Her chin rose angrily. 'I wasn't always in a wheelchair, Charlie.'

'No, but you were always married,' I shot back. 'And, not only that, but you were a client. *Married* to a client, for heaven's sake!'

She swung the chair away from me with a fluid shove, the movement strangely graceful, like an astronaut working in zero gravity. She grabbed the corner of the desk to swing round and tuck herself in behind it, back firmly in her seat of power.

The desk had been chosen with great care, I realised, to minimise any sign of weakness. Anyone sitting across that polished surface from Lorna Witney, here in her personal domain, would see only the reins of cool command.

'My marriage was on the rocks before then,' she said quietly. 'Liam's death blew it apart, in a way it couldn't have done if the cracks weren't there already. Parker probably saved my sanity. Just as I believe Randall Bane saved Thomas.'

'Why?' I asked, stark.

'Why do I believe it, you mean?' She reached absently for her glasses again, toyed with them. 'Liam's death affected us both, of course, but it hit Thomas particularly hard. He blamed me.'

'Blamed you?'

'For taking Liam with me on explorations when he was still a child. Better that than leaving him at home, or so I believed at the time. But Thomas was the one who taught him geology, ecology, when he was barely old enough to pronounce the words. We thought we'd produced a child who would grow up with a responsible attitude to the world around him. Instead, he became an eco-terrorist, and it killed him.'

She stopped, broke off, refused to show a chink, but I saw her knuckles bulge regardless. As if aware of the telltale action, she put the glasses down abruptly.

I said, 'I thought Thomas blamed himself?'

'He blamed everybody, at one time or another, the way people lash out when they're hurt. But most of all he blamed Bane for corrupting Liam. He believed that if Fourth Day hadn't influenced him, Liam never would have joined Debacle, that he would never have died. Before Thomas decided to go into that damned cult and bring down Bane, he'd been slowly driving himself crazy for over a year. I-I was scared for him, if you must know.'

Scared of him. She didn't say the words out loud, but I heard them anyway.

'But when Parker went to see him after six months, he was cured?' I said, sceptical.

'We both went. I wasn't about to shirk that responsibility.' She flushed again, less angrily this time. 'You may not want to believe it,' she said. '*I* didn't want to believe it, but in twenty years I'd never seen Thomas so centred, so... comfortable inside his own skin, his own mind. Bane worked miracles with him, somehow. And if Thomas was living in his own little dreamworld, who was I to drag him kicking and screaming back into mine?' Her gaze was both defiant and pleading. Wanting desperately for my approval, yet at the same time telling me to go to hell.

'Was that the last time you saw your husband?' I asked. 'The last contact you had with him?'

'Yes, and if I'd known what Parker was planning – to get him out – I would have damn well begged him not to. What right did anybody have to take that peace away from Thomas?'

'*Tell Mrs Witney she should have left well alone,*' the Debacle member with the surfer dude looks had said to me. Did he think she was, however belatedly, behind the extraction?

'It wasn't Parker's call,' I said quickly.

'Someone held a gun to his head and forced him, did they?' she shot back, close to jeering. I thought of the kind of pressure Epps could apply – if not a loaded gun then pretty close.

But I could understand her anger. After all, we had taken Thomas Witney's peace away, I acknowledged, and it had been the death of him. Who was to say that Parker's decision to leave him alone, five years ago, hadn't been the right one?

Whatever the reasons behind it...

And where did that leave us now?

Suddenly I was aware of an overwhelming weariness, of spirit as much as body. I would have trusted my life to Parker, but I'd been shaken by his secrecy over this job. I liked to think that, had it been me, I would have confided in those closest to me, and to hell with Epps's paranoid directives on Need To Know.

But I was even more shaken by his secrecy involving his relationship with Thomas Witney's wife, regardless of the state of their marriage at the time.

I tried to tighten my grip on what I knew was right, but the more I grasped at it, the more it slipped through my fingers like sand. After all, I was keeping secrets from Sean far more important, and personal.

I looked up and found Lorna Witney watching my expression intently.

'Can I offer you coffee?' she asked in a dispassionate voice. 'Tea? Something stronger?'

'Coffee would be fine.'

She jerked her head. 'There's a pot on the side over there. Help yourself. I'd ask my secretary, but Alice murders coffee like you wouldn't believe. She can only make tea.'

I moved to the coffee pot near the window. The pot itself was a masterpiece of style in black and chrome that clashed with its surroundings. The rest of the office was old-fashioned in design and furnishing, all dull gentlemen's club colours and dark wood panelling to match the desk. The walls were lined with bookcases and box file racks, none of them reaching higher than about five feet from the ground. Above were maps, framed articles from a variety of newspapers and magazines, and photographs going back years – the history of the company in pictorial form.

Below me, outside, I could see the Debacle crew, huddled together as a gust of wind blew in eastwards from the North Sea, bringing with it the sting of snow from Norway. It seemed a long way from the Pacific Coast Highway at Malibu.

'You made the acquaintance of our uninvited guests, I

understand,' Lorna Witney murmured. I turned to find she had wheeled out from behind her desk again. She moved close enough to the window to be able to lean forwards and look down at the protesters outside. There was no emotion in her face, as if her earlier burst of anger had never happened.

'How long have they been bothering you?' I asked.

'About a week this time.'

'This time?'

'They turn up every year,' Lorna Witney said in a slightly detached voice, 'around the anniversary of Liam's death. Stay a few weeks, make a nuisance of themselves, and then they're gone.'

I watched the ginger-haired guy I'd tackled make what I imagined was some raucous joke, laughing, clapping an aggressive hand on another's shoulder, trying to reassert his bruised masculinity. 'Always the same group?'

She shook her head, her gaze still focused out of the window. 'No, only the tall blond kid. The others call him Dexter – I don't know if that's a first name or a last. The rest come and go. I don't recognise any of the others.'

'Why do they keep coming back?'

'Presumably, lest I forget,' she said with a twisted smile. 'But I don't know for sure. We're not exactly on speaking terms.'

I poured coffee into two plain cups. It was hot enough to steam and I registered the expensive smooth aroma of Jamaican Blue Mountain, which was a favourite of Parker's. Coincidence?

'They asked me to pass on a message,' I said, and repeated what the surfer dude, Dexter, had said to me through the gate.

Lorna Witney absorbed the information in frozen silence for a moment. 'Yes, well, I figured it was something like that,' she said at last. 'We stand on the opposite sides of an ideological abyss. There can be no common ground between us.' She made it sound like a decision.

'Is that why Liam joined Debacle in the first place – as an act of rebellion?'

Her gaze narrowed. 'He always was a headstrong child,' she said, without particular affection. 'Bright, but a butterfly, flitting from one enthusiasm to the next, never settling. "Unfocused" his teachers said and I suppose they thought him maybe a little spoiled.' She glanced over at me then, as if checking for signs of censure. I showed her none. 'He tried a lot of things and never put enough of himself into any of them to succeed.' She sounded vaguely disappointed rather than saddened.

He was your child, a product of your genes, your nurturing. Is that the best you can say about him?

'So, when he joined Fourth Day, you thought it was just another of his enthusiasms?' I asked.

She looked momentarily surprised, then nodded. 'Until it was too late.' She swung the chair round away from the window and added over her shoulder, almost dismissively, 'That's him, in the photo just above you. Right before he dropped out of college.'

I glanced up, found the picture she meant and peered closer. It was a framed snapshot of a young couple, side by side on what looked like the seating of a sports stadium, their heads tilted together. The boy was Liam. Now I'd met them, I could see the unmistakable elements of both parents' bone structure morphed together.

The girl next to him was pushing her hair back out of her eyes where the breeze had caught it. They were both grinning for the camera, like they'd genuinely been having a good time.

I unhooked the framed picture off the wall, turned it to face Lorna Witney and tapped a fingernail on the glass over the girl. 'Do you know her?'

'Oh, one of his girlfriends, I think,' Lorna said, barely glancing across, her voice flat. 'We never met.'

'Her name's Maria,' I murmured.

The girl from Fourth Day.

CHAPTER TWENTY-THREE

'A child?' Lorna Witney said blankly.

I picked up my coffee cup from the edge of her desk. The liquid had cooled to tepid in the time it had taken me to explain about Maria's presence in Fourth Day, and about the existence of her infant son. I sipped it anyway. It gave me something to do with my hands while I watched her take it in.

She sat in complete silence for a long time with only her eyes moving, as if scanning a page of hidden text in front of her.

Eventually she gave a brief nod, like she'd reached the end of her mental report and agreed with its conclusions. She looked up and swallowed, face tightening.

'So, is he Liam's son?'

I shrugged. 'I have no idea.'

She gave an impatient little twitch, as if I was being deliberately obstructive rather than uninformed. 'Well...how old was he?'

I suppressed a sigh. 'I don't know – a child. Older than

a baby, certainly not in double figures. I only saw him in Maria's arms, so it was hard to judge his size. And I'm no expert,' I added. 'He seemed quite big for a toddler, I suppose, but she's very slight.'

'But he could have been the right age?' she persisted. 'He'd be around five by now, I guess.'

Her sudden intensity had me shifting in my seat. 'It's possible,' I allowed cautiously. 'But I never got close enough to the boy to tell one way or another.'

She fell silent again. I drained the dregs of my coffee.

'Of course,' she murmured, almost to herself. 'Why else would Thomas stay in that place?'

This time, I didn't bite back my sharp exhale. 'Any number of reasons,' I said. *Many of which you've already outlined when you were trying to justify yourself.* 'OK, so Maria was once Liam's girlfriend, but it's a big leap to speculate—'

'If he is my grandson, I want him out of there,' she cut in, gaze sweeping over me. 'I'm sure you can arrange that. It is, after all, what you people do.'

I didn't like the way her curled lip made her voice so bitter, but suddenly I remembered what Thomas Witney said to me about Maria, the morning after his extraction.

'She would be harmed more than you can know if you try to take her away from her family as you did me.'

I'd assumed he was talking more about Maria than himself, but perhaps there had been a double meaning to his words?

'At this stage, we don't know *who* the father is,' I said quickly, as much to cover my own doubts. 'And kidnapping is a serious offence.'

'It didn't seem to bother you as far as Thomas was

concerned,' she pointed out with damnable logic. 'And if you don't know about the child, then find out – you can do that, can't you?' She stared at me, remote and resolute. 'I want him out of there, Charlie. Perhaps that was what Dexter was referring to out there, when he said what else do I have to lose? I've already lost my husband and my son. I *will not* lose my grandchild as well.'

'I can't make that decision,' I hedged, saw the triumph in her eyes.

'Parker will do this for me,' she said with utter conviction in her tone. 'Whatever it takes, whatever it costs, I don't care. I want it done.'

There wasn't much I could say to that, other than she would have to take it up with Parker personally. My boss would need all his negotiating skills, I reckoned, to stand firm in the face of such determination.

I looked up and found Lorna Witney watching my expression.

'You must be tired after your flight,' she said, glancing at her watch, sensing victory and magnanimous enough not to crow. 'I never could get much sleep on an airplane, even before my accident. Give me ten minutes to finish up here and I'll drop you at your hotel on my way home.'

'There's no need,' I said. 'Tell me the address and I'll grab a taxi.'

'It's no trouble,' she said, her ominous tone daring me to make an issue of it. 'It's the least I can do.'

I waited in the outer office, fully expecting the promised ten minutes to turn into an hour, just to drive the point home, but she was disarmingly prompt when she appeared, with her laptop, handbag and coat slung across her knees.

I went ahead and pressed the call button for the lift while she spoke briefly to her secretary. She arrived alongside me just as the lift doors pinged and slid open.

As she wheeled past me, I was treated to a single upward glance. 'At least you don't fuss, offer to carry things,' she said grudgingly.

'I have my own bag,' I said, tapping the strap of my rucksack. I could have given her the professional hands-free excuse, too, but I didn't. I smiled instead. 'You don't strike me as someone who's shy about asking for what she wants, Mrs Witney.'

She raised her eyebrows at that, trying to work out whether to be offended, deciding against.

The lift only went down one floor and the time it took the doors to close and open again was longer than the ride itself. She stopped again to speak to the two security men who were loitering in reception, and then led me out through the back exit to the car park, where a BMW 750i on a private plate was parked next to the doorway. The five-litre petrol engine alone, I noted, was enough to send even the mildest green protester into a frothing frenzy.

Lorna Witney completed the transfer of herself from chair to driving seat with the minimum of fuss. From there, she folded the chair down far enough to swing it across and slot it into the passenger footwell, obviously well practised. I climbed into the rear.

She cranked the engine, barely audible inside the luxurious cabin. The BMW was automatic and had been converted to hand controls.

As we pulled round towards the main gate, the light had begun to drop fast, triggering the sodium lights on the outside of the building. The two security men let us out, giving their boss a casual wave as they did so.

Despite my concerns, the protesters parted meekly as we drove through, their silence somehow more unnerving than a barrage of abuse. I looked for Dexter and the squat ginger-haired guy, but there was no sign of them.

'Most people can't resist asking what happened to me,' Lorna Witney said, apropos of nothing as we accelerated along the road out of the industrial area, chicaning round parked eighteen wheelers loaded with huge pipes and chains and other, unidentifiable chunks of machinery. If it wasn't for the fact that most of it was painted Day-Glo colours, I'd suspect it was all part of the latest supergun, destined for Iraq.

'I assumed, if you wanted me to know, you'd tell me.'

That cynical smile again. 'Helicopter,' she said briefly, and I remembered one of the photographs on the wall behind her desk. It had showed a group shot of people wearing hard hats and company logos, posing between two Bell Jet Rangers.

'Catastrophic engine failure coming in from one of the rigs three years ago. We ditched a hundred yards short of the beach, came in a lot hotter and a lot heavier than anyone would have liked, least of all me. Everybody else got out with relatively minor injuries.' Her voice was cool, as if recounting a story about a stranger, one she'd told a thousand times before. 'I was just unlucky, I guess.'

'I'm sorry,' I said. 'Adapting must have been tough.'

'Coping with my injuries has not been as difficult as coping with other people's reaction to them,' she said blandly.

'They underestimate you,' I said, a statement rather than a question.

'Not for long.' Her lips twisted. 'Even before that, I recognised that I didn't exactly fit the stereotype of a roughneck. I still have all my fingers, for a start.' She glanced across. 'You must have found the same thing yourself, in your line of work. I can imagine that people sometimes make the mistake of underestimating you, Charlie.'

'Not for long,' I said, with a wry smile of my own. 'Where are we going, by the way?'

'Trying to get a room at short notice is a nightmare in this town,' Lorna Witney said. 'But the company has so many people coming in and out that we have something permanently reserved at the Calley.' At my raised eyebrow, she gave a slight twitch of her lips that might even have been a smile. 'Listen to me, talking like a local. The Caledonian Thistle, on Union Terrace. It's only a mile or so from here. It's pretty good and it's central. You should be comfortable there.'

'As long as it's got a bed without bugs and a shower that works, I'm not fussy,' I said, looking around me at the darkening buildings, at the traffic behind us in the door mirror. 'So, this guy Dexter. You said he comes back every year. Has he ever made threats before?'

She frowned in recall. 'No,' she said slowly, 'nothing like that. They just hang around the gates and generally make a damned nuisance of themselves.'

'I see,' I said. 'So, why is he following us now?'

CHAPTER TWENTY-FOUR

'He's what?' Lorna Witney's head ducked between the mirrors, as if she expected Dexter to be looming large there. 'My God,' she murmured. 'I mean, are you sure? Where is he?'

'The white Renault, two cars back,' I said. 'It was parked on the other side of the road when I arrived, so I clocked the number. It's been on our tail since we left your office.'

'How do you know it's him?'

'I can see two people inside, and Dexter and his mate weren't by the gate when we drove out.' I checked again, caught another glimpse of the suspect Renault, and cursed the fact that travelling with carry-on baggage meant I didn't even have my Swiss Army knife on me. 'Besides, it does no harm to plan for the worst.'

She gave a brief laugh, harsh with tension. 'You sound just like Parker.'

'You say that like it's a bad thing,' I muttered. 'Do you use hairspray?'

'Do I what?' she said, baffled now. 'Yes, I do. What the

hell has that got to do with anything? I have a can of it in my bag.'

I reached forwards and grabbed her handbag off the passenger seat. 'Squirt or aerosol?'

'Oh, for heaven's sake – aerosol,' she said crossly. 'Another thing those eco-freaks would hate me for, no doubt.'

'Not me.' I dug through the bag, found what I was after and flipped off the lid. 'I'll need to borrow this, if I may?'

'You go right ahead. What are you planning to do – give them a makeover?'

'Not quite,' I said.

The vehicles ahead bunched up on the approach to a roundabout, leading to a bridge across the river, and we slowed accordingly.

'Don't go home,' I said, one hand on the door handle, watching for a gap in traffic. 'Stay somewhere public. I'll call you later. Parker gave me your numbers.'

When I turned back, she was pale and grim in the dashboard lights. 'I'll wait for you at the Calley,' she said shortly. 'This I have to hear.'

'Fine.' I nodded to my rucksack. 'In that case, I'll leave you my luggage.'

We crawled to a halt, nothing but the red glare of brake lights ahead of us, cars now stationary in both directions. I hopped out of the BMW, the can of hairspray half-hidden in my jacket pocket, and jogged to the pavement, slipping between the people hurrying along its length. It was just starting to spit with rain and most of them had their heads down and their collars up.

I used a man walking at about the same speed for cover as I drew alongside the Renault. A quick glance confirmed the occupants, even though the windows were misting up on the inside. Dexter was behind the wheel, the stocky ginger-haired guy in the front passenger seat.

I took a deep, nerve-steadying breath, stepped down into the road, and flipped open the rear door.

The two men twisted, slack-jawed, as I dived in, scooting across into the centre. They did not look happy. Dexter's foot came off the clutch. The Renault lurched forwards and stalled. Good job he hadn't pulled up too close to the car in front.

'Hi, guys,' I said cheerfully. 'Don't give up the day job, will you? Because you're crap at tailing people.'

Ginger, his recent defeat no doubt preying heavy on his mind, immediately tried to strike back at me with his clenched fist, hampered by the awkward angle and his buckled seat belt.

I blocked his wildly swinging arm, jamming it hard against the side of the headrest, and squirted him full in the face with the hairspray, a prolonged burst, just like it tells you not to in the small print on the side of the can.

He squealed, thrashing against my restraining arm. The air bloomed ripe with the hairspray's soggy cloying scent. I let go of his arm, swapped the can into my other hand, and pressed it against Dexter's cheekbone, the nozzle half an inch from his left eye.

'Do something that makes me nervous, and I will blind you,' I said calmly, loud enough to be heard over the howling. That made Dexter comply as much as the threat. We sat there for a moment, the only sound the intermittent slap of the wipers across the front screen, and Ginger's retching cries.

'For God's sake, Tony, don't rub at it,' Dexter snapped through stiff lips. 'You'll make it ten times worse.'

'There speaks a man who's been gassed by riot police,' I said. 'You'll know to wash it out with cold water, then?' I'd been through all the CS gas drills in the army. The first thing you learn is that warm water opens up your pores and sends the irritant deeper, prolonging the sear.

But Ginger – Tony – ignored his friend's advice, pawing at his eyes like they were on fire. To be fair, that's probably just how it felt.

The car in front of us moved off and the driver behind gave an impatient toot of his horn. I nudged Dexter's cheek with the can.

'Move.'

'Where to?' he asked, reaching slowly and carefully for the ignition key.

'That's rather up to you,' I said. 'If you were following me, I was on my way to the Caledonian Thistle Hotel. And if it was Lorna Witney, that's where she's waiting for me.'

The wipers stuttered as he recranked the engine, put the car into gear and closed the gap that had opened up, all of four or five metres.

'What do you want?' he asked then, speaking carefully, as though afraid to move his facial muscles.

'I was going to ask you much the same question,' I said. 'And from where I'm sitting, I think I can insist you go first.'

'Don't tell that bitch nothin'!' Tony yelped in a muffled London accent. 'Christ, mate, my *eyes*! She burnt my eyes.'

'Shut up, Tony,' Dexter said. Then, to me, 'If you want

to talk, OK, let's talk, but take that damn spray can out of my face or you're gonna get zip.'

I considered, then withdrew my hand, keeping my finger on the nozzle, just in case.

Dexter let his breath out, risked a backward glance. 'Should have known you'd spot us,' he muttered. 'Way you handled Tony, you gotta be some kinda field agent, something like that, right?'

'Something like that,' I agreed.

The traffic hutched forwards again. Ahead of us, Lorna Witney's BMW made it onto the roundabout and swung out of sight. One less thing to worry about.

Dexter said, 'So, this is where you give us the spiel, huh? Stop making waves, and leave Lorna Witney alone, or you blind the pair of us for real, huh?'

Tony gave a strangled squawk. 'What d'you mean, *for real*?' He was hunched forwards now, rocking, his head nearly on the dashboard and his face in his hands. 'Bitch.'

'Do you honestly think,' I said, conversational, 'if someone wanted to scare you off, that I'm the kind of person they'd send?'

Dexter frowned and I saw his eyes flick to mine in the rear-view mirror. 'No,' he said then. 'I would guess you're more the kind of person they'd send if they wanted the pair of us found in a burned-out wreck at the bottom of a cliff.'

'I'm flattered,' I said dryly, 'although I should point out that, if I were any good, you'd never be found at all.' I waited a moment. 'So, to take up where you left off earlier, what exactly should Mrs Witney have *left well alone*, and – since she's already lost her son, her mobility and her husband – what else *does* she have to lose?'

'You're so clever,' he tossed back, 'figure it out for yourself.'

I moved the can closer to his face again, noting the flinch he couldn't quite control. 'And if I were to ask very nicely?'

His breath escaped on a hiss. 'Don't play dumb, kiddo,' he spat. 'I know the kind of people you work for. You're all the same. You just care about the bottom line and you don't give a damn about the consequences.'

'What consequences?' I asked, but his initial shock was fading, his bravado beginning to return. I knew I didn't have much time, otherwise I wouldn't have risked asking, 'For Maria? And what about her child? Is that why Thomas Witney stayed inside Fourth Day – because he found out the child was Liam's?'

For a moment Dexter's head reared back. 'Is that what the Ice Maiden told you?' He let out a derisive snort. His driving had lost its jerky edge, smoothing out as we reached the roundabout ourselves. 'My God, she's a manipulative bitch, that one.'

'What would Mrs Witney gain by it, if it's not true?'

'A smokescreen. To keep you from looking at what really happened in Alaska.'

'Which is?'

Tony lifted his head, his mucus membranes still streaming where the lacquer and the propellant had inflamed them. I didn't envy him washing that beard. 'Dex—'

But Dexter shrugged aside the warning growl. 'We mounted a well-planned operation, but they knew we were coming. Someone betrayed us.'

'Liam?' I queried.

Dexter twitched the Renault through the roundabout on the far side of the bridge and gunned onto a street that ran parallel to the railway line. I had no idea where the hotel was, and had to trust that we were heading in the right direction.

He shook his head. 'All Liam did was warn his mother not to be there. That was all she had to do – stay away. Instead, she set him up.'

'And to make sure she wasn't embarrassed afterwards,' Tony put in, 'she made damn sure those private-security bastards picked Liam out and planted that gun in his hand.'

'Right,' I said slowly, not trying to keep the cynical note out of my voice. 'You were there, were you? Saw it happen?'

Tony's eyes flicked to Dexter, who took his eyes off the road long enough to glare at him. I was glad the traffic seemed to have thinned slightly. Less to hit.

'No,' Dexter said quietly, and there was something in his tone I couldn't pin down. 'But I was.'

'Surely, if she had that kind of pull, she could have arranged a convenient accident for Liam?'

'Like she tried with Thomas, you mean?' Tony demanded. 'She had him run off the road in California – didn't work. And Randall organised his own security people to make sure it didn't happen again. So she called in you lot.'

I shook my head. 'Mrs Witney had nothing to do with Thomas's extraction.'

He flashed me a pitying look. 'No? He was safe inside Randall Bane's place, but *somebody* springs him, and within twenty-four hours he's dead. Go figure.'

'How the hell do you know about that?' I demanded, shaken.

'I know plenty,' he said, dignified enough that I moved the can further back, saw his shoulders drop a fraction.

'Perhaps Thomas knew things about Fourth Day that Bane didn't want made public,' I suggested.

'Randall?' He snorted. 'Now *you're* the one who's way off base! You want answers, kiddo, look closer to home.'

I knew he meant Lorna Witney, but Parker had covered up the link to Epps, had not told us about his own far more personal connection to the grieving widow. And she seemed strangely detached...

Suddenly, Dexter swerved over to the side of the road without indicating and pulled up, yanking on the Renault's handbrake so the mechanism ratcheted noisily. I glanced at the building alongside and read THISTLE and THE CALEDONIAN in large letters above the covered portico.

'Ride's over, kiddo,' he said, nodding to the entrance. 'You want to know more, you're going to have to find it out for yourself.'

I glanced at the stubborn set of his jaw, debated briefly on forcing the issue further. But even Tony, I reasoned, would not be so easily caught a second time, and I wasn't prepared to go further than I had done already.

Quit while you're ahead, Fox.

I climbed out of the car, but hadn't taken more than a couple of steps across the pavement when Dexter's voice called me back.

'Hey, kiddo,' he said. I turned to find Tony had lowered

his window and the American was leaning across from the driver's seat.

'Just one thing you might wanna give some thought to. When Thomas went into Fourth Day, he was convinced Randall Bane had somehow caused Liam's death. So, why else would he stay – unless he couldn't face the truth of who really *was* behind it?'

CHAPTER TWENTY-FIVE

'Well, Parker always did like redheads,' Sean said. 'I'm often relieved that your hair's more blond than red, although—'

'Sean, this is serious. We don't know what the hell is going on, or what we're really involved in.'

I was in my hotel room, lying on my bed in the semidarkness, talking with Sean on my cellphone. The phone was a recent upgrade, one that came with a radio function, which I never used, and twin earpieces, which I did. They were great for blocking out unwanted sound in a noisy location, and using them now seemed to bring his voice directly into the centre of my head. The line was good, with no echoes or delays. It felt close and intimate, almost like he was alongside me rather than three thousand miles away.

'OK,' he said, sobering. 'But I don't see what all this has to do with Witney, or with what Bane might be up to. Don't let yourself get sidetracked by rumours. I'd be more inclined to take this intel seriously if it came from a slightly more reliable source.'

'They had no reason to lie to me.'

'Charlie, they had *every* reason to lie to you. Create anarchy and chaos. Standard operating procedure for that kind of organisation. And it's worked, hasn't it? Here you are, doubting everybody's motives – including your own. I very much doubt Parker will agree to this one, so forget it. The job's over.'

But I remembered Lorna Witney's conviction of his compliance and didn't share Sean's confidence. 'Not if she has anything to do with it, it isn't,' I said. 'And there's no way I'm being a part of grabbing that kid out of Fourth Day until we know for certain we have a legitimate reason.'

I heard Sean sigh. He was at home in the apartment. In the background I could hear the classical music he only liked to listen to when he was alone. A requiem piece of such soaring sadness it made my throat constrict.

'OK. If Parker gives this the green light – and that's a big *if* – you can be sure we'll check out Maria's background pretty bloody carefully before we do anything.'

'If she and Liam were together in college, just before he dropped out, that kid of hers *is* just about the right age.'

'You think Witney discovered he had a grandchild and decided to give up everything just to stay close?' Sean asked, and I winced at the sheer disbelief in his voice.

'He'd just lost a son,' I said quietly. 'Maybe the prospect of being with his grandson was too tempting to pass up.'

Sean sighed again. 'OK, leave it with me,' he said. 'You haven't told me how Lorna Witney reacted to these accusations when you got to the hotel, by the way.'

'How do you expect?' I said, grim.

'Did she offer any kind of explanation?'

'Not really, although she *did* admit she was involved with

the exploration project Debacle were protesting against in Alaska.'

'All right,' Sean said, giving in. 'I'll ask Parker to see what he can dig out.'

'Whatever it is, Parker should have already dug it out,' I said sharply. 'What makes me most uneasy is why didn't he? What's he trying to hide? Who's he trying to protect?'

As I spoke, the conversation I'd had with Lorna Witney in the hotel bar came to mind. She'd been angry and insulted when I repeated what Dexter and Tony had just told me, and I couldn't be entirely sure if the cause of her fury was because she'd been wrongly accused, or because – after more than five years – she thought she'd got away with it.

'You think I'm a cold-hearted bitch, don't you?' she'd thrown at me. 'My God, you must, if you think *anything* would be worth the deliberate murder of my only child. What would I gain from it that could possibly be worth so high a price?'

Her voice had risen and she suddenly became aware of heads turning, the barman glancing over uneasily. She leant closer. 'Shall I tell you what I gained?' she demanded, low and bitter. 'Heartache and pain, that's what. The kind of pain I carry with me every single day, because there's not an *hour* goes by when I don't think of Liam, and it's like being told of his death for the first time all over again.'

'Everybody responds to tragedy in their own way,' Sean said now, when I reported her words. He paused, as if picking his way with care. 'Look at what happened to you in the army, Charlie. It would have been enough to finish most people, but you didn't let it finish you.'

'It changed me, though.'

'Every action, every chance meeting and hesitation – even every breath we take – changes us.'

'For the better?'

'It brought you here,' he said gently. 'Everything you've ever done has combined to bring you to this point. Only you can say if "here" is the place you want to be.'

He waited, but for some reason the confirmation wouldn't come and I found myself listening to my own silence, reflected back at me down the line.

Eventually he sighed. 'Look, you've got an early flight tomorrow. Get some rest, Charlie,' he said. 'You'll think more clearly in the morning.'

'Everything you've ever done has combined to bring you to this point.'

Hours later, the words still echoed in my mind as I lay, restless, staring at the darkened ceiling.

I thought about the combination of circumstances that had crossed Sean's path with mine in the first place. By all rights, we should never have met.

He was a working-class lad from a run-down council estate in the north of England. If he'd followed the example of his father, he'd have married early, bullied his kids, and died young. Most likely with a can of triple-strength lager in one hand and a steering wheel in the other.

Sean's only career prospects had been a dead-end factory job, or on the wrong side of the law. In his teens he had flirted with right-wing yob culture before he'd somehow pulled himself out of that self-destructive nosedive. His chance of escape had come via the army. Joining up had given him discipline, purpose, and broadened his views in every sense.

The only organisations I'd been a member of in my teens were the Girl Guides and the Pony Club. Compared to Sean, I'd grown up in rarefied and privileged surroundings. My own path into the military had been by chance, not so much to rebel against my parents, but trying to provoke a reaction from them.

If I'd followed my own father's footsteps, I would have gone into medicine and probably spent my entire life trying to measure up to his impossible standards. I remembered again taking down the three men from the van. Perhaps that arrogant disregard for consequences showed I had inherited enough of his ruthlessness to have become a top-flight surgeon. After all, you had to act with absolute conviction that the operation you were performing was right, even if the patient died.

I'd never really discovered what my mother's plans had been for me, only that I'd been a quiet and constant disappointment to her. Perhaps my biggest failing had been never to quite work out what she had expected.

I wondered, just for a moment, if presenting them with a grandchild would have provided any compensation.

Well, that was one thing I was not going to find out.

CHAPTER TWENTY-SIX

I arrived back in the States at Newark International Airport just after two-thirty the following day, flying from Aberdeen via Manchester. Without a coffin in tow, the return journey was a lot more straightforward than the outward leg.

As soon as we were on the ground in New Jersey, I switched my cellphone back on and received voicemail while we were still taxiing to the gate. The woman next to me rolled her eyes exaggeratedly.

'Life and death, is it?' she asked.

I didn't look up from the screen. 'Yes,' I said, 'it usually is, actually.'

The message was from Sean. 'Call me as soon as you get this,' he said, voice grim. 'There've been developments.'

Not having hold baggage meant as soon as I'd cleared Customs and Immigration I could head straight for the New Jersey Transit rail system, which was the fastest and most convenient way from the airport to the centre of Manhattan. As I rode the escalator, I was dialling Sean's number.

'Where are you?' he asked without greeting.

I paused only fractionally. 'On my way to get the train in.'

'Don't bother,' he said. 'I'll meet you outside Arrivals in five minutes.'

'Sean, what's going—?'

'I'll brief you on the way in,' he said, and cut the connection.

I stared briefly at the dead phone. 'And I'm fine,' I muttered. 'Thank you for asking...'

I walked out of the air-conditioned airport building into a gutsy wind that whipped through the traffic and curled itself brutally around my legs. That wasn't the only reason I was glad to see one of the company Lincoln Navigators swing in to the kerb a few minutes later.

I jumped into the front seat and Sean clutched at my cold fingers for a moment before he was muscling his way back out into the traffic flow.

'Turn up the heat,' he said. 'You're freezing.'

Instead, I jabbed the button for the heated seats and stuffed my hands under my thighs against the leather upholstery.

'So, are you going to tell me what's with the VIP treatment?' I asked cautiously.

Sean flicked a glance at me and smiled, said in a soft voice, 'Am I not allowed to come and pick you up, for no other reason than I missed you?'

I gazed at him blankly for a moment, pleased out of all proportion. 'Of course you are,' I said faintly.

'And, next time I question your female intuition, or casting of bloody runes, or whatever else goes on inside that head of yours, Charlie,' he said, 'tell me to just shut up and get on with it, will you?'

'Thank you...I think,' I said dryly. 'Why? What's happened?'

'Parker's agreed to take on Lorna Witney as a client for the possible extraction of the kid from Fourth Day.'

I took in that one in silence for a moment, idly watching a Continental jet lumbering heavy out of the airport. 'You sound surprised,' I said then. 'But you didn't see her, Sean. The look in her eyes. Whatever she and Parker had going might have been brief, but it must have been memorable.'

'Well, after we spoke last night I went to see Parker and we...straightened out a few things. Yes, he admits he had a brief fling with her. I told him he was a bloody idiot, but it was not long after his wife died, apparently. Caught him at a bad time.'

'Parker was *married*?' I said, wondering why that fact should surprise me so much. Parker had no personal photographs on his desk, and although we'd been to his home on numerous occasions, I hadn't picked up the faintest echo of a woman there, and he'd never mentioned a wife. He didn't want for female company, that was for sure. I'd just assumed – wrongly, it now appeared – that his work kept him at a certain distance.

'Yeah, it was news to me, too,' Sean said. 'Anyway, he claims it's never happened before or since. I believe him.'

'O...K,' I said slowly. 'Did you ask him if he investigated the circumstances surrounding Liam's death five years ago, when he agreed to be Witney's safety net?'

He nodded. 'Liam joined this group you encountered straight out of Fourth Day, just months before his death. The Witneys had never heard of Debacle, despite the industry Lorna was involved in. They formed in the early Eighties, but didn't appear on anyone's radar until they suddenly got an influx of cash and new members after the Exxon Valdez oil spill in 'eighty-nine.'

'Well, Debacle's not exactly a promising kind of name, is it?' I said. 'Doesn't it mean a failure or disaster?'

'It also means a complete collapse; the breaking up of ice on a river; a violent disruption as of an army; or a sudden flood which leaves its path strewn with debris.' His eyes flicked across again. 'They have a website. A lot of rhetoric, but some interesting stuff on there, if you like your environmental issues on the inflammatory side.'

'That interpretation of the name suggests their aim was disorder as much as environmental protection,' I said. 'Where did the money come from?'

'Parker's still digging on that one. He did manage to find out some more about this Dexter guy you mentioned, though.'

He waved towards the glovebox. Inside, I found a thin manila folder containing a couple of colour prints. Dexter's good-looking face stared defiantly into the camera, formal mug shots with the height lines behind him. His full name was Marlon Dexter – hardly surprising he dropped the first part. Underneath the photos were copies of Dexter's arrest record. It ran to several pages. Basic public order offences, turning to trespass, property damage and vandalism, escalating over a relatively short time period into full-blown assault and arson.

'If you check out the one listed for Galveston,' Sean said, braking for an intersection, 'you'll find that at the time Liam Witney was killed in Alaska, Dexter was getting himself arrested outside a chemical plant in Texas. There's no way he witnessed what happened.'

'If Dexter wasn't there,' I said, suddenly back in the white Renault in Aberdeen, 'then he's a bloody good actor.' I shook my head slowly. 'There was something so intense about the way he spoke. It just didn't sound like he was making it all up.'

Sean shrugged as we moved off again, accelerating into the outside lane out of habit, making progress. 'Well, we've double-checked the dates. Sorry, he was spinning you a line.'

I was silent for a moment, listening to the roar of badly mended asphalt under the Navigator's tyres, then asked, 'What was Debacle doing in Alaska, anyway?'

'According to Parker, there's been controversy for years about oil exploration in the ANWR – the Arctic National Wildlife Refuge,' he added, sensing my automatic next question. 'When the company Lorna Witney was subcontracted to at the time were granted rights to do some exploratory drilling, it caused an uproar. Not just the potential for pollution, but something about caribou breeding grounds, from what I could make out. It's a real political hot potato.'

'There's a surprise.'

'Well, there were a lot of threats of action against equipment and personnel, and the exploration company called in a number of outside contractors to handle their security.'

'Anyone we know?'

Sean reeled off a list of names, some of which were familiar and some not. 'The guys who shot Liam Witney worked for an outfit who had a reputation for putting the boot in first and asking questions later. They now do a lot of private work in Iraq, incidentally.'

'Now, why doesn't that fill me with confidence?'
I murmured, reminded of Dexter's comment about
consequences. Had we ignored the repercussions, too?

Sean smiled slightly. 'Parker managed to sneak a look at
the official report on the shooting. I didn't ask how. It was
judged to be justified at the time, by the way.'

'And did he feel there was anything dodgy about it?'

'It was brief, put it that way, but he said it seemed pretty
clear-cut. They caught a bunch of intruders planting what
were later found to be improvised explosive devices on
certain key pieces of equipment. They were challenged, at
which point the intruders started shooting. Security returned
fire with some enthusiasm. When the dust settled, Witney was
dead with the proverbial smoking gun still in his hand.'

'All neat and tidy,' I agreed. 'No independent witnesses,
I assume?'

'Liam wasn't alone, but nobody else has ever come
forwards – not that you can blame them. Debacle issued a
statement – more of a rant, I suppose you'd call it – giving
much the same version of events Dexter told you, so maybe
that's why it sounded so slick.'

I closed the folder, slid it back into the glovebox. 'So,
it's a dead end.'

Sean's head ducked. 'Not necessarily. It would seem that
your pal Dexter had more in common with Liam than he
was prepared to tell. Before joining Debacle, Marlon Dexter
was also a member of Fourth Day.'

'So, *that's* how he knew so much about Witney,' I
murmured. 'But it's not in his file.'

'It's only just come to light,' Sean said. 'Parker widened

out the search. Ex-members of Fourth Day have turned up in all kinds of radical and extremist groups. Not just environmental, but animal liberation, human rights, pro life.'

'If that's the case, then surely Epps has every reason to turn Fourth Day upside down.' I frowned. 'What's stopping him?'

'Ah well, Comrade Epps moves in mysterious ways,' Sean said dryly.

He took the Lincoln Tunnel under the Hudson, and we were silent for the next mile or so, then I said suddenly, 'If Bane was recruiting people for organisations like that, then surely Thomas Witney wouldn't have stayed inside Fourth Day unless he had a bloody good reason.'

'Maybe his ex-wife is right, and he had some kind of spiritual epiphany.'

'Or maybe I'm right about Liam's relationship with Maria, and Witney stayed for the child.' I checked his face, found he was frowning. 'You find anything out about her?'

He gave a half shrug. 'Not much. Her name's Maria Gonzalez. The kid was born seven months after Liam's death, so the dates would line up. There's no father's name listed on the birth certificate, but his name is Billy.'

Billy and Liam, both diminutives of William. 'It's not enough to warrant kidnapping him on the off chance.'

'I agree,' Sean said. 'There's no father's name listed on Maria's birth certificate, either, so maybe it's a kind of family tradition. Maybe the only way's a DNA comparison between the kid and Lorna Witney, after we've got him out.'

A flash of Maria's ragged flight and capture sprang unbidden to mind. 'From what we saw of the girl, she's not exactly stable. How's she going to react if we grab the kid and make a mistake?' I murmured, remembering, too, her total subjugation in the face of the cult's leader. 'We'd have to be sure.'

'Yeah, but that's not the kind of thing you can find out in a covert night-time raid.'

I shrugged. 'So I'll go in and talk to her.'

'What makes you think she'll talk to you, after what we did to Witney?' Sean glanced across at me, his expression hooded. 'And what makes you think Bane will let someone like you within a mile of her?'

'Who says he's going to know who I am?'

'No,' Sean said, jaw hardening. 'No way Parker will risk something like that, whatever his feelings for Lorna Witney.'

'He might not,' I said. 'But Epps would.'

CHAPTER TWENTY-SEVEN

'I don't like it,' Epps said, not taking his eyes off me while he spoke. For a moment it was hard to tell if he was expressing his dislike for the proposal we'd put forward, or me in particular. Probably both.

'We're not asking you to,' Sean said, and though there was apparently nothing more than idle amusement in his voice, his own eyes were very cold.

If Epps registered this composed hostility, he didn't show it. Instead, he said calmly, 'If you expect my cooperation and approval for this exercise, Mr Meyer – not to mention access of any kind to my resources – then I do believe it's a requirement.'

My turn to butt in. 'What makes you think we're asking for anything?'

Epps continued to stare at me for a long time. I smiled back blandly and thought I caught the faintest tic in his face, just before he finally gave in. He swept a slightly pitying gaze over Parker, and there was something patronising about it, as though he took being contradicted as a sign Parker lacked control over his men – and I'm damned sure that's how he thought of us collectively. None of Epps's own people – all male – would have dared speak unless directly questioned.

It was three days after my return from Scotland. We were in Parker's office, with Conrad Epps in one of the comfortable client chairs in front of the desk, and Parker, Sean and I ranged against him. Epps was outnumbered and off his home ground, and still managed to look like he was running the show, elbows propped on the armrests with fingers linked, legs crossed. There was no telltale tension in his arms or hands, and his loose foot dangled, relaxed.

It was interesting that he'd ordered his usual protection detail to stay out in the reception area. If they were offended by this exclusion, they took it stoically, and were currently involved in a monumental stare-out competition with Bill Rendelson across the polished floor. I'd been almost unbearably tempted to whistle some Morricone spaghetti western theme while crossing between them.

'I would have thought,' Parker said now, matching his tone to Sean's, 'that after the failure of your last operation against Fourth Day, you'd have been glad of this new opportunity to gather valuable intel without any further risk to your own personnel.'

There was nothing in Parker's voice to give away the fact that both he and Sean had tried hard to dissuade me from going back into the cult. Not under cover of night, with a highly trained backup team surrounding me and a SIG on my hip, like last time. But alone, unarmed, in broad daylight.

Perversely, the more they'd argued against it, the more determined I'd become. Parker's frustration, even bordering on dismay, had been more than evident at the time. Now it was imperceptible.

'You make an interesting case, Mr Armstrong,' Epps said. 'But you have nothing concrete to support it.'

'We've traced major donations from shell companies based in the Caymans to both Debacle and Fourth Day, and it seems Witney is not the first former member of the cult to die in violent circumstances,' Parker said. 'Four in the last year – home invasions and hit-and-run accidents – all unsolved. How much more do you want?'

'And what does this have to do with your client?' Epps asked.

'It makes her even more anxious to remove her grandson from their influence and from possible danger,' Parker said. He waited a beat. 'You of all people should appreciate what it is to lose a child.'

'Your daughter, wasn't it?' Sean supplied.

For the first time, Epps looked smaller, almost human, his shoulders a little less square and his back less ramrod straight. His silver hair no longer seemed a distinguished badge of rank, was simply a sign of age.

'Do not go there, gentlemen,' he growled, moustache bristling. 'You've made your point. I still do not see what this has to do with your client. If she wants the child out, surely it's a simple job to extract him?'

'Not until we're sure of his identity,' Parker said. 'And in order to do that, Charlie is volunteering to go in there and see what she can find out. You admitted that your investigation is stalled. We're offering you a chance to move it forward, without things turning into another Waco.'

Epps responded to Parker's sly digs with less subtlety.

'It has been my experience that women do not make reliable undercover operatives,' he said flatly. 'They do not have the mental resilience, and they become emotionally involved.'

'I have no intention of sleeping with Bane,' I said mildly. 'Or staying awake with him, either, for that matter.'

Epps's stony expression never varied at my flippancy, but his loose foot bounced betrayingly, just once, and his voice was dangerously soft. 'And how do you know that isn't one of his stipulations for entry?'

'If it was, I'm sure Chris Sagar would have included that fact in his dossier,' I said, nodding to the document itself, which lay open on the table between us. 'If there's one thing Bane *has* done since he took over Fourth Day, it's clean up the cult's previous unsavoury reputation.'

But I closed my mind to the memory of Bane himself stepping out to meet Maria as she was brought back to him, weeping and on her knees. That strangely gentle caress.

'Just as well,' Epps said, quiet and deliberate, 'because I very much doubt you would cope well with that kind of treatment, would you, Charlie?'

I froze, as much at his silky use of familiarity as the threat itself, felt rather than saw Sean's sudden stillness alongside me.

'Nobody copes *well* with violation, Mr Epps,' I said, managing to keep my voice cool and colourless. 'You just cope. Male or female has no bearing.' I paused. 'Trust me – you would fare no better than most.' *And probably a lot worse than many.*

Epps continued to meet my gaze, but something recoiled behind his eyes. He looked away and I didn't need to watch that twitchy foot flap again to know the barb had hit home.

'I'm afraid, gentlemen, that I still don't like it.'

Gentlemen. Neither Sean nor Parker seemed to notice this casual sexism. It was endemic in the field. And seeing the three of them together now, their similarities sent a sudden, unaccountable chill across my bones. Like they were all members of the same exclusive club, and I was the outsider here.

Sean smiled at him. 'This isn't a request,' he said. 'It's just a heads-up out of courtesy.'

Epps absorbed that in brief silence. 'So far, we have been unable to link the three men apprehended in California either to the deaths of my agents, or to the kidnap and murder of Thomas Witney,' he said at last. Then, with reluctance, 'However, one of my dead agents had gambling debts he'd suddenly promised to repay. It looks like whoever hired him decided to save themselves the money. That case is still open and I would very much like to close it.'

Parker inclined his head, acknowledging the concession for what it was. 'Anything Charlie learns that's of relevance,' he said gravely, 'we will, of course, pass on.' He rose, the dismissal obvious.

'Oh, we'll be keeping a close eye on things, Mr Armstrong, make no mistake about that.' Epps stood, treated us all to a slow survey while he buttoned his coat. 'Her cover story will need to be good. They *will* pressure-test it,' he said finally, eyes on Parker again. 'If you want to place an agent into Bane's wilderness programme, I would strongly advise that you make use of Mr Sagar's expertise to construct something...suitable.'

'We intend to,' Sean said sharply. 'But if Bane's looking for the kind of people we suspect, he'll pick out Charlie. Some qualities you just can't hide.'

He sounded confident, but it was ironic that, the moment I'd suggested going back, he and Parker had voiced much the same doubts as Epps. The fact that their minds ran along similar grooves did not please him, I could tell.

Epps nodded briefly to Parker but made no immediate moves for the door.

'What happens if she cracks?' he asked. 'What happens if she goes over as easily as Witney did, five years ago?'

That last bit surprised me. So, for all his snide comments, Epps still thought I might be of some value to the enemy.

'I'm not planning on being in there for more than a few days,' I said. 'And if I buckle that quickly, I won't be much use to him, will I?'

'I meant as a bargaining chip,' Epps said. His eyes skimmed across me again, merciless and chilling. 'She doesn't have to remain functional for that.'

'If we become concerned in any way for Charlie's mental or physical well-being,' Sean said, 'we'll get her out – whatever it takes.'

Parker slid behind his desk, smoothing down his tie. 'Thank you for your input. We'll take it under advisement,' he said. 'Sean, would you see Mr Epps and his people out of the building.'

Sean briefly showed his teeth. 'It would be my pleasure.'

Epps thought about making a stand, for no other reason than because he could. I saw the urge to pull rank cross his features and narrowly lose out to some darker consideration

I couldn't quite catch the meaning of. I was impressed by his willpower, if nothing else.

Maybe he just thought that anything we might conceivably provide was better than nothing and left it at that.

Sean was already holding the door open, careful to keep any hint of provocation out of his demeanour. So, his willpower was on a level with Epps's.

As I made to follow them out, Parker said, 'Charlie – a moment?' and I turned back, but not before I'd caught Sean's eye. There was no more expression on his face now than when he'd looked at Epps. It almost made me shiver.

'Close the door,' Parker said quietly.

I complied, walked sedately to stand in front of his desk and clasped my hands loosely behind me like I was back in the army.

Parker leant back in his chair and stared up at me. 'Don't do this,' he said calmly. 'You don't have to do this, Charlie. Nobody expects or even wants this of you. Not me and certainly not Sean.'

'I want it,' I said. 'I promised Witney he would be safe with us, then helped deliver him to his death, and I don't like the feeling I lied to him. If Bane had a hand in that, or he knows something – or was involved in what happened to Liam – I want to find out. I *need* to put this to rest.'

He made a small gesture of impatience. 'We still suspect that Bane may have arranged the kidnap, torture and execution of Thomas Witney. You're asking me to put you naked into the arena with a tiger.'

'From what Sagar's told us, he's not a stupid man. Even if he suspects who I am, he'll know that if anything happens to me after I go in, that's just the excuse Epps needs to tear the place apart.'

'Epps would have to wait his turn,' Parker said with a grim smile.

'Right now, we don't know who killed Witney, or why,' I said. 'If it *was* Bane, to stop him talking about what's going on inside Fourth Day, we need to know. And if it was because Witney found out his wife was somehow connected to the death of his son, then...' I shrugged, '...we need to know that, too.'

'But—'

'And most of all,' I cut in, 'if that's Liam's child – Lorna Witney's grandchild – in there, I couldn't live with myself if I left him to his fate.'

'Is that what this is all about, Charlie?' Parker snapped, a mix of anguish and temper in his eyes. 'You lost a child and now you're trying to save them all?'

'I...' I paused, swallowed, said in a low voice, 'Honestly? I don't know.'

Parker was silent, then he sighed and got to his feet. At the window, his back to me, he said, 'We haven't lost an operative for more than a year. I don't want to spoil that run. Especially not with you.'

'We put our lives on the line every day, Parker. I accept that as a normal part of the job. You should consider me no different from anyone else who works for you.'

'Our job is to expect trouble, and to prevent or deflect it. We don't go seek it out.' Parker turned abruptly, gaze skating over me. 'Besides, you *are* different, you know that. And this job is hardly normal, Charlie – you know that, too.'

He moved round the desk, smooth and fast, and put his hands on my shoulders. Just for a moment I felt his fingers tighten and wondered if he was about to try and shake some sense into me, the frustration plain on his face. 'Any decisions you face at the moment are not yours alone to make, and I don't want to have to be the one who breaks it to Sean, if anything should happen to you,' he said tightly. 'You still haven't told him, have you?'

'I—'

The door opened and Sean took a stride into the office, then froze momentarily when he saw us. Such a brief hesitation, gone before it fully formed.

He glanced at Parker, said, 'Still trying to talk her out of it?'

'Yeah,' Parker said, wry. He let his hands drop and regarded me almost glumly. 'I don't suppose there's any chance I've succeeded, is there?'

I let my gaze take in both of them. 'No,' I said. 'None at all.'

CHAPTER TWENTY-EIGHT

I walked in to Fourth Day's land with the sunrise, dressed in cargo trousers and a lightweight cotton shirt, neither chosen with camouflage in mind. My booted feet scuffed at the dirt, not attempting to hide my trail. I had a bush hat with a floppy brim to keep the sun off and a sports-type water bottle in a neoprene holder slung on a strap over my shoulder.

On my back was a canvas rucksack containing two switched-off cellphones, a deactivated radio distress beacon, a map, two chocolate bars, a bundle of cash, a knife, a first-aid kit which included shots of morphine and adrenaline, my SIG, and a box of 9 mm Hydra-Shoks. The gun, wrapped in an oiled cloth, had a single round in the chamber, but the magazine was out and empty. Everything was packed into two plastic Tupperware boxes to keep out the elements. It was like going on the most bizarre picnic ever.

Apart from that I carried no bag, no wallet, no ID, and no weapon other than what lurked inside my own head.

Sean dropped me by the side of the road that bordered

the cult land, almost the same point of entry we'd used for our surveillance of Thomas Witney. He gave me a brief 'good luck', but we'd said our farewells before leaving Van Nuys in the dark, and had been largely silent on the drive.

There was nothing left to say.

For the last mile, the only sign of habitation had been a wind-blown roadside bar, hunkered down by the side of the road, its neon faded and blinking in the pre-dawn glow.

By the time I'd climbed carefully through the barbed-wire fence, Sean was already accelerating away. I didn't look back and, I suspect, neither did he.

I struck out roughly east, using the hour hand of my watch to work out a rough north-south bearing from the sun, and ready-reckoning from there. The watch was a cheap analogue I'd bought purely for this purpose, with a simple face and a rubber strap. It would be a classic disorientation technique for them to take it away from me, and I didn't want to lose the Tag that Sean had given me.

The sun lifted solemnly from the horizon, stately in its progress, a pinkish globe that slowly lost definition as it began to burn more fiercely. The misty light hardened, the shadows of the dumpy trees shrinking back towards their trunks as if compressed by the heat. Overhead, some large bird of prey drifted lazily, feathering at the high thermals with wing tips splayed.

It was a long walk, which gave me plenty of time to think about the briefings I'd had from Chris Sagar over the past few days, sitting in a cramped office in the government hangar where we'd set up a temporary base of operations. This time, we had taken no chances with security.

'Fourth Day use a form of attack therapy,' he told me.

'Think of it as a hostile encounter group. The object is to jar you out of your personal belief system.'

'How physical are they likely to get?' I asked, but he shook his head.

'Unless things have changed a whole hell of a lot since my time, they're not,' he said, and I didn't hide my relief. 'But there'll be a strong element of psychological abuse.'

'Sounds like fun. What does that mean in English?'

He sighed, absently pushing those little round glasses back up his nose. 'I look at you and I see someone who's strong, self-confident. You have a pretty good idea of who you are and where you're going in life, and you believe in your own moral code, am I right?'

'Of course,' I said, only mildly surprised at the even note I managed to inject into my voice. *You have no idea...*

'You must, Charlie. I saw you in action. You never hesitated, I mean, not for a second! You can't act that way and not believe absolutely in what you're doing.' He looked down at his hands. 'Well, Bane will do everything he can to strip that certainty away from you. Make no mistake, it's gonna be brutal.'

'How does he justify such a technique in order to get people to submit to what is, basically, brainwashing?'

'I was a computer geek in college,' Sagar said, and it wasn't hard to believe it, looking at his ageing rock band T-shirt and baggy cargoes. 'The way Bane described it, someone who seeks sanctuary in Fourth Day is like a computer riddled with a virus. They're useless. They can't function. But you can't go after the virus a bit at a time, which is kinda his view on conventional therapy. He believes you have to wipe the hard drive completely and rebuild the system with clean programs. Start again from the ground up.'

I reached for my cup of coffee from the corner of the desk. It was dark and bitter. 'Is that what happened to Thomas Witney?'

'He wasn't just riddled with that virus,' Sagar said. 'He'd crashed. Bane didn't need to break him down, because Witney was already at rock bottom. He'd suffered enough.'

'And suffering is what it's all about?'

'Bane believes that if people haven't suffered enough, they can't or won't change. Not on the kinda fundamental level he's aiming for.' He shook his head. 'You might think you can fight him, Charlie, but you can't. Not for ever. He'll get to you in the end.'

'Like I said, sounds like fun...'

Now, the sun continued to arc into a cloudless sky above me. I checked my heading and walked on.

The temperature would have been pleasant if I'd been sitting on a lounger by a swimming pool, with a tall ice-filled glass by my elbow. Sadly, all I had was tepid water and slightly greasy chocolate that was beginning to melt. I drank sparingly, just a few mouthfuls, and ate half a chocolate bar, licking the excess off the wrapper. I'd stocked up on Cadbury's before I left Aberdeen. Hershey bars just didn't do it for me.

Amid sparse vegetation and rounded rock formations, I was completely out of sight of the road now. There were no man-made structures or signs of habitation. I moved more careful of where I put my feet, but saw no animal or reptile life either. Even the bird of prey seemed to have abandoned me. The silence took on a shape all of its own, surrounding and engulfing me. I was achingly aware of my own vulnerability, of being utterly alone.

By the time I saw the first of Fourth Day's armed patrols, I'd been walking for over an hour. My shirt was stuck to my back and my water was half gone. I ducked behind some scrubby bushes and waited to see what path they would follow. I hadn't come across a regular worn route, but it would be good practice not to follow one.

As soon as they'd passed, I looked round for a suitable landmark. There was a tall rock just ahead that looked, from this angle, vaguely like a dog sitting on its haunches, head down. I circled it twice, just to be sure it was distinctive, then knelt at the base of what would have been the dog's tail and began to dig in the soft sandy earth, first with my hands, then using a flat stone as a shovel.

It took a while to dig a hole big enough to take the rucksack, and I worked with concentration, stopping every minute or so to listen for the guards' return. When Sean and I had been watching the cult compound, we'd timed their patrols in and out but, even so, I knew I was cutting it fine. The second hole I dug was smaller, and took less time.

When I was done, I made another slow circuit of the rock. This was my emergency escape kit, and being unable to locate it again if I needed to was not a healthy scenario.

As it was, I had my tracks brushed away and the worst of the dirt washed from my hands, using almost all the remainder of my water, before I heard the patrol on their way back.

I stepped out onto my original course and kept walking, apparently oblivious but on a deliberate closing heading. I tried to keep my shoulders down and my mind empty.

One question kept coming back to haunt me.

'Why are you doing this?' Chris Sagar had asked.

Sean and Parker had asked me that one, too, and I'd given them both the same answer. 'Quite apart from finding out if Billy *is* Lorna Witney's grandchild, I'm doing it because we took Witney out of there and we lost him, and I want to know why.'

They'd both accepted it, in the end, but I couldn't tell Sagar about our new client's brief.

'Come on, Charlie,' he'd said quietly. 'I spent most of my time inside Fourth Day asking people, "Why are you here?" Everybody who wanted in, I asked them that, and you know what I discovered inside a month of doing it?'

'What?'

'That the first answer they give you is never the real one. It just never is.' He shook his head sadly. 'Half of them, they didn't even know it themselves, what finally drove them under. But you? You *got* to have an answer. A good one. One that sounds real, even if it isn't. Because, if you don't, Bane will kick your ass straight back out again.' His face pinched. 'That's if you're lucky.'

'So, it's a cover story within a story,' I said.

'Yeah, you got that right. It's like peeling an onion. Your outer layers can be kinda flaky, but once you let him under your skin, your story's gonna have to be solid. So, you need to look deep inside yourself. Why are you doing this?'

I paused, idly swishing the silt around the bottom of my cup. What could I tell him? A cynical part of my mind recognised a certain amount of clutching at straws about the whole thing. I'd been through plenty of conventional therapy of sorts, and I knew how to do the self-analysis thing. The problem was, my attitudes had been wholly shaped by experience.

If I hadn't learnt to release my latent ability to kill, I'd be dead by now. I'd been through pain and utter humiliation, and come out stronger on the other side. And while there were those who'd tried to persuade me to let go of my anger, I knew I needed it, and had kept it close like a secret.

But discovering I was pregnant had changed everything, as it was supposed to. The desire for change on a fundamental level had overwhelmed me, along with a burst of hormones and the sudden urge for Marmite-and-banana sandwiches.

I put the empty cup down on the desktop, noted that my hands were as steady as they had been after I'd shot the three men in the van on the road out of the canyon, and couldn't work out if I'd been more surprised then or now.

'I don't know,' I said calmly, 'but I'm sure, when the time comes, I'll think of something.'

Now, I timed it so that I crossed the path of the guards about ten metres ahead of them. Unless they had their eyes shut, they couldn't fail to notice me. They hadn't, and they did.

I felt the vibrations through the ground as they began to run, saw one closing on my right, knew the other would be circling behind me. I let my gait falter.

'So,' Sagar had said, last night, just before we'd turned in, 'bottom line, Charlie, give it to me straight. When Bane breaks through those outer layers, when he gets to the heart of you, and you're all out of excuses and there's no bullshit left, what is it you're gonna tell him that you want from Fourth Day?'

I heard the guards shouting at me to stop, felt the

pounding of their feet grow heavier and stronger through the soft earth. As if at the end of my reserves of strength, I staggered and went down on my knees, hands half-raised out by my sides and my head bowed, like I'd made a last effort to get here and, now I had, I was spent.

'*What is it you're gonna tell him that you want from Fourth Day?*'

'Redemption.'

One of the guards stepped round in front of me, careful not to bisect his partner's line of fire. It was the big black ex-Marine, Tyrone Yancy. One of the pair who'd gone after Maria, the day we'd seen Witney teaching his little class under the juniper tree.

The second man was a stranger. He stayed back just far enough to slot me if I looked like making trouble, keeping the M16 pulled up tight into his shoulder, eyes checking the vicinity. They were well trained. Question was, what for?

'You're on private property. Didn't you see the signs?' Yancy demanded. 'You lost or crazy?'

Squinting into the sun, I looked up at him.

'Both,' I said.

CHAPTER TWENTY-NINE

Tyrone Yancy radioed in before getting me on my feet and patting me down. He was thorough but brisk, taking no apparent pleasure in it, which was lucky for both of us.

'You think I might have a weapon?' I asked.

He shrugged. 'People sometimes try to bring in drugs. They think it will ease their transition.'

'I'm not a junkie.'

'This stage, we don't know what you are.' He stepped back. 'Please come with us.'

Despite his politeness, a certain amount of caution seemed appropriate. 'Where are you taking me?'

He glanced back, his eyes dark and expressionless. 'You're beat,' he said. 'Out of water, too, huh? We get that settled, then we decide.'

I fell into ragged step alongside him, on his right, so the barrel of the M16 was pointing down and away from me. The other guard stayed a few paces behind, not crowding, but not going out of his way to reassure, either.

I trudged between them, sweat-stained and feigning a

measure of exhaustion. As we passed through the open area in the centre of the compound, there was a small group of about a dozen adults going through morning t'ai chi ch'uan practice, their movements flowing and serene. They ignored our passing, concentration total.

I glanced across at the old juniper tree, but the bench circling its base was deserted. Thomas Witney's little class, it seemed, had not yet found a substitute teacher.

We reached the main accommodation building and went inside, the two men shouldering their rifles. The lobby looked different in daylight. Yancy detoured briefly into a side room, came back with two bottles of water and handed them over. They weren't cold, but the seals were unbroken, so I didn't care, finishing one straight down and making inroads into the other. He jerked his head to his companion.

'Message from the boss,' he said. 'He wants to see her.'

The other man didn't comment, just raised an eyebrow. I concentrated on keeping my face relaxed, on looking tired and grateful, and stopping the muscles bunch across my shoulders. I wasn't altogether successful, but they didn't seem to notice.

They led me along a corridor, remaining alert but not seeming overly tense. Sagar had told us that Fourth Day had two or three walk-ins a month, so this was hardly a new experience for them. But were all new arrivals summoned for an audience with Bane, the moment they arrived?

We continued through the main building. At one point we passed an open doorway to an office. I glanced inside, saw desks and filing cabinets. Two people were working on computer terminals like any other administrators. The very normality of it seemed bizarre.

I was led into an annexe, close but separated from the rest. Bane's personal quarters, I surmised. I'd expected to meet with him eventually, just not yet. Tension buzzed up through my shins and curled unpleasantly in my belly.

We halted outside a closed door. Yancy knocked, waiting until he heard a muffled invitation before walking in. I stepped through after him and had my first direct encounter with the man himself. On the whole, I preferred it when there'd been a sheet of one-way glass between us.

The room was large, more like a study than an office, and lined with lighted bookcases in a pale golden wood that smelt of cedar. There were blinds at the window but they were drawn against the harsh California sun. For a moment I wondered what took place in that room that Bane didn't want seen. Or was he simply trying to keep his book collection from fading?

He was reading when we came in, sitting in an old-fashioned wingback chair in deep-buttoned dark-green leather, over by an unlit fireplace on the far side of the room. There was a small round table by his arm, containing a tall glass of clear liquid that could have been anything from tap water to gin, and plenty of ice, as if he'd been privy to my earlier fantasy.

Behind the chair was a standard lamp, positioned so the light would fall onto the page. It also made it very difficult to see the man's face, which was thrown into shadow, but I could tell from his tilted head that he was watching me.

'Found this one wandering out toward the south-west corner, out of water and just about done,' Yancy told him. 'Said she was lost.'

Bane carefully placed a marker between the pages and set

the book down. He said, 'Thank you, Tyrone,' and something in that deep-set voice sent a sudden shimmer through my ribcage, like a harmonic vibration.

Yancy ducked his head in acknowledgement and stepped back to the door. When he opened it, I could see the other guard loitering in the corridor outside, just before it closed behind him with a soft click. I guessed they wouldn't leave quite yet, but I couldn't work out if their purpose was to prevent my escape, or to drag me out screaming.

Bane gestured me to a chair opposite. I glanced ruefully at my grubby cargo trousers and crusted shirt.

'What's a little honest dirt?' he asked.

I shrugged, unaccountably nervous, and perched on the edge of the seat, uncapping the second bottle of water and taking another swig while I eyed him.

'So,' he said at last, 'Miss...?'

'Foxcroft,' I said without hesitation. 'Charlotte Foxcroft. My friends call me Charlie.'

Using my full name was deliberate on my part. Oh, to Parker and Sean I'd explained it by saying I wasn't trained for undercover work to the point where I could slip automatically into another identity. I'd legally shortened my last name to Fox shortly after I'd left the army, an attempt to distance myself from the events that had led to my downfall and dismissal. It was only partially successful. But Charlotte Foxcroft – failed Special Forces trainee and unwitting fodder for the tabloids – had been very different from the person I'd since become. More trusting, more gullible.

Going back to her now seemed somehow symbolic, in my own mind at least.

'Charlie,' he said in that cultured voice, as if experimenting with the feel and the weight of the name. My scalp prickled. 'There are no trails through this land. The boundary is securely fenced and clearly signed as private property. How did you come to be lost?'

I gave a cynical laugh I didn't have to force. 'I ask myself that question every day.'

'So you are not here by accident.' He paused. 'You are fully aware of where "here" is?'

'This is Fourth Day,' I said. 'And you are Randall Bane. I was told you could help me.'

'Really? By whom?'

I shrugged, let my eyes drift down and right. 'It's doesn't matter now. He's dead anyway.'

In the periphery of my vision, I saw Bane's head shift, but I didn't react. Then he asked quietly, 'How, exactly, do you believe I can help you?'

I shrugged again, still staring at a spot where the polished wooden floor met the edge of the rug. 'I went through some shit a few years ago – a lot of shit, if I'm honest – and I thought I was past it, but it keeps coming back to haunt me,' I said, putting intensity into the words. 'And now I'm scared all the time, of what it's doing to me, and of what I might do.' I looked up, straight into Bane's face. 'I need to change and I don't know how.'

He stared at me for a long time unmoving, piercing me with eyes so pale brown they were almost golden. 'What about your family?'

'They're in the UK, and...we don't talk much anymore.'

'What brought you to America?'

'Boyfriend.' I gave a fractional twitch of my lips. 'About six months ago.'

'You still together?'

'I'm here, aren't I?' I said, injecting a bitter note. 'So, I suppose not. I've been pushing him away for months.' *No lie there, then.*

'Is he violent? Abusive? Into drugs? Crime?'

Violent? After only minimal hesitation, I shook my head.

Bane sighed. 'You don't need my help,' he said gently. 'Go back to your boyfriend, Charlie. If he's clean, like you say, make your peace with him. If he isn't, then leave him. Get in contact with your parents. Break the silence while you still have the chance. Take responsibility for your own actions and stop looking for the easy way out.'

He pressed a bell push on the table and picked up his book again. As if turning from a fire, I felt the heat and light of his interest go away from me.

Behind me, the door opened again. Footsteps closed on either side of my chair. The panic reached into my throat, churning like acid.

'Ah, Tyrone,' Bane said, not looking up. 'Give Charlie here some food and drive her out to the nearest bus station, would you? She will not be staying.'

I half-rose, reaching towards him, prepared to plead if I had to. 'Wait—'

One of the men grabbed my shoulder. I flinched instinctively at the pressure and intent, saw Bane's head lift with narrowed eyes, and that fraction of a second was all it took.

I made a snap decision, without thought to risk or consequences, knowing it might easily be the worst – or the last – I ever made. What had Sagar said of Thomas Witney? *'He'd suffered enough.'*

If Bane was looking for damaged souls to twist to his own design, I could give him twisted. In fact, sometimes it was more of a stretch to pretend not to be. To keep the anger penned up inside and to pretend to be just like everybody else, every day.

Now, I needed that rage. I took a breath and called on every ounce and shard of it, felt it come howling up out of the depths of my psyche in visceral response, all teeth and claws like a monstrous predator too long denied the kill.

The taste of it was sour in my mouth, flooding my senses, deafening me, and for once, instead of battling for control and subjugation, I gave it free rein to savage and destroy in wanton rampage.

Suddenly, I was blind with it, sick with it, in the grip of a madness long since denied its true potential and glorying in vicious release. And if, as the first blows began to fall, there was an inner voice, somewhere deep at the back of my mind, that recoiled, keening at this final breach, it was a small voice, and quickly silenced.

I was vaguely aware of Bane himself stepping back, an observer, of more bodies pouring through the doorway, of raised voices and broken furniture. Of fearfulness and, before the end, screaming.

But I don't fully remember what I did in that room. I don't know how long it went on for.

When I came round, nauseous and bruised and aching, I found they'd taken away my belt and my boots – and, yes, my watch – and I was locked up alone in the dark.

CHAPTER THIRTY

The door to my cell opened. I half-expected Bane again, come for the next round, but it was the Brit ex-Para with the slightly regal Eurasian features who stood there. Parker had identified him as John Nu, I recalled. He was wearing neatly pressed desert camouflage, his combat boots bulled to a workmanlike shine, and he was carrying a tray.

I didn't remember him taking part in the altercation in Bane's study, but then he turned his head slightly and I saw a line of Steri-Strip dressings closing a small cut across his eyebrow.

Oh yeah, sunshine. You were there.

Someone held the door and he stepped through, checking both ways as well as up, cautious as any good soldier. Behind him, the door was pushed to, but not latched. I guessed he wanted a quick escape route, just in case.

Nu put the tray down on the end of the bed furthest from me, moved back to lean against the wall near the doorway.

I glanced at his offering. A sandwich of what looked like

cheese and salad, wrapped in a paper napkin, an oversize muffin, and a banana. All finger food that could be eaten without the potential weaponry of a knife and fork. The irony wasn't lost on me.

'How you doing?' Nu asked, without apparent resentment for whatever injuries I might have caused. From the distinctive vowel sounds, his accent was West Midlands. The area around Wolverhampton known as the Black Country because of the coal.

'So-so,' I said, cautious myself. I flapped a languid hand. 'Don't think much of the rooms at this hotel, though.'

He half-smiled. 'Yeah, well, we get a lot of junkies, don't we? Got to have somewhere safe and sound to put 'em while they dry out.'

'Speaking of dry,' I said, 'did you bring anything to drink?'

He reached into the front pocket of his tunic and handed across a can of full-fat Coke. I normally drank Diet, but I reckoned I could probably do with the sugar hit.

The can was still reasonably cold, enough for the dampness of condensation to have formed on the outside. I held it to the inflamed area around my eye, letting it soothe for a moment, then picked up the sandwich. I wasn't hungry, but it was fuel, and voluntary starvation gained me nothing.

Nu watched me bite into the thick bread. Chewing made the side of my face ache, but I hadn't taken a sock in the mouth, so at least my teeth were still solid.

'Can always tell a squaddie,' he said after a moment. 'Never pass up the chance to get some scran down your neck, eh?'

'You should know,' I said. 'Miss it?'

'Nah.' He grinned at me. 'Who'd want to be on stag all night in bloody Baghdad when they could be living it up in California?'

'I would have thought, by the time you got out, you'd have had enough of taking orders to last a lifetime,' I said. 'Why join this lot?'

'Depends what you mean by "join", love,' he said, still smiling. 'Me and the lads, we was hired to take care of security and training. Don't mean we're followers.' He touched a rueful finger to the cut above his eye. 'Not that you need much training, eh?'

I finished the sandwich, wiped my fingers carefully on the napkin and took a slug of Coke. 'Yeah, well, I learnt the hard way.'

'You did at that,' he murmured, and for the first time, the humour was wiped clean from his voice. When I looked up, it was gone from his face, too. I lowered the Coke slowly but kept the can in my hand, gauged the distance between us, and waited.

'I remember you, Charlie,' he said quietly. 'How could I not? Made a right splash in all the papers, didn't you?'

I said, 'You shouldn't believe everything you read,' but caught the frozen note in my voice, and knew he'd heard it, too.

Nu nodded. 'I was on the next intake. Fancied myself in Special Forces, just like you did, working undercover in Belfast – better than patrolling the Falls Road as a grunt with the Paras, getting rocks chucked at me by five-year-old kiddies.'

I couldn't bring myself to ask what he'd heard, what lies the Powers That Be had told those who followed the disastrous training course I'd been on. Instead, I tilted my head back and forced myself to bring the can up to my lips, even if I couldn't stomach actually taking a drink once it was there.

'So,' I asked, 'did it turn out to be all you were hoping for?'

He shrugged. 'Nah. Chucked it in, didn't I?'

Roughly translated, that meant he hadn't made the grade – had been Returned To Unit. The majority of those who started the training were RTU'd, I'd been warned at the outset, with the clear implication that's what they expected would happen to me and, hey, no hard feelings. Certainly, the instructors seemed to make it their mission in life to keep the odds stacked against us. Like Epps, most hadn't believed the few women trainees had what it took.

But I'd been good enough, I knew. I'd thought that making it through the selection process was the hard part, that the training itself was going to be a breeze by comparison.

I'd been wrong.

I looked up, found Nu watching me again. Something flickered in his face.

'I served with one of them, you know,' he said then, suddenly. 'Couple of years after – in Bosnia. Lad called Hackett.'

Donalson, Hackett, Morton and Clay.

The names of my four attackers danced inside my head, the faces parading behind my eyes, vivid, vicious, causing a physical response I struggled to confine. I wondered if there'd ever be a time when I could hear their names and genuinely feel nothing. When the memory alone no longer sent that burst of pure anger scalding through my hands.

'I don't suppose,' I managed dryly, 'there's any chance he died horribly in the line of duty?'

'There was one or two who wouldn't have minded if he'd stepped on a landmine, love, that was for sure,' Nu said. 'Nasty bugger. Not the sort of bloke you'd want behind you if it all went bad, know what I mean?'

Oh, yeah. Been there, done that...

'Anyway, he got pissed one night, and he talked about it – what him and the others did to you,' Nu went on, his gaze as measured as his tone. 'Said you didn't put up much of a fight, all things considered. Reckoned you must have enjoyed it, on the quiet.'

Sure. That's why they had to beat me half to death to get me to lie still long enough...

I swallowed, but held my peace. Nu shrugged as if I'd spoken anyway.

'Hackett reckoned they done you a favour. Said what they gave you was only a taster of what them Provo bastards would have done, if you'd gone and got yourself caught after they sent you across the water.'

'If you should ever happen to see him again,' I said, aware that some vaguely human quality was missing from my voice, 'you can tell him I've acquired a whole new skill set since those days. One I'd be delighted to demonstrate to him, first hand.'

Nu's mouth twitched. He straightened and picked up the tray, sliding the untouched muffin and the banana onto the bed, held out his hand for the can. I finished the last few mouthfuls and handed it over.

He moved for the door, then paused. 'There was a sergeant on that course, one of the instructors. A bloke called Meyer, known for being one of the hardest bastards in the army,' Nu said casually. 'I found out later that you'd been shagging him while you was there, and I remembered something else Hackett said about you – that you liked a bit of pain.' His gaze flicked over me, lingering on the expanding bruise around my eye. 'Might be some truth in that, eh?'

CHAPTER THIRTY-ONE

The next time the door opened, it was the ex-Marine, Yancy, who stood there.

I was on the floor of my cell, braced on my toes and the palms of my hands, running through my third set of press-ups. The back of my shoulder – the same place I'd been shot – burned at the exertion. Somebody, I reckoned, had probably put the boot in during the struggle and it was taking a while to come back to me.

Still, it could have been a lot worse.

I looked up sharply when I heard the bolts go back, blinking as a ribbon of sweat rolled into my eyes. By the time the door cracked fully, I'd jacked to my feet.

'Your turn, is it?' I asked dryly.

Yancy didn't rise to that, just eyed me from the corridor, unwilling to venture into my cell now I was upright and obviously mobile, but my attention was grabbed by the object clutched in his fist.

'Found something belongs to you,' he said, and threw it at my feet.

The rucksack landed in a shimmer of dust. I recognised it instantly, could tell by the way it had fallen that it was empty. It crumpled sulkily onto the concrete, like it was embarrassed at being so easily unearthed. I knew I'd buried it in a hurry, but how the hell had they found it so fast?

I shifted my weight, noted Yancy's twitch of reaction.

'So,' I said at last, 'what happens now?'

'You come with me,' he said with a jerk of his head. 'Bring that with you.'

I glanced down at my bare feet. 'Some boots would be good.'

He nudged something just outside the doorway with his foot, kicking my boots across the floor towards me with more force than was strictly necessary. I stamped on them before they clouted my ankles, and sat on the edge of the bed to put them on. Yancy watched me in impervious silence.

I picked the rucksack up, slapped it a couple of times to knock the worst off it, then stepped out of my little cell with a certain trepidation.

Yancy stood to one side, indicating I was to walk ahead of him, taking no chances. I slung the rucksack onto my shoulder. It weighed almost nothing.

'You might have left me the chocolate,' I said in mock reproach, but received not a flicker by way of reply. There were no obvious marks on him and I wondered about that. His scowl was enough to tell me I must have injured something, if only his pride.

I didn't remember the area outside my cell from the way in, so took the opportunity to scan the wide, windowless corridor. The rough wall to my left was solid-block cool when I brushed my hand against it, and slightly damp to the touch. There'd been no indication of a basement level on the plans Parker had pulled, but this had a subterranean feel.

To my right was a line of three other doors, leading to what I assumed were more cells. I'd heard no sign of company during my incarceration, but that didn't mean they were empty. I remembered Nu's comment about junkies. Was making them go cold turkey down here all part of Bane's much-vaunted programme of breakdown and reconstruction?

As soon as we started moving, one of the doors opened abruptly ahead of us and Nu came out, cradling an M4 carbine.

Just for a second, it flashed through my mind that, having found my main emergency kit, the two men had set this up as a shot-during-escape-attempt, during which I could be conveniently dealt with.

Nu had his right hand draped across the stock of the rifle, his index finger hooked almost casually inside the trigger guard, but his upper body was betrayingly stiff.

As soon as I saw the gun I tensed in reflex, started to drop. The M4 shared many parts with its larger M16 brother, and was a superb close-quarter weapon, particularly compact with the stock folded. At anything over twenty-five metres, an M4 carbine would put a standard 5.56 mm NATO round through a blockwork wall like butter. But at this kind of ultraclose range, the high-velocity round was more likely to ricochet and fragment rather than penetrate.

Then I realised that Nu had not shifted his stance. With Yancy directly behind me, he would not risk a shot anyway. I straightened slowly and Nu grinned at my overreaction.

'Still sharp, aren't you, love?' His eyes slid past me. 'Sharper than you, eh, mate?'

Yancy glowered again and waved me forwards. He did not, I noted, make the mistake of grabbing me again.

Nu began to close the door to the cell he'd just vacated, and I glanced inside as we passed, another automatic response, an inbuilt desire to be minutely aware of my surroundings. The first thing that hit me was that the cramped space was almost entirely filled with boxes, draped in dust sheets. And in that instant I knew it was more than just a storeroom.

There was nothing sinister about dust sheets. Bare concrete, unless it's been treated with sealant, creates a gritty dust that's corrosive to precision equipment or electronics. But one of the sheets was hooked up a little at the corner, and I caught a triangular glimpse of the casing underneath.

I kept my face blank, my breathing steady, while my mind stepped up into overdrive.

During our surveillance of Fourth Day, we'd worked out that Bane had an eight-man security force, split into four teams of two on a standard rotating shift pattern. On the sparse side, but adequate and efficient.

Eight men. That meant a primary weapon each, plus sidearms. Even allowing for replacements and breakages and spares, maybe two dozen suitable weapons overall. The outside patrols we'd observed had all been carrying M16s. That was a logical choice, a decent weapon, with the advantage that anyone with military experience could handle one in their sleep.

As a Para, Nu would have carried the standard British Army assault rifle, the SA80. Or, if he'd joined early, the old faithful 7.62 mm SLR. During his Special Forces training, he would have been familiarised with a whole range of different firearms, including the M16.

So, why did Bane feel the need to supplement his men with M4 carbines, RPGs and hand grenades, unless he was preparing them for all-out urban warfare?

And why did he need a storeroom filled to the rafters with gun cases – unless he was training every man, woman and child in the place for combat?

'*We can't afford another Waco,*' Epps had said.

I thought again of his initial reluctance for me to enter Fourth Day, how quickly he'd allowed himself to be talked round. Too quickly, I realised now. He'd lost two men. There was no way a man like Epps would take that lying down...

So, I'd been played.

Yancy drew level with Nu, swept his gaze over the gun in his hands. 'No need,' he said, almost disdainfully. 'Put it away.'

Nu grinned at him, but ducked back inside the storeroom, reappearing empty-handed a moment later, closing and locking the door behind him. 'Happy now?' he asked.

Yancy grunted and Nu moved ahead of us, giving me a wink as he passed.

'Them Marines don't half take themselves seriously, eh?'

We went through another door and up a short flight of steps. I'd been right about the building being partially underground. I squinted as we stepped out into sunlight, shaded my eyes and glanced up. The sun was reaching its noon zenith, but I couldn't be sure of the day. In high-stress situations, people in captivity invariably imagine they've been held longer than they actually have. Time has a habit of slowing down when you have no accurate way to measure it.

So, while I knew it felt like I'd been in that little cell for days, it was probably only one or two at the most. The random light pattern had further served to disorientate me, as it was supposed to.

I glanced around, saw a group of people unloading groceries out of a dusty 4x4, others hanging out washing. All very ordinary and domestic – on the surface, at least. They paused in their labours and watched us pass, faces carefully expressionless. I looked for Maria, but she wasn't among them.

I wondered if Sean was watching somewhere out there in the undergrowth, just as we'd watched Thomas Witney. The only difference was, he would no doubt be tracking us through the sights of a long gun. And, if he was, the first we'd know about it would be the two men alongside me dropping lifeless in their tracks.

Part of me hoped he wasn't watching.

'No chains?' I asked Nu over my shoulder, keeping my movements fluid, trying not to look as though I was hurting, or under duress. 'You *are* trusting.'

'I don't think you're the type to cut and run, are you, love?' he said, and the smile didn't quite reach his eyes. 'Not after all the trouble you took to get yourself in, eh?'

CHAPTER THIRTY-TWO

The study looked much as I remembered it. The little side table and one of the wingback chairs had gone, and the rug had been thoroughly cleaned.

Randall Bane was behind his desk this time, hands loosely resting on the satin polished wood.

Laid out on a sheet of cloth to protect the surface was my gun and the box of hollow points that went with it, one of the two mobile phones I'd buried, the distress beacon, the first-aid kit, and my chocolate bars. The contents, in other words, of only one of the plastic boxes I'd brought in with me.

I kept my expression neutral as I inventoried what was there, then allowed my shoulders to slump fractionally, as if in defeat. As if they'd got everything.

But, how had they known to look for it at all? I remembered Thomas Witney's unexpected familiarity with psychoactive drugs, and wondered briefly if Bane had taken that opportunity with me.

If they had, they would have found both boxes. Why didn't they find the other?

'This is not the kind of baggage people usually bring when they're asking for my help,' Bane said, almost gently, indicating the array with a dismissive flick of his fingers.

I jerked my head in Yancy's direction. 'He told me junkies sometimes try and bring in drugs. *To ease their transition*, I think he said.' I paused. 'You know I was a soldier. Maybe I'm just having trouble letting go.'

A faint smile crossed his lips. 'If I suggested it might be better for you to leave us now, are you going to...erupt again?'

I put my head on one side. 'Perhaps,' I said evenly. 'Why? Are you planning to suggest that?'

He sighed. 'We know you were sent to spy on us, Charlie,' he said at last. 'Tell me, what did Parker Armstrong hope to achieve by it?'

I didn't show surprise at his use of Parker's name, because it didn't come as one. Wherever Bane was getting his information, it was good. And the Debacle pair, Tony and Dexter, certainly knew who I worked for. The connections were there to be made.

'The truth,' I said. 'What else is there?'

He murmured, 'What else, indeed?'

'I've never lied to you,' I said. 'That doesn't mean I've told you the whole story, either. The truth is, Parker didn't send me. Nobody *sent* me. I wanted to come and I talked him into allowing it, and you already know why.'

Bane was silent for a moment, frowning, regarding me steadily. His eyes had a darker ring around the edge of the iris, I noticed for the first time, merging to gold near the pupil. Mesmeric. I peeled my gaze away with effort, aware of a breathlessness I couldn't quite explain.

'So, this has nothing to do with the murder of Thomas Witney?'

There was no way I was going to mention our interest in Maria. 'If I said no, I *would* be lying,' I said calmly. 'Witney never wanted to leave here. We forced the issue – not entirely by choice – and I'm living with the consequences of my part in that. But it's nowhere near the whole reason.'

His head tilted slightly. 'This is not the place to find those kind of answers.'

I let out a long, shaky breath. 'Well, right now, I can't think of anywhere else to try.'

'I did not kill Thomas,' Bane said, and his voice was very sure and very steady, like his eyes, bearing down into mine. If he was a liar, he was the best I'd ever come across. It was suddenly very hot in that room, stifling. 'I had no reason to want him dead. Do you believe me?'

But out of the corner of my eye I saw Yancy move, just a fraction. Hardly more than the easing of his weight from one foot to the other. Bane's eyes, on my face, must have seen the flare of reaction.

He nodded, as if that was my answer, and stretched a hand towards the collection of my belongings. Just for a second, I thought he was reaching for the SIG. I braced almost subconsciously, but he passed over the gun and picked up my cellphone instead, stabbed the power button with his thumb.

'No doubt you have people on the outside,' he said as the unit booted up, 'ready to stage an intervention, should you fail to contact them?'

'Yes.' There was no point in denying it.

He held the phone out to me. 'Then you had best call them.'

'And say what?' I was suddenly wary, like this was some kind of trap.

'That is up to you, Charlie,' he said gravely. 'But think of this as a statement of your intent. A second step on your journey.'

'My journey to where?'

'What you seek – absolution.'

Slowly, I reached for the phone, keyed in Sean's number. As soon as it connected, I hit the speaker button. Bane raised his eyebrow.

'I've nothing to say that you can't hear,' I said.

The phone rang out half a dozen times. Longer than it would normally take Sean to answer. I assumed he was activating a recorder, or hooking it up to a satellite tracker. Epps was in this, and he had all the toys at his disposal.

'Yeah?' Sean's voice, a little gruff. A non-committal opener in case of listeners, of strangers, or anyone who'd heard him speak and might recognise him.

'It's Charlie,' I said. *I am not alone.*

There was a pause. 'Are you OK?' *Is there an immediate danger?*

'I'm fine.' *I don't think so.*

'You sure?' *What do you mean, you don't* think *so?* 'I've been worried about you.' *The team's on standby. Say the word.*

'I'm not ready to come home.' *My mission is not yet complete.* Then I sighed, abandoned our carefully worked-out covert language of coded signals and shrouded meaning. 'Sean, they know who I am,' I said. 'They know why I'm here.'

'Charlie—' he began, then stopped. I could picture his

face, shut down, bleached of emotion, thinking like a soldier because that's all he could afford to be right now. 'What do you need?'

I swallowed, meeting Bane's gaze across the desk and trying not to shift, restless, beneath it. His features formed an impassive mask, giving me nothing in return. Not a trap, but a test. *Had* he arranged for Thomas Witney to be snatched away from Epps and murdered? Personally stood in that squalid little motel room off Sunset Boulevard and watched his men – maybe even these men – beat Witney half to death and then deliver the final *coup de grâce*?

'I don't need anything,' I said, holding eye contact. 'I'm OK. I'll contact you when I'm ready. I'm just calling to say…please, don't come for me.'

There was a long period of silence at the other end of the phone. 'All right, but I have some questions.' Sean said then, cool and flat and so utterly detached it made my heart weep. 'Do you mind?' *Are you being forced to do this?*

'I understand.' *No.*

'Where did I first send you in Germany?'

No hidden messages here. Simple control questions, designed to expose distress, duress, danger. Checks and balances.

'A place called Einsbaden, just outside Stuttgart,' I said sedately, knowing that Epps's people would be analysing the recordings afterwards, listening for stress patterns in my voice, off cadences in my speech, and wanting to give them everything and nothing to go on. 'To a close-protection training school run by an ex-army major called Gilby.'

Sean barely paused, changing tack. 'What was the name of my family cat?'

'You didn't have a cat,' I said easily. 'You had a dog.'

'OK, last one,' he said, and his voice was softer now, more dangerous. 'The first time we went away – spent our first night together – where did we go?'

Our first time together had been on a forty-eight hour pass from camp. A glorious weekend during which only hunger had driven us out of bed. And then right back into it again.

But I understood the message there. He was giving me just one more night before they pulled the plug. More than that, he was reminding me of what we shared. Telling me not to let go of it. Not to throw it away.

'We went to that little chalet on the cliff, just outside Colwyn Bay on the North Wales coast,' I said. I paused, then added gently, 'And it was a week, Sean, not a single night.' *Give me more time!*

He was quiet for so long that I almost spoke again, just to check the signal hadn't dropped out, but then he said, 'I won't pretend I understand, but I'll respect your decision, Charlie. You'll call me?'

'I—' Across the other side of the desk, Bane broke his stasis to give a single shake of his head. 'I can't,' I said. 'I have a lot of things to work through, to get straight, and to do that, I need to be alone. I need to be here.' A whole raft of emotions came bubbling up in a disordered jumble, everything distilled down into a couple of meaningless words. 'I'm...sorry.'

'Yeah,' he said and for the first time he sounded tired. 'So am I.'

CHAPTER THIRTY-THREE

I wasn't returned to my subterranean cell after my audience with Bane, which was, I suppose, the one bright spot of the day.

Instead, Nu walked me back through the main building. The people we encountered stepped back to silently watch me pass. Even if they hadn't been in Bane's study that first day, this was a small place and they knew what had happened there. Or enough of it to regard me with curious and slightly fearful eyes, at any rate.

Their covert attention lay between my shoulder blades like an unscratched itch. I felt like what I was – a freak. Maybe that was the whole point of it.

Well, you asked for that, too.

In the small entrance lobby, Nu ignored the door to the outside and headed off down another corridor, turning back when my footsteps paused behind him.

'Come on then, love,' he said, almost a challenge. 'Taking you to new quarters, aren't I?'

The last time I'd ventured into this part of the building,

it had been dark, and my only concern had been getting the team in to retrieve Thomas Witney from his apparent captivity.

Sagar had told me Bane liked to play mind games, but even *he* wouldn't...

'Here you go,' Nu said, halting outside a doorway. 'Home, sweet home.'

Oh yes, he would.

They'd put me in Thomas Witney's old room.

I threw a searching gaze at Nu as I moved past him, but he stared back blandly. Inside, the room was unchanged, with the single bed, the desk and the simple chair. The glass of water and the book were even still on the table by the bed, as if in deliberate provocation.

The only difference was a girl who was just in the process of throwing a new sheet over the bed. She straightened with a gasp at the sound of Nu's voice. When she jerked towards us, I recognised the thin, nervous figure of Maria Gonzalez.

As soon as I saw her, I realised that finding out if Liam Witney was the father of her child was going to take a lot more than asking probing questions, or putting pressure on her to reveal the truth. The girl had the wild eyes and jittery stance of someone half a step from the edge. It was hard to credit she was the same girl who appeared, smiling and carefree, alongside Liam in the photograph on his mother's office wall.

What kind of breakdown had she suffered, and – more to the point – what had caused it?

If we'd obeyed Sean's instinct to take Maria out with us that night, I wondered, what would have become of her?

Even if she hadn't been snatched away, like Witney, a stint with Epps would have done nothing for her clearly fragile state of mind.

Maria, meanwhile, gaped at us, immobile.

'Here, let me give you a hand with that,' I said, offering to take one end of the sheet, smiling.

Just for a moment, she clutched the ironed cotton closer to her chest, as if I'd caught her naked coming out of the shower and was now suggesting removing her towel. Her gaze flitted to Nu, as if seeking his approval, then she nodded to me, a little shyly, and released her grip.

I smiled again and we quickly tucked the sheet under the mattress, added a blanket, and folded the corners with military precision.

When we were done, Maria gave me a mumbled, 'Thank you,' but she wouldn't meet my eyes.

'Come along, love,' Nu said from the doorway, an underlying tension to his voice. 'Let's give Charlie here a chance to settle in, eh?'

Maria flushed and nodded, scooping up the old linen she'd dropped onto the floor, and grabbing the book and the glass from the night table. I wanted to find some excuse to prolong her visit, build up some kind of relationship, but she was stretched taut as a bowstring with the urge to flee.

Nu's arm across the doorway blocked her exit, spiking her unease. I shifted my stance, knew he registered the movement by the way he let his arm drop.

'What's the book?' he asked, lifting it out of her grasp and staring, nonplussed at the old-fashioned jacket. As he turned it over in his hands, I saw the title. JD Salinger's *The Catcher in the Rye.*

He pursed his lips. 'Ever read it?' he asked me.

'A long time ago.'

'Might as well hang onto this one then,' he said, and put the book down onto the corner of the desk.

Maria took advantage of his distraction to make a bolt for it. We heard the slap of her shoes along the corridor as she hurried away. Not quite running, but not far off it.

Nu grinned and I turned towards him very slowly.

Bait her, and you'll answer to me.

I didn't have to say the words out loud. His grin faded.

'What's her story?' I asked. I didn't expect to get the truth, but even the official lie might be instructive.

'Mad as a box of frogs, that one,' Nu said, dismissive, turning away. 'You don't want to pay much attention to anything little Maria says.'

I raised an eyebrow and the grin was back, full force, just before he closed the door behind him. I wasn't at all surprised to hear the key turn pointedly in the lock on the outside.

So, I'd exchanged one locked room for another. At least this one had natural light and a few more creature comforts.

I sighed, kicked off my boots and lay on the bed with the pillows bunched up behind my head, thinking back over the stilted conversation I'd just had with Sean. Difficult to say a fraction of what I'd wanted to, over an open line with numerous eavesdroppers at both ends. The words were almost immaterial, but I replayed his defeated tone over and over.

There was a part of me, I knew, that almost wished he'd argued harder about the extra time I'd asked for, even though I would have fought him for it, if he'd insisted. I supposed there was still a chance he was out there, at this very moment, watching the compound, and had identified where I'd been brought.

And, suddenly, I was achingly aware of the gulf that had opened up between us, and just how much I missed him.

I massaged my temples vigorously, as if that would help refocus me on the job. I'd come to find out about Maria's son, I reminded myself. Why Thomas Witney had decided to stay, or what had made him afraid to leave, was a side issue.

I got up, restless, pulled open the single desk drawer, as if expecting it to be anything other than empty. The room was totally devoid of personality. Witney had lived there for five years, and yet had failed to leave a mark on the place beyond a half-drunk glass of water and a fifty-year-old book.

I picked up the Salinger, wondering how far he'd got with it, flipped through the yellow-edged pages. They riffled softly beneath my thumb, then jumped a section. I stopped, went back, opened the book up more fully and found, slipped between the pages down close to the spine, a flat key.

I picked the key out slowly, remembered Witney's claim that it had been on his night table all the time. I'd thought he was deluding himself, but that wasn't so. And if he was not a prisoner here, then he'd chosen to lock himself in at night.

So, who had he really been afraid of?

CHAPTER THIRTY-FOUR

Bane said, 'Tell me about your first kill.'

It was afternoon. I'd spent a couple of hours lying in my room, staring up at the ceiling, before the door had been unlocked by a motherly woman whose face was vaguely familiar from our surveillance. Her name was Ann, she told me, and she'd been with Fourth Day for a year and a half.

She took me to a small workshop at the rear of the main building, indicated that I should take a seat, as if keeping each other company was the most natural thing in the world.

On the workbench in front of her was a cheap dismantled radio, the type people throw away rather than repair, but she was soon absorbed in tracing the cause of its demise. I sat alongside her and listened as, without guile, she recounted her life story.

Abusive parents leading to an abusive husband, a downward spiral into alcohol and drugs, a brush with prostitution. All recounted in a matter-of-fact tone, punctuated by prosaic requests to pass the soldering iron and to reposition the lit magnifier she was using to aid her painstaking task.

With her wiry greying hair tied back in a loose ponytail, she looked like someone my mother might have served with on a Women's Institute committee. But for the rolled-back sleeves, which revealed the evidence of her past addiction comprehensively tattooed in the crook of both arms.

I'd asked her why she bothered to mend something costing maybe a few dollars when it was new. She explained it was part of what Fourth Day did, a kind of recycling and therapy, all rolled into one. 'I have no artistic talent to create from scratch,' she said simply, 'so I bring things back to life instead.' She smiled. 'Both satisfying and productive.'

Afterwards, she peacefully delivered me into Bane's study, leaving me there with a quiet smile and a quieter hand on my shoulder, as if commanding me to stay.

Now, I sat back in my chair. 'Who says I've killed anyone?'

'I know something of your history, Charlie, which I'm sure was your intention. Why else would you use your real name, if you did not want or hope for me to uncover your past?'

Yes, but how? And so fast...

Bane sat motionless as I struggled to find a way into the story, then said, 'Was it the man who cut your throat?' and there was nothing to react to in that dark-brown voice.

I forced myself not to reach towards the faded scar that encircled the base of my throat. It took physical effort.

'Yes, I killed him,' I said, flat and even. 'He had a knife. He broke my ribs, my cheekbone, and my arm in two places.' I still had the calcified lumps on the radius and ulna of my left arm, reminders of a pair of neat fracture lines that had saved me a shattered skull – his intention. Dazed, bleeding, scared, I'd thought I was finished. He had thought so, too.

I looked straight at Bane. 'He was a rapist and a murderer. It was a split-second decision – him or me.'

'A very sanitised version of events,' Bane said. I flushed, but there was no condemnation in his tone. 'John has told me something of your time in the military. That four of your brothers-in-arms beat and raped you. And yet you made no attempt to kill them. I wonder why.'

That was an image I didn't want to return to, a whole series of them, in fact. Rape isn't sexual, it's all about power, so why did Bane make this feel like foreplay? I shifted in my seat, suddenly restless, unable to find a place for my hands.

'I would have done,' I said, chest tightening. 'At the time I didn't know how.'

'But you had passed your Special Forces selection course, and were training for highly dangerous undercover work, I understand,' Bane said, no trace of taunt about him. 'How could you have been so helpless?'

I shot him a barbed look, but none of them penetrated that cool facade.

'We'd all been through exactly the same unarmed combat courses. Whatever moves I had, they knew the counters,' I said, bitter. 'And there were four of them.' I gave a short, mirthless laugh. 'I was a first-class shot. If I'd had a gun I would have slotted all of them, but they were supposed to be my comrades. I was *supposed* to be able to trust them.' And I heard the note of longing in my voice. It was the betrayal as much as the violence that had charred to the bone.

'How far had they gone before you finally believed what they intended to do?'

'Too far.'

'So, you were raped,' Bane said, his words sliding softly over my skin like a verbal caress, 'and afterwards you taught yourself the skills to prevent a recurrence, is that it?'

I shivered and my chin came up. 'Wouldn't you have done the same thing?'

He shook his head. 'We're not talking about me, Charlie. We're not talking hypothetical "what ifs". We're talking about *your* life, what happened to *you*, because or in spite of the choices *you* made.'

The anger rose fast and hard, building up instant pressure behind my eyes, prickling in my vision. 'You think I *chose* to be raped? You think I wanted that? Was asking for it?' I demanded, harsh, almost shouting now. 'OK, yes, afterwards, I trained. When I was past feeling bloody sorry for myself, and past the shame and the shock, I studied every discipline I thought might be of use to me. I vowed I'd never let anyone do that to me again. Ever.'

He took the outburst calmly. 'So, you had already made the decision to kill, a long time before the opportunity presented itself?'

He made it sound calculated, cold-blooded, as though I'd cruised the streets like some damned vigilante, praying for my chance to get even. It took the heat and the colour straight out of me. 'No! No, I...things were different.'

'How?'

I took a shaky breath. 'Because it wasn't just me he was

trying to hurt. He'd taken...someone else. Someone I cared about. A friend. And when he was done with me, he was going to start on her. And I didn't...I couldn't let her go through that. Not knowing I was capable of preventing it. I couldn't have lived with myself.'

'So that was your catalyst,' Bane said simply. 'When you were driven to kill, it was not to save your own life, but somebody else's.' And watching me across the desk, he saw the dawning truth of his words, and gave a slight nod. 'You are far from a lost cause, Charlie. However much you might wish to be.'

'Logically, rationally, I know what I did was entirely justifiable,' I said. 'The police and the courts agreed...'

'But?'

I looked down at my hands, clasped loosely in my lap. They were unremarkable hands, neither large nor small for my height and build, straight fingers, short nails. Capable hands.

Hands capable of killing.

I looked up. 'The kind of people who become mothers do not kill people.'

Bane shook his head. 'But surely parents are the epitome of the perfect bodyguard?' he said, and it was the mild surprise in his voice that echoed, lasting through my mind. 'And mothers are the fiercest of all.'

CHAPTER THIRTY-FIVE

I waited until it was completely dark before I used the key I'd found in Witney's book to let myself quietly out of my room and along the corridor. As I slipped into the tiny lobby area, I halted briefly, eyes closed, listening to the quality of silence around me.

After a moment, I turned away from the external door. I knew the security patrols had the area immediately surrounding the compound covered during the night, and they had all the equipment to do so. Going out there was foolish when we hadn't spotted anything amiss in our previous surveillance. Whatever was going on here, it was happening inside.

I remembered the gun cases I'd seen as they'd brought me out of confinement, could calculate from the height and depth of them just how many there had been. A lot. Too many to be easily explained, that was for sure.

So, what was Bane up to that he needed to stockpile armaments? And was that why Thomas Witney had been silenced?

I gave myself a mental shake. *That's not why you're here, Fox!*

I thought of the dossier Chris Sagar had put together from his time on the inside of Fourth Day, about their methods and their ideology. So far, they'd shown me little sign of the psychological brutality I'd been led to expect.

I guessed, after my initial outburst, they were waiting until I was deemed more stable before that began in earnest. Meanwhile, far from breaking me down, my sessions with Bane actually made me feel...better about myself.

Much better.

Maybe that was part of the process – lull you into a false sense of security, then take your legs out from under you.

I shook my head, stepped cautiously across the lobby and passed through into the corridor leading towards Bane's study.

Along the way, I tried the handles of every door I passed. The ratio of locked to unlocked was pretty even. I found a storeroom, a kind of first-aid station with rudimentary equipment but apparently no drugs.

In the corner was a three-drawer filing cabinet – the most likely place to find any records relating to Billy's medical history. I tugged experimentally at the upper drawer, marked A–G. Not surprisingly, it didn't open, but the cabinet was an older type. It didn't take more than a few moments to carefully walk it forwards far enough to tilt the upper half back against the wall to locate the exposed end of the locking rod underneath. I pushed it up, disengaging the locking system with a soft clunk, and smiled into the gloom. Another little gift from Sean.

Gently, I set the cabinet upright. The top drawer slid

open without complaint and I leafed through the manila dividers until I came to 'GONZALEZ, B'. It contained a slim folder, listing the usual childhood illnesses and his blood type, which was O negative. The universal donor – too common to be remotely useful.

I shuffled the cabinet back into position without marking the floor. There wasn't much I could do to relock it, but I'd just have to hope that was put down to oversight. At least it hadn't been obviously forced.

I moved deeper into the building, remembering the admin office I'd seen that first day. I really didn't expect the door to be open, but it was.

Inside, I found the layout as I remembered. Two desks at ninety degrees to each other, each topped by a dark computer flat screen, paperwork trays, and a telephone. More filing cabinets lined one wall with a small photocopier on top. Mundane, ordinary.

I hesitated. Working in close protection does not prepare you for searching an office, and I had no real idea what I was hoping to find. I almost turned back when a sheet of paper on the nearest desktop caught my eye and I canted my head to read it.

It was a list of names and addresses, maybe twenty of them, laid out in two columns in alphabetical order.

It could have been anything, from a Christmas card list to a roster for digging latrines, apart from the fact that half a dozen of the names had been crossed out. Last on the list was Thomas Witney. And there – just above him – his son, Liam. Both names had been struck through with a thin black line.

Quickly, I scanned the others, and something shimmied

down my spine as I recognised two more from Parker's briefing on former Fourth Day members. Both had met sudden, violent ends.

I picked up the sheet, carefully noting its exact position on the desktop, and shoved it under the lid of the photocopier, hitting the 'On' button as I did so.

The machine let out an eerie glow as it powered up. Heart pounding in the darkness, I glanced over at the small window, knowing that any passing security patrols would be instantly alerted. Shielding the light as much as I could, I ran off a single copy of the list and switched the machine off again. It took for ever.

I put the original back on the desktop, lining it up precisely, folding my still-warm copy and shoving it inside my underwear, where they wouldn't find it without a hell of a fight.

I slipped out of the admin office, had just reached the communal dining hall when I heard the unmistakable sound of the main outer door opening, and two sets of booted feet entering the lobby behind me.

I bolted across the dining hall on the balls of my feet. One door on the far side was slightly ajar. I dived through it, closing it fast and quiet behind me, and stood flattened against the wall, as if that would save me from discovery if they walked in.

Had they seen the light from the photocopier, or was this just a routine patrol?

Outside the door, I heard measured footsteps, indefinably male, growing louder as they approached. I shut my eyes, but there was no urgency in their even cadence. *Routine, then.*

I tried to control my ragged breathing as they passed and faded. It was hard to judge time but, maybe five interminable minutes later, I heard the steps retrace across the dining hall, and the outer door close behind them.

Only then did I relax enough to look around. I found myself in a small classroom with an old-fashioned blackboard and a jaunty alphabet frieze around it. Light came in from a line of windows set close to the ceiling along one wall. High enough for ventilation, but not for distraction. The room was probably used when the weather wasn't good enough for the kids to have their lessons outside.

Unless little Billy had ever been asked to write an essay entitled 'My Daddy', there was nothing for me here. But, just as I was about to slip out again, something on a nearby desktop caught my eye.

A folded newspaper and a pack of cigarettes.

The newspaper I could understand, but the cigarettes were something else again. Bane was big on mind, body and spirit and I hadn't seen or even smelt anyone here who smoked. It was not exactly the kind of teaching aid I expected anyone to use, unless they forced the kids to take a puff and throw up as aversion therapy at an early age.

I moved forwards, cautious. The pack was open and there was a loose cigarette lying next to it. Something about it tapped at the back of my mind. In the low light, I had to bend in close to see what it was. And the moment I did, realisation came down over me in a cold wash. In that instant, I knew exactly why it was there, and what kind of lessons were being taught in that classroom.

And I hoped to hell it wasn't to children.

CHAPTER THIRTY-SIX

The loose cigarette had a small hole pierced through it, and a piece of thread inserted at that point, almost exactly two inches from the tip.

Suggestive on its own, but hardly conclusive. Carefully, I held the pack in position and lifted the lid of the desk. Inside, I found several wooden clothes pegs, a small reel of thin copper wire, and a familiar-looking slim buff-coloured book. A reprint of an old 1960s US Army training manual called the *Improvised Munitions Handbook*.

I didn't need to leaf through the pages to find where the oddments from the desk fitted in.

A cigarette, in still air, burns at a rate of roughly seven minutes per inch, depending on the brand and conditions. What I was looking at here was the bare bones of a rudimentary time-delay fuse.

It was a simple enough improvised device. Wrap the copper wire around the jaws of the clothes peg and secure the thread around the legs to hold the jaws open. In this case, the ends of the peg had even been notched slightly, to ensure the thread sat firmly in place without slipping. Then all you have to do is light the cigarette and walk away. The cigarette burns until it reaches the thread, releases the peg, the jaws close, the copper wire completes the circuit and...

And what? Boom?

Was *that* what Bane was doing here? Sagar had seemed certain of it and now, it seemed, I had proof. The radical eco-group, Debacle, I recalled, had been disturbed setting an IED in Alaska on the night Liam Witney was killed. There had been nothing in the report about the type of device, but had bomb-making been one of the skills he'd acquired in Fourth Day?

I thought again of Ann's finesse with electronics, her delicate touch on a printed circuit board. I was pretty sure that she had the expertise to put together a much more sophisticated type of timer, so why this crude device?

As I carefully replaced the items, I noticed the folded newspaper had the lower right-hand quarter of the page on view. One story had been circled several times in pen.

I scanned it quickly, catching the gist. A visiting delegation from the Middle Eastern oil-producing countries was due to tour the Long Beach refineries the following week. A total protest by environmentalists was expected. Naturally, security was going to be tight.

That would explain the primitive approach...but to what end?

I shivered. Something just didn't feel right about this that I couldn't put my finger on. Maybe, I admitted to myself, I just didn't *want* it to be true.

And suddenly, all I felt was an anger, that Bane was throwing away the genuine good he could do here. While there was no denying that former Fourth Day members had sought out organisations like Debacle, many others left the cult to join nothing more daring than a gym.

And now, a number of them are dead.

I had a brief snapshot of the damning list of crossed-out names tucked inside my waistband. It could have just been a note of back pay no longer due.

Or it could have been a kill sheet.

Cautiously, I opened the door a crack, reassured myself I was alone, and headed back across the dining hall.

Just off it was a kitchen area, shut down and squared away for the night. There was a bug zapper high on the far wall, illuminating the space with an eerie blue glow.

By its light, I padded across the scrubbed tiles, noting the array of professional-looking cook's knives on display. Briefly, I considered taking one, rejecting the idea just as fast. Decent chefs tend to notice if the tools of their trade go missing.

Under the workstations at one side of the kitchen were rows of drawers. I pulled the first one open. It ran smooth on its runners, no squeaks or rattles, and I quickly found what I was after. Odds and ends of cutlery used for preparation rather than service. Quietly, I dug to the bottom of the tray for an old, cheap-looking table fork, flexed it experimentally in my hands. It bent easily. Perfect.

I slipped the fork into my pocket and paused in the doorway to check the kitchen appeared undisturbed, then moved back through the dining hall, out into the corridor again.

As I passed the admin office, I ducked inside, moving straight for the phone on the nearest desk. But, when I picked up the receiver there was no dialling tone, only silence. I cursed under my breath. Was Bane so paranoid that he cut the phones at night?

It occurred to me that, still out there apparently undiscovered, was a backup emergency kit containing a second cellphone. I hurried for the lobby, got as far as crossing to the outside door to grip the handle, then wavered.

Not because of concern about more guards. I'd passed my Escape and Evasion courses, and Fourth Day didn't have dedicated trackers or dogs. And not because, after this evening's discovery, I was worried that they might have found the second plastic box I'd buried and booby-trapped it, just for an eventuality like this.

But because, once I'd reported what I'd seen, I knew Epps would take over and set in motion a train of events over which I had no control. And whatever I might think about Bane's possible motives, he had shown a level of compassion, where Conrad Epps had none.

'You don't like letting go of control – on any level,' Bane had said. 'That scares you, doesn't it?'

Was that it?

Or was it just that I was nowhere near uncovering the truth about Billy's parentage? Without proof that he *was* Lorna Witney's grandson, we had no justification for taking him out of there before Epps descended on the place.

Maybe that threat alone would be enough to convince her to take the risk, but I'd seen first hand the state Maria was in. I'd lost a child I'd never had the chance to know. How much worse would it be for her?

I tightened my grip on the door handle, and slipped out into the blood-warm night.

CHAPTER THIRTY-SEVEN

A little before eight the following morning, I sat on the bench under the old juniper tree, surrounded by a small group of children. They ranged in age from probably about two or three, to around five. As I'd told Lorna Witney back in Scotland, I never was very good at judging ages.

Beside me was Ann. She'd told me over breakfast that she'd taken over Thomas Witney's teaching duties and asked, apparently without guile, if I'd help her with her class.

I agreed, although not without trepidation. It was a good opportunity to observe Maria's son and have a semi-legitimate reason to ask about him, but I was not entirely comfortable with kids. Like horses, they could instinctively tell if you were uneasy around them, enough to take gleeful advantage wherever possible.

Ann was telling the children a story, something about pirates and a treasure trove. She had a wonderful storyteller's voice, soft and rhythmic, as if reciting an old poem rather than making it up as she went along. Completely unselfconscious, she put all of herself into the tale, her manner easy and unforced.

The children obviously adored her. She seemed to know immediately how much free rein to allow the more boisterous without them getting out of hand, and how much gentle coaxing was needed for the shy to blossom.

My input was minimal at best. I caught the odd little sideways glance, when they thought I wasn't looking, wary curiosity in their faces. Maybe my fading black eye had something to do with that, or maybe they'd seen too many bruises for it to make any difference.

Billy sat cross-legged on the ground, front and centre. I kept covert watch, trying to detect Liam's bone structure behind Maria's Latin influence, largely without success.

Sipping from my bottle of water, I stared across the dusty compound, where a pair of Fourth Day guards returned from another patrol. One was the Brit ex-Para, Nu. As he and the other man ambled past, Nu raised a hand from the stock of his M16, formed a gun with his forefinger and thumb, and shot me with it, a cheery grin on his face.

There was something far too knowing about the gesture and I realised, in that instant, they'd been waiting for me to venture out last night.

So, it had been another test, after all.

I'd only made it as far as the open doorway before my doubts got the better of me. It had all been too easy, moving through the darkened building. The deserted rooms, the unlocked doors. The conveniently placed pack of cigarettes with that telltale thread so casually displayed, the helpfully folded newspaper, the list of names.

I'd stood for a minute or so, staring up at a clear skyful of stars glittering above me. And then I'd turned around and walked inside, locking the door to my room behind me and slipping the key back between the pages of the Salinger.

But just before I climbed into bed, I'd taken my stolen table fork and used one of the sturdy legs of the bed as a makeshift vice to bend it until the handle fitted snugly over my fist and the tines splayed outwards like claws. Knowing I had it, hidden within easy reach under my pillow, made me feel a little less vulnerable. Makeshift as a prison shank, it would open up someone's face, if the need arose, but be hard even for an expert to take away from me.

And there seemed to be no shortage of experts in Fourth Day. This morning's t'ai chi ch'uan class was now being followed by straightforward self-defence, with Yancy in charge.

He was good, I saw. Knew the moves and how best to instil them, even if he did like to hold his 'victims' a little too tightly, a little too long. Maybe he just liked showing off his bulging biceps as he demonstrated a rear chokehold on one woman, clasping her body hard against his. I mentally ran through the ways I could have disabled him in the time he took to explain the principle.

Yancy caught my stare and released her. The woman stumbled away from him, flushed, rubbing her neck.

'Hey, Charlie,' he called across. 'Wanna come show us how you Brits do it?'

I gave a non-committal smile, indicating the class. 'Maybe next time.'

He didn't answer, but his face called me chicken.

Now, Ann finished her story and sent the children off to find some small object from the compound that had featured in it. 'Back here in fifteen minutes,' she said with mock sternness, watching them scatter with an indulgent smile.

Good job she didn't set me the same task, because I hadn't been paying enough attention to be sure of completing it.

'You're very good with them,' I said. 'Were you a teacher?'

'Me? Oh no, I never finished high school.' She laughed, wry. 'Too busy having kids of my own by then. So, I guess you could say I've had a lot of practice. But I'm a poor substitute for Thomas – he had the gift.' Her voice apparently held no reproof. 'They miss him.'

'Well, he was a teacher by profession,' I said, neutral.

'He was the best of us,' she said, fierce now, covering her sadness. 'He didn't deserve any of it.'

I couldn't quite tell if she meant his life, abduction, or death. 'Very few people get what they deserve.'

She turned, head on one side. 'So, what do *you* deserve, Charlie?'

'I don't know.' I shrugged. 'It's one of the things I was hoping to find out here.'

Her focus left me and ranged out across the compound, watching the children as they ran haphazardly about the place in their quest.

'Randall Bane won't give you answers,' she said at last. 'He'll just help you ask yourself the right questions. Help you see what's important to you.'

'Is that why Thomas stayed?'

Was it my imagination, or did she glance towards Billy? She smiled. 'When you've been here long enough,' she said, 'you'll understand.'

I would have pushed, but Billy came sidling back then, with a chubby little girl of a similar age. He tugged at Ann's skirt.

'Hello,' Ann said gently. 'And what have you found?'

The children whispered together for a moment, then Billy solemnly presented her with a flat grey pebble, which she took carefully and examined in the sun. 'Hmm, is this the pirate's buried treasure?'

The boy stopped trying to cram what appeared to be his entire grubby fist into his mouth and nodded. The girl was flapping her skirt up and down, exposing cotton knickers covered in cartoon seahorses.

To my consternation, Ann turned to me. 'What do you think, Charlie?' she asked, handing over the pebble. 'Is it treasure?'

For a moment, I floundered, smoothing my thumb across the surface. My hands were damp with condensation from the water bottle, leaving a bright smear across the surface of the stone.

I uncapped the bottle and splashed water onto the pebble. At once, the drab grey flourished into a host of colours. I handed the wet stone back to Billy. He and the girl stared at it, apparently dumbfounded by the transformation.

'*Now* it looks like treasure.'

Billy looked up at the sound of my voice, squinting into the light, and then his face slowly crumpled with disappointment. He let the pebble drop into the dust at my feet. Then he and his silent companion turned and ran away on stumpy little legs. I'd taken beatings that hurt less.

'O...K,' I said, rueful. 'I guess *that* was the wrong answer.'

Ann leant across, put her hand on mine. Her skin was thin and dry, like an old lady's. 'Don't be upset,' she said placidly. 'Billy can be a strange child. His mother, well, she's been through difficult times.'

I watched the boy, squatting in the dust, searching for another stone that was as perfectly dull as the first, before I'd gone and ruined it for him.

'What happened to Billy's father?' I asked, as casually as I could manage.

Ann didn't answer right away, and when she did, her voice was guarded. 'He's gone,' she said, which could have meant anything from no longer with Fourth Day, to six feet under.

'He walked out on them?' I pressed.

Ann quietly folded in on herself. 'Not quite, honey,' she said. 'Some things are just not meant to be, that's all.'

The silence yawned like a cat. I picked up the rapidly drying stone, turned it in my hands. 'I guess this proves I'm not cut out for parenthood.'

'You would have managed fine,' Ann said. When I glanced at her sharply, she added, 'Motherhood isn't something they measure you up for. It just arrives, and you make it fit, best you can.'

I opened my mouth to ask how she could tell, then closed it again. She was just one of those women who *knew*. 'Well, looks like I won't be finding that one out.'

'You're young,' she said, with irritating complacency. 'There's still time.'

'Not for me.'

Before she could refute that, if she'd a mind to, Maria stepped out of the main building. She headed towards us, nervous as a fat rabbit in hawk country, halting a metre or so away.

'Hello, Maria,' Ann said easily. 'Billy's over there, see? Searching for hidden treasure.'

Maria shook her head. 'I know he's safe with you.' Her gaze met mine, the first deliberate direct eye contact she'd made with me. 'I came for Charlie,' she mumbled. 'He says it's time.'

Ann flicked a quick look in my direction and nodded, almost to herself.

'Time for what?' I queried.

'You'll find out soon enough,' Ann said. 'Go, child, and don't look so anxious.'

It was difficult to tell which of us she was speaking to.

CHAPTER THIRTY-EIGHT

Maria led me through the building without speaking. When we reached Bane's study she knocked, waiting dutifully until invited to enter.

Randall Bane came out from behind his desk to greet us. He was wearing a cream linen shirt hanging loose over pale trousers, and his feet were bare. They were tanned and long, almost slender.

Bane put his hands on Maria's upper arms, turning her into the light to stare down into her face, his own eyes hooded.

'Are you ready?' he asked gently.

Her answering smile was shy, almost tremulous. 'I think so.'

She had an eagerness to please that tightened all the muscles across my stomach. I let my gaze flit around the room, identified a dozen items I could use to kill him if he made a move on either of us. When I glanced back, Bane was watching me with something close to amusement.

'Tell me, Charlie, do you ever tire of always expecting the worst of people?'

'Frequently,' I bit out, 'but it has the advantage that I'm rarely disappointed by them.'

He regarded me for a moment. Once again, I had the unnerving impression that he could see straight into the back of my mind. 'It means you are also often disappointed by yourself.'

He let go of Maria and stepped back, spread an arm. 'Come.' An invitation with the hint of an order beneath it.

He moved across to another doorway in the far corner of the room. Without hesitation, Maria followed and, more warily, I did, too. I found myself in another corridor, windowed on one side, doorways on the other. We passed a tiled bathroom, a small kitchen area – Bane's private quarters.

And I realised that Bane was right. I was thoroughly disappointed for trusting him, for believing he was different, when all the time he was leading up to this. Cursing inwardly, I told myself it was just fear and adrenaline that had pumped up my heart rate and evaporated every drop of saliva on my tongue.

Bane reached the far end of the corridor. He paused, looked back at me with a smile that made the roots of my hair prickle, as if he knew exactly what I was thinking, feeling. Then he opened the door and went through.

On the other side, I found myself back in the ripening heat of the day, standing next to a low open-fronted building that had once been intended for horses. Now it housed vehicles, keeping them out of direct sunlight. One was an ugly four-door Chevrolet with the bonnet open. Two men I vaguely recognised from breakfast were leaning into the dusty engine bay.

They looked up as we approached, nodded to Bane and Maria, stared at me. I glanced at what they were doing, recognised polished engine cam covers and the open impeller housing of a turbocharger. I'm no expert on cars, but that motor did not look factory in such an old, sedate body. So, either this was another example of Fourth Day's make-do-and-mend ethos, or they were deliberately creating a street sleeper. For a quick getaway, perhaps?

Sensing my interest, one of the men wiped his hands on a rag sticking out of his back pocket and casually reached up to pull the Chevrolet's bonnet closed. I offered him my best clueless girlie smile. If his answering scowl was anything to go by, he wasn't convinced.

Next to the Chevy, along with four dust-filmed Kawasaki quad bikes, was an open Jeep. The Jeep's weathered seats clearly showed that the soft top was never raised – if one was fitted in the first place.

Bane rested a hand on the rollover bar. 'You're all set.'

'Set for what, exactly?' I asked as Maria climbed into the driver's seat.

'For your journey.'

'Hang on a minute,' I said, uneasy now. 'I'm not going anywhere.'

'And that is part of your problem.'

'I—'

It was Maria who cut across me, her voice unexpectedly strong. 'The greatest journey anyone can make,' she said, fastening her seat belt, 'is inside their own head.'

Bane smiled at her, the first full-blown smile I'd seen him crack. It transported his features back to a time when he might have been carefree. There was something strong between them, I realised. Just for a second I wondered if *he* was the father of Maria's child. I tried not to think about the age gap between them.

The back of the Jeep, I saw, was loaded with containers of water, food, camping equipment. 'So why does this inner journey need so much outer gear?'

Bane took pity on me. 'Everyone who comes here is required to spend time in the wilderness,' he said. 'Time away from the distractions of the community, to listen to their own thoughts and discover what's important to them. To think about where they want to focus their life.' He nodded towards the Jeep. 'Maria is simply there to keep you out of trouble for the first night, to be your guide.'

'But I've only been here a few days,' I said blankly. *Most of them in splendid isolation.* 'What makes you think I'm ready for this?' Besides, whatever was happening inside Fourth Day was happening *here*, not in the middle of nowhere. This felt suspiciously like Bane was shunting me off into the sidelines.

He stared at me for a moment longer. 'You've always been ready.' When still I hesitated, he added, 'And what's a few more days, if it helps you to understand where your life has been, and where it's going?'

Reluctantly, I swung myself up into the passenger seat. Maria smiled at me for the first time, as if grateful for my acquiescence. She cranked the engine. Bane stepped back with a little dip of his head. The last glimpse I caught of him was reflected motionless in the door mirror, framed by swirling eddies of dust.

* * *

We drove for what seemed like a long time. Far enough that it would have taken half a day to hike back on foot. Further out, the terrain became more ragged. Maria drove with an easy competence I hadn't been expecting, not clinging to the steering wheel as the vehicle scrambled over the rough ground. She crouched forwards, animated by the challenge. The frightened girl Sean and I had seen running from the compound might have never existed.

'You're good at this,' I said after a while.

'I grew up on the Baja peninsula,' she said, not taking her eyes off the way ahead. 'We did a lot of four-wheeling down there.'

I wedged myself sideways in my seat, one hand braced on the dashboard. I still had a lot of bruises, and the ride quality did little for them. 'How long have you been with Fourth Day?'

'A while.' She flicked me a quick sideways look from behind her fringe. 'I came and went again,' she said then, something wistful in her voice. 'It took me too long to realise I belonged here.'

'Is that why you joined – to find somewhere you felt you belonged?'

She shook her head. 'My mother died when I was seventeen,' she said. 'Without her it all seemed...pointless.' The corner of her mouth curved upwards. 'I found family here – for me and for Billy.'

Ah!

'What about Billy's father?'

The smile blinked out. 'He's gone,' she said. It seemed to be the company line on the subject.

'It must have been hard, raising Billy alone,' I said carefully. 'What happened?'

'It hasn't been easy,' Maria said stiffly. 'Billy can be awkward, moody. After he was born I...did not always love him as I should.' Her voice trailed off and she shrugged. It didn't take a genius to work out she had suffered from post-natal depression. Had that developed into other disorders? 'But here, with Randall's people, we are not alone.'

'Ann told me Thomas was very good with the children,' I said, trying another approach to break through the distance in her voice, but that only increased her agitation.

'He left,' she muttered. 'He promised me he wouldn't go, but he never even said goodbye.'

'He didn't have a choice, Maria,' I said quietly, trying to keep the self-recrimination out of my voice.

But she didn't hear me. 'They all leave,' she said, almost to herself. 'They say they won't, but they do. As soon as you allow yourself to love someone, they go. They leave you and they don't come back.'

I winced as the Jeep bounced over another rock, graunching the front chassis cross member as it hit, and almost jerking the wheel right out of Maria's hands. Maybe this was one conversation I should have saved for later.

But I knew I didn't have much time and might not get another chance like this. I took a breath.

'Did Billy's father abandon you, or didn't he have a choice, either?'

She took so long to respond that I didn't think she was going to. We battered on, but her flair, her enjoyment was gone, turning it into a gritted-teeth endurance ride.

'I never wanted him to go,' she said at last, her voice brimming with pain and anger.

Even then, I couldn't leave it. 'Go where?' I demanded. 'With Debacle?'

Maria's foot lurched off the throttle and the Jeep rolled slowly to a halt. Soundlessly, her shoulders began to shake until great sobs wracked her body.

I put my hand on her arm. It took a moment before she even realised it was there.

She sat up, tried to scrub away the tears with the heel of her hand. 'We need to keep going. Randall's relying on me.'

'Maria,' I said gently. 'We're in the middle of nowhere. Can't you stop here? Won't this do?'

She looked around as if seeing the landscape for the first time, dazed. 'OK,' she said. 'This place is as good as any.'

We set up camp in a sheltered area behind a rocky outcrop, working quickly to unload the Jeep and put up our tents. Or rather, Maria put up the tents, which seemed to involve emptying them out of their bags and letting go of them, whereupon they sprang to full-size shape like a magician's stage prop. I, meanwhile, gathered a dozen large stones into a rough circle to make a fire pit.

My attempts to re-engage Maria in conversation were largely unsuccessful.

'You are supposed to be listening to yourself,' she told me stiffly. 'I am not here.'

I shrugged, climbing onto the nearest rock, which stood about four metres high, its surface abraded smooth by wind and time. The compound had disappeared from view, with nothing but scrub and distant mountains, as far as the eye could see.

'How far does the cult land stretch?' I called down to Maria.

She stared up, shading her eyes with one hand. 'We are not a cult,' she said, sounding defensive.

'O...K,' I agreed. 'How far does *Fourth Day's* land stretch?'

'I don't know – many miles,' she said. 'Thousands of acres. Randall's been buying it up for years, I think.' Her voice was steady now. When I slithered down the rock, though, she was still frowning. 'It's important, Charlie,' she said. 'We're not some bunch of religious wackos. We're a community, one that is strong because we stay together and we learn from one another. Haven't you realised that by now?'

I touched a finger to the lingering bruise around my eye. 'Oh, I don't think you're a bunch of religious wackos, Maria,' I said. 'As for learning from each other, I've been wondering about that. I've been wondering where a schoolteacher like Thomas Witney learnt all about martial arts and the uses of psychoactive drugs. Did Bane teach him that?'

'Randall?' Maria repeated, her voice catching. 'Of course not! Whatever Thomas learned was to protect us. He—' She broke off abruptly, aware she'd said more than she'd been intending to. More than she should.

'Protect you from what?' I persisted, but she backed away, both hands up as if to warn me off. I took a step after her. 'Maria—'

'From trouble. From outsiders!' She glared at me, eyes very bright. 'From people like you!'

CHAPTER THIRTY-NINE

It was dark. I lay on top of the rock that sheltered our little camp, staring up at the stars again. The rock was curved on top, and I was just over the crown of it, so the campfire didn't interfere with my night vision. All I could see of it was a reflected orange glow and the occasional dying ember floating upwards on the rising air. It was pleasant enough not to need a jacket, and mine was rolled, pillowing my head.

Idly, I picked out the curve of the Plough above me, the bright W of Cassiopeia overlaying the misty swirl of the Milky Way. And between them, as if signposted, the Pole Star.

I'd climbed up there after Maria had zipped herself pointedly into her tent for the night, and I'd lain long enough to see the star map rotate slightly in the heavens, as it would do regardless of my existence or anyone else's. Lying on my back on a still-warm rock in the middle of nowhere, I was overwhelmed by my own insignificance.

Perhaps that was what Bane had in mind.

My thoughts returned to Maria, apparently asleep in her tent. She had not spoken much after her outburst. I'd tried to draw her out again, but we'd moved warily around each other within the confines of the camp, cooking and eating and squaring away with minimal communication.

Afterwards, she'd walked out into the golden sunset with just a brusque order to stay put. I ignored her, of course, following at a careful distance. Eventually, Maria halted, looked around guiltily, and pulled a small cellphone from her pocket. I'd edged close enough to hear her opening words.

'Ann? It's Maria. Yes, I know I'm not supposed to... Look, I just wanted to check Billy went to bed OK... You know how he can be sometimes...' Her voice trailed off, as if all out of excuses.

Slowly, carefully, I'd backed away. By the time she'd returned, I was sitting near the fire, staring into the flames. So, Maria had brought a cellphone with her, which sounded like it was against the rules, just so she could check on her son. She'd learnt to love him. Would I have done the same?

And then, in the darkness, I heard a quiet crackle of noise below me. I lifted my head, trying to focus on the sound. There were all kinds of large wild animals out here, I knew, from coyotes to bobcats to black bears. I didn't know much about their habits, but I didn't fancy becoming light supper for any of them.

But when I looked down, the predator who crept towards our campsite was far more dangerous – human.

The figure of a man passed so close below me, I could have reached down and touched the top of his head. In the weak moonlight, I made out night vision goggles covering his eyes, covert clothing.

I flattened against the warm stone until he'd passed, then rolled silently onto my stomach and low-crawled to the crown of the rock on my elbows and toes, moving one limb at a time, body suspended to reduce any possible scrape of sound.

As he neared our damped-down campfire, the intruder lifted the NV goggles up onto his forehead. He turned a slow circle, checking, keeping his awareness open, and I got my first look at his face.

It wasn't really a surprise to recognise John Nu. I'd already subconsciously placed the size and the shape of him. And you don't forget the way a man moves. Still, I waited. Had Bane sent him to check on us?

I waited longer than I should have to find out, letting him advance, soft-footed, into the camp, careful not to silhouette himself between the tents and the fire. He stopped again, cocked his head to listen for sign of occupation.

From inside Maria's tent, I heard a faint rustle as she shifted in her sleep. Nu heard it, too. He paused as if to confirm it, or to steel himself. I wasn't sure which.

Then he reached for something at his side and started to bring his right arm up. In the dancing flames' reflection, the outline of the gun was starkly familiar.

Scrabbling for compression, I launched myself off the top of the rock and landed heavy on his back, just as he took up the tension on the trigger. Reacting rather than acting, I was a fraction slow.

His arm lurched, hand tightening reflexively. The brutal sound of the gun discharging catapulted away into the distant darkness, hard and hot and bright. The shot went high, punching a small, seemingly trivial hole through the fabric of the tent above where Maria lay sleeping.

The momentum of my attack took Nu down to his knees. I wedged my right forearm into the nape of his neck and looped my left around his throat, felt his muscles bunch to counter.

If I'd hoped to win myself a second or so to complete the lock, Nu disappointed me. He instantly whipped the gun back and pulled the trigger twice more in quick succession, no panic, no hesitation. I jerked my head sideways instinctively, the hearing in one ear exploding into numbness by the proximity of the blasts. The pressure wave flattened my hair, particles from the cordite stinging the side of my head, vision buzzing. *Shit!*

Dazed, I fell backwards, landing with a whump in the sandy soil. Nu spun, crouched, swinging the gun round as he came. I pivoted onto my hip and kicked his left knee out from under him, aiming low under the patella and driving the kneecap up and back with the sole of my foot.

Nu grunted, but kept the gun up as he went down. I shifted and sprang, landing sprawled along the length of him, driving my own knee into his solar plexus, bringing the other up hard into his groin. Air gushed out of him in a fast hiss as he curled around the blows. And as his head came into range, I slammed my elbow round into his temple, knew it was a solid connection by the way his head snapped to the side.

Still Nu hadn't let go of the gun. I asked myself, afterwards, if it would have made a difference if he had. He was more or less out of it, certainly groggy, but a dogged survival instinct had him still struggling to aim.

I lurched to my feet and lashed out towards his head, my booted foot cracking hard against his jaw. He splayed backwards, the gun finally spilling from nerveless fingers. His skull bounced off the ground with a dull, wet thump.

Balance gone, I staggered over and snatched up the gun, recognising it as a SIG that was almost undoubtedly my own. I shoved the gun into the leg pocket of my trousers, almost falling.

The ringing in my ears wouldn't clear. It had become high-pitched, erratic, and I realised that Maria was out of her tent, in a skinny top and shorts, eyes wild, and she was screaming on and on, eyes fixed on Nu's body.

The rise and fall of his ribcage told me he was still breathing, if shallowly. But the earth around his head was turning slowly dark, and that was very bad news.

'Maria!' She jerked, and I realised I was shouting. 'We need a medic. Where's your phone?'

She was starting to shiver now and didn't respond, didn't take her eyes off him. I tottered across and grabbed her arms, gave her a shake.

'Is he dead?' Her face was white, eyes huge. 'Is he dead?'

'No,' I said, ignoring the voice in my head that told me I'd fractured his skull. 'But he will be if we don't get him to a hospital. Listen to me, Maria! Where's your phone?'

I took the flicker of her eyes as permission to scramble into her tent, quickly locating last night's clothes. I dug in the pockets until my hand closed over the shape of the phone in the gloom. Above me, there were two holes in the canvas walls, on opposite sides, where the round had penetrated and continued on, harmlessly, into the night.

I backed out of the tent again, stabbed my thumb on the power button for the phone and cursed its seemingly interminable start-up routine.

'He's shot,' Maria murmured. When I glanced across, she still hadn't taken her eyes away from Nu.

'Nobody's been shot. He missed,' I snapped. Aware of a tickle at the side of my neck, I dabbed a hand to it. My fingers came away greasy with blood, muttered, 'Not by much, but he missed.'

'He's shot,' Maria repeated, mumbling. 'I saw the blood. I saw him fall. I saw...'

Her voice drifted off and I realised from the shock-bound stare that whatever she was seeing, it wasn't here and now.

'Who, Maria?' I asked, more gently now, although part of me already knew the answer. 'Who did you see?'

Her head turned in my direction, but her streaming eyes were a long way from me. 'Liam,' she said.

CHAPTER FORTY

'When Maria and Liam left here five years ago, they joined Debacle together,' Randall Bane said. 'She didn't tell me what she planned to do.'

'Would you have tried to talk her out of it?' I asked dryly. 'I thought you encouraged everyone to find their own path?'

'I do.' For a moment his eyes were very dark and very difficult to read. 'But Debacle was Liam's choice, not Maria's. She went only to be with him.'

'I see.'

'Do you?' There was a hint of bitterness in his voice that I'd never heard there before. 'Afterwards...she was never quite the same again.'

'She witnessed his death, didn't she?' I said. 'That would be enough to break anybody.'

'Perhaps.' He glanced at me again, fathomless and brooding. 'It would not have broken you.'

I was sitting on the folded-down tailgate of a big Ford crew cab pickup truck, which had brought Bane out to the campsite, together with Yancy and a couple of the other security men.

They'd found me keeping a watch over the still-unconscious Nu. Maria had closed down into shock by the time they arrived. I'd wrapped her in blankets and stayed close, but she hadn't spoken again, just sat silently rocking herself into a protective trance.

Nu hadn't moved. I'd checked his airway and his pulse, which was a steady tremble in his veins. There was a protruding rock beneath his skull and he'd landed on it hard enough to break the skin, and the bone beneath. The fluid coming from his ears – not a good sign – told me he was beyond my medical abilities, so I'd left him where he'd fallen.

About an hour after my 911 call, I'd heard the first approaching vehicle and assumed it must be the paramedics, but stayed put. Our fire was the only light showing out here, so they didn't need additional guidance from me. I left the SIG in my leg pocket, albeit with the flap open.

It was my gun. Not just the same make and model, but my personal weapon. I didn't need to check the serial number. I'd know it anywhere. The one I'd buried on the way into Fourth Day and had last seen on the desk in Bane's study. I could hazard a pretty good guess at Nu's plan. Shoot Maria first, then suicide me and leave the SIG in my own dead hand.

What I didn't know was why.

But when the vehicle engine finally stopped and I heard doors slam, it was Bane who strode into the camp, followed by Yancy and the others, fanning out, M16s ready.

Bane faltered, taking in Maria's almost catatonic state

and Nu's immobile body. Yancy shouldered his weapon and bent over Nu.

'I thought this was supposed to be quality alone-time,' I said, aware my voice was still too loud and there was a vicious throbbing in my ears. 'It's turning into quite a party.'

'One of the patrols heard gunshots,' Bane dismissed, face satanic in the firelight. 'What happened here?'

I nodded towards Nu. 'Your boy there decided to use us for target practice.'

Yancy twisted. 'He's alive,' he said, eyes flicking over me. 'Hurt bad, though.'

'Yeah, well, he had it coming.' Still unsteady, I got to my feet, vibrating with tiredness as the adrenaline hangover kicked in. The blood had dried on my neck and was starting to itch. 'I can understand you wanting rid of me, Bane, but what the hell has Maria done to you?'

Bane didn't answer immediately. I saw his gaze range round the campsite, taking it all in. He spotted the bullet hole in Maria's tent, so either he was sharp, or he'd devised the plan and was just checking how far Nu had managed to get before being so unexpectedly thwarted.

'Maria is an innocent,' he said at last. 'I have no idea why John would try to harm her, as you say.'

'Well, think harder.'

Bane fell silent. Eventually, he glanced at Yancy. 'Tyrone, please take Maria out of here.'

'She stays.' I held up the cellphone I'd taken from Maria. 'I've already called this in. Trying to cover up for her will only make it worse when the cops interview Nu...*if* he ever comes round, of course. He landed with quite a crack.'

Yancy's eyes flicked over Nu. 'I knew this Brit bastard was up to something,' he muttered.

Bane silenced him with a single look. 'What happened?' he asked again, something subdued about him.

'A convenient opportunity for you,' I said. 'Or an engineered one – I'm not sure which. A chance to get rid of two liabilities at the same time.'

'And in what way, exactly, might you both be considered liabilities?'

'Well, I've seen things I really shouldn't have done,' I said, glancing at Yancy, who'd straightened and moved closer. I deliberately ignored him, skimmed my eyes over Maria's huddled figure instead. 'And her because people are closing in on you, Bane. Heavy people, and she's just too delicate to hold the line. What are you afraid she might tell them about you?'

'Not everyone is as resilient as you are, Charlie,' he said, evasive, 'but if you think I'd sanction something like this, you are gravely mistaken. I have always tried to protect Maria.'

'I saw her run from you, scared, days before we took Witney,' I said flatly. 'Now you send the pair of us out here, prepped as sacrificial lambs. Nu was even using *my* gun, just to make it look good.' I fished the SIG out of my pocket and displayed it loosely, partly to show it to him, and partly to disguise the fact that I was reaching for it at all.

'Bastard,' Yancy repeated. He swung round and glared at the supine figure, shifting his weight so that for a moment I thought he meant to put the boot in.

As for Bane, something flashed through his face, emphasized by the light from the fire. Anger and sorrow.

Suddenly, I realised this was as much a shock to him as it had been to me. Whatever Nu had been up to, he'd done it without Bane's blessing. And possibly without Yancy's knowledge.

And that...changed things.

'I sent Maria out here as your guide because I thought she could learn something from you, not the other way around,' Bane admitted. 'I hoped she would absorb something of that resilience I mentioned. Something of your strength.'

'Why?'

Those eyes pierced me again. 'Because I spend my life trying to help people, but my biggest regret has always been that I seem unable to help the one person who means most to me – my own daughter.'

CHAPTER FORTY-ONE

The police and paramedics arrived at the same time, and from then on the activity became frenetic. I let the uniforms take away my SIG with gloved hands, dropping it into an evidence bag. This was getting to be a habit.

The paramedics quickly decided to airlift Nu to the nearest trauma centre. They wanted to take Maria in as well, but I pointed out that transporting the victim to the same hospital as the man who'd tried to kill her might not be good for her state of mind. Bane intervened. I don't know what he said to them, but eventually they entrusted a sedated Maria to his care. He left with her, in the big pickup, shortly afterwards.

The female paramedic who checked me over told me I'd been lucky, and that my hearing should recover in a day or two. It wasn't the first time I'd experienced gunshots at close proximity, but the muffled whine was starting to annoy. I hedged when she asked careful questions about my residual black eye.

By the time the air ambulance helicopter lifted off with

Nu on board, the sky was lightening towards another mild day.

Yancy appeared at my elbow. 'I'm gonna drive you back to the compound in the Jeep,' he told me. 'There's a Detective Gardner waiting on you there.'

'Oh, goody,' I murmured. Still, at least I hadn't shot anyone this time, although Nu might have been better off if I had.

Yancy was not as good an off-road driver as Maria, so the first part of the ride was a lot rougher, leaving very little room for conversation. That might have been the idea.

As we neared habitation, however, the terrain smoothed out and I was finally able to ask, 'So, who's Nu working for?'

Yancy shrugged, eyes on the track ahead. 'Don't know. But he's been acting kinda strange lately.' His eyes flicked sideways. 'He was harder on you than he had reason to. Thought it was because of what you are, but now?' He shrugged again, an annoyed twitch. 'Who knows how that mother's mind works.'

We reached the barn behind Bane's quarters and Yancy swung the Jeep back into its allotted bay. The sun was rising faster now, the light changing every minute, warmth seeping through.

As we climbed down, Bane himself appeared through the same doorway Maria and I had used the day before.

'How's she doing?' Yancy asked immediately.

'Maria's sleeping.'

Yancy picked his M16 off the back seat of the Jeep and cradled it meaningfully. 'I'll go watch over her,' he said. He nodded briefly, and strode away, head hunched into his sizeable shoulders, as though he took the attempt on the girl as a personal affront.

Knowing this might be my last chance, I put a hand on Bane's arm as he turned away.

'Was Liam Billy's father?' I asked, and felt him tense momentarily under my fingers, then relax.

'Of course not,' he said, so blandly I couldn't distinguish truth from lie. 'This way.'

He led me back into the building and along the corridor to his study. When he opened the door and ushered me through with a gentle hand at the small of my back, Detective Gardner was sitting casually behind Bane's desk. She was in jeans and a linen jacket today, the hem hooked back to show the gun on her hip.

Another plain-clothes man stood by one of the bookcases, head tilted to read the titles. He was wearing a sober suit with a police shield tucked into his belt. He turned as we came in and I faltered at his grim expression.

'Thank you, Mr Bane,' Gardner said. 'We'll take it from here.'

Was it deliberate that her words were a direct echo of Conrad Epps, that day on the canyon road in Calabasas, or were they too throwaway to have hidden meaning?

Bane considered for a moment, as if her order was a request, then turned to me, almost solicitous. 'Charlie?'

'I'm fine,' I said, zeroed on Gardner. 'Let's just get this done, shall we?'

Bane's fingers hooked under my chin, snapping my eyes to his. He stared down into them for a long searching moment before releasing me, apparently satisfied.

'All right, Detective,' he said, stepping back. 'Please

remember that Miss Fox has been through an ordeal last night, and treat her accordingly.'

'We'll be gentle with her,' Gardner promised coldly.

Bane nodded shortly and went out, closing the door behind him. Out of the corner of my eye I saw Gardner's companion move away from the bookcase, swing to face me. I turned my head and he pinned me with a near-black gaze.

'Hello, Miss *Fox*,' Sean said softly. 'Abandoned your cover pretty quickly, didn't you?'

'It was already hopelessly compromised.' I glanced at Gardner again, but she seemed content to let Sean do the talking for now, watching us like we were playing a chess final. 'Bane knew exactly who I was, the day after I arrived. They knew I'd brought an emergency kit, and could work out where to look for it. Either Epps hasn't plugged that leak, or Parker has one of his own.'

Sean said nothing. I swallowed, added, 'And Nu recognised me.' My lips twisted. 'Turns out he applied for Special Forces – was part of the intake after mine. He knew all about me.'

Sean frowned. 'I don't remember him.'

'He washed out,' I said, 'but he remembered you.'

Sean prowled round in front of me, narrowed eyes raking my face and lingering, as I knew they would, on the stubborn bruise around my eye. For a long moment, neither of us spoke. He was waiting for an explanation. I couldn't find one that wasn't far too defensive.

At last, it was Gardner who said, in that world-weary cop's tone, 'So, you gonna tell us what happened?' And I heard the unspoken *this time* curl around the end of her question.

I took a breath and ran through the events of the night, quick and concise. Sean leant against the edge of Bane's desk and crossed his arms while I spoke, shutting me out. I tried to blank the gesture, kept my voice calm and level as I recounted Nu's ambush, Yancy's anger, and Bane's revelation about Maria.

'It's pretty clear that *she* was the one – not Dexter – who witnessed Liam Witney's death in Alaska,' I finished.

'So, why didn't she come forward?' Gardner asked.

'Because she'd fall to pieces under questioning,' I said. 'You didn't see her after the shooting last night. She's an emotional train wreck. I'm not surprised Bane wants to protect her.'

Witney had tried to do the same thing, too, I recalled. Maybe he'd coaxed the story from Maria, but realised there was no way he could ever ask her to testify. Was that why he stayed close – a last link to his dead son?

'And you definitely don't think Nu was following Bane's orders to get rid of the pair of you?' Sean said. 'An emotionally unstable daughter might be enough of a handicap...?

I shook my head, aware only of the annoying buzz still present at the periphery of my hearing range, of a dragging tiredness. 'No way.'

He and Gardner exchanged another silent glance, but I didn't catch the meaning. It was like being excluded from a private conversation in a public place.

'It's very unfortunate that Nu should be...incapacitated at this time,' Gardner said then, neutral. 'I was planning on coming out here today to question him about the kidnapping and murder of Thomas Witney.'

'What?'

'We got security tapes from the office building across the street, puts him at the motel on Sunset right about the time Witney was getting his brains blown out.'

'I thought Epps took everything and you'd been told to lay off.'

'So I'm stubborn – sue me.' She shrugged. 'Tape quality was poor, but the lab cleaned it up some. This is not like on TV – they got a constant backlog, and we've only just gotten the tape back,' Gardner said. 'So it's sure convenient for Bane that suddenly Nu can't answer questions.'

'Wait a minute. You think...?' I shook my head. 'Actually, I don't know what the hell you think!'

'We know Witney was taken by someone he trusted,' Sean said. 'Otherwise, they wouldn't have uncuffed him. He thought he was being rescued – until it was too late.'

'We think we can prove Nu's involved,' Gardner said. 'Question is, was Bane pulling his strings?'

I had a sudden flash of images – the kill list of ex-members now safely hidden inside the hollow leg of the bed in my room, of the circled newspaper story, the training manual and the doctored cigarette. And I knew I should tell Sean all this, but I couldn't shake the feeling there was something *off* about the whole thing.

Like someone was pulling *my* strings.

'No,' I said.

Sean let his breath out fast. 'You're covering for him, Charlie. Why?'

'I just don't believe Bane is the big villain he's being painted, all right?' I rubbed a hand across my face. 'Epps thinks he's Bin Laden by another name, and Sagar told me all kinds of horror stories about what goes on in here. So far, I've seen no evidence to support any of it.'

Sean jerked upright, crossed to me in a couple of long strides and grabbed my arms before I could react, spinning me round. If I hadn't been running on no sleep, I might even have countered him in time. But I didn't.

He propelled me forwards, almost roughly, fingers biting, until I was in line with a mirror on the far wall. In it I saw a ragged figure with slightly singed hair and a marked face. The remains of the black eye were probably at their most colourful, I realised, although the tenderness had diminished along with the swelling.

Looming behind me, Sean's face was tight and pale. He bent close to my good ear. 'Just look at yourself, Charlie,' he whispered, somewhere between anguish and savagery. 'You think I don't know you well enough to tell you're in pain just by the way you move?'

I opened my mouth to protest, but he twisted me sideways and, oblivious to our audience, slipped his hand under the loose tails of my shirt, dragging it up to half expose my back.

I knew without needing to see them that other bruises had formed and bloomed and spread across my torso. I heard Gardner's sucked-in breath and was unreasonably irritated by it. Clumsily jerking myself loose, I yanked my shirt straight again and backed away from him.

'I had to make it look good, you know that.'

Sean made no moves to follow, just stood expressionless. 'Christ Jesus,' he muttered at last. 'Bane had the shit kicked out of you, and you're *defending* him?'

'*He* didn't do anything,' I snapped. 'Why the hell can't you keep an open mind?'

Sean folded his arms again. 'It's not *my* mind we're concerned about.'

'What?' I demanded softly.

'This operation's over, Charlie,' he said, final as a prison door closing. 'You're coming out of here with us, right now. By force, if necessary, if you feel the need to make it *look good.*'

I glanced across at Gardner, but her face told me she was way past supporting any actions I might take. 'And what will that achieve, exactly? I don't have anything concrete to report to Lorna Witney.'

'If you haven't found out anything by now, you're not going to,' Sean countered, brutal. 'What will staying here do for you?'

I opened my mouth, closed it again, but before I could get much further than that, Gardner's cellphone began to blare. She answered it without taking her eyes off the pair of us, spoke briefly, and closed the phone up again.

'We're ready to leave,' she said, getting to her feet. There was a long pause and her focus switched to Sean. 'I'll wait outside.'

But as she strolled towards the door, she took something off her belt and tossed it to Sean, who caught it one-handed. I saw enough to recognise a set of handcuffs.

'Just in case.' She gave me a dark look and went out.

When Sean and I were alone, I asked roughly, 'You think you'll need those?'

'You tell me,' he said, voice low. 'Why are you really here, Charlie?'

'Because I need to be.' I sighed. 'Because I'm a mess and, believe it or not, Bane is helping me to get my head together.'

'And this…problem, whatever it is – you couldn't bring it to me?' he demanded. 'After everything we've been through together?' The bitterness was starting to leach out like contaminated groundwater. 'I thought what we had was stronger than that.'

I heard the past tense and closed my heart to the sudden pain. 'Sean, you were all part of it…' I broke off, aware from his face I'd said the wrong thing. 'Shit, I'm making such a bloody hash of this.' I sank into the chair near the desk, staring at my own tightly clasped hands. Sean hadn't moved, I noted, but he seemed much further away than he had ever done. A worm of fear uncoiled deep in my belly.

'You remember when we got back from Texas – after that business with my parents?' I asked, and when he nodded I took a deep breath and said baldly, 'I discovered I was pregnant.'

I expected a reaction. What I got was nothing for the longest time. Anticipation pushed a narrow blade very slowly into my chest, burning as it went.

Eventually, Sean said, 'Pregnant,' his voice totally without inflection. 'And you didn't tell me.'

'I was in a tailspin,' I said, aware my knuckles had turned white under the skin. 'I didn't know what to do.'

'"Do" in what way?' he queried, dangerously soft. 'Didn't you think something like that was important enough to discuss with me?'

'You weren't there, Sean!' I burst out. 'I was freaked out. I thought I'd lose everything – you, my job, my green card. I thought I'd get sent home and I was in a total panic. You were working away when I found out.' If that wasn't entirely true, it was close enough to make no difference.

But I felt my face heat at the minor lie, knew he'd seen the involuntary reaction by the narrowing of his eyes. Still I blundered on. 'How could I tell you something like that over the phone?'

He launched across the study to bend over me. 'You're talking in the past tense,' he said, white-faced, grabbing my arms like he wanted to shake me until my teeth fell out. 'What the fuck *did* you do, Charlie?'

'What do you think I did?' I broke his grip, shoved to my feet, hurt and angry, wanting to punish him for his lack of faith and only punishing myself. Logic didn't come into it.

'Did you have an abortion – is that why you were in hospital after Texas? Those "after-effects" you so casually mentioned?' he demanded, face twisted with contempt.

'Do you honestly believe I'd do that – abort your child without even *consulting* you?' My voice had risen to an outraged squawk. I stopped, continued more quietly but no less brittle, 'Is that how little you think of me?'

'I don't know,' he said, weary. 'I thought I knew you.' He'd said that once before, I recalled bleakly, when he thought I'd betrayed him. He'd been wrong then, too, and it seemed he'd learnt nothing from the experience.

I watched him turn away, then said in a small voice, 'I lost the baby.'

He stilled but didn't turn back right away. 'When – in here?'

I swallowed the howl forming in my throat, found it left an acid taste behind. 'Do you think I'd have volunteered for this – knowing what happened to Witney – if I'd still been pregnant?'

He did face me then, ashen. 'OK, when?'

I groped for the chair again, grateful for the support. 'You came back from Mexico and I was going to tell you then, but within a couple of days the Lopez boy had been kidnapped and you headed straight back down there again to sort it out. By the time you'd negotiated his release, it was too late...'

'You miscarried?'

The doubt in his voice goaded me into carelessness. 'Yes! Ask Parker if you don't believe me...'

'Ah, so *Parker* knows about this.' Sean's tone was absolutely deadly.

'He came to the hospital. I begged him not to tell you,' I admitted, aware only that I was making the most God-awful shambles of this whole thing. I scrubbed at my face again, wished I'd had some sleep, a chance to think it through instead of stumbling into this half-cocked cock-up.

'I'm sorry,' I said, utterly wretched. 'I wanted to tell you. You don't know how many times I tried.'

'But not hard enough. Why is that, I wonder?' Sean murmured. 'What were you afraid of – that I wouldn't want a child? That I'd try and coerce you into getting rid of it?'

'I—'

'Or maybe you were more afraid that I *wouldn't* ask you do to that.'

My face flooded with a mix of anger and confusion and shame, and I'd be willing to bet that Sean saw and identified every emotion as it surfaced. 'I don't know *what* I thought. Yes, I was afraid! I was fucking terrified, if you must know. The thought of having a baby would have meant the end of everything I've worked for.'

'What about everything *we've* worked for? Did you really

think I'd let you walk away and take my child with you?'
He paused. 'Was it a boy or a girl, by the way? Did you
care enough to find out?'

I was so numb I hardly even flinched at that one. 'It was
too early to tell,' I muttered. 'Eight and a half weeks.'

I saw him still as he did the mental calculations, worked
back the dates. That blade finally slid all the way home,
lancing my heart and freezing the air in my lungs.

'Sean, I'm so—'

'Don't say it,' he snapped. 'Don't tell me you're fucking
sorry! I remember the relief in your eyes when I got back
from Mexico.'

My voice was barely a whisper. 'So, that couldn't have
been simply because I was glad to have you home?'

'It might. I even allowed myself to believe it was,' he
said sourly. 'But all the time you were keeping secrets—'
He broke off, looked away with his jaw bunched, no doubt
remembering all recent mention of secrets and lies. Small
lies, one piling on top of another until their own weight
finally brought them crashing down.

'Sean, I love you,' I said, heard the desperation in my
voice. 'Nothing's changed about that.'

'But you didn't trust me to stand by you, did you, Charlie?
You didn't trust me enough to share your pain. To allow
me to grieve alongside you? Instead, you wrapped yourself
up in your own misery and went running off here to some
crackpot guru for absolution. What kind of love is that?'

Lashed by the bitter spill of rage, I knew that defending
Bane on any level would only make things worse. 'I can't
begin to explain it, but he's helping me.'

Sean's face went black, closed down. 'You say nothing's

changed,' he said, terrifyingly calm now. 'But from where I'm standing, nothing's ever going to be quite the same again.'

And with that he turned and walked out, closing the door with quiet finality behind him.

CHAPTER FORTY-TWO

Randall Bane found me still there, after Sean and Detective Gardner had departed. I had no idea how long it was. Part of my mind had shut down as firmly as Maria's.

Bane came into the room quietly, paused by the doorway as if waiting for a reaction I was too insulated by shock to give. He moved round in front of me and leant his hip on the leading edge of the desk, very much as Sean had done.

'That did not go well, I take it,' he said at last.

I managed a wry smile that actually hurt to produce. 'Not as well as it could have done,' I said mechanically. 'No.'

Bane was silent for a time, then said, 'You told him about the baby.'

That brought my head up sharply. 'How the hell did you know who he was?'

Bane folded his arms across his chest, smooth-shaven head tilted slightly. 'There's a chemistry between you that can't easily be hidden,' he said darkly. 'And he did not like me touching you.'

I swallowed. 'Is that why you did it?'

'It was...instructive.' He paused. 'So you told him, in anger and in haste, and he responded in kind.'

I gave a strangled laugh. 'Oh yeah, that about sums it up.'

'And now you are sitting here, wallowing in your isolation.'

There was nothing mocking in his voice, but I shot him a poisonous look anyway. 'I was faced with an impossible choice. I never wanted to be in that kind of position,' I said. 'Christ knows, I was at the back of the queue when maternal instinct was handed out. It would be madness to have kids in this job, and I...need to work.'

'Of course.' Bane's chest rose and fell slowly. 'Because, otherwise, what would you do with that killer instinct you're so proud of – is that it?'

I let my own breath hiss out between my teeth. 'Yes.'

'When you first came here, I told you the thing that scared you the most was losing control,' he said. 'For you, your pregnancy and miscarriage represented the ultimate loss of control. You never planned to conceive,' he went on, relentless, 'and then when you had inadvertently done so, the decision of if and when to terminate that pregnancy was also removed from your hands.'

'You really think I would have had an abortion?' I demanded. 'There wasn't time to make *any* decisions, one way or another. And I wouldn't have done anything without...' My voice trailed away.

'...talking with Sean,' Bane finished for me. 'But Mother Nature beat you to it, and now you feel angry not to have been consulted, and resentful that your own body betrayed you and deemed you somehow unfit for the task. And, most of all, I suspect you even felt relief.'

'You missed out guilty as hell,' I said tightly. 'Guilty for keeping it secret from Sean in the first place. More guilty for keeping quiet after. And yes,' my chin came up, defiant now, 'guilty for feeling relieved that I didn't have to make that choice.'

'Those are natural reactions, in the circumstances,' Bane said. 'Your mistake was to try and exclude Sean from the process. He had every right, as the father of your child, to be involved, to be allowed to come to terms with this in his own way. Instead, you threw it at him.'

'Badly.'

He nodded, face grave. 'When we're hurt, instinct makes us lash out at those closest, trying to drive them away,' he said. 'It reinforces our sense of self-hatred. See, you tell yourself – even those who claim to love me, abandon me. See how worthless I am?'

He paused, unfolded himself and reached down to tilt my face upwards, fingers cool and dry under my chin. Those strangely compelling eyes locked onto mine. He smoothed his thumb across the corner of my mouth and I felt it tremble at his touch. 'It's a vicious downward spiral, Charlie,' he said gently. 'Break out of it, or it will destroy you.'

Too late.

As if I'd spoken out loud, he sighed and released me, almost with reluctance. I let my head drop, staring at the floor.

'I know Sean. He won't forgive this.'

'Only if you will not allow it,' Bane agreed. 'If you believe you do not deserve to be forgiven. And where will that lead?'

Sean and I had separated before, after our disastrous time in the army. He had been told I'd tried to sell him out, and events had conspired to reinforce that opinion. We'd been apart for four years before chance brought us together again. Now, I couldn't contemplate a future without him in it. I would have died for him.

Bombarded by images, aching with fatigue, I shut my eyes. 'I don't know,' I murmured. 'How did it come to this? How could he...?'

'A part of you *wanted* to see the worst of him, and he revealed himself accordingly. But before you condemn him, tell me – what could he possibly have said that wouldn't make you think less of him, one way or another?'

I opened my mouth, but no words came out.

Bane nodded. 'If his feelings for you are strong, his reaction was always going to be a violent one. Maybe not physically, but certainly emotionally. And a part of you craved that.'

It was my turn to be silent. Eventually, I said, 'There was never going to be a right way to tell him, was there?'

Bane shook his head. 'No,' he said. 'And if he's a logical man, he'll come to realise that himself, despite the damage to his pride.' He rose, self-contained, within himself, and looked down at me. 'The only question is, how mortally did you maul each other on the way to this epiphany?'

I looked up at him, tired enough to weep. 'Damn,' I said quietly. 'Why couldn't we have had this conversation *before* I spoke to Sean?'

CHAPTER FORTY-THREE

Maria did not resurface until the day after Sean and Gardner's visit. She emerged after lunch into the dusty warmth of the central compound, clinging to Ann's steadying arm, walking slowly by her side.

From the shady bench under the juniper tree, I watched their halting progress in my direction, almost holding my breath. The bulky ex-Marine, Tyrone Yancy, shadowed the pair, not crowding but always there. Three paces away, Maria faltered to a standstill.

I rose, stuffed my hands into my pockets, waited.

'Thank you,' she said at last, her voice husky, like she'd ripped her throat up screaming. She offered a tentative smile. I did the same.

I craved longer with her, to try and explain that she had to fight back, to fight forwards, to find her anger and release it instead of letting it crush her, but her mind had already faded from me. As Ann led her away, Yancy gave me the slightest of nods.

I watched Fourth Day's inhabitants at their latest self-defence practice, delegated by Yancy to another of the security team. Their concentration seemed more sharply focused than previously, as if this was no longer just a theoretical discipline, but an imminent probability.

The overall reaction towards me was mixed. Some had eased up, but most clearly blamed me. As if I'd brought this down onto Maria. As if Nu hadn't been a traitor long before I came along.

Time alone had another side effect, though, and that was for me to think about Sean.

I'd lost him once before and had drifted, without direction or focus. It had taken time, after he'd come back into my life, to recognise how right we were for each other. Both of us scarred by experience, we'd healed far more effectively together than either of us would have managed alone.

But in the shock and bewilderment of my unexpected pregnancy and the miscarriage that followed, I'd lost sight of the strength of that union. Of the fact that neither of us stood a hope in hell of finding happiness with anyone else. That, for me, Sean was my balance.

And at that moment, sitting under the ancient juniper tree, I knew with certainty that I would do anything, sacrifice everything, to rescue what I had with Sean. Because the idea of a future without him, of the course my life might follow, was a dark road that must remain untravelled at all costs.

Bane had accused me of wallowing in my isolation. If it wasn't true then, it certainly was now.

He had been cool towards me. That morning, I'd taken him and Yancy back into the subterranean building where I'd initially been contained. I'd shown Bane the stocks of M16s and M4 assault rifles I'd noted when they'd brought me out of my cell. Bane had surveyed the contents of the opened packing cases with no more than a slight frown on his face. I couldn't tell what thought currents swirled beneath the surface.

'And you never knew this lot was here?' I queried.

He gave a nominal shake of his head. 'These are storerooms,' he said, eyes flicking to Yancy. 'I have little reason to come here unless we have someone who needs confinement, both for their safety and our own.'

The ex-Marine had remained equally impassive, displaying neither guilt nor surprise. He checked over all the boxes for himself, inspecting the weapons as though he was about to make a buy, or he thought I might have planted them.

'Nu had some kind of deal going,' he said at last. 'But I don't ask, and he don't tell.'

'Well, as soon as Gardner gets hold of him, he *will* tell,' I said, exasperated by their stoicism. 'He's facing at least one attempted murder charge, if not two. If he thinks he has anything to bargain with, he'll use it. And, right now, the authorities believe you're the bad guys. Possibly with good reason.'

'Meaning?' Bane's voice was colder than I'd heard it.

I jerked my head. 'Come with me, and I'll show you.'

Bane paused, as if weighing up the consequences, then made his decision.

'After you,' he said. And as I passed him, he glanced back at Yancy, swept an arm to indicate the room at large. 'Dispose of all this...equipment, would you?'

'How?' Yancy asked.

'Anywhere it won't come back to haunt us.'

Yancy looked doubtful. 'Lot of dough here,' he said.

Bane silenced him with a look of his own. 'Break it up. Bury it. Nothing is worth bringing down such trouble onto us.'

We moved above ground again, walked through the main building and across the dining hall, ignoring the stares from those in occupation. I opened the door to the classroom on the far side without knocking, which turned out to be a mistake. Ann was in the middle of chalking up sums onto the blackboard at the far end. She froze in mid equation and I more or less followed suit, mentally cursing for not expecting the room to be occupied. I glanced at the desktops, but the only thing in evidence was wax crayons and sheets of paper.

Twenty small faces turned in the direction of this interruption, their gaze passing over me without seeming to register, but lightening noticeably when they recognised Bane.

'Randall.' Ann's serenity faltered slightly as it transferred to me. 'Is there something I can do for you?'

Bane's eyes slipped to mine and issued a silent challenge. I stepped forwards, offered an awkward smile and a muttered, 'Excuse me,' to the children sitting at the nearest desk, and lifted the lid.

It was empty. I lifted the lids on either side, but they were empty, too. No annotated newspaper, cigarette pack, no copper wire, no book on how to make improvised munitions of any kind. No real surprises there, then. Nu was hardly going to leave such incriminating items lying around for the children to discover. So, why had they been left there before?

Bane leant over my shoulder – unnecessarily, I thought – and stared at my lack of discovery.

'Have you lost something, Charlie?' Ann asked blankly, but it was Bane who answered for me.

'It would seem not,' he said, straightening. 'We're sorry to have disturbed you.'

But word must have got round and now I found myself sitting under the old tree, pointedly alone.

Well, Fox, you didn't come here to win a popularity contest...

Idly, I wondered about Nu's overall game plan. Who was he working for, other than himself, and why had he tried to kill Maria as well as me – unless she was purely collateral damage? Or, alternatively, what reason did he have to try and take out Bane's daughter, for which I would have been the convenient scapegoat?

The more I pulled at it, the more tangled it became.

Then, at the far side of the compound I saw heads begin to turn towards the dirt road in, and a moment later saw dust rising and heard the sound of vehicles approaching, two of them.

As they neared, I recognised the lead car. It was the old Chevy I'd seen before, the low, sweet growl of its engine belying its elderly bodywork. The other car was the nondescript saloon type favoured by rental agencies.

They pulled up and began to disgorge passengers. Half a dozen people, young and dressed in lightweight clothing as though prepared for an expedition.

I sat watching as the new arrivals were greeted like long-lost relatives, all hugs and kisses, and little squeaks of delight. It wasn't until the driver of the second car emerged that I realised who they were.

The driver was a tall blond guy with surfer dude good

looks. Dexter. I quickly skimmed the others, noted two or three of the people who'd been with him in Aberdeen at Debacle's annual blockade of Lorna Witney's company gates. The squat ginger-haired figure of Tony, already pinking in the sun, and the girl who'd complained about my mode of transport. They were obviously not strangers, but what were they doing here?

Maria, meanwhile, had stumbled to a halt, a look of bewilderment on her face. Ann was watching her carefully.

Dexter, in the act of lifting his bag out of the car, suddenly caught sight of her. He let out a shout, dropped the bag and ran across, gathering her up close. I was near enough to hear his words, even though he spoke with his face muffled into her hair.

'I'm sorry, baby,' he said, voice shaking. 'I'm so sorry I wasn't here for you.'

Maria flung her arms around him, hands gripped into fists in the fabric of his shirt, body starting to quiver with wracking emotion. She looked like never letting go.

And, in that moment, things became clear. Like why Dexter had claimed to be the one who saw Liam die in Alaska. Unless I was very much mistaken, this also answered the question of Billy's missing father. 'No longer with us,' I'd been told. It was all a matter of interpretation.

Dexter continued to hold Maria, rocking her gently as if slow-dancing to some melody only they could hear. I told myself it was that, and nothing else, which brought a strangely poignant lump to my throat, and made it difficult to swallow.

The door to the main building opened and Bane stepped out. Dexter saw him approaching and straightened automatically, the way a private soldier reacts to the presence of a general. If the serious expression on Bane's face was anything to go by, his apprehension was justified.

Bane halted a few metres away and waited until Dexter had disentangled himself, something he achieved not without difficulty. He handed the girl off into Ann's care. Maria's eyes never left him.

'Dex,' Bane said, his tone easy enough, but his face was brooding. 'This visit was probably unwise.'

'Blame me,' Ann said quickly. 'I called him. He had a right to know.'

'You expected me to stay away?' Dexter demanded, a faint flush in his cheeks. 'He could have killed her!'

'I think you'll find Maria had her own guardian angel,' Bane said, and for the first time, he glanced across at me. Dexter did the same, but there was something altogether darker in his gaze.

'Yeah,' he said, 'but what about the rest of us?'

CHAPTER FORTY-FOUR

Later, in my room, I was twenty pages into *The Catcher in the Rye* when there was a tentative knock at my door. I was finding it hard to concentrate on the printed page and was glad of the excuse to put it down without feeling like a literary peasant.

'It's not locked,' I said, which, for once, was the case.

I'd been hoping for Maria – although not as much as I'd been hoping for Bane – so Dexter's lanky presence came as a surprise. He'd changed his clothes and his fair hair was damp from a shower. I swung my feet down off the bed and put the book aside, careful not to spill the key I was still using as a bookmark. He took his time about speaking.

Eventually, with a sliver of defiance, he said, 'I'm told I oughta thank you.'

Double-edged, but not outright hostile.

I shrugged. 'That depends.'

'On what?'

'On why Maria was targeted in the first place.'

Dexter moved across to the window, leant on the wall

nearest and stared out through the glass. 'How do you know Nu wasn't after you and Maria got in the way?'

I shook my head. 'He had plenty of other opportunities, but I think he wanted to get us both together. Any ideas why?'

It was Dexter's turn to shrug. 'You tell me. Things were fine here until you came.' He tore his eyes away from the view of the compound outside. 'Until you took Thomas away to his death.'

'From what I've been told, it looks like Nu may have had a hand in that one, too. This thing is centred here,' I said mildly. I paused, thinking of the circled newspaper story about the oil refinery visit. *Right up Debacle's street.* Fishing, I added, 'What I don't know...is why now? We were tasked to extract Witney, and it had to be done quickly, but he'd been here five years. What's kicked all this off now?'

Dexter ignored that. He twitched restlessly away from the wall, hands in his pockets and shoulders hunched, then said abruptly, 'Thomas had been helping us – Debacle, I mean.'

'His son died for your cause,' I said. 'Why would Thomas help you?'

'Because he came to believe in Randall.'

'Helping you with what?'

'Whatever we needed. Research, mainly, but if things got tight, he organised an escape route across the border to Mexico. Maria's extended family would give us shelter when we needed it.' The affection in his voice told me he'd needed it more than once.

'So, it was all bullshit, that stuff you fed me back in Scotland – about the reasons Thomas Witney stayed in Fourth Day.'

Dexter smiled thinly. 'We wanted to throw you off track. I remembered the name Parker Armstrong soon as you said it. He was the guy they hired to grab Liam when he first came here.' A flash of contempt lit his eyes. 'He missed.'

Understanding made me ignore the jibe. 'Ah, so when I started asking questions about Billy...'

He nodded, sober. 'Randall thinks I'm a fool to have come back here, but I couldn't come before, when Maria needed me, so...'

No, you were already in custody in another state, I thought, but noted the 'back' and said carefully, 'You were all here – you and Maria and Liam – before you went off to join Debacle.' I made it a neutral statement of fact, then asked, 'Whose idea was that?'

'It was kind of a joint decision,' Dexter said, a little defensive even so. 'Randall encourages everyone who comes here to find what's important to them. For us, it was the environment. I mean, what's more important than the planet we all live on, right?'

'Right,' I echoed. 'And for Liam, of course, protesting against oil exploration had the additional appeal of sticking it to his parents. Or, more particularly, his mother.'

Dexter shrugged again. 'Liam was into Debacle, right from the start. But when Randall held out, that really did it for him.'

'Held out?'

'Against temptation,' Dexter said. He shook his head, wonder in his voice. 'You gotta be real firm in your beliefs, to turn your back on all that dough.' He gave a rueful smile. 'But I guess it kinda helps if you don't need the money.'

Something prickled at the base of my neck, the back of my skull.

'Held out against what temptation?' I repeated and something in my voice brought him up short.

'You mean nobody's told you about the oil?' he said, looking confused. 'Jesus, I assumed that was the whole reason you people were here.' He lifted his hands in exasperation, let them drop again, bitterness twisting his mouth. 'That's what it's always about, isn't it? You think this great country of ours would ever have gone in to "rescue" Kuwait if they hadn't had a shitload of oil under their sand?'

'Nothing to do with Kuwait being invaded by a hostile nation, then?' I asked mildly.

'If you believe that, kiddo, you're living in a dreamworld.'

I paused, then pointed out, 'I seem to recall we went to war over the Falklands.'

'Yeah, and you notice *we* didn't help you guys out on that one, even though it was practically in our own backyard.'

'So, you're trying to tell me that there's enough oil under Fourth Day's little patch of land to be worth murdering for?' I asked, not bothering to hide the cynical note.

He snorted. 'Some neighbourhoods in LA, they'll cut your throat for your sneakers. And there's enough oil under parts of Utah, Wyoming and Colorado to last into the next millennium.' His face grew serious. 'You telling me *that's* not worth killing for?'

'OK, let's say you're right,' I agreed. 'Why is it only just coming to light now? Why has the US allowed the Middle East to hold it to ransom for decades? However difficult the oil is to get at, surely it's cheaper than going to war in the

Gulf – twice? So, why aren't there oil drilling platforms all over the Midwest and tanker ships lining up halfway along the Pacific coast?'

That provoked a full-fledged laugh. 'Because it's not that simple, kiddo. This is oil *shale*.'

I frowned. 'What's the difference?'

He sighed, as if talking to someone woefully ignorant. 'They've known about oil shale for nearly one hundred fifty years,' he said. 'The problem is extracting it. They used to use a process called "retorting". What happens is—'

'I'm not an engineering student, so spare me the gory details,' I interrupted. 'Just cut to the chase. What's the big problem?'

'Using the retorting method – environmental catastrophe is what,' Dexter said flatly. 'Once the shale is mined, they have to crush and heat it to extract kerogen, which can then be distilled into oil and gas. But this produces huge amounts of waste, and I mean *huge* – like, the heat desiccates the rock and expands it, so by the time you're done, there's too much of it even to shove back into the hole it came out of.' He raked his hands through his hair in frustration. 'Not that you'd want to put it back, of course, because it's now contaminated with heavy metals and a load of other highly toxic crap, just waiting to poison the nearest groundwater.' He gave a caustic smile. 'And there wouldn't be much groundwater left, 'cause the refining process uses so much it sucks the area dry.'

'So, what's changed?' I asked carefully. He stopped, pulled his focus back onto me. His breathing was elevated, I noted, cheeks flushed. 'Has the price of oil finally risen to the point where the benefits now outweigh the concerns?'

'The oil companies claim they've been working on an *in situ* conversion process, which means you don't have to mine the shale at all. Instead, they drill down and insert heating elements into the rock, then heat the whole of the subsurface up to like seven hundred degrees, for several *years*.'

This was clearly supposed to provoke some kind of a reaction, but I just blinked. 'What does that do? Boil it off?'

'No, it speeds up the natural development of the oil and gas by *millions* of years. But, of course, nobody knows about the long-term consequences,' he added glumly, 'and I doubt they care.'

I asked, 'Surely it can't be cost-effective to heat up something to that temperature, for so long?'

'Compared to conventional oilfields, you'd be amazed,' Dexter said. 'They're still developing the process, but the word is, they've got it just about cracked. Soon as they do, any pockets of oil shale the government doesn't own already are going to suddenly become prime real estate. We're talking a million barrels an acre.'

OK, *now* it was something worth killing over. 'And there's oil shale under Fourth Day's land?'

'Yeah. Liam discovered it, not long after we came here, but Randall, of course, wasn't interested in exploiting it.' He gave a smile that was a mixture of pride and sadness. 'Which is why they're trying to get rid of him.'

'Who is?' I said. 'Nu?'

Another derisive snort. 'John Nu doesn't have the *cojones* for something like that – not on his own,' Dexter muttered, 'but I know who has.'

'Epps.' The name came to my lips almost unbidden.

His head jerked. 'Whoa – that bastard's involved, is he?'

'You know him?'

'Our paths have crossed, let me put it that way,' Dexter said, lips twisting. 'He tried to get me to rat out Debacle after the Feds grabbed me in Texas a few years ago.'

'Which is where you were when Liam was killed in Alaska.'

He paused a moment. 'Sharp, aren't you?'

'It has been said,' I returned dryly. 'I know Maria was there and saw what happened.' When he raised an eyebrow at that, I added, 'Things she said, after Nu took a potshot at her. She had kind of a flashback.'

'Shit, poor kid.' He looked away, swallowed. 'It destroyed her. She only joined Debacle to be close to Liam. He was like the big brother she never had.'

'You knew, last time we met, that I believed Billy might be Liam's kid,' I said. 'You do realise, don't you, that if you'd told me the truth – that he was yours – I would never have come here? You could have saved yourself a lot of bother.'

His mouth twisted. 'Yeah, and painted a damn great target on the kid's back while I was at it. You've met Epps. You think he'd hesitate to use Billy to get to us?' His eyes looked through me, then he said, 'I would have married her – I *wanted* to marry her, but she said no. That made me angry for a while, but I guess it runs in the family, what with her mom and all.'

'What happened to Maria's mother?'

'She and Bane had a thing going, then she went home to Mexico, joined some bunch of fanatics down there. Never told Randall she'd gotten pregnant,' Dexter said. 'Maria only found out about him after her mom died while we were at college. She tracked Randall down, wanted to meet him.' He shrugged. 'Liked what she found.'

I let my breath out slowly. Well, *that* explained a lot. For a moment, I wondered if Bane had allowed his personal feelings to colour his advice, and telling Sean of my own pregnancy might well turn out to be the worst thing I could possibly have done.

He had to know some time.

I pushed the thought aside. 'You said you didn't think Nu was the brains of the operation, so who was?'

'The only person I can think of is the one who was trying hardest to persuade Randall to go ahead with the exploration project,' Dexter said. 'That little bastard, Sagar.'

'Chris Sagar?' I demanded faintly, mouth dry, skin shimmying in reaction. 'But wasn't he Bane's second in command?'

Dexter laughed again, and it wasn't a pleasant sound. 'Second in command? What is this now, the military? He wasn't good enough to scrape the shit from Randall's shoes.'

'So, who is he?'

'He was part of the old Fourth Day, before Randall bought them out. Sagar stayed on, but Randall cleaned out all the rot and Chris Sagar was rotten, believe me, all the way through. He's the one who campaigned hardest to develop the oil shale. He hounded Liam for figures on how much could be made out of it. Eventually, Randall threw Sagar out.'

I jerked to my feet. 'We've got to talk to Bane,' I said,

agitated. 'Epps is using Sagar as his Fourth Day advisor. Either he had no idea Sagar's got some kind of personal vendetta going, or he doesn't care.'

'It's a little late to consider that, I'm afraid,' said a deep voice from the doorway. We both turned, to find Bane himself standing in the opening, regarding the pair of us gravely. I wondered how long he'd been there. Dexter flushed.

I said quickly, 'What's happened?'

'Tyrone has reported some disturbing activity around our boundaries,' Bane said, eyeing the way Dexter's face had turned corpse white beneath his tan. 'It would seem there is a significant SWAT presence surrounding us.'

'They've come for me,' Dexter whispered, sinking onto the edge of the bed. 'You were right, Randall. I shoulda never come back. I've put you all at risk.'

'Oh, I don't think you're the one to blame,' Bane said, looking straight at me as he spoke.

That hurt more than I expected, a physical pain in my chest. 'Bane, listen—'

He held up a hand. 'I've heard all I need to. If Chris has been feeding those people with enough lies to have brought them this far, the time for talking is over.'

I felt the blood drop from my face. 'You can't make a stand,' I said, thinking suddenly of those twenty little faces who'd turned towards me in the classroom. 'It will be another Ruby Ridge. Another Waco. You'll be slaughtered.'

'You speak as if we're a cult,' he said, nothing more than moderate distaste in his voice. 'How long do you have to be among us before you realise that's not the case?'

'I know you're not,' I said. *Now.* 'But what *I* believe is immaterial. You should be worrying about the guys out there. The ones dressed in black with the armoured Humvees and the fifty-cal machine guns because, right now, what *they* think is pretty bloody vital to your survival.'

Bane didn't respond, just switched his gaze to Dexter. 'If you're done here,' he said to him, 'we have arrangements to make.'

'Of course,' Dexter muttered, getting to his feet.

'What can I do?' I demanded. 'If you need help with defensive—'

Again, Bane held up that silencing hand, cutting me dead. 'You've done enough,' he said, face grave. 'I trust you won't take it as a personal insult if I insist that you remain here?' And he held out his hand. For an absurd moment I thought he wanted to shake on it, then I realised he wanted the Salinger, and the key it contained.

'"Trust" is an interesting choice of word,' I said, acidic, as I handed it over.

'I'm sorry, Charlie,' he said. 'But we now have to consider you a possible danger to us. The safety of this community is my responsibility.' He ushered Dexter out. Dexter threw a final reproachful glance in my direction as he went.

'Yeah,' I murmured as the door closed behind the pair of them and I heard the lock turn. 'Good luck with that.'

After they'd gone, I lay on the bed staring up at the ceiling for what seemed like a long time. The sun dropped towards the horizon and I tracked the passage of the long shadows around the walls like a giant sundial.

I didn't expect sleep to come, but eventually it did, restless and disturbed.

So, when I came bolting into wakefulness with a gasp in the dark, for a few seconds I wasn't sure if it was something real or imaginary that had roused me.

A fraction later, senses screaming, I registered a presence in my room, a bulky slither of sound, a proximate breath. I closed my hand around the makeshift knuckleduster I'd moulded out of the old table fork, and catapulted upright in my bed, lashing out blindly. I caught something a glancing blow that elicited a pained grunt in response, but only served to accelerate my nightmare.

Flailing, I began to scramble from under the entanglement of bedclothes, needing mobility, a clear fighting ground. Adrenaline injected into my system with a raw whisky blast.

The lock dropped onto me seemingly out of nowhere, pinning my throat, my neck. I saw wild colours and black static, felt the sudden compression of blood inside my head, the pressure behind my eyes as the clenched muscles restricted the supply. In utter panic, I knew what came next.

I barely felt the scratch as the needle went into my thigh.

'*Bastards*,' I said, but my voice was already beginning to slur.

And after that, I remembered nothing.

CHAPTER FORTY-FIVE

I came round sitting upright in a hard-backed chair, sluggish and groggy, with a foul taste in my mouth. Even through closed eyelids, the room was lit with irritating brightness. When I tried to lift a hand to my face, something snagged sharply at my wrist.

My eyes snapped open. *Mistake.* I flinched, blinded, tried moving my limbs but found them constricted and heard the jingle of metal on metal. I stilled abruptly, fighting the terror that bubbled up in my throat. If anything brought me the rest of the way out of it, dismayed, betrayed, that was it.

A man's voice said, 'She's all yours,' and there were footsteps and a door closing. I opened my eyes again, cautiously this time, and looked out through slitted lids.

The first thing I saw was Sean, leaning his hip against a table with his ankles crossed and arms folded, watching me. He was dressed in DPM trousers and combat boots, and an olive drab T-shirt that showed the delineated muscle in his arms and shoulders. His clothes were stained with the sweat of prolonged effort, and crumpled like he'd been wearing them all night and well into what must have been the following day.

I was wearing yesterday's clothes, too, but stripped down to my thin undershirt. I shivered in the clammy atmosphere as I eyed Sean for a moment without speaking, then turned my head slowly and surveyed the rest of the room.

It was not much bigger than the interview room where Detective Gardner had first confronted Bane. It even had the obviously fake mirror set into one wall, and heavy-duty spotlights in the ceiling. There was a camera mounted high into one corner, pointing down at us through a rage-proof grille. The recording light was on.

Initially, I had no idea of location and there was little to be gained from the room. Just the quiet hum of air conditioning overlaying the flat nothing of good sound insulation. But, every now and again, I felt a slight vibration coming up through the concrete beneath my feet as another heavy plane took off or landed. Probably Van Nuys, I considered. The government hangar at the airport was an ideal location for Epps to interrogate a less-than-cooperative subject. Not just from a security standpoint, but because of its seclusion, also.

Nobody can hear you scream over the sound of a jet engine primed for take-off.

I lifted my hands to the limit of the handcuffs that fastened my wrists to the steel arms of the chair, rattled them slightly. 'So,' I said, more calmly than I felt, 'is this how it is between us now?'

'We had every reason to be cautious. That was some improvised shiv you were using,' Sean said, voice neutral. 'And are you really saying – if we'd simply asked you to walk out of there with us – you would have come?'

'We'll never know, will we?' I said, icy. 'But some choice in the matter would have been nice.'

He came upright so fast I hardly saw him move, more a lurch of reaction. In front of me, staring down, he said with quiet vehemence, 'Don't talk to me about choice, Charlie.'

I swallowed, head tilted back to meet his eyes. 'I know you don't want to hear it when I say I'm sorry, but there *were* no choices to be made, Sean. *I* wasn't given a choice.'

He stepped back, as if he didn't trust himself to be near me. 'Are you talking about our child,' he said coldly, 'or the fact you *chose* not to tell us about the terrorist attack Bane's planning on the Middle Eastern delegation visiting the oil refineries in Long Beach? Or the fact he's been hoarding enough small arms to start a war?'

For a moment I was stunned to silence. Thomas Witney had assumed that we would take advantage of the effects of the midazolam to question him as a matter of course, either during or immediately after his extraction. We had not done so, and I recalled feeling vaguely insulted that he would think we'd stoop to such measures.

But Epps had no such scruples.

The reason for having my arms bare suddenly dawned. They had wanted free access to my veins.

The sense of violation swept down over me like a bucket of cold water, drenching through my skin to chill the bones beneath. I struggled to suppress a shudder, and it took everything I'd got to fix Sean with a ruthless, unwavering gaze.

'Well, it looks like you were right,' I said then, matching my delivery to his.

'Meaning?'

'Right to chain me up before I realised what you'd let them do to me.'

I thought I caught a momentary twitch, then it was gone. 'It had to be done, Charlie.' *This was out of my hands.* He paused, almost a hesitation, then said quietly, 'And do you honestly think I would have let anyone else question you?'

The anger rose hot and fast, a spurt of rage that starred my vision with pinpricks of exploding light. 'Oh, and you think that makes it all OK?' I demanded. 'We're back to choices again, and this wasn't questioning – this was mental rape!'

His head reared back like I'd slapped him. 'Charlie—'

'What the fuck else would you call it?' My voice had risen, harsh and bitter. 'You came in here and you took what you wanted from me, regardless of my wishes. Regardless of whether I was even aware of what you were doing. But because it was *you*, you think that makes it *better*?' I was close to shouting now, hands clawed, arms rigid and shaking, so the handcuffs quivered against the chair like the chains of a tortured ghost. 'You think, when those four bastards raped me, years ago, the fact they weren't total strangers somehow MADE IT BETTER?'

The silence that followed my outburst was deafening. Sean's face set stone white, stone hard, with the exception of a muscle that jumped at the hinge of his jaw.

'So, why didn't you bring it up, yesterday, that you'd found those guns? he asked then, dogged.

'Bane didn't know about the guns – it was Nu,' I said. 'As soon as Bane found out about them, he ordered them broken up, got rid of.'

'Convenient,' Sean said dryly. 'What about the getaway car they were tuning up – a Chevy wasn't it? Or the list of dead ex-members?' He paused. 'You should have told us, Charlie.'

'Ah! So, I was asking for it, is that what you're saying?'

He brushed the jeer aside, ploughing on regardless of the pain I recognised this was causing him, even through the haze of my own. 'Why didn't you tell us that members of a known terrorist group had arrived at the compound?'

'Because they hadn't,' I said, wrestling for control, to sound reasonable and rational. 'The Debacle crew only turned up after you left. And there's nothing sinister about it. As soon as they heard about the attack on Maria, there was no way Dexter was going to stay away. He's father of her child, not Liam Witney.'

'And if you knew that, the job was over.' Sean let out a long breath and gave a sad little smile, glanced back towards the mirror. 'I have to hand it to you,' he said bleakly, speaking not to me but to someone behind the glass. 'You knew exactly what bullshit story they were going to feed her.'

CHAPTER FORTY-SIX

Story? What the hell...?

Before I could argue, the door opened and Chris Sagar came in, smiling, smug with satisfaction. I jerked at my bindings in automatic response, the reflex snarl of a cornered animal. Less cocky, Sagar darted away, sidling around the far side of the table and taking the chair behind it. Sean leant on the wall to one side, watching us both.

'You think you know the truth, Charlie, but they've been messing with your head. You see, *I'm* Billy's father,' Sagar said gently, as though breaking news I might find upsetting. 'That's why I left Fourth Day. Maria and I fell in love, but Bane decided I just wasn't good enough for daddy's little girl. He forced me out, and then broke her mind. All I'm trying to do here is rescue my son and see justice done. These people are dangerous fanatics.'

'Fanatics?' I snapped. 'The only fanatic here is you, Sagar. What proof do you have? Does Epps know you've been feeding him bullshit about Bane running some mind-control cult, when all the time you're just desperate to get your hands on the land.'

Sagar laughed. 'You must be even weaker than we thought, Charlie. I've never seen anyone swallow the line Bane's selling so fast.' He chuckled a moment longer, then shook his head, solemn. 'The land's worthless. I should know – it was offered to me at a rock-bottom price before Bane took over Fourth Day, and Epps knows that, but I can see from your face that Bane didn't quite bring you up to speed. You can't build on it or farm it. What possible value could it have?'

That rocked me. I glanced at Sean, unable to work out why he was allowing Sagar to lie to me. His expression gave no comfort. 'What about the oil shale?' But I heard the doubt in my own voice.

Sagar didn't quite laugh again, but it was a close-run thing. Instead, he grinned at me. 'Liam Witney found one or two interesting rocks, but they amounted to nothing,' he said. 'You think he would have gone all the way to Alaska if there'd been something worth protesting right there on his doorstep?' He shook his head with sham regret. 'Such a shame about that kid.'

'What about the rest of it?' I said, beginning to slip. 'What about all the "psychological abuse" you claimed they'd subject me to?' I checked Sean's face again. 'Surely you took the opportunity to ask what happened to me in there, when we were having our...cosy little chat.'

But it was Sagar who answered, all amusement gone. He indicated the last of the fading bruise on my cheek with a twist of his fingers. 'You didn't have to say a word for us to realise that Bane's moved on a long way from mind games,' he said with quiet seriousness.

'Disappointed, Chris?' I tossed at him. 'That how you got your kicks, was it – breaking in the newbies?'

For a moment something flared behind the lenses of his glasses, then he caught himself and shook his head. 'Nice try, Charlie,' he said, sitting back in his chair. 'You see, I told them, before you were brought in, *exactly* what fantasies you'd come out with. I know Bane's methods well.'

'Ah, yes, when you were his mythical "second in command", hmm?'

He shrugged almost helpless to Sean. 'What did I tell you?' he said, conspiratorial now. 'Next thing, she'll be trying to convince you I sent John Nu after her.'

Before I could respond, the door opened again and Conrad Epps walked in. He looked arrogant and rested. Sean, by comparison, had the hollow-eyed stare of battle-weary troops during a brigadier's front-line visit. And although Sean came upright, there was a tense readiness about him that was a long way from deferential respect.

Behind Epps, Parker Armstrong also stepped into the room, followed by Bill Rendelson. *Come to gloat have you, Bill?* It was starting to feel crowded in there.

Parker and Rendelson were in suits, and from the way my boss glanced sharply between us with narrowed eyes, he hadn't been behind the glass for my interrogation. I couldn't bring myself to look at Rendelson, not wanting to see the bitter recrimination on his face.

'Thank you for your expertise, Mr Meyer,' Epps said deliberately, ignoring me. 'You're finished here.'

Sean moved towards me, but Epps blocked him. I saw the way Sean's eyes flicked and knew, if Epps attempted to physically restrain him, Sean was liable to break all the man's fingers before security laid theirs on a weapon.

'Stand down,' Epps said, the force of a cracked whip in his quiet voice. 'We require Miss Fox's presence for a while longer. You can have her back when we're done.'

'Done fucking with her head, you mean?' Sean said, deceptively light. 'No.'

Epps rocked back, moustache flaring like cat fur. He turned his head towards Parker as if expecting him to intercede. I couldn't see Parker's face, but if Epps's reaction was anything to go by, it showed no sign of capitulation.

Sagar's eyes, meanwhile, danced everywhere. Was his glee really only obvious to me?

'No,' Parker echoed. 'I'm doing what I should have done last night, and taking Charlie out of here, right now.'

'She may have vital intel about the internal layout of the compound, their current strength,' Epps said. 'She stays.'

To my shock, it was Rendelson who muscled forwards, got right in Epps's face. He was shorter, but of a width, even if he was an arm down on the other man.

'Enough,' Rendelson growled. 'You cut one of us, we all bleed. Go have your fun someplace else.'

Parker lifted a hand, as if to hold him back, and Rendelson subsided, glowering.

'You're the one who owes me the favour now, Conrad, so I'm calling in that marker,' Parker said silkily. 'Trust me on this, you do not want to get into a pissing contest with me right now. Not before a highly sensitive operation on US soil.'

'Are you threatening me, Mr Armstrong?' Epps sounded amused.

'If that's what it takes,' Parker said. 'Besides, I'm sure Mr

Sagar will be only too happy to draw all the diagrams you need on Fourth Day.'

It was satisfying that Sagar himself didn't look thrilled at the prospect, but at least Epps was unlikely to pump him full of drugs before he asked for a map.

Epps nodded to someone on the other side of the glass, and a moment later one of his minions arrived with the keys for my cuffs. I rubbed at my wrists where the metal bracelets had rested, attempting to rid myself of their symbolic presence.

As I pushed out of my chair, I staggered and nearly fell. Sean caught me before I'd got anywhere near going down, was about to lift me into his arms when I said in a brittle voice, 'Don't.'

He froze.

'If there's one thing I want very much to do,' I said steadily, 'it's to walk out of here under my own steam.'

He nodded at that, kept his arm around me until my legs had stabilised, then released me and stepped back. Much as I could hardly bear to have him touch me, having him let go was worse.

I glanced towards Bill Rendelson, but that brief flash of solidarity was hidden beneath his usual scowling countenance.

Epps's people shadowed us back through a maze of offices and corridors until we finally reached the main floor of the hangar. As we passed through the final door, the noise levels rose dramatically. Not just from the normal activity of the airport going on outside the hangar, I realised with a sickening lurch, but the highly abnormal activity going on within it.

The place was swarming with personnel. Black-clad guys in SWAT uniforms, cleaning weapons and repacking kit. I recognised the rituals such men go through, just before a major fight.

At the far side of the hangar, near the entrance, were two Chevy Suburbans. Joe McGregor was leaning against the front wing of one, careful to keep the protective bulk of the engine block between himself and Epps's men, I noted. His body language was casual, but his eyes never stopped moving.

As we reached the vehicles, our escort peeled away, formed a perimeter. Beyond them, I could see a couple of M3 Bradley Fighting Vehicles, and M728 Combat Engineering Vehicles, which were basically a tank with a bulldozer blade on the front. Epps must have brought them in by heavy-transport aircraft.

My God, I thought. *They're going to start a war.*

'Charlie will ride with me.' Parker cut across my thoughts, and his voice was the same one he'd used on Epps. For a moment, I thought Sean would argue anyway, but with a last dark look in my direction, he turned away without a word and climbed in alongside McGregor. Bill Rendelson slid awkwardly into the rear seat.

It was only when the reinforced door of the Suburban closed solidly behind me, and Parker cranked the engine, that I let my head drop back against the headrest and my breath escape me.

'When are they going in?' I asked as he swung a tight circle and headed out.

'I don't know, but the oil refinery visit is less than five days away, so you can bet it will be soon,' Parker said as we cleared the hangar and drove out into the brutal sunshine of a California afternoon.

'Do you know how many women and children there are in Fourth Day?' I asked. And when he shook his head, I added bitterly, 'No, and I'm betting Epps doesn't, either. I thought he wanted to avoid another Waco?'

Parker's eyes slid sideways, met mine. 'I think it's too late for that now.'

CHAPTER FORTY-SEVEN

'You OK?'

By the time Parker asked the quiet question, Van Nuys was behind us and we were heading east into steadily thickening afternoon traffic on Roscoe Boulevard.

I twisted in my seat to face him. Behind us loomed the bulk of the other Suburban. Rendelson was hidden, but beneath the passing reflections on the windscreen, I caught glimpses of McGregor and Sean, grim-faced like they were on their way to an execution.

Maybe, professionally, that's what this is.

'I don't know,' I said evenly. 'Would you be?'

Parker was silent for a moment before he said, rueful, 'No, I guess not.'

'It was you and Sean who went in for me, I assume?'

He nodded. 'With Joe. You're not easy to take, if that's any consolation.'

It wasn't. How did I tell Parker that he and McGregor might have had better luck by themselves? Living with Sean had made me minutely aware of him in every sense and I always woke to him. Last night, his unique scent had registered on some deep subconscious level, reaching through the layers of sleep.

I glanced away, the tail lights of bunched-up cars ahead suddenly blurring in front of me.

Parker braked until we were barely crawling. I half-considered jumping from the car, but knew Sean would be after me before I'd made it ten metres, and I was in no fit state to outrun him without a miracle.

I was so tired that even my hair ached.

'You should have reported in as soon as you found out Dexter was the kid's father,' Parker said then. 'Our duty to the client ended there.'

'I know.'

'As for the rest of it...' He sighed. 'Why didn't you tell us? Why make us find out this way?'

Because I've been brainwashed, apparently.

'I knew I was being used,' I said instead. 'And I wanted to find out who and why before Epps took over with his usual sledgehammer diplomacy.'

There was a light-controlled intersection ahead. Beyond it, I saw we were edging into roadworks, giant orange-and-white-striped bollards squeezing the vehicles down into a single lane while a group of guys who looked like they were auditioning for the Village People dug up the central reservation.

'You holding out on us gave significant cause for concern,' Parker said.

'Sufficient to drug me to the eyeballs and let Sean prise it out of me that way, you mean?'

For the first time, I saw Parker's temper flash out. 'OK,

so you were questioned harder than any of us would have liked, using methods we would rather not have employed,' he snapped, 'but Sean did what he had to when you lied to us, when you forced our hand. So suck it up, Charlie! You knew what you were getting into. And did you really expect Sean to stand by and *watch* while Epps worked you over? Or would that just have given you a bigger stick to beat him with, huh?'

For a moment I sat in stunned silence, disbelieving Parker could be so cruel, then the heat flooded into my face. He was right, I realised to my shame. Like Sean's response to the news of my pregnancy and miscarriage. There was no ideal way to react – for either of us.

Even as the apology formed, I was interrupted by the trilling of a cellphone. Parker dug in a pocket, one-handed, and stabbed the button for speaker to make it nominally hands-free.

'Boss?' came McGregor's voice, distorted by the tinny speaker. 'Traffic reports are bad from here all the way down I-five. We better detour or we're gonna miss our flight.'

'OK,' Parker said. 'We'll make a right on Lankershim and stay off the freeway.'

He ended the call and snapped the phone shut, dumping it into the centre console. We crept forwards another few metres, just as the light overhead flipped to amber. I glanced back and saw McGregor had been cut off by the closing red. Parker kept rolling, just managing to squeak the Suburban into the bottleneck on the far side as cross traffic began to pour through behind us.

'What flight?' I demanded, heart beginning to pump.

'We're booked onto Air Alaska out of Burbank,' Parker

said. 'Two changes back to JFK. Not ideal, but they were the first seats available.'

'Why the big rush?' I said. 'Why do you want to get the hell out of Dodge unless...' I stopped abruptly. 'Epps is going in tonight, isn't he?'

Parker hesitated. 'Look, Charlie, I'm sorry...'

'Not as sorry as I am.'

In one move, I hit my seat belt release and grabbed the phone from the console, at the same time yanking the door open and piling out into the roadway.

We were barely rolling by that point. I managed to stay on my feet as I hit the ground and ran, shaky, parallel to the line of near-stationary cars, heading directly forwards, away from the Suburban, and then cutting in towards the construction as the traffic alongside me began to move. I leapt the barrier and dropped down onto the exposed hardcore.

Behind me, I heard a yell, car horns blaring, knew Parker could not abandon his vehicle, and Sean was hampered by the heavy traffic cutting across behind us.

But not for long.

I ducked under the swinging arm of a mechanical digger, ignoring the yells from the workmen who converged on me as though this was some giant game of tag. The rough ground was stony underfoot, making running slow and perilous. And quite apart from being sleep-deprived, I had no idea what kind of chemical cocktail Epps's people had pumped into me. Already, I was nearly spent.

A big guy in a stained vest, fluorescent bib and hard hat made a grab for my arm. He just managed to snag my shirt and drag me off balance. I stumbled and went to my knees.

'Hey, lady! You crazy?' he demanded. 'You tryin'a get yourself killed?'

Just for a second, I debated on putting him down, knew I could do it fast, but it would still take time I didn't have.

So I looked up at him, let my face crumple, knew by the way his eyes flickered that he'd clocked the bruise around my eye. And, despite the fact that the grubby vest he wore was known as a wife-beater in the States, he didn't look the type.

I glanced back as if fearful, and saw that Sean had managed to negotiate his way through the stream of cars and was sprinting for our position, exuding anger and menace like a heat haze as he bore down on us.

'*Please...*' I begged, and hoped he'd mistake the sweat on my face for tears.

The big guy hesitated just for a second, then hoisted me to my feet and gave me a gentle shove.

'Go on, get outta here,' he said, jerking his head. 'We'll slow him down for ya.'

'Thank you!' I sobbed, and fled.

I reached the far side of the roadworks without looking back. The traffic moving in the opposite direction was travelling more freely, faster. I couldn't afford to stop, just launched into it and hoped for the best. I just about dodged through one lane unscathed, until a car door mirror clipped my hip and sent me tumbling.

Unable to tell if rolling sideways would save or kill me, I hunched into a defensive ball, arms wrapped around my head, heard monstrous tyre squeal approaching.

Then nothing.

I opened my eyes, looked up and found the fly-splattered

grille of a Honda Civic staring down at me. The car had slewed sideways a little, although not enough to block traffic, which edged round us on both sides. I caught shocked faces through the glass as they drove by. Something to tell their families about when they got home, but God forbid they should think about stopping.

A car door slammed and a young woman's head appeared over the corner of the bonnet, staring down at me. She had dark hair done in braids along her head, pale skin and a thin, sinewy build. Unusually for someone dressed in workout gear, she looked like she might actually just have come from the gym.

'Holy crap! I thought I'd killed you. Are you all right?'

'Please,' I said, squinting up at her, 'help me!'

She glanced across to where four or five of the construction workers now surrounded Sean, brandishing a variety of tools. He crouched, dirty and dangerous at the centre. I hoped none of the men were foolish enough to actually take a swing at him. If he'd been in a suit like Parker, I realised, I would likely have been the one they'd run to earth.

'Can you walk?' the woman said. She reached down to grab my arm and I lurched to my feet, wincing. 'Get in!'

She scrambled back behind the wheel and, as soon as I had the door shut behind me, she set off, smoking the tyres as she cut sharply across onto a service road and roared through a parking lot before hitting the main road again.

'First cop car we see, I'll pull him over!' the woman said, a clenched excitement in her face as she checked the rear-view mirror for signs of pursuit. She would, I sensed, be dining out on this story for months. 'You want my cellphone, call nine-one-one?'

I realised I still had Parker's phone in a death grip in my right hand and shook my head.

I dialled the emergency number. When they answered, I said, 'I need to speak to Detective Gardner, LAPD Homicide. It's urgent.'

Alongside me, the woman's eyes widened. She jammed her right foot down a little harder, reasoning, no doubt, that this was one day she was not going to get booked for speeding.

CHAPTER FORTY-EIGHT

Detective Gardner picked me up forty minutes later on a quiet street in West Hollywood. My good Samaritan, whose name was Bridget, insisted on waiting with me in her car, swivelling constantly in her seat to check for black Suburbans. Her manner was guaranteed to draw their attention had they happened to cruise past, but they did not. It felt somewhat ironic, having my own bodyguard of sorts.

Bridget was the survivor of an abusive marriage, she told me. She'd been her husband's Friday-night punchbag for seven years before seeing the light, and she advised me to do the same. She'd taken a couple of classes in judo, and was ready for the bastard, yes ma'am, if he ever tried breaking the restraining order – or her wrist – again. Plus she now spent five nights a week at the gym, soon as she got off work. Which, she said, curling her skinny bicep, was where she'd been headed when I had almost dived under her wheels.

I nodded and said it was obviously working for her,

which was greeted with a beaming smile. All the time, I was trying desperately to work out what the hell I would say to Sean, the next time we met.

The street was lined with pavement cafés and bookstores. The last place I expected Sean or Parker to come looking. After my initial call to Gardner, I'd switched off the cellphone to avoid a trace, considered dumping it altogether, but rejected that idea. I was still hopeful things hadn't gone past the point where I might actually be able to return it to Parker, with employment and friendship in some way intact. I knew Epps probably had the equipment to pinpoint the phone's location, regardless of activity, but I hoped fervently that my boss would not want to involve him.

Across the street, a dull-green Buick swung into an empty parking space and Gardner got out, looking alert and together. She was in another linen jacket over a dazzling white T-shirt and you didn't need to see a badge to read her as a cop.

'That's my ride,' I said to Bridget.

Bridget rolled down the Honda's window and gave her idea of a covert wave. Gardner headed over, put her arm on the roof and leant in. The action made her jacket gape. Bridget saw the gun, as I'm sure she was supposed to, and her eyes went suddenly big and round.

'Charlie,' Gardner greeted me, without expression. 'You look like shit.'

'Thanks,' I murmured.

'She was being kidnapped!' Bridget said. 'She had to practically throw herself under my car to get away.'

'That a fact?' Gardner's gaze stalked over me, slow and measured. 'We need to talk.'

I climbed out of the passenger seat, aware I'd started to stiffen alarmingly. Still, it was not as painful as the last time I'd been hit by a car. I paused by the driver's door, smiled down at Bridget.

'Thank you,' I said, meaning it. 'Truly. You were fantastic. I wouldn't be here without you.'

She beamed again, flustered by the praise. 'Well, if there's ever anything I can do...'

'There is just one thing,' I said, saw her expectant eyes. This whole episode was the biggest thrill she'd had in years. 'If your ex ever comes back, please, don't try to take him on. Run like hell and call the cops.' Ignoring her open mouth, I added, 'A couple of judo lessons is only enough knowledge to get you seriously hurt. Trust me.'

Gardner nodded to her. 'Drive safe now,' she said. Crossing the road towards the Buick, she asked, 'What was that all about?'

I turned, gave a last wave as Bridget pulled away still frowning. 'One good turn deserving another.'

Ten minutes later, Gardner and I sat in a booth at the back of a small Italian restaurant a couple of blocks from where she'd parked. I'd tried to persuade her that time was a factor here, that Epps's men were massing for attack on Fourth Day, and something had to be done, but she faced me down with a bland implacability.

'You wanna go? Knock yourself out,' she said easily, knowing I had no money, no credit cards, and was probably already listed as a fugitive.

She gave that one a good ten or fifteen seconds to fully

sink in, then said, 'You hungry? I'm starved. I know this great place just down the street. C'mon, let's go eat while we talk. I'm buying.'

I had little choice but to follow.

Once we were seated, she ignored the drinks menu to order a glass of half white Zinfandel and half cranberry juice with a slice of lime and no ice. If the way the waiter took this in his stride was anything to go by, she was a regular here.

'How's this for weird?' she said then. 'If you hadn't come looking for me, I woulda come looking for you.'

'Oh?'

'Nu didn't make it.'

'Oh,' I said again. 'Shit.'

'Yeah,' she murmured. 'That about sums it up. Blood clot, the doctors reckoned. He never regained consciousness.'

I sat for a moment, elbows resting on the tabletop, trying to work out how guilty I felt. I remembered the way Nu had strolled into the camp and calmly taken aim at a sleeping woman. Not very guilty, I realised.

On the way into the restaurant I'd noted out of habit there were three exits, including the one at the front, one leading to the kitchens, and another marked 'restrooms' with a propped-open door through which I could see a service alleyway at the back. I'd already logged it as my best emergency escape route, but I'd been hoping to eat before that became necessary.

The waiter brought our drinks and I sipped from my bottle of San Pellegrino. 'Are you intending to hold me on this?'

'Well, I wouldn't have been thrilled if you'd made that flight,' she said, lifting her own glass and eyeing me over the rim, 'although I think jumping from a moving vehicle to avoid it is a little drastic. Probably constitutes some kinda traffic violation, too.'

'Jaywalking, you mean?'

While we'd walked to the restaurant, I'd given her a brief rundown on events since our last meeting. Gardner had absorbed the news largely in silence until we'd sat down and had been through the ritual of ordering. Then she picked up the thread again, as if she'd never stopped mentally teasing at it.

'So, why *didn't* you come clean with us? Might have saved you a lot of grief in the long run.'

'I've been trying to work that one out since you and Sean left. The only reason I can come up with is...it just didn't *feel* right.'

'Hmm. Neither does a cult stockpiling weapons.'

'What makes you so sure Fourth Day is actually a cult?' I asked wearily. 'I mean, it might have been, once, but now?' I shrugged. 'Do they steal people away from their families? Do they trick money out of the gullible? Do they actively recruit followers to their twisted version of a "faith", whatever that might be?'

Gardner considered that for a while, then frowned. 'Thomas Witney's beef with them was the first official complaint since Bane took over,' she admitted. 'But you *did* see those guns – and that circled newspaper story, and the list of dead ex-members.'

'The thing that bothers me is the *way* I saw it all. Nu practically took that M4 out and waved it under my nose. He couldn't have been more obvious. As for everything else, well, leaving it all so carelessly on display in a children's classroom was just foolish, and Bane is no fool.'

'Ah,' she said, shrewd. 'So, is this you not wanting to believe the worst of Fourth Day...or Bane?'

I suppressed a sigh. 'Come on, Gardner, doesn't it stink of a set-up to you?'

Absently, she wiped the condensation off the sides of her glass, her face distant with concentration.

'Yeah,' she said at last. 'It smacks of overkill. If it had been presented to me as a crime scene, I woulda suspected it had been staged.'

'Exactly. Someone's been trying to ram Randall Bane down my throat as the villain of the piece from the start and, quite frankly, it's starting to make me gag.'

That provoked a twitch at the corner of her mouth that was quickly controlled.

'And you think that "someone" is this guy Sagar?' she asked. 'Why did he want Witney dead? If what you say is right, all that did was ruin Epps's case, make him back off, which would seem to be the last thing Sagar wanted.'

'I don't know,' I murmured. 'Sagar's been trying to convince Epps that Fourth Day is al-Qaeda by another name, but if Epps *had* actually got to question Witney, what would he have found out? That Witney occasionally helped fugitives across the border? Illegal, yes, but hardly enough to interest Homeland Security. The way this was set up, it looked like Bane had a lot at stake. A lot to hide. Worth killing for.'

Gardner's face was quiet for a while, then she said. 'But all that did was make Epps pull out.'

'Maybe Sagar misjudged him,' I said. 'Epps is a cold-blooded bastard and I don't think he responded the way Sagar hoped he would.'

'And you think that's when Sagar hired in local muscle to go for you.' She flicked her eyes in my direction. 'No offence, but if losing two of his own guys didn't blow Epps's skirt up, that wasn't gonna do it for him, either.'

'Killing me would have been one thing, quickly over and done, but they meant to grab me and make Parker sweat. He wouldn't have let it rest. He takes losing people very personally. He would have razed Fourth Day to the ground to get to the bottom of it.'

And as for Sean...no, better not to think about what Sean might or might not have done.

The waiter arrived at that point with our food. Gardner had ordered *penne a la vodka* with a side salad and, uncaring, I'd asked for the same. The waiter flourished a giant pepper mill over our plates and departed.

'Remember the guys who ambushed us, in the van?' I pressed, dogged. *The ones I* didn't *kill.* 'The only way they could possibly have known where we'd be was if one of us tipped them off.'

'If you say so,' Gardner said, her voice cool, and I remembered, too late, that Epps had whisked her three suspects away before she'd had a chance to question them herself.

'If it was a snatch not a kill, why weren't they told to hide their faces?' I went on quickly. 'No, the plan was to grab me then and kill me later, I'm sure of it. Sagar didn't care if I'd talked to Witney – he just wanted something to goad Parker into action.'

Gardner shrugged and took a forkful of pasta. 'So, was Nu really trying to take a potshot at Bane's daughter, or was he just taking another run at you?' she asked, circling back.

'I don't know,' I said again. 'I'm not sure he was after either of us, to be honest. It could well be that the objective was simply to draw the Debacle crew out of hiding and really get Epps's attention. And, if that was the case, it went exactly as planned.'

'Except for the part where Sagar's inside man ended up dead.'

I swallowed a mouthful of food. I knew I had to refuel, and part of my brain was aware it was good, but I couldn't identify a single flavour.

'Yeah,' I said gravely. 'Except for that, of course.'

Strange the way the mind works. I'd been troubled over my actions in dealing with the three men in the van, who had survived, more by luck than judgement. But Nu? There I had no doubt, no hesitations. I hadn't intended him to die, and there was no guarantee of his intent, but the way it went down...?

No, he'd taken his chances.

We ate on in silence. Gardner cleared her plate with the determination of someone who has a busy schedule and a fast metabolism, picked over her salad, then put her fork down and said casually, 'So, what you gonna do now?'

I shrugged. 'Contact Epps, I suppose,' I said, reluctance in my mouth. 'Try and persuade him to stop this lunacy before it's too late.'

She shook her head, immediate if regretful. 'Not a good idea, Charlie,' she said. 'Epps contacted me before I picked you up. He told me you'd gone rogue and were running out of options, and thought you might try for my help. Looks like he made the right call on that one.'

CHAPTER FORTY-NINE

For a moment, everything stopped. I tensed, rechecked my exits, the faces of the other diners, but the restaurant contained only civilians as far as I could tell.

The waiter came over, clutching the bill on a little plastic tray, his professional smile fading at our stony faces. He left the bill on the corner of the table and scarpered. Gardner picked it up, glanced at the total, and tucked a couple of twenty-dollar bills under her empty glass.

'Relax,' she said dryly. 'D'you think, if I was gonna turn you in, I woulda bought you dinner first?'

'So...why did you?' I asked, confused. 'Or, more to the point, why didn't you?'

She smiled. 'Partly because I didn't have you pegged as the easy-to-brainwash type and I kinda wanted to make up my own mind,' she said, sliding out of the booth and straightening her jacket over the gun. 'But mainly because I think Epps is an asshole.'

'We're in agreement there,' I murmured. 'But won't this get you into a shitload of trouble?'

She shook her head. '"Be on the lookout," is all he said. Fortunately, he didn't feel the need to spell out what he wanted me to do in that event.'

'This is not your fight, Gardner,' I said, still unconvinced.

'I stand for the dead,' she said quietly. 'And it's not your fight, either.'

As we stepped out of the restaurant, the sky above the street lighting was a cool blue-black, tinged with an orange glow like a distant battlefield. The heat of the day had settled back into sullen clamminess, and the breeze idly kicking litter along the street did little to refresh it. I wondered if the feeling of impending storm was simply a state of mind.

I thought of the last fleeting look of anger and disbelief on Parker's face just before I'd ejected from the Suburban, and the sad regret in Sean's eyes when he'd spoken to Sagar behind the mirror. *'You were right...'* And I tried to work out how it had come to this.

I hardened my voice, my face, my heart, said, 'What else is there?' and tasted the bitter tone.

We reached Gardner's Buick. She unlocked the doors and we climbed in and, as we threaded our way through the evening traffic towards the freeway, I wondered briefly if Parker and Sean and McGregor had cancelled their air tickets for this evening. I wondered if I still had a job. I supposed that stealing your boss's cellphone and throwing yourself out of his car was pretty much considered a resignation in any language.

But most of all, I wondered if I still had a home, and someone willing to share it. This job would have been tough enough on any relationship, but coming on top of everything else, well, could we hope to salvage it?

Would Sean even want to try?

I took a deep shaky breath, saw in the instrument lights that Gardner's head turned towards me in brief but silent enquiry. I had no intention of satisfying her curiosity.

The drive out to Fourth Day took an hour and a half, leaving behind the harsh glitter of the City of Angels and sliding into classic dark desert highway. We talked sporadically, giving away little of each other in the process.

At one point, I asked, 'So, that business card you gave me – are you going to tell me what the "B" stands for?'

Gardner gave a snort of laughter. 'If I told you, I'd have to kill you.' She paused. 'But my friends call me Ritz.'

'Ritz?' I repeated. 'As in the crackers?'

'No, as in the snazzy hotel,' she said, still smiling. 'I like to think it's 'cause I'm not a cheap date.'

Then, in the distance, I recognised the glow of the little roadside bar, the only sign of habitation near Fourth Day's land.

Gardner tensed in her seat and the smile fell. 'Looks like we've got company.'

Even in the gathering darkness, we could clearly make out the roadblock up ahead, next to the bar itself. Gardner lifted off the throttle and dropped her window as the Buick cruised to a halt. The sticky night air came tumbling into the car, humid as fevered breath after the air-con chill.

Alongside us, the bar's neon signs for Bud Light and Miller Genuine Draft were the only lights showing, but the rough dirt parking area alongside was crammed with vehicles that had government drab written all over them, bristling with antennas. At the back, I could just make out the bulky outline of a mobile command unit, an articulated truck with a trailer so black it seemed to actively suck in light from the surrounding area. There were satellite dishes on the roof, but I had no illusions the occupants were using them to watch European porn.

Epps. He was so close I could feel him.

A man in SWAT black with an H&K MP5 pulled up tight into his shoulder stepped up to the driver's side of the car, keeping in the safety zone behind the line of Gardner's shoulder. I glanced round, casual, and could make out another standing off in the gloom, keeping him covered.

'Sorry, ma'am, I'm gonna have to ask you to turn your vehicle around,' the SWAT guy said, offering no explanation. 'Find another route.'

'I'm a cop,' Gardner said, keeping her hands on the top of the steering wheel. 'I'm gonna show you some ID and, just so's you're aware of it, I'm carrying, OK?'

She reached into her jacket, nice and slow, and brought out her badge. The SWAT guy took it without a word, retreating into the darkness. We waited without speaking until he passed the ID back through the open window.

'Sorry, Detective, I'm still gonna have to ask you to turn around,' he said, and there was a subtle undercurrent of threat in his voice now, like if he had to ask again it would count against us. 'You hear me?'

'Loud and clear,' Gardner said. 'You be careful now.'

She buzzed her window up as she put the car into reverse and carved a neat, economical turn. I tried to take in as much as possible without making it obvious. The manpower Epps commanded was impressive.

As we hit the darkness again and picked up speed, Gardner let out a low whistle. 'When these guys decide to throw a party,' she murmured, 'they *really* decide to throw a party.'

'Is that it?' I demanded. 'We just turn tail and run?'

Gardner's expression in the dash lighting was neutral. 'Bane's a clever guy,' she said. 'I'm sure he'll figure it out.'

'That's not what worries me.' I thought again of the two SWAT men who'd approached us, their technique and teamwork, and something unfolded with quiet menace inside my head.

Teamwork.

I must have gasped. Gardner's glance was fast, speculative. 'What you got?'

'Thomas Witney knew the men who grabbed him,' I said. 'If they'd been strangers, they wouldn't have risked taking the cuffs off him, and he would have fought them, but there wasn't time. So, he went willingly.' *At first.*

'So?'

'*Men*,' I repeated. 'Plural. Couldn't have been Sagar, because he was still in the air and he doesn't have the skills. So, who else would Nu take with him? Who would he trust?'

'Shit,' Gardner muttered. 'There's another inside man.'

CHAPTER FIFTY

I fumbled Parker's cellphone out of my pocket, stabbed the power button, muttering, '*Inside* is the operative word.'

'Here,' Gardner said, handing her own phone across. 'Main number for Fourth Day's stored. Use mine.'

I took it gratefully, but realised even as the phone rang out at the other end that I had no idea what to say to Bane when I got through.

Eventually, it was Ann who answered with a cautious greeting.

'Hey, it's Charlie. I need to speak to Bane.'

There was a long pause at the other end of the line, what sounded like a shaky breath. 'Don't you think you've done enough damage?' she asked.

'Ann, please—'

'No,' she said, firm in sadness rather than anger. 'Leave us be, Charlie. Leave Randall be.'

And before I could react to that, she'd quietly cut the connection.

'Shit,' I murmured in unconscious echo of Gardner's own

response, glanced around. 'Look, stop the car. I'll hike in from here.'

'In the dark, with no equipment?' she said, not lifting off. 'I don't think so.'

'Gardner—'

'Trust me,' the detective said. 'I ain't been a cop around here for ten years without learning a few back roads that a bunch of out-of-town Feds know nothing about.'

Gardner's alternative route took longer than the main gate would have done, but not nearly as long as tabbing in across rough, unsighted ground. She brought us around to an old service road that eventually joined up with the track Maria and I had taken into the wilderness.

Finally, we braked to a halt near the row of open garages where the Jeep and the quad bikes were sheltered. We'd barely climbed out of the car before the outline of another man in black, carrying another readied long gun, materialised from the darkness.

'We're here to see Bane,' Gardner said, keeping her hands where he could see them.

The figure stepped forwards, looked at me.

'The prodigal returns,' Yancy said.

'Yeah,' I said. 'Lucky for you, huh?'

He led us without comment in through the back door and along the corridor to Bane's study. The room looked exactly the way I remembered it. I had to remind myself it was only yesterday since I was last there. It seemed like a lot had happened since then.

Bane was not alone. Clustered around his desk, looking at what appeared to be blueprints or architect's plans, were

Dexter and his thickset friend, Tony. The one I'd disabled with a can of Lorna Witney's hairspray, back in Aberdeen. If I'd been hoping he'd already forgotten the incident, I was quickly disabused of the idea.

'You've got a bloody nerve!' He started round the desk, fists clenching as if to manually inflate his blood pressure as well as his muscles.

'Tony.' Bane's voice was soft, but it halted the eco-warrior in mid stride. Then Bane's gaze fell upon me and he smiled. I couldn't help the way my nerve endings lit up at that smile, even if I had the nasty sneaky feeling that by coming back here I'd just done something altogether predictable.

'Charlie,' he said gravely, a hint of challenge in his stare. 'We thought you had decided to leave us.'

'That decision was made for me,' I said, 'and I wasn't exactly consulted.' *Or fully conscious, for that matter.*

'I see.'

'Don't give her a hard time,' Gardner broke in. 'She's probably landed herself the number one spot on the Most Wanted list for what she's doing.'

And when Bane raised his eyebrow at that, I added, roughly, 'Epps is on his way to take this place and he's bringing all his biggest and best toys. Tonight, most likely.'

Bane paused, but we weren't telling him anything he didn't already know. 'Thank you for the warning,' he said at last. 'Both of you.'

'That's not why I'm here – officially, at least,' Gardner said easily. 'I wanted to update you personally on the situation with John Nu.'

Out of the corner of my eye, I saw Dexter flex at the mention of Nu's name, but my attention was more firmly on Yancy. The big ex-Marine showed no apparent emotion. His face was calm, almost placid, but I didn't miss the subtle way he redistributed his weight onto the balls of his feet.

'Maria will not be bringing charges aginst John,' Bane said. 'It's enough that he's gone from here. I will take out a restraining order, if necessary, to prevent him coming back onto the property.' He glanced at me. 'I cannot, of course, speak for Charlie.'

'Things have kinda moved on a little from assault,' Gardner said, voice dry. 'We have evidence that places Mr Nu at the scene of Thomas Witney's murder.' She paused, let that cool cop's stare circle the room. 'And we have reason to believe he had an accomplice.'

'Nu wasn't good enough to take out two of Epps's people single-handed,' I said. *Hell, he wasn't good enough to take out two unarmed women, even when one of them was asleep in her tent.* 'Still think it's in Maria's best interests not to press charges?'

'The docs haven't exactly said when we'll be able to speak with Nu,' Gardner went on, casually lying through her teeth. 'But, hypothetically, I daresay the DA might offer to cut a deal. The way things are looking right now, he's got nothing to lose.'

She managed all this with a totally straight face and a vaguely weary air, as though it didn't matter much to her one way or another if one murderer was exchanged for another. It was just another case in a procession of ones just like it, day in and day out. Not a bad act, but I had the feeling the ones that got away haunted Gardner's dreams as well as her waking hours, for all the toughened outer shell.

'Unless, of course,' Gardner said into the silence that

followed her last statement, 'that accomplice decides to turn himself in before we can talk to Nu.' She shrugged. 'It's kinda first come, first served.'

I turned my head, met Yancy's eyes. 'So, Tyrone,' I said softly, 'what's it to be?'

Yancy's eyes swivelled, saw the realisation on the faces ranged against him – especially in Dexter's. But most of all Yancy saw the regret in Bane's eyes. His expression twitched for the first time, as if he'd still been hoping, right to the last moment, to brazen this out.

He said, 'What kinda evidence?'

'Security cameras in the lobby of the building opposite,' Gardner said. Her eyes were on Yancy's hands, still resting on the stock of the M16, but she'd shifted a little, I noticed, putting her right hip forwards so she could better reach the gun on her left, bending slightly forwards from the waist. Pure cop stance.

Only trouble was, Yancy had been a soldier. Probably a very good soldier. I felt the familiar tightness in my chest, even as a weight seemed to lift from my mind. The only time I never had any doubts, it seemed, was when I faced the possibility of killing or being killed.

Yancy stepped back, smooth and fast, moving his feet into a wide base, knees bent, bringing the M16 up to ready position. I heard him flip the safety off as he slipped his finger inside the guard.

But as soon as I saw his hands begin to move, I moved, too. Even as he dropped his right hand down to the trigger, brought his left up to the stock, I was already closing the gap between us. I pivoted sideways and grabbed the barrel with my right hand as it came up, forcing it round and away from the room's occupants, in the direction of his trigger hand.

At the same time, I snapped my right foot up and stamped down hard onto his leading knee, yanking sharply on the barrel to pull him off balance. He gave a grunt as his injured leg collapsed, tipping his upper body forwards and neatly presenting the back of his neck for an elbow strike that had him hitting the floor hard enough to bounce. He was a big guy, layered with muscle. There was no way I wanted to risk breaking a knuckle on him if I didn't have to.

I peeled the M16 out of his hands as he went down, thumbed the release for the magazine and worked the action to eject the chambered round. When I looked up, breathing hard, it was to find Gardner watching me over the sights of her own weapon.

Tony, I noticed, was staring like he'd just eaten something unexpectedly sour. He was the first one to speak, just a faint profanity uttered under his breath.

A long time ago, back in the army when Sean had first taught me hand-to-hand, he'd pointed an Armalite at my stomach and coolly ordered me to try taking it away from him. Instinct tells you to shove the barrel to your right, so it doesn't track across your body, but that pushes it away from your opponent's trigger hand. Reflexive army training makes him simply accelerate through that arc to lash out at your head with the butt as it sweeps round, and Sean was nothing if not very well trained. Then he told me to get up and try again. It was a lesson I didn't need to learn twice.

Now, as I stalked past Gardner, I said, 'He's all yours,' and put the M16 and the magazine down on the desktop, which gave me a good opportunity to have a nosy at what they'd been studying when I came in.

The papers were indeed the architect's drawings for the compound, with various buildings added at different stages. The majority of the main accommodation block and Bane's own quarters were relatively new. And that probably meant Epps would have had little trouble accessing the same plans. That wasn't all it meant.

I turned away from the desk, looked at Bane. 'You already knew Epps was coming, didn't you?'

Bane glanced at the man on the floor. Gardner had holstered her gun and pulled out a set of cuffs, was busy dragging Yancy's wrists together behind his back, reeling off his rights as she did so.

'Tyrone indicated this afternoon that there was some kind of obvious surveillance operation in progress,' Bane said with a hooded gaze. 'I thought it wise to take some basic precautions.'

Saddened, sickened, I shook my head. 'Epps will almost undoubtedly see anything you've done to prepare a defence as a sign you're escalating the situation,' I said, as Gardner rolled Yancy onto his side and sat him up. 'Which was, no doubt, the object of the exercise.'

Dexter came forwards then, white-faced, the cords in his neck standing out as his shoulders flexed. 'Give me half an hour alone with him,' he muttered. 'He'll tell us what the game is.'

'Nobody's getting any time alone with him,' Gardner said, stony. 'This man's now my prisoner.' She looked down at Yancy. 'That deal I mentioned. Either you or Nu takes the rap for Witney. If I can't get one, I'll settle for the other

– up to you. Just don't insult me by telling me it was all Nu's idea, huh?'

Yancy manoeuvred himself to a sitting position, shook his head a little and winced. I could tell by the way he was hunched forwards that the knee was hurting like a bastard, but I couldn't bring myself to care. They'd done far worse to Thomas Witney.

'No, I recruited him, when Bane started having all that *trouble*, a while back.' The sly emphasis made me suddenly realise that Yancy probably knew a lot more about Thomas Witney's car accident than he was prepared to admit. He lifted his head, proud. 'We both knew what we was signing on for.'

'So, you created the demand for extra security, then got yourselves taken on to provide it,' I said. 'Clever. What did Sagar promise you for all this effort?'

'Plenty.' He started to shake his head again, stopped abruptly. 'Man, he was talking telephone numbers. Chance to make more money than I ever seen in my life.'

'And what were you expected to do for this spectacular reward?' Gardner asked, keeping her voice bland.

Yancy scowled nevertheless. 'Keep the field clear,' he said. 'Take care of problems.'

'And Thomas was just one of the problems you took care of, was he?' I put in, icy.

'Sagar was still here when Thomas first came, but nobody knew Thomas was Liam's old man. He didn't exactly shout about that, huh? Sagar told me he approached the guy, thought he could confirm the oil shale find. I mean, he was a geologist – what better qualification, huh? But Thomas strung him along for a while, then said there was nothing there. The land was worthless.'

'Thomas came to me,' Bane said quietly. We turned, found him frowning. 'He told me about Chris's offer and asked how I squared my conscience with encouraging young people to go and risk their lives in the name of the environment, when one of my own was aiming to exploit the resources on my own land. It was at that time I came to the decision that Chris could no longer remain with us.'

He looked down at Yancy, nothing in his face, but it still made the big ex-Marine shift uncomfortably on the floor. Maybe it was the pain from his knee, or maybe from his own conscience, I wasn't sure which.

'Wait a minute,' Gardner said. '*Is* there oil under Fourth Day or not?'

'Liam discovered it, quite by chance, and Thomas confirmed it,' Bane said. 'But this is supposed to be a place of retreat, of sanctuary and quiet contemplation, not of heavy industry and pollution and greed.'

'You could have moved someplace else,' Gardner said with hardly a flicker.

'Why should I?' Bane barely glanced at her. 'I don't need the money. And I understand this latest method of oil shale extraction is entirely unproven. It could be decades before the removal of whatever lies here becomes a viable proposition.'

'Is that why you tortured Thomas Witney?' I asked Yancy. 'To find out the truth about the oil shale?'

'Partly,' Yancy admitted. 'Partly to find out what he told you about Sagar.'

'Nothing at all,' I said bitterly. 'As you now well know.'

Yancy had the grace to look ashamed. 'He looked relieved when we hijacked the van, poor bastard,' he murmured. 'Then he saw what we'd done to...he saw what we'd done.'

'There were easier ways to get the truth out of him than beating him to death,' I pointed out, thinking of Parker and Epps, and the drugs they'd employed.

'Sagar told us to make it look good, but the Feds still wouldn't play ball.'

'Is that why Sagar hired those no-hopers to make a run at me – to try and goad Parker into taking independent action?'

'Told him he shoulda gotten more men.' Yancy's mouth twisted with disdain to show his opinion of amateurs, then subjected me to a long appraisal. 'When you showed up here, we already knew all about you, Charlie, and we just about bent over backwards to show you everything you needed to see, all laid out, but you just wouldn't bite, huh?'

'You weren't exactly being subtle,' I said. 'Was that why you made a play for Maria?'

'Hey, that was Nu. I didn't have nothing—'

'Toss a coin for it, did you?' I cut in, and he went so abruptly silent that I realised they may well have done just that. 'What was that supposed to achieve?'

He gave a half-hearted smile. 'Exactly what it did – bring both your people, Meyer and...,' he jerked his head towards Dex, '...lover boy there, running. Sagar covered all the bases.'

'Not quite,' Gardner said. 'John Nu died early this morning.'

Yancy's mouth gaped. 'But, you said—'

'I said, if I couldn't pin this on one of you, I'd settle for the other,' she said with a grim little smile. 'There is no deal. There never was. Congratulations, Tyrone. You win tonight's star prize.'

Expertly for a woman of her stature, she wrestled Yancy to his feet, hands still cuffed behind his back, took a firm grip on his elbow and looked at me. 'Decision time, Charlie,' she said. 'I'm taking him out of here. You gonna come with me, or you gonna stay?'

CHAPTER FIFTY-ONE

I chose to stay. Of course I did. How could I do otherwise when an arrogant little voice in my head whispered that by being here I might be able to prevent the worst of this? Epps's men might not blink at taking me down along with the rest, but I clung to the hope that Parker or Sean would hesitate, if only for a second...

Now, though, I tried to concentrate purely on the practical.

'From a defensive point of view, it's a nightmare,' I said, shaking my head over the architect's plans spread across Bane's desk. 'The construction's mainly timber frame rather than block, which won't stop anything remotely heavy calibre. We can't hope to defend all points of entry, because they could come through a wall as easily as a doorway.'

Gardner was stowing a manacled Yancy into the back seat of her car as we spoke, and Dexter's crew were helping Fourth Day's frightened inhabitants to prepare for whatever was to come.

'It was not built as a fortress,' Bane pointed out mildly.
'I—'

At that moment, the phone rang. It was a modern sleek
silver handset, sitting flush with its cradle on the desk and
it had a piercing ringtone. Bane's hand hovered over the
receiver for a moment, then he pressed the button for the
speaker and said a calm, 'Yes?'

'Mr Bane,' said a controlled voice at the other end of the
line. 'My name is Epps, Homeland Security. I'm sure you
remember me.'

Bane's face locked. Smooth and sleek, he had never
resembled a statue as much as he did then, but when he
spoke his tone was almost lazy.

'How could I forget?'

'I imagine that Miss Fox and Detective Gardner have,
by now, brought you up to speed on the gravity of your
situation.'

Bane's eyes flickered to me. 'What is it that you want,
Mr Epps?'

I heard Epps sigh. 'A satisfactory conclusion. Peaceful if
possible, but I believe you'll find we are prepared for any
eventuality.' There was indifference in his tone, as if it didn't
matter much to him whichever way we played it.

'I'm sure you are,' Bane murmured. 'Just as I'm sure you
are aware that we have women and children here.'

I frowned at him. It was useless to appeal to Epps's finer
feelings. The man didn't have any.

'Then I expect you will want to do everything possible
to avoid... unpleasantness.'

'And how can I do that?'

'By giving yourself up, Mr Bane.'

'I wasn't aware of being in a position where I needed to do so,' Bane said mildly. 'If you want to talk, come in and we'll talk.'

Epps made a noise that might have signified amusement. 'Thank you for the generous offer of hospitality,' he said dryly, 'but we'll do this on my terms, I think. I will send a vehicle in to collect you. With a chase car. They'll come via the main approach road in twenty minutes. Be waiting. Any sign of a weapon, and I will not be able to guarantee the safety of those women and children you mentioned.'

Bane's face hardened, but his voice stayed smooth. 'I'll be expecting you,' he said. 'Detective Gardner was just on her way out with a prisoner you might be interested in – Tyrone Yancy. He has confessed in front of witnesses to killing your men, and to the murder of Thomas Witney. I think you should hear what else he has to say.'

'Nobody leaves until we get there,' Epps said, and cut the connection without waiting for argument.

'You two know each other,' I said flatly. 'How?'

He sighed. 'I made a great deal of money in the Eastern Bloc, shortly after the collapse of the old Soviet Union, by dealing with, shall we say, a diverse selection of people,' he said at last. 'In those days, Epps was concerned with overseas intel. He tried to induce me to pass information on my business associates back to certain government agencies.'

'Nice.'

He nodded absently. 'Had I been exposed, the consequences would have been lethal – not just for me, but the families of the people involved. I refused. Since then, Epps has had me in his sights.'

'So, it's personal.' I stuffed my hands into my trouser

pockets, jerked my head towards the laden bookcases. 'Well, I hope you haven't read all those books, because where you're going, you'll have nothing to do *but* read.'

Bane glanced up. 'What choices do I have?' he asked, sounding weary for the first time. 'Making a stand is not an option. You said so yourself.'

'At least don't take it lying down,' I said. 'If you have contacts in the media, now's the time to exploit them. And if you have any high-priced lawyers on retainer, I'd be putting them on standby, if you haven't done so already.'

He reached for the phone again, but this time when he pressed the on-hook dial button, the speaker replayed only an edgy silence. Bane lifted the receiver and jiggled it a few times, without result.

'They cut the phones – standard operating procedure,' I said. I peeled Parker's stolen cellphone out of my pocket and hit the power button, watched it search fruitlessly for a signal. *Shit.* 'And they knocked out the nearest cell tower, by the looks of it. That means your Internet connection's down as well. Epps is nothing if not thorough.'

'That settles it, then.' Bane moved round the desk, put his hands on my shoulders and gazed down at me. 'Go forward from this if you can, Charlie,' he said. 'When we first met, I believed you were one of the most troubled souls I'd ever met.'

'I know.'

'I was wrong,' he said. 'You're one of the most fearless. And the most courageous. You do what most of us dread, what most of us fear. I have never believed that violence was the answer to anything, but giving in to violence is not the answer either.'

'Which is precisely what you're doing with Epps,' I said roughly.

He shook his head. 'I have the responsibility of others on my shoulders,' he said. 'Their needs outweigh my own. But you would do what is right, and have the nerve to see it through.' He paused, smiled. 'Don't doubt yourself, Charlie. You have good instincts. Trust them.'

'You can say that, knowing what I've done?'

His eyes searched mine for a moment. I don't know what he was looking for, but he seemed to find it. 'It has always been my hope that if there is one thing people take away with them when they leave here, it is the courage of their convictions,' he said, his voice very deep, almost resonant. 'Quite often, it seems, they are prepared to die for what they believe in.'

'Like Liam,' I murmured.

'Like Liam,' he agreed. 'But you have a rarer quality. You are prepared not just to die for what you believe in, but to kill for it. Why should that make you any less principled than they are?'

Unaccountably, my eyes started to fill and burn. His hand came up, thumb brushing the dent of my chin where it had begun to tremble.

With infinite gentleness, those long elegant fingers slipped around the base of my skull and tilted my head back. The brush of his lips over mine was little more than a whisper that raised a thunder of shouting. He'd stepped back before the echo of it died, leaving me adrift and utterly bewildered.

'Now, go tell the others,' Bane said quietly. 'Ann will know what to do. I have certain arrangements to make, and we don't have much time.'

I broke away, headed for the door.

'Oh, and Charlie?'

I glanced back to find Bane seated at his desk, had begun writing on a plain piece of paper.

'It has always been a source of great sorrow that I allowed Maria's mother to push me away. I should have fought harder to stay with her. If I had, I might not have missed Maria's childhood, her adolescence. I might have been there for her sooner. But I walked away in anger and pride. Don't make the same mistake.'

'I'll try,' I said, and went out, closing the door quietly behind me.

CHAPTER FIFTY-TWO

Detective 'Ritz' Gardner lay full-length in the dusty scrub, resting on her elbows, her voice coming out slightly muffled behind the set of night vision glasses.

'I have *got* to get me some of these.'

'Do many surveillance ops in total darkness, do you?' I asked. 'Any street lamps or artificial light and all you get is massive flare-out.'

'Really?' She sounded disappointed. 'Still...'

The moon was coming and going behind high fast-moving cloud, giving patches of clarity amid the darkness. Far over to the west of us, Los Angeles glowed an angry orange that stained the heavens.

'See anything yet?'

'Not unless Epps's guys are disguised as deer and gophers,' she said, scanning. 'What are we hoping to achieve out here, anyway?'

'Honestly? Bugger all,' I said. 'But it's better than sitting around inside waiting for them to come.'

And if they just decide to execute him, right here in the

desert, you'll stand witness. A cop. Someone they'll listen to. Someone with credibility.

After the order from Epps to stay put, Gardner had stashed Yancy in the very cell I'd so recently occupied, and agreed to my suggestion that we ventured out to check for signs of a double-cross. She had retrieved her official body armour from the boot of her car, but I'd drawn the line when she lifted out the Mossberg pump-action shotgun.

'If they get close enough for that thing to be any real use, we're screwed anyway,' I told her. 'And besides, you have your standard side arm. Use that and you can claim self-defence. Anything else and it looks like premeditation.'

Reluctantly, I felt, she lay the shotgun back in the boot and tightened one of the Velcro straps for the vest, settled it on her shoulders. 'What is it, exactly, you're intending we should do?'

'Watch for a double-cross,' I said. 'I trust Epps about as far as I could throw him.'

'But they're jamming the radios as well as the phones,' Gardner pointed out, as we'd picked up the night vision goggles from the depleted security team and headed out into the scrubland beyond the compound fence. Her voice softened. 'There won't be anything you can do, Charlie.'

'Oh, I'm sure we'll think of something if we have to.'

Now, I swung my own NVGs across the approach road. It was like looking at an alien seabed through green-tinted water, ambient light artificially boosted so the picture was slightly out of kilter, ghostly. I panned across, half-expecting to see a scatter of fish suspended in mid-air, and stilled suddenly.

'We've got movement,' I said, refocusing. 'Two vehicles, just turning in. Could be Suburbans.'

'Uh-huh,' Gardner murmured. 'And right on time. Nice to see our tax dollars efficiently at work.'

I shifted to check the luminous dial on my watch, then realised the cheap replacement for my Tag did not have that facility. I wondered if I'd ever see the Tag – or Sean – again.

I remembered Bane's words. Could we find a way past this? As the Suburbans rolled closer, leaving a plume of pale dust rising behind them into the night air, I felt a sudden tightness in my belly.

Not long now, and you'll find out...

And then, without warning, the tail of the lead Suburban bucked into the air in a ball of light and flame so hot and bright it blasted through the green spectrum and straight into hard, cold white. I'd already whipped the goggles away from my face as the sound of the explosion reached us.

By the fire, I watched the vehicle bounce down again and veer wildly, the driver fighting for control. I saw sparks from the ripped-out rear axle hitting rocks and stones as it skidded along the track.

Gardner squawked, 'What the—?'

I didn't answer, eyes fixed on the wrecked Suburban. As soon as it stopped moving, the doors were opening and a group of black-clad figures emerged. I counted four, some staggering, but all able to move under their own steam.

The driver of the second vehicle had already reacted, braking hard enough to slew sideways. A moment later, another team, obviously well armed, were debussing with experienced military haste.

'What was that?' Gardner's voice was hoarse. 'Was it a bomb? Who—?'

I pulled back my focus, saw another vivid blazing streak race in from the far right and hit the second vehicle amidships, turning it into an instant fireball.

'No, it's a bloody grenade launcher,' I said, scrambling to my feet. 'Come on!'

To her credit, Gardner was on her feet and only half a stride behind me. 'Those are Epps's people out there,' she said, gasping as she ran. 'Who in the hell is firing at them?'

That is what I want to find out.

I clamped the goggles back to my face. The heavy green cast made identifying obstacles difficult and unfamiliar. We ran in halting steps, wary of falling. As we neared the scene, the light from the blazing vehicle made them almost ineffective anyway. At least we'd seen the men inside bail out before the second grenade hit, but I wasn't interested in checking for casualties. They could do that for themselves.

With the homicide detective alongside me, we plunged deeper into the scrub.

I knew we weren't looking for an expert, and that ruled out the rest of Fourth Day's security, who were all ex-military of some type. They would have known to aim further forwards of the lead vehicle in order to hit it cleanly. I remembered the way the fire-trail seemed to hang in the air as it ran. Whoever was on the trigger badly miscalculated the relatively slow muzzle velocity of a rocket-propelled grenade.

If our shooter was an amateur, he wouldn't have risked firing from the maximum effective distance for the weapon.

That meant he was close, and we could catch him.

Or her.

Even so, I was unprepared for how soon Gardner shouted, 'Police! Drop your weapon! Drop your weapon and get down on the ground!'

The reply she received to her challenge was two sharp staccato barks from a small-calibre semi-automatic. We both ducked instinctively, hearing the high whine of the rounds disappearing into the night.

'Shit,' Gardner muttered. 'There's never any backup when you need it.'

'Are you telling me you don't carry a clinch piece?'

'What, like a snub-nose thirty-eight in an ankle holster?' she demanded in a savage whisper. 'Tried it, my first month out of uniform. Throws your back out like you wouldn't believe.' I heard the grimace in her voice. 'And I never needed it, 'til now.'

'I'll circle round, try and draw him out. You better be ready to take him down. Just try not to shoot me by mistake, Ritz. I've been there and done that, and it bloody hurts.'

'OK,' she said tightly.

'And remember to shut your eyes when you fire, otherwise the muzzle flash will ruin your night vision.'

'I'm not some damned rookie, Charlie! Just go, and let's get this done.'

I cut away from her, not making any attempt at stealth, sweeping round in a long looping arc designed to flush our assailant out of cover, just noisy enough to be a tempting target. It occurred to me, too late to do anything about it, that I should have asked if Gardner had any qualms when it came to pulling the trigger. Many cops, I knew, never got to fire their weapons in anger during the entire length of their career. Just because LA had over four hundred homicides in a year didn't mean Gardner herself was willing to add to that number.

I hoped the evidence of murderous intent, still blazing fiercely over to our left, would silence any last flutterings of conscience.

I paused, closed my eyes as if to divert auxiliary power to my still-dodgy hearing, heard a shuffle off to one side. My eyes snapped open. I caught a flicker of shape between me and the fire and was already ducking when the blow came.

It still landed across my shoulders hard enough to blast the air from my lungs, drop me to my knees. I twisted as I went down, flung up an arm and deflected a second blow away to the side. He was using something long and heavy, already pulling back for a third swing. I couldn't survive much more of this.

For God's sake, what are you waiting for?

'Drop it! Drop it!' Gardner's voice was tight with tension as she came forwards. 'Down on the ground!'

I felt the dirt kick up in my face as my attacker obeyed the command and dropped whatever he'd used to clobber me, but I saw his hands move, saw the glint in them, and yelled, 'Gun!'

Still Gardner hesitated. The gun in the man's hands – and I was damned sure it was a man now – jerked as he fired. It all seemed to happen very slowly. I saw the shaft of flame spit from the end of the barrel as the action cycled. The empty brass came spinning out of the eject port and I flinched as it bounced against my neck, marking me instantly with a small cigarette-end burn.

The report was a painful crack that exploded in my tender ears, so I didn't immediately register the two shots Gardner fired in return.

But I heard him grunt as both rounds took him in the torso, heard the dull thump of the gun landing in the dirt next to me. I fumbled at the shadowed ground, snatching the weapon up, but knew at once I didn't need to use it.

Gardner stumbled forwards, eyes made wide and wild by the fire, found me bending over the fallen figure.

'Did I...?'

'Near enough,' I said curtly, feeling my way along his body. He was vibrating with fear and pain and the rapid onset of shock. The whole of his chest was greasy with blood, his breath coming in ragged gasps.

Gardner dragged out a pen flashlight and clicked it on, cupping her hand around the bulb to keep it shielded. She panned across his body, faltering as the beam caught the shine of the blood, the rattle and the shake, and settled on his face. As soon as I saw it, I knew him. I think I probably knew him before then anyway.

Tony. Dexter's comrade from Debacle. What he hoped to gain from this, I had no idea. Gardner's flashlight beam clipped the edge of the weapon he'd used to clobber me and I saw it was an M16 with the M203 grenade launcher slung under the barrel. Twentieth-century weapon transformed into Neanderthal-era club in the blink of an eye.

The M203's 40 mm projectile had an effective range of a hundred and fifty metres and a muzzle velocity of only around seventy-five metres a second. A fraction of the speed that a 5.56 mm round would have left the assault rifle the launcher was attached to. The same guns and the same launchers I'd seen stacked in boxes in the subterranean storerooms. The guns the fake-faithful Yancy was supposed to have destroyed.

'Why?' I asked.

Tony bared bloodied teeth. 'The money,' he gasped. 'Why else?'

Noises off made Gardner and I both start, eyes raking the surrounding gloom. 'They're coming,' I said, rising. 'We have to go.'

'But, we can't just leave him,' she protested.

'They'll take care of him,' I said, mentally crossing my fingers as my mind put several connotations on the words. 'Even if we could get him back to the compound without killing him, we can't treat him there. Leave him. Now!'

And without a backward glance at the men from the two wrecked Suburbans, now advancing on our position, we ran.

CHAPTER FIFTY-THREE

'They'll come for us in the dark,' I said, snapping the magazine out of another M16 and laying it flat on the desktop. 'In the early hours, before the sky starts to lighten, with the Bradleys up front, most likely. They'll put down smoke for extra cover. If we're lucky we might smell it in advance. And they'll come soon. If not tonight, then tomorrow at the latest.'

Bane threw me a speculative glance, raised an eyebrow in Gardner's direction as if asking for confirmation. She was loading dismantled stocks and barrels into storage boxes to be distributed around the compound, as far apart as we could place them to try and prove Bane's non-violent intent.

We were in the little classroom where I'd found Nu's planted fuse and the report of the oil refinery visit that had created the timetable for this tragedy of errors. There was no significance to the location – it was just a convenient place to work on the weapons.

Outside, in the background, I could hear the steady chug

of the diesel generators that were providing power. The next thing Epps had done, after cutting the phones, was to cut the mains power.

'They'll wait,' she said, but I heard the edge in her voice, as though she was trying to force confidence into it. 'Try to starve us out first – break our nerve.'

'After what Tony did?' I shook my head. 'No, they're going to want to take us down quickly.'

We'd watched Epps's men cluster round the spot where Tony had fallen, but if their lack of urgency was any indication, either he was already dead, or they'd decided that he should be. It was a cold foretaste, I considered, of what might be to come.

I glanced at Bane. 'Sean's with them. He knows, the more chance he gives us to dig in, the worse it will be for them.'

Bane fixed me with a long stare that slipped between the cracks of my armour like rain. 'You mean, the more chance he gives *you* to prepare,' he said, and it wasn't a question.

I shrugged, picked up the next weapon and worked the action. The sharp, mechanical slither of the M16's internal scales was ugly as blasphemy amid the jaunty alphabet frieze and childish writing on the blackboard.

'He knows you,' Bane said.

I set to work, practised enough now that I didn't have to watch my hands. 'Not as well as he thinks he does,' I said. *Or we won't survive this night.*

'And you know him.'

I looked up then, caught both the stillness in him, and the pace. 'No,' I said. 'I'm not sure I know him at all.'

* * *

By the time Gardner and I had reached the main entrance, sweating and breathless, the fire from the two vehicles was a fierce bright light in the near distance. Half of Fourth Day seemed to be outside waiting for us, including Bane, with Dexter alongside him.

'What the hell did you do, kiddo?' Dexter demanded. I looked down, saw I still had Tony's gun, a Ruger P89 semi-automatic, clutched tightly in my bloodied fist.

Taking it from the scene was a grave mistake, I acknowledged. When Epps's people searched his body, there was nothing to show he'd been armed with anything other than the RPG, and yet he'd been taken down in a clinical way that suggested execution rather than self-defence.

Ah well, too late for regrets now.

'Not us.' Gardner shook her head, bent over, one hand braced on her knee while she caught her wind. 'Your pal, Tony.'

'What?' Dexter backed a step, and for a moment I thought it was guilt rather than denial that caused his instinctive retreat. 'No,' he said. 'Oh, no.'

'Oh, yes,' I muttered, indicating the conflagration. 'He blew the vehicles Epps sent in.' Bane's face was shocked. 'Used an M203 grenade launcher. Yancy obviously didn't quite follow your instructions regarding their disposal.'

'How do you know it was Tony?' Dexter said, voice rough. 'It couldn't be. I've known him for... Why, for God's sake?'

'We saw him, Dexter,' Gardner said flatly.

'Well, where is he? I want to see the sonofabitch. I want—' And then his eyes flickered to my hands again and an awful understanding came over him. Ann put a hand on Dexter's shoulder, but he twisted out from under it, shouldered past us and ran.

I thought he meant to go to his friend, but when Gardner and I charged after him, he was heading in the direction of the underground storerooms where Yancy had been safely locked away.

By the time we caught up with him, Dexter had the door to Yancy's cell flung open and was inside, staring down at the ex-Marine as he sat, apparently unconcerned, on the hard mattress.

'Tell me why, you bastard!' Dexter yelled, breathing hard through his nose, jaw thrust forwards.

Gardner grabbed Dexter's shoulders and, when he would have resisted, casually twisted one arm into a standard lock behind his back.

'OK, Tyrone,' I said, aware of people crowding in behind us, of more in the corridor outside, 'how many more are there?'

He eyed us all with something akin to slow amusement on his face. 'I already said way too much.'

I glared at him. 'Tony just fired a forty-mil grenade at Epps's guys on their way in.'

Yancy's gaze drifted over the blood drying on my hands. 'I'm guessing that didn't go well for him.'

'Bane was going to give himself up,' I said with a burst of useless anger. 'As it is, Epps's guys will be coming in here with all guns blazing. You think you're likely to survive if they do?'

'Say I do.' He shrugged. 'Where's that gonna get me? Next twenty years in San Quentin, waiting for a needle in my arm.'

Dexter stopped struggling and Gardner released him. He flicked her a poisonous glance as he pointedly stepped away from her. 'I thought Tony was my friend,' he said in a pathetic little voice. 'What the fuck *happened*?'

Yancy threw him a look of contempt, but said, 'The kid was broke and desperate. Same old story. He sees you rich kids playing at being eco-warriors, and still drawing on your monthly allowance from mommy and daddy. Playing at it. And he wants his share.'

'And in return, he tries to take out two armoured Suburbans with a short-range grenade launcher – on the move, in the dark?' I queried. 'Come off it, Yancy. He was an amateur and he missed. That should have been your job.'

Yancy shook his head, gave a low chuckle. 'You ain't worked it out yet, have you?' he asked. 'Tony? He's been on the payroll for a *long* time. Making sure nobody say nothing about no oil shale find in California. You get me?'

And suddenly I did get him. A final piece of the puzzle, one that had shown no signs of fitting, suddenly rotated and fell into place.

'It was Tony who was in Alaska, wasn't it?' I said slowly. 'Tell me, did he kill Liam himself, or just deliberately compromise him?'

Yancy grinned, deep-cut lines appearing around his eyes as they crinkled. 'You got it,' he said. 'Takes you a while, but you get there in the end.'

Now, close to midnight, I walked through the hastily barricaded rooms of the main building, shoulder to shoulder with Randall Bane, the man I'd once been sent to betray.

We stayed away from the windows, knowing who was out there in the darkness, watching.

Bane walked slowly among his people, radiating calm, touching a shoulder here and there, and I watched something of the fear go out of them, as if beneath a blessing. The glances they stole in my direction were darker, but if they felt I should have been thrown to the wolves by way of sacrifice, they held their tongues. Bane had spoken for me, and for most of them that was enough. And without Yancy, without Nu, they knew they needed me. What I stood for. What I was.

We'd collected everybody into the very centre of the main structure, reinforcing the walls with sandbags, hastily concocted using earth shovelled up from under the floorboards, into pillowcases and backpacks and sports bags. Anything that would hold it.

It wouldn't be enough to stop the kind of rounds our attackers would be using, of course, but it was better than nothing. Better than doing nothing, too.

Dotted at points around the room were fire buckets and piles of sopping blankets against smoke or gas, and bottled water.

It was a surreal situation. The thing that brought it home, even though it was my own suggestion, was that each person had their blood group written in large clear letters on the skin of their forearm, in indelible marker.

The children sat in a huddled group in the centre of the room, where the illusion of safety was strongest. The older ones had been organised as runners. There weren't enough medical kits to go around, so we'd located them at several centralised points to be distributed according to need. The children would carry them, like powder monkeys on a Napoleonic man-o'-war. I hoped they would make less tempting targets for the SWAT team.

Now, Bane approached and crouched to their level, murmuring reassurances. They watched him with frightened eyes in pinched faces, innocently accusing. I ignored the way my heart contracted, shrivelling in my chest at what I'd helped contrive they be a part of.

Maria was there, cradling Billy in her arms. She'd taken no chances with her son's blood group, writing it on both arms and across his neck. Universal donors, I knew, could only receive blood from a like source. Would Epps's people take the trouble to find a match for him, if it came to it?

I turned away. 'You should have got them out while we had the chance,' I murmured.

Bane glanced at me, and his gaze was heavy. 'I doubt they would have agreed to go,' he said.

'They shouldn't have been given the choice.'

'But it's all about choice, Charlie,' he said gently, and his eyes lingered on the little girl holding Billy's hand – she of the seahorse knickers. I vaguely recalled her name was Maisie. She had AB+ scrawled along her arm in jerky lettering and I wondered if Bane knew that, with that type, her chances of survival were markedly better than his grandson's. 'We didn't start this.'

'And you won't finish it, either,' I said, brutal, watching their tightly intertwined fingers. 'How does that square with your ideals and your choices?'

He didn't answer. We passed on, out of the flickering, diesel-generated light and into a dimmer passageway. I put my hand on his arm.

'You've got to get to Epps, face to face,' I said. 'Convince him what's really going on, however it's been made to look.'

'You think he'll listen to reason?'

I let my breath out. 'You think he'll listen any better if you wait for him to come through the walls with CS gas?'

Bane walked on another few paces, then said, 'What do you propose?'

'Epps has set up a mobile command post out on the main road. Gardner and I passed it on the way in.' I paused, smiled faintly. 'You're probably the most persuasive bastard I've ever met, Bane. If I can get you to him, can you stop this?'

His mouth quirked slightly but his face was thoughtful rather than surprised, as though he'd known what I was about to say, if not quite the wording. 'It's unlikely they will let us simply walk in,' he pointed out.

'I'll deal with that.' I made a gesture of impatience. 'Sagar has engineered it so that you won't get another chance to come quietly. What's the alternative?'

'And what if it's Sean who stands against you?'

My face hardened. 'I'll deal with that, too...'

CHAPTER FIFTY-FOUR

It was a long time since I'd ridden a quad bike. Astride one now, struggling to follow Bane's tracks in the dark, I rapidly came to the conclusion that I preferred two wheels over four. The quads, it seemed, combined all the ungainliness of a car, with the vulnerability of a bike.

Just because I'd had a road bike licence for years did not make me a good rider on the rough stuff. Bane, of course, piloted his machine over the loose dirt with a natural agility born of long practice.

I could see him ahead of me now, standing up on the footpegs to absorb the jolts and letting the quad do all the work underneath him as he picked his way around the larger rocks.

The Kawasaki quads were the ones I'd seen the day Maria and I had made our abortive trip out into the wilderness, parked alongside the Jeep. Both Bane and I wore NVGs and kept the headlights switched off. We had taped over the rear brake lights, which made finding our way even more alien in the green-tinted gloom.

Gardner had not been in favour of letting the two of us go alone, but even she couldn't fault the logic of it. Bane was the one Epps wanted. And if Epps couldn't come to us, we would have to go to him. Preferably before he C4'd the main door off its hinges and ransacked the place.

'Keep them safe, Ritz,' I said as she watched us mount up.

'Same back at you.' She leant over and gave me a quick hug, patting my back awkwardly around the rucksack I wore, then drew back with a smile that contained more than its share of bravado. 'If the worst happens, my stamp collection goes to my niece,' she added. 'She always loved the ones of the waterfalls.'

'It won't come to that.' *Not if I can help it.*

Now, thumping across the uneven surface with a warm breeze blowing grit into our faces, I wondered what I had to bequeath, and to whom I'd choose to leave it. It was a sad reflection on my life, I thought, that nothing immediately sprang to mind.

I had my bikes, of course. The Honda FireBlade, laid up under dust sheets and layers of protective grease in the back of my parents' garage in rural Cheshire. And the Buell in the underground parking garage beneath the apartment in New York. What else? The majority of the last year's salary stashed away in an investment account, a decent watch, a good pair of boots, a few handguns. Not much to show for nearly twenty-nine years on the planet.

Sean and I shared a travel-light mentality. We didn't collect mementos of our time together, weren't big on stuff and clutter. When we had managed to get time to slip away together for a holiday, we'd brought back no souvenirs and taken no happy snaps. I couldn't remember the last picture of just the two of us together.

And if a good number of people were still alive because of us, in circumstances where they might otherwise have perished, there were possibly an equal number who had died by our collective hand.

Someone once said that people are remembered by the shape they leave in the world. When I looked back at my life so far, all I could see were holes.

We travelled north for perhaps half a mile, slowly enough for tension and effort to bathe me in sweat. Then we turned directly west until we hit the road Gardner and I had initially travelled in on. In the distance, south of us, we could see our objective, the faint neon-lit bar, its car park suddenly a blaze of halogen that reached far into the night sky. We did not make the mistake of heading directly towards it. I remembered the SWAT guys who'd materialised alongside Gardner's car and knew we wouldn't get within five hundred metres of Epps before they took us down.

Traffic on the road was sporadic, but we could guess its nature and did not want to risk being seen or challenged by anyone else, either. I was prepared to fight if I had to, but doing so would serve no tactical purpose. In fact, it would actively work against us. It was going to be difficult enough to convince Epps we came in peace, without arriving with yet more blood on our hands.

So, we hung back, beyond the periphery of the headlights until there was a large enough gap, then crossed quickly, keeping the quads nose to tail and plunging rapidly into the scrub on the far side. We struck out west for a distance, until the lights from the road were obscured by the terrain and barely visible, and then headed south, running parallel.

The ground seemed a little easier over here, or I was finally falling into some kind of rhythm where I was able, like Bane, to let the quad work underneath me, without tensing in anticipation of disaster at every bump and jar.

Part of my mind stayed alert, keeping my body's guidance systems functioning, monitoring the sensory input from the NVGs, listening for external noise above the quads' engines. But another part turned inwards, looking for answers in the only place I would ever find them.

It seemed like a long trip but, even so, I was no wiser at the end of it than at the beginning.

Eventually, Bane eased his right hand off the throttle and glanced back over his shoulder. I nodded and he swung the quad on its final heading, directly westwards, back towards where we knew the bar was located. For speed, we would ride in as close as we dared, then continue on foot. Now the moment was close, my mind was strangely calm amid the other uncertainties.

Twenty minutes later, I lay alongside Randall Bane, flattened against the sandy ground, watching the activity surrounding Epps's mobile command post on the far side of the road. We were maybe twenty-five metres back from the shoulder, plenty close enough to see the bulky trailer's gloss-black gleam under the harsh lighting, like a giant shark.

The earth felt warm under me and I was suddenly reminded of my first glimpse of Bane, lying like this with Sean as we watched Fourth Day's compound.

'I assume you have not brought us this far without a plan

for getting us inside there,' Bane murmured, nodding to the trailer, 'preferably without getting our heads blown off.'

Since Gardner and I had passed, the whole of the parking area next to the bar was now lit up like a football stadium by arc lights on extendable poles, a generator running at the foot of each. Whenever anyone walked across, they were starkly illuminated, throwing out multiple shadows.

'In a manner of speaking,' I said. 'My inclination is a repeat of how I got into Fourth Day.'

I felt the frown in his voice. 'You mean, walk in and see how far we get before someone accosts us with a gun?' he asked. 'And what if Epps decides not to satisfy his curiosity about me until *after* the raid on the compound is over?'

'Oh, I don't believe he'll do that,' said a voice above and behind us, disembodied in the darkness. 'I think you'll find Comrade Epps can't *wait* to talk to you.'

CHAPTER FIFTY-FIVE

'Hello, Sean,' I said calmly, without moving my head. 'Right on time, I see.'

'Up slowly to your knees, Charlie, if you please. Hands where we can see them.' It was Parker who spoke now, his voice completely emotionless. He was a little further back than Sean, I judged, and standing off to his right. 'Let's not do anything that any of us would have cause to regret.' And I got the feeling he was speaking as much to Sean as to me.

Carefully, Bane and I pushed up to our knees, hands out from our sides and fingers loose. Parker appeared around from behind us, moving cautiously. He was dressed in the black of the SWAT teams and armed with an M4.

Bane glanced at me, his expression unreadable. '*This* was your plan?'

I shrugged. 'You were right, Sean does know me,' I said. 'But better this than trying to fight our way in, don't you think?'

'We got them,' Parker said, and I saw he was wearing

a throat mic, the words not directed at us. 'We're bringing them in now.' He nodded to Sean, still behind us. Next thing, Sean's hands began a rough pat-down search of Bane. He went over him twice, seeming surprised not to find a weapon.

'There's a Ruger nine-mil in my backpack,' I said mildly, when Sean moved on to me. 'I took it away from Tony, after he tried to take out the two Suburbans Epps sent in for Bane.'

'Oh, I know all about that,' Sean said softly, and finally stepped round in front of us. There was a livid gash along his cheekbone which had been hastily Steri-Stripped back together. Any saliva in my mouth turned instantly to ashes.

'Oh, shit,' I murmured. 'You were in one of them.'

'Lead vehicle,' he said shortly. 'We found Tony's body. If you hadn't killed the little bastard, I would have done it myself.'

I didn't think passing on the blame – or perhaps the credit – to Gardner would have gained me anything, nor would denying prior knowledge of Tony's abortive ambush. Either Sean knew, at some deep inner level, that I would not have been a part of it, or he was past believing me anyway.

I kept silent.

'OK,' Parker said. 'On your feet.'

'You really think we should take him to Epps?' Sean asked. 'The fact it's what he wants makes me suspicious in itself.' His cold stare swept over Bane's impassive features. 'It's not as if he can tell us anything operationally useful.'

'For God's sake,' I said. 'What do you think this is –

some kind of half-arsed assassination attempt? Why do you think we're here, if not to try and stop this before it goes any further?'

And when Sean would have reacted in anger, I'm sure, Parker silenced him with a single look. 'All right,' he said. 'You really want so badly to see Epps? Let's go.'

They escorted us across to the command centre truck, not exactly as prisoners, but not exactly as guests, either. They didn't cuff us, as I'd half-expected that they might, but both Sean and Parker stayed slightly back, where they could read any body movements that were remotely hostile. I snuck a quick sideways look at Bane. If he had fears about what was to come, he didn't show it.

Only when we reached the steps up into the back of the trailer did Parker move ahead, knocking and waiting for the door to be opened. The rear half of the interior was a mass of flat-screen monitors and communications equipment, manned by three of Epps's personnel, all male. I wondered almost idly if Epps employed *any* women, and, if so, in what capacity.

Parker led us straight past the technicians, who barely glanced up from their monitors as we passed. They might have been geeks, but they were still all carrying Glocks, I noted.

Out of the corner of my eye I saw one screen carried what appeared to be a satellite image of the compound. Interesting to know that Epps had that kind of clout, and no wonder Parker and Sean had been waiting for us. They must have tracked us from the moment we left. But did that also mean...?

'Didn't you see Tony waiting for you?' I asked,

nodding to the image on the screen.

'Epps only got the OK to retask the bird *after* the RPG attack,' Sean said darkly. 'Before then, it wasn't deemed necessary.'

And by the way the technicians studiously avoided his eye, I surmised that had been a bone of contention.

Parker walked straight to the front half of the trailer and opened a door without waiting for an answer to his perfunctory knock. Inside, we found Conrad Epps sitting behind a surprisingly utilitarian desk with just a phone and a laptop in front of him. Against the far wall, perched on a low sofa, was Chris Sagar.

At the sight of us, Sagar jerked to his feet, would have backed away if the base of the sofa hadn't already been hard up behind his knees. I had to make a physical effort to stop myself reaching for his throat. If Bane felt the same way, he didn't let that show, either. I'd never met a man with so much self-control.

Apart, maybe, from Sean.

I glanced at him, but he was like a stranger to me. He stayed by the door, making no bones about blocking our exit. It was hard to remember, watching him now, that we had shared a bed, a life, and intimacy. Parker moved round so he was against the far wall, to Epps's right, providing diffuse targets.

'Mr Bane,' Epps said, leaning back in his chair. There was no satisfaction in his voice, no gloat. Me, he completely ignored, as I thought he probably would.

'Mr Epps,' Bane returned gravely. He folded his hands neatly in front of him, allowed his shaven head to tilt as he surveyed his nemesis with something close to indifference.

'You wanted me, so here I am,' he said. 'Now, perhaps you would be so kind as to leave my people alone.'

'What a pity you weren't always so amenable,' Epps said coldly. 'And it's a little late for that, don't you think? They seem to have involved themselves.'

'It doesn't have to be too late,' Bane said. 'I'm prepared to answer any questions you'd care to ask. My only stipulation is that first you hear what I have to say.'

'In case it escaped your notice, Mr Bane,' Epps said coldly, 'you're in no position to lay down conditions.'

'Neither are you,' Bane said, his gaze sweeping over an increasingly nervous-looking Sagar, 'when this whole sorry tale becomes public knowledge.'

Such was his conviction that Epps paused a moment, eyes flicking to his consultant, then said, 'What is it you have to say, Mr Bane?'

'Wait a minute!' Sagar protested. 'Surely, you're not—?'

'Rest assured that I am not an easy man to convince,' Epps said easily. His gaze shifted back to Bane. 'What evidence do you have to support that statement?'

'None that would convince a jury. But, tell me, was it you who approached Chris Sagar for advice on cults in general and Fourth Day in particular, or was it the other way around?' he asked, his voice calm and measured. 'He has no doubt told you that he was a former member of the subversive cult called Fourth Day, that he was the trusted second in command, and that's all true.'

Into the stunned silence that followed, Bane added, 'But what Chris failed to admit is that this was before I was involved with Fourth Day. All the excesses and practices he claims went on did indeed happen, but under his guiding hand. He was not rescued and rehabilitated, but cast out and shunned.'

'Lies!' Sagar shouted, stabbing a finger in Bane's direction. 'I warned you he'd—'

'Be quiet, Mr Sagar,' Epps said with a faint snap like bones breaking.

'The old owner of Fourth Day had no children, no close relatives, and Chris was positioning himself nicely to inherit, both the cult and the property that went with it. Then the old guy was forced to sell out. There was a private lawsuit by the familes of several young girls, who were abused at Fourth Day's hands, and he sold to me. It was settled out of court, with the minimum of publicity, but there are ways of finding out these things.' Bane paused, glancing at the set faces before him.

Epps leant forwards on the desktop, linking his hands together as if to keep them under control. 'Go on.'

'I have sworn depositions from the victims and their families, naming Chris for his part in this tragedy. How he escaped jail time is a mystery. It's all there, and you are welcome to examine the documents all you like, in my lawyer's offices, during normal business hours.'

Parker regarded him with just a touch of scepticism still. 'Are you saying he set this whole thing up as some kind of revenge deal?'

'Not at all,' Bane said. 'This is all about simple greed. It always has been.'

Sagar took a pace forwards. 'He's lying!' he said, but there was an underlying desperation that we all heard. He swallowed it down as best he could. 'He had Witney murdered to stop him talking to you, for fuck's sake!'

'Detective Gardner has a confession from Tyrone Yancy about that,' I put in. 'He claims that he and Nu killed Witney on your orders, Sagar.'

'You can't listen to her,' Sagar jeered. 'She was too weak to resist him. She's gone over, just like you said she would.'

Epps regarded me for a moment in granite silence, then turned back to Bane. 'Greed?'

'Liam Witney first discovered the oil shale deposits, and he made the mistake of telling Christopher. Of course, the big oil companies have been researching an economical method of extracting oil shale for decades, but now they may finally have made a breakthrough. I had a geological survey carried out that confirms the presence of enough oil-bearing shale to produce millions of barrels.'

'I didn't know,' Sagar protested. 'C'mon! I would have bought the damned land myself if I'd known.' He gave a short, high laugh. 'I told you, I thought the shale deposits were minimal at best. Worthless.'

'At the time you had no means of raising the capital to buy the land,' Bane said, allowing a flick of steel to lash through his voice for the first time. His eyes slid back across to Epps. 'And now he's trading futures for favours. How much did you offer Tyrone to keep the ball rolling in the right directions, Chris?' When Sagar merely glared, he went on, 'What I don't know is how he managed to enlist my security personnel in the first place.'

'Fourth Day used to have ties to various militia groups,' Parker said suddenly. 'Both Nu and Yancy were members of different groups after the military, and it was in their interest to bring about a return to the old regime. They could well have been behind the original attacks – supply and demand.'

Supply and demand. I remembered Yancy's confession back at the compound, and was heartened that Parker had come to the same conclusion unaided.

Epps regarded Bane through narrowed eyes. 'Why did you not approach us with this counter-intelligence right at the start, Mr Bane?'

Bane gave a sad half smile. 'You and I have a history together, and I knew I was unlikely to be believed,' he said simply. 'Chris had told you that Fourth Day was a brainwashing cult, and you were only too ready to accept that.' He looked right into Epps's eyes, straight in and through and down deep. 'I believe,' he said gently, 'that Mr Sagar may have found out that your daughter took her own life after her involvement with a cult in Tennessee, and manipulated that knowledge in order to convince you. He's an excellent psychologist. All conmen are.'

Epps's face went blank white, so that even his gunmetal grey moustache seemed to fade and something of the steel went out of his frame as he deflated before our eyes like a slow puncture.

'I took over Fourth Day in order to turn it into a place of refuge, not to found my own religion,' Bane said calmly into the silence. 'Maria's mother was involved with fanatics, and it has had a profound and detrimental effect on my daughter's life. She still has nightmares and day terrors. People come to me damaged, and I try and help them to heal themselves.'

'Like Charlie, you mean?' It was Sean who spoke, surprising me with the dusty hoarseness of his voice. 'Just how, exactly, have you been helping her to heal?'

When I turned, I found his face almost as pale as that of Epps, and a desperate anguish in his eyes. Because, I realised, it had finally come home to him that if what Bane was saying was true, then half of what he'd believed of me – what Sagar had twisted to fit the apparent facts – was not.

Bane's eyes skimmed over him and I could tell from the gentleness in his face, his voice, that he realised it, too. 'Charlie needed very little help to let her inner beauty shine,' he murmured. He turned back to Epps. 'I entirely understand that you will need further proof of Chris's machinations,' he went on, but to my surprise Epps shook his head.

'I might have done,' he admitted slowly, 'had Mr Sagar not demanded, in return for his expertise in this matter, that the US government make over all Fourth Day's property to him.'

Bane showed no triumph, no relief, didn't smile, just nodded with the quiet dignity of a statesman. 'Now,' he said, 'please, call off your dogs.'

CHAPTER FIFTY-SIX

Cancelling the planned assault on Fourth Day's compound was not a five-minute job. Oh, standing down the SWAT teams was achieved with one phone call, but restoring communications proved slightly more complicated. Eventually, Epps ordered up another couple of Suburbans, of which he seemed to have a limitless supply, and announced we would go in.

Sagar had lapsed into a dull-eyed silence, sitting hunched on the sofa. Parker had to scoop a hand under his elbow and lever him upright when word came through that the vehicles were waiting for us outside.

Parker handed off Sagar none too gently to Sean, who opened the door and nudged him through. Because of the confined space behind the technicians' seats, we went through the communications area of the trailer in single file, Sagar leading with Sean directly behind, then Bane, me, Epps, and Parker bringing up the rear.

And even as we stepped out into that narrow space, an uneasiness came over me, a sense of trepidation I couldn't quite identify.

Surely Epps won't pull a double-cross on us – not now...

I glanced back over my shoulder, but there was nothing in Epps's face to alarm me. *Perhaps I'm just getting paranoid in my—*

I felt rather than heard the stumble through the suspended floor, twisted back just in time to see Sagar trip, cannoning clumsily into the technician sitting closest to the door. And in that instant I had a flash image of him stumbling like that once before, when the three men in the van had ambushed us. I'd told him to run, but he'd apparently fallen over his own feet and gone down, and I'd been forced to face our attackers when my instinct had been to flee.

As I watched, almost in slow motion, Sagar landed on the seated technician, driving the man's upper body forwards so that his forehead smacked into his own keyboard. Sagar let out a convincing 'oof' as he hit, but his right hand snaked for the gun sitting at high ride on the man's belt, with all the speed and sureness of a card cheat switching to a cold deck.

'Sean!'

Even as I shouted the warning, Sagar jammed the stolen Glock nine into the technician's ribs and, without hesitation, pulled the trigger.

The noise of the report was concussively loud inside the confines of the trailer. Unarmed, helpless, I took the only option open to me, jumping on top of Bane and powering him down, swinging him round to keep my body between him and the gun.

Sean was already reacting before the technician knew he was hit. He had the fastest reactions of anyone I ever met. The M4 was slung over his shoulder on its strap but he didn't bother trying to raise it, reaching instead for the .45-calibre Glock 21 he carried in a Kramer paddle holster at his side. He fired as soon as he cleared leather, aiming by grip and muscle memory and instinct.

But Sagar was already moving as the first shot landed, ducking and spinning away, so the round grazed across the back of his shoulder blade rather than landing solidly in his upper body, as it had been intended.

Sagar let out a grunt of pain and fired again as he bolted for the doorway, four rapid shots let off straight-armed behind him, blindly, as fast as he could work the trigger. The muzzle oscillated crazily as the action cycled, but his rounds were intended purely to cause havoc and confusion, to delay pursuit, fired without any clear target in mind.

But they found one anyway.

I couldn't tell which of those wild shots hit Sean. All I saw was his head snap back and to the side, the mist of blood and something else, some heavier debris, sluice upwards across the clinical white wall of the trailer, then he went down.

No staggering halt. No controlled descent. No realisation of pain or damage. Just a sudden total overwhelming collapse as all motor function ceased.

Inside my own head, someone started screaming.

I don't remember jacking upright, but next thing I knew I was on my feet, snatching up Sean's Glock where it had dropped from his lifeless hand. Lights exploded behind my eyes, a howling filled my ears, the smell of blood was in my nose, my mouth.

And I wanted it.

I threw myself at the closing door before it had time to swing fully shut behind Sagar's fleeing figure.

He'd got to the bottom of the steps and had started to run, awkward, stooped because of the shoulder injury Sean had inflicted. Sagar wore a pale-blue shirt and the blood was already soaking through the back of it in a spreading diagonal slash as if from the blade of a sword, his ponytail lank with it.

With a snarl I barely recognised, I bounded off the top flight of steps at full stretch, aiming straight for the blood like a starving predator going after wounded prey. I landed hard on his back and felt the almost irresistible urge to sink my teeth into the back of his neck and keep crushing until they met bone.

The weight and speed of my attack sent Sagar face first into the dirt, spilling me over his shoulder. He had time to let out a wail of pain and anger and shock before the air thumped out of his lungs.

As I rolled through the fall, he was fighting for breath, but still had enough left in him to swing the gun up towards me. I grabbed his arm and broke it cleanly at the elbow across my knee. He shrieked.

But the noise was cut off, sharp and abrupt, when I shoved him onto his back, knelt astride his chest and, as his mouth fell open on a gasp, thrust the muzzle of Sean's Glock into it. I pushed the barrel all the way in, until the curve of the trigger guard crushed his bottom lip against his teeth and the front sight gouged into the roof of his mouth, and the hot steel burnt his tongue.

He went rigid under me, eyes jammed open, wild with panic as he looked into my face and saw his own death there waiting for him.

Around me, I was vaguely aware of torrential movement, of running boots and shouting, of the mechanical rasp of weapons being brought to bear. Gradually, as the initial burst of rage subsided into a cold ruthless flame, the sounds began to individuate.

Someone was yelling for a medic, someone else for backup, and just about everyone was yelling at me to put the gun down.

Not a chance.

Slowly, minutely, I felt the muscles in my forearm contract, through my wrist and the tendons in the back of my hand, and into my right index finger. I began to take up the trigger, first the tiny blade that forms part of the Glock's safety mechanism, then the curve of the trigger itself, balancing against the slight restriction. In my imagination, it quivered like a drawn bow.

'Charlie!' Parker's voice finally penetrated, tight and shaken. I took my eyes away from Sagar's face briefly. After all, it wasn't like I needed to aim.

Parker had moved carefully round into my field of view. His hands, his shirt, the legs of his trousers, were all covered in blood, gleaming dark against the black of his gear, and a stark bright velvet crimson against his skin.

Sean's blood.

'Stand down, Charlie!' Parker said, and in all the time I'd known him, it was the first time I'd heard him sound afraid. 'He's not dead. *Sean is not dead.* Do you understand me? They're working on him. The medics are working on him, right now.'

In my mind's eye, I saw again the pink mist and the shards at the moment of impact, the way Sean had dropped and folded. I'd seen people go down like that before. None of them had ever got up again.

'I'm sorry, Parker, but I don't believe you,' I said, the words very clear and calm.

Another man moved round into my line of sight. Conrad Epps. And if I'd seen a momentary vulnerability in him, back there when Bane had mentioned his daughter, any weakness was well buried now.

'If you pull that trigger, Fox, my men have orders to take you out,' he said, and the words had a studied carelessness about them, as if discussing a garbage bag.

Parker flung him a desperate look. 'Don't do this, Charlie.' His voice cracked. 'You don't have to do this. They'll kill you if you do this. They won't have any choice.'

I closed my eyes for a moment. Back in Fourth Day, I'd made the decision that I didn't want to go on without Sean, but I'd never expected to be faced with the prospect of going on so totally alone. Not like this. A great keening sob welled in my chest and wailed inside my mind. All I could hear was the sound of my heart tearing.

Perhaps this is the answer.

'You can't do it, Charlie.'

I opened my eyes and found Bane had joined the others, outside the circle of the SWAT team, with their M16s all pointed at me. I glanced at Sagar's bulging face. He'd begun to gag as the blood from the roof of his mouth trickled into his throat. His tongue fought convulsively against the intrusion of the barrel, bloodied saliva stringing from his mouth.

In that second I not only hated but also despised him. For Sean to go down to an amateur blind-luck shot seemed the ultimate insult, somehow.

'Trust me,' I said acidly, 'I can hardly miss.'

Bane shook his head, almost sadly. 'You are not a killer without consequence, Charlie, you never have been,' he said with utter certainty. 'You will never shy away from what needs to be done, but this...does not. If he was still fleeing, you would not hesitate, but you have him at your mercy.'

He tilted his head and looked down into me, the way he had done when I'd first arrived at Fourth Day, when he'd said that all he saw in me was rage and sorrow, and without them I'd have nothing to sustain me.

I eyed him bitterly. 'Sure of that now, are you?'

'Yes, I'm sure,' Bane said calmly. 'Your only reason for killing this man would be revenge. Parker, here, is afraid you will take that path, but I know you will not. It would go against everything you are, everything you have made of yourself.'

I was silent. In the distance I heard the steady chop of rotor blades, coming in fast and low. Afterwards, I told myself it was the possible arrival of a medevac helicopter that swayed it for me. That what Parker had said might be true.

That Sean might not be dead.

A tiny sliver of doubt crept in, hope hitching along for the ride.

I looked down again, dispassionate, at Sagar. The blood from the wound in his back had leached out to halo his body, so my knees were soaked in it. He was weeping, eyes squeezed shut as if to stem the flow.

His left arm thrashed weakly. The right flopped, disengaged from the broken elbow downwards. The gun he'd taken from the technician lay within a finger's length of the useless hand. A part of me willed him to find the strength to pick it up, just to make the decision for me.

'It's all about choices, Charlie,' Bane said softly, as if he could read my swirling thoughts. 'And if Sean chooses to live, why shouldn't you?'

The noise of the helicopter grew louder, almost on top of us now, the downwash from the rotor blades blasting grit and gravel across the parking area in a sudden surge as the air ambulance pilot saw the stand-off on the ground and put the machine into a reflexive hover. He was not combat-trained, I realised, was not going to risk his life to come into a hot zone to drag out casualties, however seriously they might be injured.

I dragged the Glock out of Sagar's mouth, chipping his teeth, brought both hands up in a gesture of surrender that could not be mistaken from the air. The SWAT team converged, whipped the gun out of my grasp and lifted me bodily away from Sagar, hauling me back a few metres. Hands on my shoulders forced me, unresisting, onto my face with a knee rammed into my back until they had the PlastiCuffs zipped tight around my wrists.

I just managed to turn my head in time to see another two of Epps's men haul Sagar up and cuff him, too, careless of the gunshot injury that made him squeal. I waited until he met my eyes, until I had him.

'If he dies,' I said, loud enough to be heard over the increased thrust of the landing heli, 'you'll wish I'd pulled that bloody trigger.'

And after that? Who knows?

Sometimes, living is harder than dying, but I never did take the easy path, did I?

EPILOGUE

Hospitals smell the same and look the same everywhere in the world, and the Los Angeles County/USC Medical Center was no exception. The sharp tang of antiseptic and disinfectant overlying the faintest trace of fear.

I'd been told that County General, as it was known, was one of the finest teaching hospitals in California, that its Level One trauma centre was second to none. That it provided immediate treatment for more than a quarter of all serious emergency cases in the city and the southern half of the state.

But none of this excellent pedigree could alter the fact that Sean had nearly died on the flight in, and again on the table during the seven hours of surgery to remove the shattered fragments of bone from his brain.

The 9 mm Hydra-Shok round had entered his forehead just above the outside corner of his left eyebrow, and ploughed a destructive deadly furrow rearwards through his temple before exiting just above his ear. Along the way it had cleaved a path through the side of his skull like an ice-breaker, scattering deadly shrapnel as it went.

The damage, the surgeons told us in sombre tones, was confined to the left frontal and parietal lobes. If the shock of the injury itself didn't kill him, then some level of brain damage was almost a certainty. It was not their business to give us false hope.

They used a confusing mixture of technical medical phraseology interspersed with oversimplified terms, as if speaking to children. In the glazed eye of my mind, it sounded like another language altogether, where only some of the words were familiar and others were completely incomprehensible.

No doubt my father would have been able to translate their prognosis into simple, logical, and unflinching terms. Just one of the many reasons I did not call him. I did not call anyone. As if by not telling them what had happened, I could make it all go away.

Of course, there was a slim chance Sean would awaken and be almost normal, but the odds were not in favour. It was far more likely, the doctors announced, taking the areas of injury into account, that he would have significant cognitive, memory, movement and coordination problems. We should prepare ourselves. They would not know more until he woke from his coma.

If he woke.

Until then, I lived in twenty-minute snatches, three times a day, which was as long as they'd let me into Intensive Care to sit by his bedside and listen to the ventilator pushing air in and out of his lungs, and to clutch at his waxy fingers. As if by doing so I could physically pull him back into this world.

The rest of the time I haunted the waiting area, dead-eyed. As much in limbo, in my way, as Sean.

*　*　*

Detective Gardner came in, sat with me in the waiting area and told me, in hushed tones, how the siege of Fourth Day had ended before it had begun, with no casualties except for Tony. She'd been informed, unofficially, that his death would be judged a good shooting and she was in the clear. If I read the hand of Conrad Epps behind the suspicious speed with which the incident had been laid to rest, I didn't say so.

'It's Beatrice, by the way,' she said as she was leaving.

Foggy, distracted, I could only stare at her.

'The "B" on my card.'

'Oh, right.' I paused. 'Does this mean you have to kill me now?'

She smiled, told me to look after myself, and departed.

Randall Bane paid me a visit, seeming to bring with him a little oasis of calm. He was treated with a reverence by the staff that I could not initially understand, until they explained, shocked by my ignorance, that he was a considerable benefactor.

Bane thanked me gravely for my part in proceedings, only too aware of the cost. He told me that, miraculously, by the time the police did finally start taking statements from the members of Fourth Day, Dexter and the remaining Debacle crew had slipped away like they'd never been.

Maria was still shaken from the attack by Nu and disturbed by the upheaval. She had her good days and bad days, he said. Being with Billy helped. Being close to her father helped. He hoped, in time, she would be able to put it all behind her and move on.

Just as, he hoped, I would be able to do the same.

'That's not up to me,' I said, eyes drifting along the corridor in the direction of the ICU.

'For the moment, just try to think of the reasons to stay, Charlie,' he said, deep as a winter lake, 'rather than the reasons to leave.'

Conrad Epps never put in an appearance. I would have been more surprised if he had. But I learnt from Parker that Chris Sagar had been spirited away somewhere, as had Yancy. I guessed their debriefing would not be as passive as my own.

I was briefly assailed by fears that Sagar would manage to strike some kind of deal, end up with his freedom and a new identity, but I reassured myself with the knowledge that he had caused the deaths of three of Epps's people. Not only the two men guarding Thomas Witney, but the technician from the mobile command post. He'd been airlifted out on the same helicopter flight as Sean, but massive internal injuries saw him dead on arrival.

I clung to the tenacity that had kept Sean alive through that same short flight, as if proof of his determination to survive.

Parker Armstrong took complete charge of me, offering neither questions nor condemnation. He arranged somewhere close by to sleep and shower, and brought me food I didn't want at regular intervals, which he then coaxed me into eating.

On the fourth day, in a nearby diner, he said, 'Sean wanted you back, you know. He thought he'd blown his chances after we had to debrief you and then you bailed.

It was like you'd chosen Bane over him.'

I pushed away my half-eaten omelette and sat back. 'I didn't want to accept it, but Sean did the right thing – the *only* thing – he could do,' I said dully. 'I put you in an impossible situation and, knowing Epps, he gave you no choice.'

Parker nodded. 'Either Sean did the interrogation, or Epps let his own people handle it. No way was Sean going to let anyone else in there with you. He knew you'd go crazy when you realised what had been done, but he also knew it was better than the alternative.' He went quiet, settling his fork on his empty plate very precisely, as if he was looking for a way into what he had to say and was totally at a loss how to begin.

'What else, Parker?'

His eyes flicked to mine, troubled. 'Apparently, when they were almost done, he told Epps's guys to turn off the recorders and he sent everyone out.'

The unease formed a lump behind my breastbone. 'What for?' I asked. 'What else did he want out of me that he didn't want the rest to hear?' But I already knew.

'I would guess it was about the baby,' Parker said. 'How you really felt about the pregnancy. What you were planning to do, if you hadn't miscarried.'

The lump began to thunder, as if trying to hammer its way to freedom or escape. I had to swallow before I could speak. 'And what did I say?'

He shook his head. 'Sean never told me,' he said. 'That was private between you and him. I don't know.'

'That makes two of us,' I muttered.

'Well, whatever it was, it must have been the right answer.

Last thing he did before we went out to wait for you and Bane was ask for leave so he could take you away for a while, after this was over. Do some talking, he said, get things straightened out.'

I clutched gratefully at the consolation his words offered with a fervour that was almost pathetic in its intensity.

His voice softened. 'Soulmates come along once in a lifetime, Charlie, if that. You find one, you'd be a fool to let them slip away. And Sean is no fool.'

His face dissolved suddenly in front of me. I ducked my head sharply, blinked a few times and gazed out through the tinted glass to the traffic running past outside, the shadows knife-edged and defined in the California sunshine.

But sitting there, I was overcome with a sense of utter desolation. Who knew what Sean would be, if and when he woke? In the meantime, I was told not to hope, yet robbed of the freedom to grieve. Stuck in the No Man's Land between holding on and letting go.

And a part of me began to wish, when I'd had the chance to do so, that I'd pulled the trigger and saved myself this pain.

ACKNOWLEDGEMENTS

As always, there are a lot of people without whom this book would not have made it into print. The following folk provided the usual help, inspiration and advice, some of which I took on board absolutely, and some of which I ignored at my peril, or twisted for my own sinister ends. The facts are probably theirs – the mistakes are undoubtedly my own.

DP Lyle MD is my first port of call for all medical information and he came up trumps yet again; Douglas Giacobbe provided SWAT info; Robin Burcell told me how the LAPD would conduct an interview; Linda L Richards pointed me in the direction regarding the behaviour of cults; travel consultant Chris Sagar explained how to transport a corpse from one country to another; Stuart and Fiona MacBride gave me a virtual tour of the seedier side of Aberdeen; JT Ellison very kindly corrected my accidental Britishisms, and my UK copyeditors, Fliss and Simon Bage, corrected just about everything else.

I'd also like to thank everyone on the *www.Murderati.com* blog site, who diligently answered obscure questions like how the doors operate on a Gulfstream G550 and the availability of free walk-in medical clinics in Manhattan.

Of course, the real hard work to make something of this book was done by the amazing team at my literary agents, Gregory and Company, including Jane Gregory herself, Stephanie Glencross, Jemma McDonagh, Claire Morris and Tess Barum.

I'm immensely grateful to my UK publisher, Susie Dunlop, and all the talented crew at Allison & Busby; to my new US publishers, Pegasus and Busted Flush; and to all the sales and marketing people, and the bookstores and libraries on both sides of the Atlantic. Thank you all.

Various people read this at the early stages, and made great suggestions and comments, including Iris, Sheila and Graham from the Lune Valley Writers' Group, Derek Harrison, Shell Willbye, and Dina Willner. And my husband, Andy, of course, read every chapter as it was written, and kept me going right to the end. You are all stars.

Finally, a big thank you to BG Ritts, who made the winning bid in the charity auction at the Bouchercon World Mystery Convention in Baltimore, to become a character in this book. I have included her very carefully, in accordance with her instructions (I hope!) and I was delighted to do so. The auction was in aid of Viva House, a Catholic Worker House of Hospitality and Resistance, and the Enoch Pratt Free Library.